D0386844

DO UNTO OTHERS...

Baen Books by
MICHAEL Z. WILLIAMSON

Freehold
The Weapon
Contact with Chaos
Better to Beg Forgiveness...
Do Unto Others...

The Hero (with John Ringo)

DO UNTO OTHERS...

MICHAEL Z. WILLIAMSON

BAEN

DO UNTO OTHERS . . .

This is a work of fiction. All the characters and events portrayed in this book are fictional, and any resemblance to real people or incidents is purely coincidental.

Copyright © 2010 by Michael Z. Williamson.

All rights reserved, including the right to reproduce this book or portions thereof in any form.

A Baen Books Original

Baen Publishing Enterprises
P.O. Box 1403
Riverdale, NY 10471
www.baen.com

ISBN: 978-1-4391-3383-5

Cover art by Kurt Miller

First printing, August 2010

Distributed by Simon & Schuster
1230 Avenue of the Americas
New York, NY 10020

Library of Congress Cataloging-in-Publication Data

Williamson, Michael Z.
Do unto others— / Michael Z. Williamson.
p. cm.
ISBN 978-1-4391-3383-5
1. Miners—Fiction. 2. Business intelligence.—Fiction. 3. Political fiction. I. Title.
PS3623.I573D68 2010
813'.6—dc22

2010022797

10 9 8 7 6 5 4 3 2 1

Pages by Joy Freeman (www.pagesbyjoy.com)
Printed in the United States of America

To Jim Fuson

For a sincere kindness.

PROLOGUE

Aramis Anderson flinched as a bullet cracked past his head. That was a bit closer than he liked. He took the suggestion though, and rolled low past Elke Sykora. She fired again at one of the targets appearing through a doorway.

He returned the favor, gapping one just as it jumped into view, straight through the right eye.

"Egress!" he heard. That was Alex Marlow, team commander, and Aramis bounced forward to make a hole between two doorways. That put him squarely into view of another doorway, and he kept his weapon loose and ready.

Except that another figure popped past the window, firing as it went. He got it, but a bullet whizzed past him simultaneously. Behind him, four team members carried their civilian principal struggling and screaming out the front door. Elke shouted *"Fireinthehole!"*

His heart went schizo and tried to go two directions at once. If Elke was about to set off a charge, he needed to be outside, fast. He slipstepped back, feeling assorted debris under and around his feet, but he cleared the front doorway without trouble, and went into low zigzag. More bullets snapped past to bury themselves in the walls, as Bart and Jason provided cover fire around him.

Behind him he heard *pop, pop, WHAM!* and he guessed Elke had set a charge of smoke, incapacitance gas and explosive. Bits of something stung him like annoying insects, with an occasional numbing smack of something a little larger.

Alex said, "Flames. Call the fire department."

Elke shook her head. "No need."

A moment later another explosion blew the flames out. Whatever gases it released effectively cut off oxygen, and the smolders from her first shot drifted away in the breeze.

It was always a tremendous rush to do a live fire drill. It was also phenomenal training, an incredible team building technique, and fun. He wished they'd had time when they first met. He'd have started off a lot better with Elke. By the time they started these drills, he already knew the woman could shoot, and was an explosives whiz. He regretted the way he'd talked down to her at the time. She didn't seem to hold a grudge, though. And, if she wasn't going to mention the bullet he'd put centimeters past her ear, he wasn't going to mention the one she'd put past his.

Their "principal" was also their company CEO, who pushed up from the dirt he was lying in. The screams had been acting for effect. He was completely calm now, which most people would not be after six heavily armed troops shot up the kidnappers around them and blew the building up.

"That was sexy," he said with a grin. "And very, very smooth. I'll be sure to find more work for you."

They shook hands all around, smiling. Aramis felt a load lift.

That was, until Shaman Mbuto, the team's surgeon said, "You appear to have a nick here, Aramis."

He twisted to look at his shoulder. Sure enough, he had a streak on the fabric, and he could feel a bruise underneath, tender to the exploratory probing. It was gel, not a real bullet, but it still counted as a hit. On the other hand, a few scrapes and dings were inevitable, and he'd had a lot worse.

On the other hand, Bart Weil announced, "So Aramis is buying the drinks tonight."

Aramis groaned. The big, grizzled German could consume beer like a bilge pump on the ships he used to crew. Some of the others had expensive tastes, but not the sheer volume Bart did.

Jason Vaughn said, "Hmm . . . I'm tasting . . . Elijah Craig? No, I think it's Ardbeg. Mmm . . . good stuff."

It was going to be a long, expensive night.

CHAPTER 1

Alex Marlow had just been tasked to guard the richest woman in the universe. He wondered why he wasn't twitchy.

Of course, his team hadn't been told that yet. Nor had he started the mission. Both of those would raise the stress level.

He and four of them were awaiting the sixth member, who was uncharacteristically late.

"Where the hell is Elke?" Aramis snapped in frustration.

"She's probably mining her apartment for practice, or defusing her comm, or having an intimate experience with her shotgun," Jason Vaughn offered. "Regardless, you're not going to make her appear faster." He smiled wryly.

Aramis was only a bit more than half Jason's age, and it showed. He twitched, all youth and energy. Jason sat in a couch, comfortable and calm.

For calm, however, Jason had nothing on Bart Weil, the big German, who leaned against the wall and barely gave evidence of being alive. His eyes took in everything, though.

That left Horace "Shaman" Mbuto, the team's surgeon, as the odd one out. He was older even than Alex, ancient by the standards of executive protection, and making use of the time to inventory a surgical kit.

They seemed a bit motley, but in the executive protection business, they were the best, and had been a team for a year now. He couldn't imagine breaking them up. The mixed skill sets meshed perfectly, and the personality clashes were minor and only added flavor. They were Ripple Creek Security's star bodyguards, and paid accordingly.

Luckily, money was not a problem for their new principal.

His musing was interrupted when he saw familiar movement out by the gate.

"Here she comes," he said.

Eleonora Sykora, called Elke, hated running late. Admittedly, she'd enjoyed the reason for it, but still.

They entered the Ripple Creek site on her password, and the gate flashed a warning that guest vehicles could go no further than the turnaround ahead.

She turned to Alaric and said, "If you want to kiss me goodbye, do it now. Last chance."

The car was on automatic. Alaric bent over and kissed her deeply, his hands roaming inside her jacket and all over her body. If he only knew how much trust she showed by letting him do that.

"Okay, stop now," she insisted, before he got too excited again.

"Why like this? What's wrong with kissing you goodbye when I drop you off?"

"Because they might think I'm a girl," she said with a smile. She measured the car's deceleration and reached for the handle.

He still looked puzzled when she jumped out. Without a word she grabbed her personal bag, closed the door and strode toward the building where she was to meet her former and again teammates.

She hoped the new job was worthwhile. Men could be fun, but explosives were so much better. Finding reasons to use them socially was the tough part.

Jason felt better when he saw Elke. He worried about her when she was late. They'd been friends a long time, and saved each others' butts more times than he could count. Probably everyone knew her persona was largely an act, but he knew the real Elke. She really was a performance artist who worked with explosives, but under that, she was very human. She just didn't let it peek out often.

Elke slipped in the door and closed it behind her. The window darkened with polarizing as Alex pushed the control, and she drew a heavy drape across. Jason activated the dampening gear on the table next to him, and a few other security measures happened. It wasn't as secure as some military areas, but it should be plenty for what they needed, he hoped. Alex seemed a bit twitchy, though he probably thought he looked dead calm.

Alex stayed sitting, but said, "I assume you all realize we have a mission."

Bart said, "I was hoping we would be told of a pay raise and free beer."

"You know better," Alex replied. "We have a medium duration project, on and off Earth, in civilian environments. That means limited weapons and explosives."

Elke said, "I will send you the usual protests on this theory."

Alex smiled back, "And I will file them in the usual way."

Banter aside, Jason understood the concern. High profile civilian missions could be worse than those in war zones. Everyone knew you were unarmed, and your response was basically to say, "Stop, or I'll call the police!" That, or throw yourself in front of incoming fire. It came down to tactics, evasion, diversion in lieu of any confrontation of any kind. That was always the goal, of course, but for putative peacetime missions it was a legal and real imperative.

Aramis said, "I notice we haven't been told who we're guarding."

Elke said, "I assume we haven't been told for a reason." She gave a hint of smile.

Alex smiled back. "You assume correctly. The OPSEC is necessary. However, you can be told now." He touched a command, which put the full screen up.

"This is our principal," he said, and gave them time to wrap their brains around it. The silence lasted about a minute.

Aramis said, "She's..."

Jason offered, "Stunning."

"Actress? Model?" Bart asked. "She's not one I recognize."

"Caron Elain Prescot," Alex said.

"The Prescot ExtraSolar Ores Group?" Elke asked.

"Yes. Daughter of the owner."

"He's worth how much?" Shaman asked.

Jason, now caught up, said, "There's no way to count. He's primary shareholder of the company, and they own an entire fucking star system full of readily exploitable minerals. More money than most governments can get to play with, and no need to worry about appeasing a populace. He treats his employees well, I understand."

"Yes," Alex said. "The employees are not likely to be a problem, other than the occasional awestruck miner who doesn't know who she is and wants a date."

"Do I recall," Shaman said, leaning back in his seat with a furrowed brow, "that several other major shareholders are unhappy with the state of affairs?"

"Former shareholders," Alex said. "It's been thirty years since Prescot Mining bought an option on mineral extraction rights for the system. The initial plan was terraforming. That proved infeasible, so the original title holders sold it off. However, Prescot was able to argue successfully that they retained rights based on capital outlay, not bundled with the rest. Several other nations and groups all bought in and out on rights to the system, in a decades-long financial poker game. Several times exploratory parties and habitats were started, and abandoned. Eventually, they all defaulted or cancelled and abandoned."

"Which puts the system up for grabs again," Jason said. "Except that Prescot's claim was never abandoned."

"Right. They basically inherited the jump point and had mineral rights to the system. They landed a habitat and laid the balance of claim, and started shipping minerals back, at a loss. Even some of the stockholders pulled out, and their consortium investors and backers dropped them."

"I remember watching that on the stock scroll," Jason said with a grin. He'd always respected accomplishment. "The volume increased as they plowed capital into development of new tech. Once they reached break even, they had this asymptotic growth curve for about a month, then it got taken off the charts completely because it buried everything else."

"From millions to billions?" Elke asked.

"From millions in a billion mark operation to trillions, quadrillions, no one knows how much," Alex said. "The Prescot family holdings went from a significant minority to majority shareholders, they basically bought their family company back, and then acquired an entire system of assets."

"And it's our job to protect his daughter against jealous rivals," Bart said. "He can afford us, and they are hiring us because they think it's worth it."

Aramis said, "So a private citizen is spending enough money to buy a small house every week to have us watch his daughter? Why does that sound like we'll be earning it?"

"Yes," Alex agreed with a nod. "It's not just us. We get the daughter. Jace Cady's team gets facilities again—she's got the estate, basically. Our pilots are going to take over any ship with a family member on it, and unannounced. The boss will assign them from a pool at the last moment, so no one can make a concrete plan. This family earns in seconds what we earn in weeks."

"That doesn't sound like fun for them," Elke said.

"Yeah, imprisoned by your wealth," Aramis said, still staring at the screen. "She can't possibly have a social life."

"I think I would rather be back in a war zone," Bart said.

Shaman said, "Yes, there are definite issues we will have to deal with. This is going to be very rough."

"I can handle it," Aramis said confidently. "Despite the vomitously obscene wealth, I plan to be as cold and professional as possible. I won't comment on her at all."

Jason said, "Aramis, she's a high risk principal. You'll have to escort her up close, stay with her even in the shower, check her clothes when she dresses, check her skin for darts or poison patches."

Aramis paused and stared.

"Man, you're bullshitting me!"

"Well, yeah, but you started it."

Even Aramis howled with laughter at that.

Alex was glad to see it. A lot of the early personal clashes had dissipated over the last year serving together.

"Still," he said, "she is a beautiful young college woman, and that makes her a lot different from either a celebrity with fans or a politician with enemies. I don't know that any of us have handled a specific mission like this. Bart?"

Bart shook his head. "Celebrities, yes. Occasional executives personally. No one at this level, and not family members subject to kidnapping or death."

"So I want everyone to review their training, text, video and interactive. They're inadequate, but at least will help keep us in the right mindset."

Everyone nodded.

✧ ✧ ✧

The Prescot industries were almost too large to manage. There was a board of directors, and various officers and departments, all of whom managed their share. However, as CEO of the Group, Bryan Prescot had to track all of it to some degree. Details were almost impossible. It was just too large.

He did, however, make daily overviews, and occasionally zero in, on things that specifically interested him, or were of immediate concern.

The list was long, though. Tourism and casinos were easy; they were contracted out. The contractors paid up front, and a percentage of gross over minimum. His brother handled all that. Scientific research was officially a loss. The research agency ate up a lot of money to look at rocks, space, whatever it wanted. Those were charged against company profits. Of course, as always, the average was for the research to lead to new sources of revenue and improvements in operational efficiency. They were good PR as well.

Charities. The only real concern was giving away too much and causing destabilization. It was a serious worry. Prescot could easily make entire classes of people dependent, and Bryan did not want that.

Bio sciences produced the organics, hydroponics, vat grown meats, O_2 producing bacteria, other bacteria that excreted assorted chemicals and enzymes, or cracked rocks. They were even trying to tailor one for that environment.

Materials science, physics, space transport—all interesting stuff.

His first love, though, was the mines. They were where the family started, and what they did. Digging rock, crushing it, extracting ore. The technology meant the human race would effectively never run out of resources, and made transmutation research a poor investment for the near future. Every mine on Earth, and even those of the asteroid mining concerns, was shutting down. They simply could not compete with a company that imported refined raw metal five hundred million tons at a time, with the power to produce it supplied on site, effectively for free.

There he'd done what he felt was right, and hired as many of his former competitors as he could, and paid for their employees to be retrained. He was making large areas of Canada, Germany, Russia, China, Africa and South America into parks, but the people who'd depended on the former mines would have starved. They liked him well enough now, and their families were not suffering, which was the important part. The goddammed eco twits, however, still hated him despite the free parks he'd built. They'd never be happy.

Hundreds of petty, pointless lawsuits to stop his "corporate greed" and "facism" as they misspelled it, and "elitist concentration of power and wealth." They cost the company, at most, a few hundred thousand a month out of billions. They had to be watched, though, because a lucky strike with a commiserating judge could cost a lot more to fix.

Caron smiled to Ewan and Garrick as she left the lift. They were fixtures here, had been guarding the family since before she was born. They were like uncles to her, as much as Uncle Joe was. Ewan gripped the door handle and opened it for her. They still used manual doors here. Tradition.

"*Diolch*, Ewan," she said and smiled.

Her father was at his desk, and she held the smile until Ewan closed the door. It was traditional in look, but modern in its soundproofing. Once private she was less composed.

"*Tad*, I got the briefing on the Ripple Creek bodyguards," she said.

"Good, I got mine, too," he said.

"I don't like it. It's going to affect my studies," she said. She breathed a dramatic sigh to emphasize it. Was it too much? If he caught it . . .

He swiveled in his chair. "Come here," he said, and opened his arms.

She did enjoy his closeness, and his empathy meant she'd given just enough.

"I love you, *Merch*," he said, gripping her tightly.

"I love you, *Tad*," she agreed. "That means you're not going to change, doesn't it?"

He leaned back. "Caron, we need them. I wouldn't spend the money if I didn't think we did. I'm almost sorry we've done so well, for the hatred we've gotten."

"Only almost?" she replied, feeling anger and jealousy. "Unload some of it. Let other companies buy in."

"Caron, you know that's impossible. The economic repercussions would be huge. We also can't exploit Govannon forever. We have to drag the resources out now, and keep control of the technology, which is where the real future is. Times change and so must we."

"Yes, I know we're not drift miners carting out coal anymore. I know we're beyond the Industrial Revolution and don't have children in the mines anymore. I'm being selfish by insisting on a normal personal life—"

"And melodramatic," he said.

Damn him.

He continued, "You've never had a normal personal life, and I'm sorry. On the other hand, you've always had friends to play with, even if they're retainers rather than peers. I try never to treat our staff as anything less than friends and compatriots, and I know you do, too."

"They're not exactly poor, and they are part of the extended family, in a way," she said. "But I can't just go out and make friends."

"The irony is that if we were merely millionaires you could ignore the money. With what happened since you took your tests, it's now impossible."

"I know, and I want to be a normal college girl. I'm half tempted to just drop it entirely and get tutors."

"I considered that," he said. "But I think the socialization is important, even as limited as it is. The environment isn't ideal, but you'll be more separated with tutors. You can't develop in a vacuum." He frowned and looked sad.

"Govannon is a vacuum, outside the dome," she said.

He grinned. "No, it's a toxic atmosphere at high pressure. Caron," he said more seriously, "I wish we didn't have to spend money on things like public affairs and security. I'd rather give more of it back to our workers and stockholders and keep some for ourselves. I don't like having to plan every outing around business and potential threats. But if we walk away, lots of people lose their jobs, lots of people relying on our stock for income and pension suffer, and we won't be any less hated by all those who didn't have the courage to hang on. We've had all these discussions before."

"I know, *Tad*, and I'm sorry. I'm just frustrated. I can't even . . . I can't even have a real boyfriend." She blushed. "Everyone is either trying for position, or knows they can't and are just a diversion, or doesn't get told who I am and then resents it, or . . . Hell, you know all this." She tossed a dismissive wave.

He looked a bit uncomfortable. He knew she wasn't a virgin, and had had a sex life for some time, but he never liked mention of it. She wasn't comfortable discussing it either, but it did bother her, and she'd always been able to talk to him.

"If I could sneak you off somewhere for a year, I would. I am sorry." He reached for another hug.

She gripped him back this time.

"So am I," she said.

As she left, he sighed himself. She was a grown woman, and she was still his little girl. Now that little girl needed a security force.

Ewan and Garrick came into the office with his brother Joe. Joe had gotten past the younger brother stage, eventually. Now they managed to interact as friends, after a fashion. Bryan lamented they were both too busy to actually socialize much.

That was as much his fault, of course. He checked the time. He had a vidconference in ten minutes and then a face-to-face with the County Council, just because it kept them thinking of him as a local businessman. He could skip it, but . . . And of course, his own security detail was arriving, too.

"We have to be quick," he said, "but what's the final take? Ewan?"

Ewan seemed slightly put upon, and well he might.

"They're trained for much more serious events than we are. Of course, I hope that's completely unnecessary. However, they have a reputation."

Joe wasn't as agitated as he'd been throughout the contracting process, but still wasn't comfortable.

He said, "There's the price, of course. I know we can afford it, but it's not cheap and I feel it's both unnecessary, and a copout. We're basically telling any threats we can be scared into that kind of expense. There's perception that being able to afford that kind of expense is immoral. Then, they do have a reputation for shooting things up and arrogantly disregarding any rules they don't like."

When he paused, Garrick cut in.

"They ignore rules that would hinder their ability to protect their principal. Yes, it sometimes looks bad in the press, but we know firsthand what the press is like. They are just about the best, and the only outfit that can offer the schedule and flexibility we need. I feel no moral failure in admitting I'm a Welsh hillman who's loyal to his lord, but cannot offer that level of expertise. I will, of course, manage oversight, but unless there are specifics, I'd prefer to just let them run things, and I'll be liaison to them."

Bryan pretty well knew all this, but he liked having everyone face to face. It made sure everyone took it seriously and understood it was personal, not just a business calculation.

Along which lines, he had to deal with the two next items on his schedule. He'd been glancing at his screen. A nervous habit.

"Well, we'll welcome them and work with them when they arrive. I'm sure they're neither as bad nor as good as stories have it. Drinks this evening if we have time."

"Can't make it," Joe said. "But have one for me."

"Of course."

They rose and left.

CHAPTER 2

Damn, *this* is a Welsh country house?" Aramis asked. He looked and sounded impressed as he craned his neck. He was riding shotgun next to Bart. Elke leaned past him and clicked stills on top of video. Her secondary task was to document the missions, for later review.

"It's not too opulent, at least," Horace commented. He'd seen much more blatant displays of wealth. This was a quiet, if large home in the country, with a vista from its hillside meadow, near some lake or other, and surrounded by rolling, wooded hills. The two villages nearby were Cwm Irfon and Abergwesyn. He wasn't going to attempt to pronounce those.

Elke said, "It's almost as big as the Celadon Presidential Palace. That says a lot, doesn't it?"

Bart said, "I take it you mean that the former palace is not that impressive, as this house is not too large."

"Large enough," Jason commented. "My family would be more than comfortable with one floor of one wing."

"They do have a staff we'll have to deal with," Alex said.

"A large one, from the looks of things."

Shaman said, "I believe the brief said two families are retainers. Almost feudal, except they're well paid these days."

Bart pulled the car up through the coded gate, and along a sweeping driveway past manicured lawns, catalog-perfect flowerbeds edged in rocks and tiles, and onto a broad apron under an almost perfectly transparent rain shed.

Horace recognized Garrick Crandall as he stepped through the door. He was a light security type for the family, meaning he chased away trespassers looking for photos or interviews, and kept the immediate space around the family clear of reporters when traveling. That had been sufficient until their fortune exploded. It was he who'd suggested them, and he looked quite glad to see them.

"Gentlemen, lady," he greeted them. "Welcome. Please come this way, inside and right, then left."

Horace waited for Bart, who set the car on auto and sent it to the carriage house. Together they brought up the rear.

He made a point not to gawk, but it was impossible not to be impressed. The place was large, hundreds of years old, and the owners had taste. The wood was carved enough to reveal grain and figure, not enough to be cluttered. The rugs were the busiest features, but they were authentic. He recognized a Bobo mask high on the mezzanine. It was real, not just a tourist fake. Cabinets lit with delicately colored tubes displayed artifacts from all over. The furniture was old style, new built, he figured, since Aramis sitting generated no squeaks of protest from the couch.

He hoped for a lot of time to explore the place in peace.

Elke, though, had that look in her eyes. She was plotting places to mine, such as behind that clock, next to the wardrobe by the door, and above that mezzanine. He should probably mention that to Alex and Jason, to ensure she didn't actually do so without permission. She was flaky that way.

Right then, he was interrupted by Garrick Crandall's wife Joanne gracefully placing a tray of hors d'oeuvres on the broad coffee table in front of the couch, or settee, or divan, or whatever it was called here. He took that as a hint to sit. The others glanced around, and followed his lead, all but Elke and Jason. He suspected Jason was acting as buddy and leash for her.

As he leaned back into the leather cushion, he hoped there was no violence, but he suspected that one way or another, the pleasant country lifestyle was at an end for this household.

Jason was comfortable in a suit. He wasn't comfortable with only a small stunner and light armor woven in. The threats here could be as great as on the battlefield, but they had to pretend to be harmless to fit Earthside civilian customs. He understood the necessity of the image for the public, family and company. He didn't have to like it. At least he had a "briefcase" that would unfold to a stun bag launcher and drop more torso armor. The delay to reach it could prove fatal, though.

That was why he was being paid more than a good doctor or lawyer.

"Here she comes," Alex warned. They all stood, casually but politely.

The door opened and a slim young lady came in. Physically, she was not large, nor did she project any particular aura of power, but . . .

Not just beautiful, but sexy. She exuded it. Her ancestry was Welsh, and Kazakh, and Maltese. Flawless skin, dark eyes with a hint of almond, dark hair tied back and casually flipped over her shoulder, but looking as if every strand was placed by an artist. Every curve and line suited her perfectly. She wore a casual tunic and jacket over tailored slacks, wholesome and classy, that couldn't hide the body underneath and didn't try.

The exotic looks that only come from having your ancestors raped by passing barbarians for a couple of millennia, part of him quipped. He choked it down.

On top of that, she was not much older than his own daughter. That disturbed him unconsciously, except he was conscious of it. Dammit.

Alex's voice snapped him back.

"Miss Prescot, a pleasure to meet you again. Please let me introduce the rest of the team. This is Jason Vaughn, who is a technical specialist."

She smiled primly and extended a hand. Her shake was firm but ladylike. Her eyes were intense and scrutinous.

"Mr. Vaughn."

"Miss Prescot," he said. "Do please call me Jason if you wish."

"I will, thank you."

She moved on, and he chuckled mentally at "technical specialist." Better than saying "gunsmith and lock cracker," which was more accurate if less socially acceptable.

"Horace Mbuto is also a surgeon."

She turned to shake hands with Shaman and he saw her from behind.

Holy crap! He looked away.

Shaman betrayed nothing. Elke didn't seem jealous, bothered or attracted. No unconscious response he'd expect from a woman facing another loaded with looks and money. Elke was ice. No, not ice, just pure business.

He felt better to see that even Bart was nonplussed, and Bart had guarded female celebrities in their dressing rooms.

Aramis tried hard not to stutter, and didn't make a fool of himself, but certainly presented as naïve and new, which he wasn't.

She sat carefully on another couch, and said, "So how will this differ from previous security? What do I need to know? Oh, please sit."

Jason sat down on the chair, and found there was powered memory foam under the leather. Very, very comfortable, and didn't everyone have ten thousand marks of seat upholstered and hidden to look like a three-century-old antique? Since money wasn't an object, of course.

Alex said, "Much of this was in the briefing I sent, but it comes across different in person."

Jason imagined that was a diplomatic way of avoiding saying, "You should have read your briefing, you arrogant young bitch." Well done.

Alex continued, "The critical point is that your safety is our only concern. If you wish to change our operational methods, please ask, but I don't have much discretion. It will have to go through Corporate and our contractee—your father. We have been trained and briefed on your specific situation and will be as discreet as possible, but given the choice between discretion and protecting you, we will always protect you."

"So I will have even less privacy than before," she said, looking sad and put upon. Jason twigged it was an act. A good one—she'd obviously had lessons, but it was just a little too perfect to be natural. She was going to be manipulative. She was left-handed, he noted. Not extremely, but certainly by default and preference. That should have been in the written brief.

"Unfortunately, yes," Alex said. "Elke will escort you anywhere sensitive or personal, or where discretion calls for avoiding males. Bart has specialized in celebrities, and will be with you at public functions as much as possible, but obviously is quite noticeable. Aramis will take over where less visibility is called for. At least one of us will be at your apartment at all times, whether you are or not. We are all trained in emergency medicine, and Jason has supplemental training, so Horace or he will be nearby as much as possible."

"Goodness, that's quite a scheduling chart you must have," she said.

"Indeed, but we're used to it." He continued his brief. "One important factor is that the first person to see a threat takes charge of the scene unless they ask for replacement or are removed from the event. I am officially in charge, but if Aramis sees a threat, I will defer to his judgment until he announces it is clear. We need you to support this, too."

"Of course," she said. Her body language didn't seem to support the statement to Jason's eye. It was a pro forma response.

Still, they had control of transport and commo. There wasn't a lot she could really do to antagonize them, in his estimation.

"We will be unseen as much as possible, and please do not acknowledge us at all. That can be a hint to a threat as to who to take down first. Also, if there is a threat, we will immediately put you somewhere safe, or take you to the ground, or cover you, or otherwise get you out of reach or aim. The best thing you can do in that case is go limp. We can pick you up and carry you if need be, or shove you in the right direction. Please let us do the thinking for you. We welcome any observations if you want to yell or point, but we need to make the response. We're trained as a team."

She seemed to draw into herself slightly. "This is so much more than I've had before."

"Yes, it is, miss," Alex agreed with a nod. "However, we were hired because that is the perceived threat level."

"I appreciate your forthrightness," she said. "So you'll be coming with me to school?"

"Us and others. There are two other teams covering your father and the house and your apartment."

"What has been done to my flat?" she asked.

"Only security. Sensors. Armor. Locks and access control. Personnel on duty. None of your personal belongings have been touched."

"Good," she said, though she continued to look put upon and faintly embarrassed. Jason understood that. Privacy was a big thing, especially on Earth. There was little enough of it.

"So," she asked, "when do we depart?"

Alex said, "Unless there's an emergency, I'd like to spend the weekend checking with our facilities team both here and at your flat. We'll get you there right after dinner Sunday, if we may?"

"That's fine," she said, looking a little relieved. "There are still some personal things I'd like to pack."

"Go right ahead, miss," Alex agreed. "Elke and Aramis will stay with you."

She twitched slightly and blushed.

"Can it be just Elke?" she asked. "Nothing personal, you understand, but..."

Aramis said, "I'll wait outside the door. I don't have to be intrusive."

"Thank you," she replied with a relieved and gracious nod.

She hesitated a moment, seemed to figure how things worked, and turned for the stairs. Elke managed to flit in front of her and lead, while Aramis followed.

Certainly there were not threats in their own home right now, and certainly every paranoid detail would be covered, Jason thought. It would be insane not to, considering the value of the principal. As they went up, he took station at the bottom of the stairs, where he was between the main outside door and the principal. Bart jogged quickly and quietly, despite his mass, to the top, with a small sonar unit. Alex and Shaman remained in the parlor, alert while checking maps and photos of the estate.

He heard Bart go through every room in the wing, checking closets, windows and halls. That had already been done, and would be done regularly. Shortly, Bart came back down and started through the downstairs rooms.

It was going to be a long, tiring assignment.

Jason was the team's barrier expert. Cady's team dealt more with perimeters, but he handled the interface. He wanted to see what he had to work with.

When asked, Garrick Crandall said, "The entire estate has hedgerows, both around the edge and in various places throughout."

"We might need to see about something localized to back that up," Jason said.

"I think they're pretty secure."

"Really? Let's take a look then." Jason wasn't convinced, but he wasn't going to call a man he had to work with a liar without checking things out, either.

Crandall gestured for Jason to follow, climbed into a buggy, and drove over the hillcrest and down to the western end of the property. He pulled up along a matted wall of growth.

Jason whistled as he got out. This "hedgerow" was pretty robust. They were what he'd call trash trees, planted perhaps three to a meter without a break, in three rows. About a half meter up, they were notched, bent and had grown into their neighbors, and a half meter above that, notched and bent back. The protruding limbs were trimmed, but the rear limbs grew into a tangled mess with the unmanaged middle row, along with those from the back half of the same growth. It was a near solid mass of wood and debris a meter thick, full of spikes, thorns, nettles, god knew what else, bugs, rot . . . a kilometers-long dreadlock of plantlife. No one was going to cut through that without a power saw, a dozer or explosives, and it wasn't likely much that was man portable would shoot through it, with the shifting densities of dirt, damp timber, weeds and decay.

"I'm convinced," he said. It must have taken decades to grow this wall, but it was completely eco friendly, required no building permits, was hard for anyone to complain about, and cost little. It didn't even really require maintenance. The less it was maintained, the better.

"We've been doing this for a few years in Wales," Crandall said with a smile. "A few thousand."

"You should be proud. That's an elegant and brilliant defense."

"Thank you."

They drove back to the house, and he admired the hedge until it was out of sight.

Back at the house, he cornered Elke.

"The hedgerows are very secure."

"They are," she agreed.

"Can you prepare something in case we need to cut out?"

"Of course. I have."

"Please don't install any devices unless you are specifically asked."

"We will never become lovers with an attitude like that," she replied with a bit of a grin masking a hint of annoyance.

"It's a sacrifice I'll have to make for the sensibilities of legions of bureaucrats who would otherwise suffer damage to their orderly worlds."

"They don't care about you the way I do," she replied, with an almost convincing glint.

"But you'll comply?"

"I will," she said. "Consider my protests to be automatic on matters like this."

If only all their disputes could be resolved so calmly, he thought.

He was back out again a few hours later to show the facilities team around.

Cady's team would normally have arrived first, but they'd first done Bryan's office and Caron's flat. Jason met Cady as she arrived, and her team spread out with more sensors and detection gear. He gave her a summary tour of their work so far.

She said, "The hedges are very secure. We have a good clear field of fire, too."

"I'm so glad they can't hear you say that."

Cady giggled. He always found that a little creepy. Yes, her chromosomes had been mixed up at birth, and she was a good looking woman . . . but that just made knowing she'd been born male that much more awkward. Culturally and legally it wasn't a problem. Personally, though, it was still something unusual. More with various religions still making an issue of it.

That aside, there were eighteen of them on this assignment, plus an open order for backup if they needed it. Eighteen operators on 24/7 was . . . a lot of money. More than some professionals made in a year, per day.

Aramis was almost certainly correct. At some point, they were going to have to earn it.

CHAPTER 3

Horace woke to his alarm. That was good. It meant nothing untoward had happened that night. He stretched, worked out a few knots, and made use of a very nice bathroom. Then he performed his eighty push-ups for the morning and, with slightly elevated pulse and respiration, made his way downstairs. Jason was on watch, as usual. The man liked late hours, and his home planet of Grainne had a long day, making it easy for him to take rotating shifts. It was just 0500 and dawning as Horace walked in and nodded.

"Nothing to report," Jason said. "It's quiet, it's a very nice house, and Elke is sulking because I wouldn't let her mine the stairs this time."

"Understood," Horace agreed. They were a quirky team, but they were a very good team.

Elke could be heard on the stairs right then. He recognized her tread. She hopped down the last few, lit lightly facing them, and spoke.

"I will be printing a form protest I can datestamp and issue each time I am bound by such cuddly rules. I was hired for my expertise in explosives. Refusing permission to use them creates a hostile working environment."

Jason grinned widely. "Good morning to you too, dear."

Horace studied her. She wasn't actually offended, he was sure, but certainly disappointed. She really did love her explosives, and setting them. The problem came afterward. If Elke had a device, she expected to use it. She never seemed truly happy unless there was a rain of rubble, twisted girders and a sharp overpressure wave. Some shooters liked recoil. Some people liked hot food. Elke liked explosions.

There was a knock at the door from the service area—kitchen, pantry, maintenance, and the morning chef pushed her way carefully in with a tray of pastries. Horace untensed and moved his hand from his holster. He could tell Jason did, too, though the man was very subtle. Elke was stonefaced as usual. She was wearing a casual shirt and slacks, with a baton readily visible on a shoulder sling under her left arm. He was positive she had a firearm tucked away somewhere. They all did, rules be damned. Jason's was a reliable, inexpensive little pocket piece. His own was a relic from the last war in Cameroon, with unknown pedigree and rather ugly, but the Serbians had made reliable stuff for centuries.

Jason eyed the cart of food and nodded, "Thank you."

"You're most welcome, gentlemen and lady," the chef said. Joanne? Yes, Joanne Malloy Crandall. She violated the rule of not trusting skinny cooks. She was lithe and well kept for her fiftyish age, and an amazing cook, they'd found out in less than two days.

A buzz on the commo indicated Bart on his way down, with Miss Prescot. That was early. Though Horace recalled she'd retired around 2100. He stepped over and took a cheese Danish and a china cup of coffee, and added real cream and a single spoon of raw sugar. He didn't care much for sweets, and these pastries were mild enough to suit him. Jason took nothing; he never ate early, and not before sleeping, which he was about to do. He handed the logscreen over to Horace and politely excused himself.

Bart and Caron came down, and she immediately focused on the cart.

"Oh, thank you, Joanne. Your timing is perfect."

"I try, miss," the chef smiled. "There are scones in the warmer."

"Excellent."

"These beignets are really good," Elke said around a polite mouthful. She'd already conducted a tactical raid on the cart. "They're made here?"

"Oh, we have those expressed in from a bakery in the French Quarter in New Orleans. I can find the name for you if you like."

Horace choked on his coffee. Her casual comment defined the gulf between them.

Elke said, "That's fine. I'll just enjoy them here."

Horace wondered if his coffee beans had been handpicked the day before by Indonesian virgins, before being roasted over mesquite grown in the Sierra Nevadas, then flown in and prepared by Irish monks. In some ways, the Prescots were very down to earth. In others, so far beyond anyone he'd ever guarded.

Horace waited with Bart and Aramis for Miss Caron to come down to the carriage house, as it was called. "Garage" was more accurate, but didn't do it justice.

They stood next to one of the family's limos, a brand new one from Bentley, in a rich, subtle cognac metallic finish.

Bart looked it over and said, "I have not driven this model in three years. It is much nicer now."

Elke and Jason were with the principal. Alex was already at her apartment giving it another once over. That made several once overs.

Caron came in followed by the two others, her bags ready for school. She had one long garment bag and two smaller ones, which seemed quite reasonable, really. Of course, she had other stuff waiting for her.

Bart climbed in the driver's compartment. Horace held the door as Jason entered first, then Miss Caron, then Elke, then Aramis, then himself.

He'd only seen the vehicles from outside. Inside was surreal.

Caron sat at a desk, and opened a slate and a comm both, to work on her classes. There were directional lamps everywhere. The upholstery was a velvet that was almost fleece, accentuated with leather.

There was a refrigerator containing cold cuts and fruit, that rolled out from under the coffee table and had recesses for cups and glasses. A glass rack was along one side. The other side was a low temperature oven, not in use, but that could hold a rack of lamb or a roast.

Two seats rolled out to beds . . .

The air-expressed beignets were probably in here somewhere, too, he assumed.

Still, Bentleys had real armor plating, and this one seemed to have a good, low center of gravity. It was electric only, but had plenty of capacity. And really, what was wrong with traveling in style?

As they rolled out, two other vehicles went with them, and parted ways within a few kilometers. Garrick Crandall and Ewan Hale were in one, one of Cady's team in the other. Straightforward distraction against anyone observing departure.

"I have two stops on the way," Caron announced.

"Very well, yes?" Alex replied.

"Just a couple of items to check at shops. Is that okay?"

Horace thought it probably wasn't. However, the risk was likely minimal and she'd need time to get used to detailed security. Alex would agree.

He did, though he looked slightly put upon.

Both stores were in a small town not far from, and en route, to the university.

The locals probably knew something was up, with a flashy car and a block of people moving en masse. Caron picked up some specialty food at a shop, then walked two doors down for a Syrian handbag she liked.

It was slightly inconvenient, but they were paid to help her keep some semblance of normality. Aramis wasn't one for shops, but he knew a lot of people, women especially, preferred hands on. Well, he did too at times. He did that at industry shows where he could test fire stuff. Clothes, he measured and ordered, except his dress suits. Then there was...

Okay, it made sense in a lot of ways, and these were personal items. Not that it mattered. Their job was to escort her.

She paid, thanked the storekeeper, an elderly Welsh woman who looked a bit confused at the five "friends" escorting the young lady, and they headed back out into the street in a block.

A young man shouted, "Hey, miss!" and sprinted toward them. A loud bang echoed off the walls.

It might be completely innocent, and it might be an attack in progress.

Elke shoved Caron sideways toward the car. Shaman moved in toward the rear, Jason toward the front. Aramis already had the door open, and Elke shoved her principal down and in. Caron sat heavily and the team tumbled in around her.

In seconds, the two men ran hands over torso, limbs and up to her head.

"Ayyahh!" she yelped.

Jason said, "Sorry. Got to check for injuries. It's strictly professional. You're fine as far as I can tell."

"Well, warn a girl in future." She grinned in relief. "It was almost a good time. And of course I'm fine."

Then she got serious. "Was there actually a threat?"

"Unknown," Elke said. She had her phone live and her fliptop open, scanning something. "Probably not, but we're not paid to take risks, only to protect you."

Jason was scanning his own gear. He said, "I show nothing. If it was a snatch, there's no commo."

"No readings here, either," Elke said. "Likely just an admirer. I've dumped the data to the police for archive. I doubt they'll follow this, but if another event happens we can document a pattern."

Bart asked "Where to, then?"

"Move us to a different route and come in from the side."

"I can do that," he agreed.

Elke ran through her system. "Audio analysis is the bang was a turbine intake catching a spark. It seems to be that older truck two spaces back. I'm amazed it hasn't been converted to the new electric yet."

Alex said, "So no apparent actual threat. Cady confirms alert, no obvious hostiles in area. They'll be watching the garage entrance."

Horace said, "Miss Caron, we'll pat you down any time there's a possibility of injury. Damage often doesn't show, and isn't felt. You did well. You relaxed, we moved you to safety, and vacated the area. That's our standard response."

She blushed. "I didn't even have time to respond. I saw the bloke running, and then you shoved me into the car. Sorry."

Jason said, "Don't apologize. That was fine, and what you should do. I'm guessing he recognized you and wanted to talk. The explosion was coincidental, it seems. However, we'd still have stopped him, and hurried you into the car, in case he was a distraction. Anyone wanting to see you needs an appointment from now on, I'm afraid."

She nodded.

"I have had random strangers try to socialize. Most mean well. Some want a favor or money. It's embarrassing, a bit awkward."

Jason said, "You're probably going to get more of that, money being what it is. There's really no good way to avoid it without looking unkind."

A few minutes later they drove into the dark, guarded cave of the garage. They fell out in formation, Caron seemed a bit more relaxed and took her position, and they walked her upstairs.

Caron found it embarrassing to have this much attention. She understood the possibility of trouble, but the money tied up in protecting her was more than her flat cost several times over, and the flat was decadent.

As she stepped out of the car, the four main goons fell in around her with Horace and Alex out front. She had to admit that Aramis was quite the toned raff. Bart wasn't unattractive, though a bit too rugged, but that body... Jason and Horace and Alex were all distinguished and interesting. Even Elke was an attractive and well-toned woman. The fitness obviously came with the job. So here they were, a wall of flesh around her, keeping her safe from the world.

Alex walked ahead into the lobby, exchanged words with someone in a work coverall, and nodded. They swept past, while a few passersby looked quizzical. She blushed.

Another in the same coverall held the lift door. They crowded in, her in the middle of a square, and went up, silently. Yet another uniform met them on her floor, and two more were at her door. They looked like caretakers, except they were too fit, alert, clean cut and intelligent looking for typical caretakers. Then she was inside and the door closed.

"You are secure, miss," Alex said. "We've swept for bugs, threats, anything out of the ordinary."

She sighed. Her last term, which should be a fun time when not buried in studies. Instead, it was going to be an emotional chore.

"What is our schedule, how will we move?" she asked, avoiding looking at her flat.

Alex said, "Much of that will be held close until the last moment. We'll vary your departure time by several minutes, it's all we can really manage. Two of us will go with you. Spontaneous trips are fine; they're harder to predict. We have the adjoining apartment and those doors connect to it."

She'd seen the doors and figured that was what they were for. Dammit, an apartment like this deserved guests, parties, luxury. Instead it was a highly decorated hermitage and prison, every luxury driving home that it was a substitute for reality and human contact.

Worse, how was she to have such contact, a date? Would she be left alone with a lover? Or would it require a background check and a guard next to the bed? She had no idea of the etiquette for this, and could not bring herself to ask.

The changes to the flat were awful. The windows had bars, charged to resist projectiles, and the latest ballistic glass behind that. They didn't open. The balcony had several layers of protection and was no longer useful nor even decorative.

So far, the flat didn't seem to indicate there was any possibility of social interaction other than through an electronic network.

Well, her registration was all taken care of, by remote and by barrister. She had nothing to do until her first class in the morning.

She did make a tour of the place. Her wardrobe had plenty of variety, hung and racked and neatly folded and ready. It was still the nice place it had been, but every door was composite armor now. The wardrobe was new, because the former one was now a vault that could protect her. It had space for two people. She wondered how her guards would decide which one of them got to be inside with her while the others stopped bullets. That was a little sobering in concept. In reality, of course, she didn't expect that to have the slightest utility. It was just that extreme professional paranoia Garrick had warned her about.

She already knew they couldn't be manipulated the way *Tad* could. A lot of this she'd just have to put up with. However, there must be some ways to counter at least some of the excess.

Elke was ready for Caron the next morning, along with Aramis. They both sat at the dinette table, geared up and ready. Aramis finished a worthy breakfast that was apparently most of a pig prepared five different ways. Elke had eaten lightly. She preferred to snack on fruits, vegetables, meat and cheese throughout the day rather than demolish calories in blocks.

She felt a little nervous about her upcoming plan. It should work, but it required things she found a little uncomfortable.

Caron seemed emotionally okay, if a little cool. That was expected. She came through in a jacket and slacks that were semi-professional. She had good taste. That likely had to do with the occasional but permanent risk of cameras. Nothing Elke had ever heard about the family sunk to the depths so many did, even though most such depths were completely average. The very wealthy were culturally prohibited from being average.

"What do I need to do this morning, then?" Caron asked.

"Just go to school as usual," Jason said. "I'm posted here, Alex back at the house, and the rest will rotate with you at school or while traveling."

"Very well," she nodded. "I have an invitation to a party for Friday. A term opener. I didn't RSVP."

"Good. I'm assuming you plan to attend?"

"If that's acceptable, yes."

"Miss, we're at your disposal. If you wish to go, we'll make it work. I just recommend never RSVPing and showing up at odd times, and not to everything, nor even everything that seems choice. It will make you less predictable. It might also give you a reputation as an even nicer lady for showing up at some of the less-regarded events."

"That's good advice," she agreed. "Yes, this Friday is a go."

"I'll plan accordingly."

Bart, Aramis and Elke rose and went with her, Bart first through the door.

Since the previous night, one of the elevators had been walled off and made private. That seemed to confuse her a bit. She gave a slight nod to Aramis.

Yup, she knew enough engineering to grasp it. She was gifted in brains as well as in . . . well, he shouldn't think like that, in case he blurted something out at some point.

A man from Cady's team, Adam Helas, stood near the limo. Everything was under both human and electronic security. Aramis was still a bit stunned himself, by the cost of all this. Money was no object. People said that. Few meant it.

Bart drove along a couple of thoroughfares, and on manual. Always manual for this. No automated system that someone could hack was allowed to control the vehicle. In fact, Jason had gutted the controls quite thoroughly. There was supposed to be a regionally assessed fine for that. Either political connections were involved or the fine was just paid. What was money?

In future, they might pull up in several locations from either direction for each location. Today, Bart simply drove past the front of the hall her first class was in, and braked.

"Out now," Elke said, and was on the pavement herself in less than a second. Caron moved fast for a civilian, though they'd need to politely work on that. Aramis followed and Bart moved.

Caron seemed embarrassed by the attention, but she took it gamely. As they left the vehicle, she managed an expression that was slightly haughty and partly casual with just a hint of amusement. She probably found it easier with only two guards, rather than the whole box, especially as Aramis held back and wasn't readily apparent.

A "temporary" security elevation had existed for close to twenty years in England, based on a couple of earlier incidents. While it wasn't practical to search everyone passing through every time, what Alex rudely called "Security theater" existed to dissuade disgruntled students. Anything obviously a weapon would probably trigger alarms.

So, Aramis walked through the atrium with minimal hardware, alongside Caron, whose doccase and comm were completely unremarkable, as if anyone would question her in the first place.

Then Elke walked past the sensors.

The scanner went schizo.

It chimed, flashed and presumably showed a variety of hardware to the monitor station. Elke helpfully pulled out her stun baton and extended it grip first to the guard.

As he started backing up, she pulled out a canister of tear gas and held it out with the other hand, with a helpfully blank expression on her face.

She said, "I didn't think you'd want these unattended on the scanner belt."

"Ma'am! Please!" the old man said. He didn't seem like a former cop. Probably a career security guard. A relatively well-armed professional was beyond him.

Elke shoved the baton into his hands, and pulled out her cuffs, then a small and legal knife that was nevertheless against campus "policy." She had a small extendable plastic baton, barely legal, as its only purpose was to physically beat on people.

She handed over a small but practical arsenal, then extended her arms to be wanded. Aramis watched her cringe slightly as she was touched and patted. The mass of students stopped and stared for a few moments.

With everyone distracted, Aramis turned, took Caron's arm and walked off. His own hardware was as objectionable to them, but forgotten in the mixup.

A point had been made. Caron's bodyguard cared nothing for university policy.

The unmade point was that Aramis had snuck in quietly.

The next day, Elke would repeat the process. Whichever covert agent was assigned to the task would shortly have a full suite of nonlethal hardware in case things turned sour.

The only downside, from Aramis's point of view, and he was sure from Elke's too, was that they were *non*lethal.

Though if Jason could accomplish a late-night survey, they might get around that limitation, too.

In the lecture hall, Elke sat next to Caron, near enough to an exit for a hasty retreat, not close enough to be easily targeted. If there was a panic, Elke might have to disable a few bodies to make a hole for her principal. She understood that bothered some people, so she wouldn't discuss it. Aramis was within sight on the far end of another row. He could easily be present for lectures with credentials that marked him as an "examiner" from the British National University Board. The credentials were real, and examiners did sit in on occasion. The Board would be surprised to find Ripple Creek had acquired those credentials. So, in fact, would the person who issued them, though not as surprised as the Board officer who had approved them without his knowledge.

However, he couldn't walk into labs without being questioned and made, so he'd spend some time in other classes for cover, as near as he could manage to Elke and Caron. Elke knew she'd be stressed in a lab full of potential explosives and weapons and a principal to guard. She reminded herself that most people, even with the theoretical knowledge, wouldn't think to whip up a device on the premises, nor were most of them hostile.

It was unfortunate that the old schools insisted on classrooms rather than remote learning, for some cultural reason. Though, it somewhat paralleled military training by keeping the students in a structured environment.

The last term was eight weeks, and Elke would be busy most hours of most days. There were other females available, but it did make sense to keep their team as a unit, and they were among the best at this work. After the term, Elke would have enough time to buy some nice things, like perhaps those multifrequency overlays for her glasses, or a couple of pairs of the Belleville pumps that flattened out to cushioned running shoes.

She noted the time, realized there were only five minutes left, and she'd managed to completely ignore a lecture on environmental impacts and the growing glaciation. She could ignore one lecture a week in each class, and the work groups would be easier to monitor as she could walk around.

As the tone sounded time, she rose and preceded Caron out the door.

Right outside, someone called, "Caron!" and Elke turned while reaching for her remaining weapon; a pocket stunner Aramis had slipped her.

Caron called back, "Mitzi! Cheers!"

"Good to see you!"

Caron looked cautiously at Elke while hugging her friend. Elke gave no response. She wasn't going to prohibit such things, but she did not endorse them.

Mitzi stepped back and said, "So, will I see you on Friday?"

"Possibly. I can't plan ahead anymore. It depends on security issues." She gestured her head toward Elke.

Mitzi turned and said, "Oh! Well, obviously you're welcome too."

Elke smiled professionally and said, "Thank you. I don't make the schedule, but I appreciate the offer, if there is opportunity."

"Great. Are you Czech, may I ask?"

"From Hradec Králové," Elke said.

"Oh, how pretty." She turned back to Caron. "Well, good luck."

"Ta, Mitzi. And you."

CHAPTER 4

Bryan Prescot disliked the extra security as much as Caron did. He wouldn't admit so, and he tolerated it because it was a good precaution, and as an example to her. He loved his daughter more than anything, and had even before Ashier left. He'd thought it rather asocial of the woman to dump the child on him, but in retrospect he was quite happy. Caron seemed to be, too.

Guards outside his office didn't bother him much; he kept the door closed. Chauffeurs and escorts were part of his life and had been for decades. A walking block of human bullet traps, though, seemed pretentious and silly. On the other hand, the building was named after him.

Joe was waiting in the Prescot Tower atrium with his own, cheaper detail. They seemed perfectly competent, and Bryan wondered if he'd overspent.

"Afternoon, Joe."

Joe grinned. "Good afternoon. You saw my report?"

"Skimmed it. It's just more money."

"Just more money? You wound me! Half a percent here, a few quid there, another billion somewhere else..."

"I'm impressed and grateful. It's just that after a while, they're just numbers. The important part is that we're now prepping the next generation of technological development for Caron to take over."

"I suppose, if you look at it that way. I still find challenge in it."

"So challenge yourself, and accept everyone's gratitude for brilliant work."

There was some jostling. The two teams had trouble interacting. Both recommended using just one contractor for all security. Bryan thought that was a good idea, but Joe could pout almost as well as Caron. He liked the team he'd had these last three months. They'd been with him while on Govannon, too, so they meshed well. The only real issue was when both teams got together.

I should have ordered security for everyone, not just recommended he get some. It wasn't an issue until now. It might not be for long, though, since they were swapping off on mine oversight. Long term, though.

Long term, the idea was not to need to live like a feudal lord. He sighed.

"I wish we could do dinner as we used to. This is very aggravating. No offense to you, of course," he said to his entourage. Two of them smiled slightly and shrugged. So reticent.

They had to take two lifts, but they were keyed and controlled, so they both reached bottom together. There was no underground for vehicles here, and no practical way to create one now. All the security people objected to that, but, while there were lots of things he could do by remote, holo and conference, some things did require a personal appearance, and the point of a headquarters was that the head was there.

They stepped out, and moved across the lobby toward the file of cars under the awning, visible through the now even better armored glass. He approved of that. It protected employees and guests, too. The awning was to be made wider and closed off somewhat, starting next week. As long as the openness was kept, he approved. He didn't want it to look like a fortress.

A waft of air blew past and outside because of the building pressure, so it was two steps before he smelt the city air. It wasn't as clean, but it felt more natural. He spent far too long cooped up. More time outside was what he needed.

A moment later, he wondered what the hell was going on, as he was stuffed into the limo's seat, while people shouted and piled around him. The car ripped away as he choked for breath, was pulled upright and patted all over.

"Sir, how are you? Any injuries?" Kent Ready, that was the man's name.

"I'm fine," he insisted. "What the hell was that?"

"Shots fired, sir. From the south. We're detouring north and will pick up the M Four before turning toward Wales. We've called Metro and National."

Shots?

"I believe you," he said, and burned red. "But I honestly didn't hear a thing. I'm sorry."

"That's why you hired us, sir."

"How's Joe? And all your people?"

"Everyone is fine, barring some scrapes from taking cover. Thanks for asking."

"Thank you for protecting me, I suppose. I mean, you did, and I'm thankful. This just isn't something I learned the manners for." Shot at? Really?

"That's fine, sir. We're out of the area and should be safe."

Someone else said, "Metro is sending a chopper to overfly."

Kent shook his head. "Negative. If they want to, I want them not to."

"Understood."

Bryan asked, "You don't trust the Metropolitan Police?"

"Sir, I don't trust anyone."

Alex, Cady and Ramon Jukov sat in the command center. What had been fliptops and portable communication gear was now built onto the back of the house, a modern, military-looking and armored sore in contrast to the old stone. It was a useful retreat if there was time.

Alex was stressed because the real world threats were becoming clear.

Jukov said, "It's relatively easy from my end. We can surround Bryan around the clock and it doesn't matter if the stockholders don't like it. The threats, though . . ."

Cady pointed at the armored roof and said, "We have this. I'm coordinating on the apartment and his office, of course. But school and travel are the weak points."

Alex said, "So, looking at it again, we have no general perception of animosity. There are the usual activists opposed to corporate whatever, but they don't tend toward more than annoying protests. The public doesn't really care about the family or the business, they're just one of those names in the news. There's no activity that would draw a lot of attention personally. But, we have two threatening notes, one delivered personally to the front door of the company HQ, and one message forwarded to a private account. Either one could be a crank. Both together in short order indicate some kind of intent, even if it's only to cause distress."

All three of their phones rang simultaneously with one of the control center's bands.

"Shit!" Alex said, echoed similarly by the others. That almost certainly meant...

Cady answered and flipped to speaker.

"We're all three here," she said.

"Shots fired," came the report. "Two shots fired at Bryan and Joseph outside HQ. No injury, no contact, local police found unmarked weapon on rooftop."

"Unmarked?" Alex asked.

"Unmarked and antique. Well over a century old, rifle firing metallic cased rimmed rounds."

"Clever enough," Jukov commented. "Untraceable, lethal, disposable."

"Response?" Cady asked.

"Both principals in limo, tag team set up, dispersal, standard plan."

"Understood. Keep us informed, use my code."

"Will do."

The three stared at each other for a second, and Alex could feel the tension trickle through the room.

"So," Jukov said, "we have hostile action. Potentially lethal, though not very effective. We can't assume the intent is just intimidation, so we have to escalate."

"The last shots fired at executives or ranking politicians in Europe was fifteen years ago," Alex said. "So this is serious enough."

Cady said, "Well, as I noted, I can reinforce facilities more and have further patrols and flights, but we have limited cleared personnel, even if Mr. Prescot allows. Personnel, though..."

"They won't hear of pulling her out of school. I'll have to make other plans," Alex said.

"On the bright side, I expect our advice will be heeded a bit more," Jukov said.

CHAPTER 5

The next day, additional security measures were put in place. Caron was publicly escorted by Elke and Bart, and Jason found a reason to skulk around after meeting with the dean and head of security. Elke felt better with backup. Security wasn't about pretending to be nice. Security was about providing force.

After a visibly uneventful day, Shaman showed up in a limo, swapped seats with Bart, who then drove to a prearranged appointment even Caron didn't know about. The car passed through three rings of London, paying a heftier fee each time to be allowed access to the roads, and pulled up in front of an old building with a simple brass sign, "Fashion by Joy."

They flowed out of the vehicle and straight through the door, and up to a first floor—meaning second floor outside of Britain—studio behind a glass and brass entrance that would stop some artillery fire.

Joy Alexander awaited, with two of Cady's men who'd swept her shop earlier.

"Welcome," she said, with a gracious sweep. "You must be Miss Prescot."

"Please do call me Caron. I've of course heard of you, Ms. Alexander."

"It's a privilege to provide you with a wardrobe."

"Yes, I appreciate it." Caron looked puzzled. "I wasn't aware I was getting more."

Elke sat back where she could watch the polarized windows and the door. With Bart outside and Aramis looking for threats across the street, she felt safe enough. All she had to do was watch and listen, as Caron got fitted for an entire wardrobe. This wardrobe would be classy, upscale, and loaded with useful tools in case of further incursions or attacks.

Joy Alexander would never be considered pretty. Elke had seen her on TV, and she dressed well enough for her figure, and wasn't unattractive. She was just rather plain, short and a bit overweight.

Still, it was not obvious. The woman really did know how to dress, which was why she got paid as much as she did. This line of clothing was specifically for clients like the Prescots, and had been designed with the aid of several experts in the field.

"First, we're going to update your accessories," Alexander said. She opened up a real but probably lab-grown leather jewelry case the size of a doccase, and unfolded the inner partitions.

Caron looked on with interest at the show. Elke kept professional eyes on it and looked up periodically to scan the room.

"That's a lot of sunglasses," Caron commented.

"You'll wear them from now on. Ten styles and colors to suit any outfit. Do you ever wonder why celebs wear them?"

"I assume to hide their faces, disguise them somewhat."

"That, and to hide their expressions. These are also self-polarizing enough for one of the military's flash bang grenades, or camera lights, or even some incendiaries. They're ballistically proof against pistol fire or some shrapnel. They all have built in transponders for location tracking, which your security team will be able to follow. They have a laminate frequency shifter to improve your vision in low light."

"So I should wear these inside as well?"

"Especially inside, and outside at night. That's where flash is most effective at stunning. If it creates a new trend, of course I will sell plain, un-upgraded versions through my brand." Alexander smiled. She did know how to make money, after all.

"I suppose I can get used to them," Caron said. She flipped open a pair, tested their mechanism, and twisted them around. In Elke's estimation, they really were fantastic sunglasses on top of everything else, and probably sold for around a thousand marks a pair. Caron slipped them on, nodded at the fit and looked in a mirror.

"Oh, I do like them," she agreed. "Mysterious, sophisticated."

"Larger eyes are seen as more attractive. While these aren't eyes, they lend a similar effect. You have oval and oblong lenses, and the angular ones. I think the angular will suit you better for daily wear. The oblong are probably more suited to evening."

"Very good," Caron said. Elke could tell she was eager to move on.

Alexander said, "Okay, these aren't jewelry, but the earbuds contain active noise-cancelling circuits. You should wear these whenever your team thinks it advisable; they help with flash bangs, too, and with sonic stunners to some extent. They are small and hard to see, but you'll still want to style your hair over them."

"Okay."

Alexander held up a necklace on a fine chain.

"Now, this is real platinum, rhodium, silver, gold. The gems are real. Each also contains a tiny transponder; we want you to have as many means of contact as possible. If you snap them off and drop them, they are a low-power, but very loud and bright flash bang."

"Am I okay using those?" Caron asked, looking up at Elke.

"I know the model," Elke said. "They will be annoying to us, but not critically debilitating. The plan is that any attackers will not know of them, and we gain the advantage for a few moments. If you feel the need if we're attacked, say if someone gets inside our perimeter, you should use them. If alone or cut off, you should use them as soon as you think you are threatened. Even with the glasses, you should close your eyes for a moment."

Caron nodded, and accepted the jewels carefully but with interest.

"Now, a variety of accessories your security detail will teach you about. These lacewood hairsticks are actually boron composite inside. One Mont Blanc pen has a single tear gas shot in it for close quarters, the other contains another stiletto. Your watches have alarms built into them. Slap down hard on the face and it will transmit. Your purse straps are reinforced cord. This looks exactly like your family ring, but has a stun gun built into it. You get two good shots, and it will need to be recharged periodically. There are two of them."

"So be careful how you hug." Elke grinned.

Caron smiled back. "This is rather spy thrillerish. I didn't know stuff like this really existed."

"It does for a few million marks," Alexander said. "Your father paid for a lot of the development, which means a little more income for both him and my sales company."

"Yes, that happens a lot," Caron said, blushing.

They were at the point, Elke thought, where any development of any kind was going to generate more income. They'd have trouble spending enough in any fashion to get poor, or even just less rich.

"Now, I have replacements for several of your outfits with me," Alexander said. "I tailored them to your new measurements."

"Good," Caron said. She smiled and shrugged at Elke. "More boob."

"You would not want to be pinched, I imagine," Elke replied smoothly.

"All your clothing other than evening gowns now has ballistic armor in it. It won't stop bullets, but it will help with any fragmentation or knives."

"Is that necessary?" Caron asked Alexander.

Alexander turned to Elke, who turned to Caron and said, "We don't expect direct attacks against you. However, if one is directed at us, you could be at risk. There's also always a risk in a hand-to-hand fight, of someone mixing up with you."

Caron looked somewhat reassured, but still rather sobered. "Okay," she said.

Alexander continued, "You'll be wearing a lot of corsets and bodices, both as outerwear and underwear. The reason is, we can incorporate better body armor into them."

Caron asked, "Do I have to regard everyone in the world as a threat at this point?"

"Only those who might consider killing or kidnapping you for a billion marks," Elke said. Caron nodded and sighed.

There was still more. Alexander said, "These belts are strong enough to rappel with, will work as tourniquets, and as belts. You should wear one in most outfits."

"They certainly are stylish. Name brand," Caron said.

"On the outside, yes. Eventually I'll secure licensing rights. For now, these are private for you. And this." Alexander grabbed a belt buckle and pulled. Out came a pair of boron fiber claws, contoured to exactly follow the curve of the belt around Caron's waist, which was coincidentally a great angle to hook someone in the guts or under the chin.

"Oh, my." Caron accepted the weapon and looked both impressed and shocked.

Alexander said, "I'll seal everything here, and your couriers will deliver it, yes?"

"That's the plan," Elke agreed. She couldn't guess if Alex would change plans partway through, just to wrench anything someone might try. "Take your time, Caron. When you are ready we'll head back."

"But how will I be able to use this properly?"

"We'll train you. Our job is to stop threats from reaching you. If we fail, you use these."

"Well, let me try the outfits then," Caron said, obviously uncomfortable. She scooped up two bodices and some slacks and headed for the dressing room.

Elke snagged her arm.

"Sorry, we need to keep you in sight anywhere out of your apartment from now on."

"Oh." That made the young woman sigh and pout. "I guess I don't have a choice."

She didn't, but the men had politely turned toward windows and doors. Elke kept her eyes on Caron and Alexander and anything in the room someone might hide behind. It was ridiculous. It was also imperative.

Caron tried the outfits, approved the fit, and seemed eager to leave.

"Follow me, then," Elke said.

Once in the limo, Elke said, "We have a couple of additional things, too."

"Oh? Like?"

"This." She handed over a small tube.

"That's a hash pipe," Caron said, looking cross.

Elke said, "Technically, it's a 'one-hitter.' You hold it up, click the igniter, and it will deliver a lungful of concentrated THC vapor, either as smoke or as a mist with flavor mixes."

"So what does it really do?"

"You exhale and it blows out a sleeping gas that will fill a car's compartment. There's also this one that looks like an asthma inhaler." She handed it over. "Acting nervous shouldn't be a problem. Then you disable everyone in the vehicle, assuming slow speed or crash webs."

"Including myself?"

"Yes. Don't inhale or you'll just collapse and leave them wondering."

Caron burst out in musical laughter.

"That is both wonderful and terrible, and I feel like I'm in some spy sensie."

"Yes, but this can disable a carful of people. You must take it seriously."

"Oh, I do. It's just . . . I understand. It's serious, but it seems so fun."

"Any of your transponders will squawk if you just snap the chain. I mean they'll be loud enough to disorient people, and draw attention. Of course, that compromises them. But you can choose to draw attention, or have us track you covertly."

"I really will need some training in all that."

Bart said, "I will do so. It's not as complicated as it seems."

"There is one more thing," Elke said.

"Yes?"

"You must discuss this with no one. Not your father or uncle, not the staff, not even our associates from other teams. This is training and gear between us and our principal."

"But doesn't Joy . . . ?"

"She provides many types of devices to many people. The specifics are tailored. None of this is beyond an expert to figure out. It just slows them down. The result is that experts are unlikely to bother, because legitimate income is easier. Amateurs will be hindranced enough we can stop them. In between is a gray shade of people who are trained enough and willing. Those are the real threat now."

"I understand," Caron said, looking serious and sober but not frightened.

Elke didn't mention the other precautions they'd taken, that they wouldn't share even with their principal. If it went well, she'd never know.

The man responsible for the shots was rather pleased. They'd not been expected to be real threats, and in fact, he'd have been rightfully pissed if they were. No, just enough to scare those macho thugs into cracking down. The daughter was more sequestered, and Bryan Prescot was more removed from his staff. That was a good thing. Separate them all from each other, and their friends and employees, then move in. Ideally, it would be bloodless.

They'd added quite a bit of security, though, and that would make further attacks more awkward. Or rather, convincingly believable ones more awkward. However, it took money to make money. Proper investments would result in more threats. This was a financial game. They didn't have to succeed, just look like they might have succeeded.

At the same time, though, there were a finite number of possible threats. He had to keep things discreet, anonymous, infrequent and unpredictable. Games theory said that each successive attack would narrow the possible origins. He had to move them where he wanted them, and do it shortly after the term ended, but without making it look like a maneuver.

The best thing, then, was to encourage amateur freelancers. He was rather sure enough chaos would cause the Ripple Creek people to recommend a withdrawal. If not, the family security almost certainly would, and if not, then Joe Prescot definitely would.

Predictability was useful at times.

"Well, the good news is I was able to do a tactical survey of the school, with the blessing of both school and local police," Jason said.

"So what's the bad?" Aramis asked from a dilapidated couch he'd arranged to have delivered to their on-site command room.

"They were pretty close to me the whole time."

"So you weren't able to hide anything?"

Aramis looked relaxed on that couch. Jason thought he might, too. Good purchase. It wasn't nice enough to worry about, unlike everything in the estate and most of the stuff across the hall in the principal's apartment.

"You know me better than that. However, I was limited to stuff that wouldn't give off a traceable signature. So no actual explosive. But, since we went past the area the chemistry labs are in, I was able to stash Elke's backup gear. It won't show."

Elke looked disgusted. "Did you also stash me some sinew and chipped flint?"

"I did what I could. Sorry."

"It's fine. I will adapt. However, every assignment, I am more and more tempted by Novaja Rossia or Grainne. There are too many rules on Earth meant simply to inconvenience me."

Alex said, "Just make sure it's not discussed anywhere else. Even our employers are timid on this subject."

Elke shook her head. "The nature of this society saddens me. For people descended from Celts, Romans and Vikings, they are pale shadows."

"We're fine, Alex. And of course you'll remind us again, because you have to."

"Yup. We understand each other."

"With that, it's dinner time. Those chickens should be roasted."

"Bring it on," Aramis said.

After that, it was up to Bart to teach tactics.

"We will go through this quickly, and we will go through it daily," Bart said. "You will quickly learn instincts for using the devices without having to stop and think."

"Good," Caron said. "I like not having to be a helpless princess."

"So what do you have?"

"I wear armor, I have the briefcase, the brolly, my glasses and the stun baton that looks like a silly talisman."

"Yes, that is the correct order. Wear the armor from the case, then open the umbrella, and use the baton or your other personal weapons as needed. We will also work on how to seek cover. We will do this regularly, and sometimes in front of staff."

"Doesn't that risk leakage? Of the information?"

"We hope so," Jason said. "If a particular item is compromised, we have a good suspect on who the leak was. That's why there are multiples of almost everything."

"I hate not being able to trust anyone. I'd give all the money away if it would help."

Bart said, "Celebrities enjoy their money but hate the fame. Not being able to walk down the street, shop, talk to anyone. You have some of that. It could be worse."

"Yes. Well, let's get to it, then."

Bart raised his headset and advised, "This is Bart. Test session. Thirty minutes." He turned back to Caron and said, "Let me see you activate your earrings."

She clutched at her ears and squeezed.

He grabbed toward her, being careful and slow, and she responded with the baton.

"Good," he said.

"That was so slow," she protested. "I could easily read you."

"Yes," he agreed. "I will get faster as we go. Within a week you will be quite fast and not have to think."

"Okay, then," she agreed.

He just hoped things stayed calm for that week.

After thirty minutes of practice, he let her sit down and relax. He'd prefer more time, but as with all principals, she had major life issues to deal with. Her classwork must be done, too.

Elke came in for the late evening shift. She was managing on two lengthy naps a day, of about four hours each. She could do this for a while, but Caron and her family would soon have to adapt to men around her even in private surroundings. More so with the threat level raised.

Caron acknowledged her but didn't speak, being busy with some project or other. Elke found a seat and studied details around the room to keep herself alert and awake. Four hours of nothing was bad enough. Four hours of nothing while Caron listened to bad music, hummed and muttered to herself, shifted and moved around and constantly stared at her with an annoyed expression was very hard on the nerves. But it was what she was paid for.

Elke noted the apartment was fairly dusty; the shelf across the room already needed to be wiped. That indicated Caron was very wrapped up in her studies, because she did a good job of maintaining the place. The dishes were done, the sonic washer empty and the kitchen quite neat. The climate control might need to be adjusted. The temperature swung a couple of degrees, and Elke could feel the breeze get warmer and cooler. She'd mention that to Jason. Caron seemed to get more and more agitated, then pull herself back down. That was partly attention to her work, but she also probably found Elke unwelcome for something private.

That continued to get worse for almost an hour, then—

"Arrrgh!" Caron slapped her fliptop closed and flung her notepad across the room.

"Yes, miss?" Elke asked at once. She relaxed as soon as she determined it was frustration, not a threat.

"Transmission design. I *hate* it."

"Ah. Tough problem?" She recovered the notepad from the couch—at least Caron wasn't the kind to smash things, only toss them in frustration. Elke handed it back to her.

Caron read from her screen.

"'A prospecting crew has left an omnidirectional beacon on a metallic planetoid with a high concentration of readily extractable ores (Subtype M Six). The beacon broadcasts a digital, spread spectrum signal containing its ID, contents, and location in space; however, when you go to the broadcast location, you find that the coordinates are in error. Directional receivers are unable to triangulate the location of the beacon due to the presence of multiple other beacons, interference from iron-containing ores, and signal bounce off intervening masses. Your prospecting ship contains a number of similar omnidirectional spread-spectrum beacons that can be set to receive instead of transmit. Describe a method for triangulating the desired beacon location using only these omnidirectional receivers.'"

"Ah. So it's a signal propagation problem."

"You're familiar with it?" Caron asked. She seemed surprised.

"I work with explosives. Signal theory is a prerequisite for proper remote detonation, and for dismantling foreign devices."

"Oh. Of course." Caron took a moment to think on that.

"I'd lay it out as a direct-sequence spread spectrum design." Elke leaned over and sketched on the notepad.

She thought for a minute to translate from Czech to English, since this was a very technical discussion.

She said, "Inverse square alone would be enough to triangulate source if there was no interference. But iron-containing asteroids and other radio sources will spoof with signal strength, so by using code division across a spread-spectrum you can calibrate the noise from interference sources and use timing differences to also estimate distance. Iron is mentioned, so correct for its reflection and absorption across the frequency spectrum. Adjust the apparent signal strength at the receivers to accurately indicate the distance to the beacon. If you need to fine tune more, take the M Six type's content average of nickel and cobalt—and iridium is a relatively very powerful interferer in Sol system, I recall. Allow for those. Don't forget the alloying structure if it's pure enough ore to alloy, and how it affects reflectivity. That should be in your metallurgy for antennae texts."

Caron squinted, seemed to grasp it, and said, "I'll try it that way. Thanks."

"You're welcome. For metallurgy or mechanical engineering, you can ask Jason. Shaman, of course, knows biology. Bart can help with steam turbines. Alex knows marine geology and history. Aramis is actually well read in surveying, cartography and the aerial geometry for it."

It was amusing to see the girl mouth silently. She'd obviously never considered that her security team was trained to do anything other than pull triggers and stop bullets.

Caron dove back into her coursework. Elke couldn't fault her work ethic, and she was a very bright girl. If she stuck to it, she had the potential to make her family business a long-lasting legacy.

Caron finally went to bed at 0135. Jason came on duty at 0200.

Jason checked the corridor to ensure he was secure. He knocked while buzzing a code. The two together, along with cameras monitored here and at Alex's desk made a pretty good protection screen.

Elke answered the door with a pistol, of course.

"Good morning," he said as he walked in. "I say that because I haven't slept yet. That's the only kind of good morning." He sat down at the dining table that was their ersatz office. He hated mornings, so he tried to stay awake late enough to sleep through them.

"Things are well enough," Elke reported as she secured the door behind him. "You should have a fairly quiet time."

"Good." It could be boring, but that was better than the alternative.

Right then, Caron's door opened and she wandered out, giving a quick nod.

"I just need a snack," she said, looking slightly shy.

He didn't think she was being a tease deliberately this time. Likely she was feeling and a bit more comfortable with her security. That was a good thing. But she was wearing a T-shirt that ended just high enough for him to wonder about panties. Damn the woman. She opened the fridge and bent, legs demurely together, and he looked away.

"No worry," Elke said, walking past the alcove toward the table.

Caron stood up with a chunk of real Cheddar cheese and a Golden Delicious apple, and padded back to her bedroom.

"G'night," she said.

"Night, miss," Jason agreed.

"No, she wasn't," Elke said, fumbling with her fliptop.

"Wasn't what?"

Elke swung the screen around.

It showed a low angle but very well-framed image of Caron from the underside. No, she wasn't wearing panties.

Very, very impressive. That was all he could think about Elke's photographic skill. The image itself was just...

"I don't know if I should thank you or hate you."

"Either way. I'm scrubbing it in ten seconds."

"I assume you're considering that recon practice."

"What else would it be? Done?"

"Yes, thank you."

"Don't mention it."

"Never."

CHAPTER 6

Caron had the invitation to the party that Friday. As instructed, all public comment was that it was unlikely she could appear, but might try. Then the team planned for her to actually attend.

Aramis found her to be a bit scatterbrained, and she was definitely not happy with heightened security. She was antsy, irritable and cast glares around her. He knew it was hard for someone to ramp up from no major security issues to high threat level, so he didn't see any need to report it, other than in the routine end of shift notes.

Still, it couldn't be easy to never enter a room unless someone else checked it first, and have the wall of meat surrounding one nonstop. She wasn't socializing much, either. A hush hood for her phone had arrived earlier, and she'd been delighted. Her phone was built into an ear hoop and headpiece. One of her phones.

Still, she was holding up well enough. Protection detail got boring in controlled spaces, but that was better than being in the open. Still, as long as it was possible for someone to rocket or mortar the building, or fly a drone, the technical gadgets and the armed troops—Aramis—were part of the package. In a case like that, all he could do was help her evacuate, or act as a portable heavy metal collection point.

So he sat at the dining table in her barely twenty-square-meter apartment, and quite nice it was, though the amenities were on the practical side, not flamboyant excess. He sat, kept alert for threats and was thoroughly bored, his brain running through the lists of neat tactical and field gear he could buy with his money and the company arranged licenses, the car at home he would upgrade yet again shortly, and perhaps he should consider Jason's advice about a kilt.

The part of his mind that watched her was his professional principal-watching sector, that saw only a body, the space around it in zones, and potential threats in those zones.

He noted as she bustled around and gathered things, and kept the bedroom door open. That lack of privacy, and the need to be in sight of someone almost constantly, was part of what still pissed her off.

She came out with a faint quizzical look on her face, puttered around, then hmmph'ed and walked toward him.

"I'm told I can trust you implicitly," she said, staring at him with challenge in her eyes.

"Absolutely. It's what I'm paid for. I could even give you references, except I won't." A lot of people didn't get that joke, but she did.

Prescot almost smiled. It was more a glint. She turned and headed for her bedroom.

Moments later she came out with three dresses. She draped them over the couch, and started unbuttoning her blouse.

The bitch, Aramis thought. Yes, she really was.

Shortly, she was naked, though turned casually away, giving him a view of that impossibly curved ass. She grabbed a gown, stood and turned, letting him see her entire profile, taut and stretched, then shimmied it down over her body.

"What do you think?

Of the dress? Because I'd kill to touch that body.

"I'm not sure red is your color," he offered calmly. It was a good thing she couldn't read his biometric monitor.

"Very well." She drew it up and off, legs just slightly spread, and tried the second.

"White's a bit better," he agreed, trying to keep completely detached. The dress clung like paint.

"I'm not sure it's what I want. Everyone will be in black or white," she said. "Perhaps the blue."

She turned demurely, and then had to bend, twist and squirm to get the snug fabric off. All the while, his view was full of the gyrations of that ass.

The blue slipped right over her head, rippled into place as

she smoothed it over her curves by hand. It really did suit her flawless olive skin.

"I think that's it," he said.

"I think so, too," she agreed, smiled, and gathered up the other two dresses. "Thanks for the help," she said as she carried them back to the bedroom.

"You're welcome, miss," he replied. If she was going to pretend that was what she was doing, so was he, until he could find a cold shower and something to dull his brain.

The local police and campus security were informed an hour before, with a previously agreed fee paid to each for responding. This wasn't an official function, nor was there an actual incident, so their presence was paid for to offset expenses. This was not a bribe, though Jason couldn't help but think it always seemed that way in cases like this.

Back home on Grainne, of course payment would be expected, and there would be no hint of impropriety, because that's how things were done. Here, it would be seen and treated almost as a bribe even though it was officially legal. Earth, especially Europe, was bipolar over such things.

The party hosts probably realized Caron was coming the moment a swarm of cops arrived and started scanning for weapons and bugs. Then Cady's team arrived to double check. Everything was aboveboard and safe, because while it would be possible to bribe some cops, bribing an entire shift, and campus security, was incredibly unlikely, so they'd support each other. Those odds also meant any dedicated threat wouldn't bother. Again, enough money could solve most such problems, either as tax, bribes, payoffs or in security. It was almost pointless. Long term, though, good security was more cost effective, and morally better.

They were already in the limo when they got the word things were clear.

"Clear," of course, was a relative term. Caron's obscurity was washing away fast in the wake of the attack on her father and uncle, and the heightened and more visible security. The entourage drove up in the Mercedes limo and stepped out. A temporary additional cordon moved the press across the street, but they took images and video of the entirely mundane act of stepping out of a car and into a residence hall for a party.

Inside, things were a bit sullen, because no one was allowed anywhere but restrooms, kitchen and the common hall without escort by cop. After a few hesitant trips, people stopped even bothering with items forgotten in rooms.

There were snacks and music and young people and limited liquor, though. No one seemed willing to pursue other mind-altering substances, even legal. The goon presence just intimidated them to withdrawal. That was not going to help Caron's social life.

Mitzi was the hostess, and her expression shifted from murderous to cheerful between Jason leading the way through the door and Caron two steps behind. Caron moved forward and hugged her.

The overall reception was about as chilly as a Finnish winter, but Bart came in last, pushing a cart of accessories, from champagne and fine beer to tequila and even off-world imports, with trays of chocolate and fine cheeses. It wasn't really in their job description, but it did help with the awkwardness, and definitely lightened the party mood. With that and a helpful DJ and light mixer, the party achieved an adequate level of levity in a few minutes.

The security was still intrusive. Everyone present was vetted by the local police and had to be checked off a list Alex compiled. Anyone with a questionable background, not initially listed or not a student didn't come in. Four supplemental RC personnel shook everyone down, then handed them back their recreational drugs and booze, after bagging potential weapons and most electronics with claim checks they could use later. Phones didn't work in here unless specifically authorized. The room used for dance wasn't dark, and it had a police officer inside. It didn't matter that his position was only to watch for real threats, not petty crimes, he was a damper on festivities.

Still, it was likely there'd be a lot less complaints of antisocial behavior compared to other college parties, though that was the point of most college parties, Jason thought.

And Aramis should be miffed.

He'd much rather their positions were reversed. Yes, the scenery was gorgeous. No, he couldn't do anything with or about it, and he just found it distracting and annoying. Aramis was young enough he'd still get a kick out of it, but to Jason, the hall full of prime young college flesh was just tedious, really.

He felt invisible enough. He might be twice their average age, but he was in top shape, didn't have many lines on his face yet, and his coat and shirt fit the general theme. He might be a professor, or a grad student, or someone's older date.

The fact was, though, he was Caron's bodyguard and everyone knew it. The occasional visible glances betrayed interest, annoyance, occasional disgust, but everyone shifted slightly when in proximity to him.

Caron knew the party was mostly façade and he suspected she was lying to herself to try to retain the masquerade of normalcy. Nor was Caron going to sneak off with anyone for any reason. She was pretty clearly sweet on the boy she was chatting with now, with occasional brushes of hands and torsos, leaning in to chat closer. It would be aggravating to be him. It would probably aggravate her, too; though Jason didn't have firsthand experience, he imagined the frustration was similar.

Ironically, if she wanted to drag the man to the limo, Bart would drive around wherever they wanted, with Elke for backup, and neither would twitch or say a word to them having sex involving whipped cream, table tennis paddles, or even a properly cleared goat of legal age. However, she did not have the experience to feel comfortable with that, and it seemed unlikely her potential paramour would, so they were cursed to be at least as frustrated as Jason.

A young woman moved into his personal space. He glanced down and kept his expression cool.

"Hello," she said.

"Good evening, miss."

"Oh, there's no need to be formal," she grinned. "I know you can't drink, but can you talk?"

"I can talk a little," he said. It would break up the monotony of tension, as he called it.

"I'm Suzie."

"Pleased to meet you," he smiled and nodded.

"And you. Do you have a name?"

"Yes, but I checked it at the door." Would she catch the cynicism?

"But I have to call you something," she said, with an almost pout.

"Bob will work. Yes, it's generic."

"A shame," she said. "You seem like you'd have an interesting name. Dylan or Martin or Brandon."

"If you like," he agreed. Truthfully, he wasn't paying much

attention. Occasional glimpses down her cleavage, nicely framed by that wrapped shirt, and peeks at whatever else she happened to show his way, were a fun diversion. That's all he was going to get out of it, and if she was going to talk to him, he was going to call it a fair trade. Her face had the characterless prettiness of the almost mature.

"You really can't talk much, can you?" she asked.

"Sorry, no. I'm on duty." He noticed Caron was reluctantly disentangling herself from that young man, and swapping codes on her public phone. Good. Smart girl. Phones were damped in here, but she could call him later.

"That can't be fun."

He wondered how she'd react to an honest answer. This aspect? No, not really. Other aspects? Challenging, sometimes dangerous, but at least they aren't boring. And it's fine, because unless you become a renowned surgeon or lawyer, I make more money doing this than you ever will, so when I'm off duty I can afford to enjoy myself.

Instead he said simply, "I can manage. It's part of the job."

She wandered away with a polite good-bye. He figured she'd been either curious, or trying for a score for points. No hard feelings either way, but it was a bust for them both.

That wasn't all. Caron was wearing high-waisted slacks tailored very snug, glossy patent boots, and one of her armored bodices. She could be a pauper with the manners of a New Social Party politician in that outfit and still be one of the three most visible women here.

Jason deliberately didn't look at the other two. He was required to look at Caron.

Yes, this was going to be one of those missions. He reminded himself about the money.

On the whole, he figured the guests rated the party at least six of ten, perhaps eight. It came off okay in the end, and they departed around 0200.

When they left, Caron spent the whole trip hunkered back in the corner of the limo, a hush screen over her face, whispering into her phone and twitching occasionally in laughter or interest. Even after they arrived at the apartment, she paid bare attention to her feet, walked between the team, and ignored them completely all the way to her bedroom, where she shut the door.

✧ ✧ ✧

Alex had an appointment with Mr. Prescot at some time Saturday morning. It would be when he said it would, and not before. Prescot accepted that, though clearly was unused to having other people dictate his schedule.

That was because Caron's schedule was made as random as possible. Even though there was unavoidable predictability to it, any variation that could be included, was.

The team drove her back from school. Crandall and Hale went up in two other vehicles, one an unremarkable Volvo, one the big limo, and with those, the Mercedes and a company Hate Truck, they danced through loading and headed out in convoy.

Alex followed it all from his HQ, with maps showing route, and occasional coded pings from Jason marking agreed upon landmarks. He did not access any traffic cameras, satellite, phone or web. It was possible to follow someone across almost every square meter of the UK. It was also possible someone could hack him if he did. A paper map with a list of landmarks in his head was much safer. Sometimes the highest tech was no tech.

The team arrived on their own schedule, entered the now very secure perimeter of the estate, with laser webs, cameras, microphones, Cady's troops on patrol carts, and various other sensors watching every mite and butterfly. There were a lot of pretty butterflies here. Alex would vaporize them all if it would stop the constant traffic of signals that generated falses he had to personally delete.

Once they were inside the house proper, he called Bryan Prescot.

"Yes?"

"Sir, I can come up for that briefing now."

"Thank you. Please do."

He waited a few moments for Jason to arrive to relieve him. Cady was already upstairs, as was Jukov.

"I apologize," he said to Mr. Prescot as he entered his office.

Bryan said, "No, you don't. You take my daughter's safety seriously, and I appreciate it."

"That is true, sir. I apologize for situations beyond our control."

Prescot smiled.

His brother looked nervous and irritated, though.

"Mr. Marlow, can you urge Bryan to see that we get Caron to Govannon? I believe that's the safest place for her. I plan to move there myself, possibly permanently. There's no advantage to fresh air and countryside if it includes gunfire. Everything else can be done inside."

"Well, ideally our principals would be locked in bombproof domes on a flat field under another dome ringed by automatic guns. As this is not feasible in any real world, we adapt."

Bryan smiled. "I'd prefer to avoid that, and Caron should be able to finish as normal a schooling as possible. It's proper."

Joe twitched in that eager tic of someone who wants to get a word in.

"It's not cost effective. No offense to your team, Mr. Marlow."

"None taken. We are not cheap. However, we've not lost a principal yet."

"So you recommend staying here?"

Alex didn't like being manipulated.

"I recommend specific approaches based on the client's needs. If Bryan and Caron need her to finish her schooling, I will devise strategies to enable that. My team will implement them. I avoid blanket lifestyle suggestions when possible. Caron is already rather miffed at the ones we've had to implement."

"I'm sensitive to that," Joe said, so flatly it was clear he really didn't give a shit. "I'm also cognizant that she can't enjoy her activities if dead."

"Should I feel she's at that level of risk I will advise accordingly."

"And if not? Why are you here?"

"The time to buy a fire extinguisher is not after the fire has consumed the kitchen," he said smoothly. Joe was one of those asocial little twits who didn't realize how abrasive he was.

Bryan cut in. "Joe, can you summarize your idea?"

Joe took a breath and pulled himself up from a hunch. "Sorry. Yes. I'm heading back to Govannon to supervise the next round of upgrades and building to the resort. The idea is that Caron is trained enough to provide mine oversight for the next cut. She will be much safer there. You can remain here to handle the government. We all know you do that better than I possibly could. I'm not good at diplomacy."

No shit. Really? Alex thought loudly.

"Alternately," Joe continued, "I could remain here and keep things in a holding pattern while you go. Either way, it reduces the target level here—is that the term I'm looking for, Mr. Marlow?"

"It works for the concept. At the same time, it's less cost effective to have widely split teams both needing logistical support at this level."

"Ah," Joe said, with a nod. He looked bothered. "Yes, that is the economic issue."

That choked his engine completely, Alex thought, but kept a professional face.

"Also," Alex offered, "it's not hard to keep you all separated except here, and we're solidly protected here. Cady?" He was only too glad to pass it off to her.

"Easily," she agreed. "There's plenty of perimeter property, and the terrain is not conducive to stealthy approaches. The air corridors are shut and monitored by several governments, all wanting to look effective. Anyone on foot we can take down, easily."

Jukov said, "I also would prefer to keep the family as a unit. Wider separation just leads to all the problems mentioned, and makes communication harder. At some point, a reunion gives a very definite timetable."

Joe shrugged in restrained exaggeration and said, "I prefer to avoid threats to our family. I want to push for that."

Bryan said, "Joe, after Caron graduates, we can both relocate. You go ahead now."

Joe grimaced. "I feel like I'm running out on you. But I do need to get back there, and I'll have things ready for your return."

"It'll all be new to me. I haven't seen it in five years. Only the mine, none of the resort or community."

"You'll be amazed. I guarantee it."

"I believe you. The images can't do it justice, I'm sure."

There was a pregnant pause that turned embarrassing, finally broken when Bryan said, "So, someone took a shot at us."

"They did," Jukov said. "Badly. Deliberately badly. The range wasn't extreme, the weapon was adequately accurate and in overhauled condition. They hired someone able to get that close, who then missed both of you by a couple of meters."

"I suppose it's good they don't actually want me dead."

"It's not impossible," Jukov said. "They might have been trying to hit either of you. Ex Ek's info doesn't give much more than what we have. We have to assume it was a legitimate attack. We must consider it was a scare tactic or political statement. The concern is that it would be stupid to use deadly force, and face the penalty for it, if not intending to follow through. But some groups are not very smart and not willing to follow through."

"So they aren't a threat, just a nuisance."

"Correct. Given time, the police will track them down."

"I won't bow down to petty threats."

Joe said, "Someone rebuilding an antique rifle to shoot at us from a sniper position is not petty."

"No, but still. That's why I hired these people."

Jukov said, "We consider it a manageable threat at this point. I've changed protocols to account for it."

Joe asked, "What kind of changes?"

Jukov said, "That's rather complicated, varies by situation, and it's policy not to discuss it with anyone. I won't even tell my compatriots here—" he indicated Cady and Alex—"except as it affects them."

Joe looked put upon, but said, "I suppose I understand that. I'd still urge announcing a plan to leave, make it look like something long in the works, which it is, then do it."

Bryan spoke, softly but firmly. "I will do so when I'm ready. Caron will do so after classes."

Alex appreciated a man with determination. It made his job easier.

Alex really didn't like the mix of Ripple Creek and Ex Ek. Not that Ex Ek were bad, but they weren't quite as highly tuned, they had different protocols and procedures, and he had no control over them. It was bad enough juggling Cady's team and Jukov's. They had to have a certain amount of autonomy, and he had to manage them as District Agent in Charge.

Now there was this requirement to include the Prescot retainers. He was sure they were nice people, devoted, knew the family and the routines and the area. They'd had some basic skill training and were probably decent observers. However, they were not trained nor equipped to deal with urban combat. He said so.

Joe Prescot had to mouth off on that one. "Do you really expect that, Mr. Marlow? Really?"

"Sir, I expect anything at any time, especially as shots have been fired."

Bryan raised a hand to his brother and said, "It's been expressed to me by my company PR staff that the perception of having that level of force is a provocation. It makes people want to challenge it."

Alex was being challenged, and knew he was getting heated, so he paused and said nothing for just a moment.

"Sir, that can happen," he said, "at certain levels. At the same time, the people who might consider it a challenge are not . . . the ones to worry about." He wanted to say more, but wasn't sure how to phrase it.

"At the same time, we have our family retainers. They are family, really. That's perceived as tradition. Dropping tradition for what you admit are combat troops doesn't play well."

Joe switched sides all of a sudden.

"Bryan, we need the pros, we really do. I'd just like Mr. Marlow to keep the environment in mind. Rural Wales, not some backwater planet in the midst of civil war."

"I'm aware we do," Bryan nodded. "So I want to have our own people along, for appearance's sake, and because they are trusted and experienced and can advise you on what people expect of us."

It was reasonable and did offer a few benefits. Alex was sure the hindrances would outweigh them, though. Not that there was anything he could do about it.

"Then I'll make it work, sir," he said.

It wasn't a massive hindrance. He already had the two retainers incorporated as distractions. Moving them closer in was awkward, though, and one more thing to juggle.

CHAPTER 7

On the way back that Sunday, Elke of course kept close to Caron.

Caron wasn't that girly, but far more than Elke. She had personal clothes and kit she picked up, and an amazing collection of bras. Elke bought athletic type bras intended for military and emergency personnel, by the pack of six. Caron's were expensive, color-coordinated, styled for various outfits, and often custom made. They collectively cost as much as a good Arnold Detonation Control Module.

The team escorted her down to the garage, in formation for practice. This time they took a Bentley, a classic Cadillac, and Crandall followed in the limo. Cady's team brought the Hate Truck.

As they traveled, eyes out in all directions, Elke admired the landscape. This area was still lightly populated by modern standards, and very pretty.

A chime sounded, Caron dove under a hood and talked into the phone. No video, that was the rule. The fewer clues to location, the better.

She seemed slightly nervous during the rest of trip. Elke chalked it up to tension over the threat level. She talked little until they arrived at the apartment.

Once in the door, with it secured and the men across the hall, Caron spoke up.

"I have a date tonight," she blurted out.

"Ah, I see. And where is this date to take place?" Elke asked.

"Um . . . here." The girl was blushing, sweating and stammering. So she definitely planned to get intimate and didn't want guards along.

Still, Elke was going to make her spell it out, after the earlier teases, hassles and general brattiness.

"Good, that's easier for us," she said. "Do please give us as much notice as possible so it's easier for us to be discreet."

Caron brightened, reading something into that that Elke hadn't said. "Good! Can you be gone from seven until say one?"

"Absolutely not," Elke said to Caron's disappointed, confused and angry expression. "That would be a breach of contract. We don't know who this man is, and even if you've known him a while, the money involved is enough to tempt anyone."

Caron didn't cry. She looked very put upon, and ready to argue the point. Her body language was aggressive and demanding, and that mixed with her status, youth and hormones meant a battle.

Then Caron took a deep breath, shifted and said, "Please?"

Elke stood and faced her. "I'm sorry," she said. "The risk is unacceptable from a professional point of view. Even if he is perfect, someone could enter your apartment. One of us stays in here, Cady's crew outside, and we clear it before you enter. That's not subject to debate. And leaving you alone with anyone is out of the question. If you get hurt, our careers are over, and our bosses disgraced, on top of you being hurt and your father taking trouble. You will have to accept this."

"Do you," Caron paused, blushing so bright she radiated, "have to be in the room with me?"

"No," Elke said. "We can give you some privacy, after we secure things properly."

"Thank you."

Elke reported it, as required.

"Argo, Babs. Social engagement. Guest to be cleared."

"Hit me."

Elke looked over at Caron. "What's his name?"

"Uh . . . Dominic. DeBurgh."

"Dominic deBurgh, nineteen hundred hours approx."

"Noted. We'll clear him."

Caron seemed really nervous after that, and irritated.

"I don't have a private life, do I?"

"Sorry, miss. Not anymore."

Caron went to prep, both herself and her classwork. Elke made another call.

"Request Aramis as second for duration. I'll stay on."

"Ooo-kay, if you like." Jason sounded surprised.

Aramis came over, looking casually professional. He was much less an arse than he had been when they first met. He'd taken a while to mature, but he was shaping up decently, and Elke trusted him completely. He'd even mostly learned to trust her.

"Why me?" he asked, casually.

"I want you to keep the date in his proper place."

"Subservient to you?" he asked with a grin.

"That's assumed. He should be cowed, you say? Quite well. If he is confident, I will be suspicious."

"That's reasonable," Aramis agreed. "I'll pile on as needed."

It was only an hour before deBurgh arrived. The phone chirped and Alex said, "He's on his way up."

"Got it."

There were polite and discreet ways to clear someone through a security check. There were times to do that. This was not such a time. Even with Caron being a college senior, they were in effect in loco parentis for her safety, and Elke wanted a stern male image. Caron needed a bit of a lesson, and any guests needed to know their place from the start. It would be socially awkward, but much safer.

The door chimed and Elke pulled it open.

Aramis was obviously going to enjoy this, and Elke let him.

"Hello," Aramis said to the young man. "I'm her personal security for the day." He extended a hand.

"Pleased to meet you," the blond-haired, fresh-faced kid said. "Dominic deBurgh."

DeBurgh stood stunned into inaction as Aramis moved from handshake to a secure hold and started searching him. His arms were swept, pockets cleaned out into a pile at his feet, collar crunched, waistline dipped, legs swept and his groin felt up.

Aramis handed him back his watch, nodded and said, "You're clean. Whatever you do tonight, don't do anything that might indicate she's hurt. No screams, no shrieks, no bondage games, not even a hickey. I *will* kick in the door and you *will* leave on a stretcher. Do we understand each other?" The look on his face was that of a cold, egoless, no-bullshit professional.

As Dominic nodded with eyes dilated and frozen, Elke chuckled silently. If the boy could get an erection after that physical and emotional assault, she'd have to consider he was either a dedicated masochist or a dedicated sadist.

Caron looked slightly amused, very embarrassed and incendiarily angry. Very angry indeed.

"Oh, stop that!" she said, though it lacked force. Aramis kept his blank face on and took it.

"Dominic is from a good family, and I won't have you treating him like a criminal. Sorry, Dom. Please have a seat."

Aramis felt good. The boy was definitely shaken, and radiated his sense of violation and nervousness. Caron was pissed, served the little bitch right. Professionally, he was sure this man wasn't a physical threat. Still, he would have to find a way to resolve the conflict of wills. It wasn't good to be at odds with the principal.

Caron kept looking around, and once made a head-tilting gesture of dismissal. Elke gave her a single twitch for a negative.

Aramis smirked inside. The girl had pissed Elke off, too. Elke was seeking revenge. He knew about that, slightly, and hoped Caron acquiesced fast. If she tried to one-up Elke, it would get ugly.

It was probably a good thing Caron was so normal generally. She and the boy played a game, twinned into her system with a headset each, and managed to laugh and talk and banter as if alone. There was some touching. She was clearly familiar with deBurgh, and comfortable.

Then they took the goggles off, and she went for a friendly kiss.

It almost worked, except he saw Aramis standing against the wall, and shied.

She drew back, looked uncomfortable, but clutched onto him and wouldn't let go. She leaned in and whispered, breathed in his ear, her hair falling over his face and shoulder. She managed to get him off the chair and stagger him back to the couch.

DeBurgh seemed torn between her attention and the guards. Caron smiled, made reassuring sounds, and kissed him.

That seemed to finally relax him a bit.

Then she looked up at Aramis with a gaze that was purely caustic.

"I got the feeling you wanted to watch, just to keep me safe, of course. So go ahead."

Dominic lay stunned, but didn't protest as she peeled naked.

Aramis kept his face blank, but inside he muttered to himself, *holy shit!*

Then she crawled over Dominic and plucked at his clothes, shoving him back onto the couch. His protestations decreased, though he did glance around a few times. Aramis didn't move. Elke, unseen to them, winked and grinned at Aramis, then dropped behind the couch and started doing push-ups.

The moaning, writhing and wrestling was certainly interesting, but Caron was obviously doing it as a challenge. Aramis wasn't going to let out a peep. He kept his attention on security, and noted that someday this would make one hell of a war story.

In a few minutes, Caron screamed triumphantly, teeth clenched, head thrown back, mussed hair flying around her head and every muscle strained in a clinch around Dominic. It took a moment for her eyes to focus, and then she looked over at Aramis, with a sadistic grin.

He maintained his neutral expression. Hers clouded up.

Then she turned her head to see Elke, head on hands, leaning over the back of the couch, hair plastered to her face with sweat. Caron didn't know the sweat was from push-ups, and Elke had a perfectly cultivated smile.

"Very exciting," Elke said. "It's a shame I'm only here professionally."

Caron strangled another scream and bounced upright, strode into her room and slammed the door. Dominic looked around in panic, embarrassment and fear. Aramis stood stock still and said nothing. Once Dominic realized nothing was going to happen, he clutched for clothes and got dressed, trying to conceal himself by hunching. He flushed red enough to be a warning beacon. After his timid knocks on her door were ignored, he moved hesitantly back and forth before leaving, closing the front door quietly, still without a word.

Loud music blared inside Caron's room, audible even out here.

Smiling at last, Aramis asked, "Would you really go there, Elke?"

"I won't stop your speculation of it. Enjoy." She grinned.

"Sadistic bitch," he snarked.

"I thought you'd figured that out by now." She grinned wider.

He wasn't going to say that that grin was evil and exciting. She knew it.

How ironic that the night before he'd been hoping Elke would get some candid shots from the bedroom or shower. It's not as if he'd publicize them. He'd keep them locked on a private system that would never connect outside. He suspected she'd beat him to a pulp for asking, though. Even asking would endanger his contract, and getting caught with them would be worse. If by some disaster anyone else did get hold of them, he'd best cut his throat.

It wouldn't be so bad if Caron wasn't determined to use her looks to express her displeasure with the circumstances. He really didn't blame her. He felt sorry for the girl, and he figured if he stuck it out long enough, so to speak, that she'd give up.

She knew he was holding out, hoping she'd get bored and give up. No chance. She had nothing better to do, and this was her only realistic way of rebelling.

They changed shifts at 0200, and Bart came in. Aramis quietly briefed the German on the events, as dispassionately and with as many generalizations as possible. "Intimate relations on the couch," was pretty specific, though.

"I wish I could find a way to dissuade her from taunting," Aramis said. "She doesn't really have a reason to stop, and is escalating to find a reaction."

Bart said, "I just told her I've seen better."

Aramis felt stupid.

"Does that actually work?" he asked.

"Aramis, no woman ever believes she is pretty enough. The prettier they are, the less they believe it. She knows I have guarded music stars and actresses, some of those she knows by reputation. I tried to avoid ones she might know in person. So she is convinced they are better looking than her, and more available, given their reputations. She knows she cannot actually touch us. The end of that conversation is she doesn't really like me, so she doesn't try to bother me. She made an attack, I ignored it as unworthy. She has no way to escalate."

"I wish that had occurred to me."

"If conversation allows, you might let her overhear you boasting of a date. I'm sure Elke or Jason will play along if I'm not around."

"And make it juicy, eh?" He'd had dates like that, but not recently enough to help.

"Very juicy, but quiet, so she must strain to hear."

"I'll consider it. It would have to be after I have a down day or two."

CHAPTER 8

Caron felt dirty the next morning. She knew it was unhealthy, but there it was. She'd treated Dom badly, put on a spectacle, annoyed her guards. In return, she wasn't sure what Elke's response meant, but it was faintly creepy, and Aramis continued to be a stone eunuch.

Jason and Horace, or Shaman, escorted her down to the garage. It seemed improper to use that nickname, but he apparently enjoyed it.

Even Ewan seemed distant. She frowned. So much for secrecy. Had he heard rumors or a report of her exploits? He'd known her since birth. A perception among the guards of her as a slut wouldn't go over well, and he'd probably talk to *Tad*, too.

She made a point of smiling though.

"Good morning, Ewan, good to have you driving for me again."

"Thank you, Caron," he said.

That wasn't like him. Either he was picking up her mood or had heard something.

She piled in and decided against her usual quiet travel. She brought up music, dug a boiled egg and some cayenne salt from the bar, and leaned back for comfort. She needed to put the weekend behind her, manage class, and apologize later, though not much later.

Caron didn't notice Ewan turning off. She was so used to varying routes it was just background. She noticed they were going slower, though, and after several minutes she asked, "Is there a problem?"

"Not at all, miss," Ewan said. "We should be arriving momentarily."

She didn't recognize the area at all, and they'd been around the school from every direction.

"Arriving where?" she asked.

At that moment he turned the wheel hard and brought them up into the dark maw of a warehouse of some kind. The overhead door was hydraulic and almost slammed closed behind them, pausing at the last moment to settle and lock into its track. She grabbed for the door. Locked. She punched the override. Nothing.

"Here," he said, and sighed. "I am very sorry, miss."

He released his safeties and was out the door in half a second.

Four goons . . . real goons, not bodyguards . . . trotted up to the door and stood in an arc around it. Their faces were hidden by masks and they carried sub-machine guns.

"Let's have no trouble," one said, and clicked the door open.

Feeling chilled and burning in a simultaneous flush, prickles all over, she carefully stepped out, one foot at a time, eyes darting back and forth.

They didn't touch her, only gestured with guns. She walked in the direction indicated.

It's not assassination, she told herself. *You're worth too much alive and unhurt. They could kill you anywhere, no need to sneak around, no need for four . . .*

It wasn't reassuring. Her world had just been smashed. Ewan had been with the family longer than she'd been alive. His father had been with them. His *grandfather*.

And now he was helping some criminal element.

She kept her eyes straight ahead and made as if to ignore their presence. She even adjusted her posture for the look-down-the-nose effect for the lower classes. She took a slow, measured breath and tried to calm the trembling, vibrating anxiety and fear. She was a Prescot, and Prescots were neither impressed nor intimidated by rabble.

She raised her left arm gracefully and pressed her neck pendant panic button. It was only the third time she'd ever done so, and the other two had been for training. She doubted the signal would get anywhere; only complete idiots wouldn't have it damped and jammed. Still, if there was a chance, or a power fluctuation, or a gap, the signal might get out.

She tried to keep track of movement. Ewan had driven south

and turned east. She was now facing south again. The warehouse was stripped and empty, lit and had few features, but there were eight other bays with lorries backed in. She gulped.

Sure enough, a few moments later they chivvied her left, east, and into the empty back of a lorry. As she turned and watched, one man rolled the door down while the others stood with their guns ready. The door rattled and latched and everything went dark. She could smell stale food and mild decay from previous cargo and spills. Then she heard other lorry doors running down. Possibly seven or more decoys, dammit.

The powerplant in the vehicle was electric. Caron shifted back against the forward bulkhead and squatted down for balance. The lorry pulled out smoothly, up a ramp and then south. South. That was definitely away from the school at this point. West. South. Soft east.

Shortly she was on the M5, she figured. She made note of the time. A moment's fumbling let her find a pen. She shot her sleeve, yanked it up and wrote backwards from the inside of her elbow up, retracing the route as best she could.

Then a wave of anger swept over her. She should have been banging on the side for attention, dammit. Yes, tracking her route was good, but getting out was better. Though realistically, the odds of anyone hearing anything and reporting it were slim. Still, she would when they stopped again. If they stopped.

"Say again?" Jason almost shouted.

Helas said, "Disappeared. Transponder off. I zapped a request for traffic cameras. They were connected in thirty seconds. Nothing."

"I fucking said we needed our people. Alex said it. Don't hire us and then . . . argggghh!"

An adrenaline panic slammed him. He took a huge draft of air, slowly exhaled, and punched for Alex as he did so. Today was about to get exciting.

Caron was sure they were back on streets, but not sure where. With no way to gauge speed, they were somewhere a few kilometers away, and not north. Still, that was a defined area. She'd work this as surveying problem.

She had some weapons and tools, but it seemed probable that any use would just get her stripped naked and abused. Whoever had her was using teams of people, not just singles. She despaired of fighting a group, even with things like the flash bang.

The lorry slowed, stopped and then the door rattled up.

"Out," a man said. She recognized him as one of the group from earlier. That meant two vehicles had come this way. Another item.

A door on the wall ahead stood open, and she assumed that was their destination.

It was. Or rather, it was hers. They reached the door in formation, and in a moment, one goon slipped her purse free and another yanked at her backpack. A pair of hands from a third shoved her firmly inside, and the door was closed.

She flushed in fear and anger again, and turned to the door. It was hinged on the outside. She wasn't going to try the knob yet, but she knew it would be locked when she did. From outside came the sound of bars being slammed into place in the concrete floor. She glanced down and saw a covered slot large enough for a tray of food but no more.

Concentrating on the cell kept her mind busy. She took a good look.

It was a locker room, or it had been. L-shaped. There were four nice toilet stalls and four sinks, with plenty of hand towels and warm air dryers. The floor was tiled, and had drains set into it. There was a bank of modern lockers with biometric locks, and four shower stalls. The plain benches had a cot set up between them with a pillow and coverlet.

So, it seemed there were plans for food and water, she had toilet facilities and showers, and bedding.

That meant they planned to keep her alive for now. Good.

She glanced up, then made it look like a gesture of frustration, while taking a surreptitious peek at the ceiling. Dropped acoustic tiles. Was it possible there was an opening above? It seemed unlikely they'd miss something like that, but they might count on her not noticing.

Another slow walkthrough didn't reveal any obvious cameras or monitors, though it was quite possible they had miniaturized ones. There was no reason not to play bored, so she opened every locker slowly in turn, scanned them, read the graffiti, and looked for signs of cameras.

Nothing. The place was bare.

✧ ✧ ✧

Alex tried hard not to steam. His professional advice had been ignored, and now his principal was missing, along with her untrained retainer. He might have attended a basic bodyguarding course, but he was not the skilled professional the rest of them were.

There was also the possibility he was corrupted, compromised or dead. Alex wouldn't mention the latter. Ewan seemed like a nice guy, but he was not Ripple Creek's responsibility. He very well might be their problem, though.

He'd advised against trusting anyone. Joe Prescot had attacked him for that, and Bryan had been soft. This was not a Ripple Creek failure, but it would play that way on the news.

So, first thing was to recover the principal, second was to keep it out of the news. The relevant parties would know, and that was all that was needed.

Jason was in the office with him, pacing. Jason did that when he couldn't shout or break something.

Jason said, "I'm not sure what we can do. We have government sanction to protect our principals, and Corporate will back us up a lot. Going looking, though . . . first, we're not PIs. Then there's the legal limits on entry, interception, et cetera."

"We have to tell Mr. Prescot."

"You do. I agree. Tell him it's a probable, not to be alarmed, and we'll keep looking, but the clock is running."

There was a knock at the door. Elke discreetly stuck her head in.

"Come in," Alex said.

She slipped in and closed the door.

"We have limited tracking resources," she said. "Some pheromones, some camera shots the police gave us free. Have you a map?"

"Yes," Alex said and spun his comm around.

"Ewan was varying his route as we told him, but he took a right here and kept going. Lost camera view here. We might have a pheromone trace here. Shaman is in that area. I suggested he deploy from the school OP."

"Good. Is Aramis still there?"

"Yes."

"No outside comments until I say so."

"Aramis says he's sure the word will leak from the cops."

"Maybe. If so, Mr. Prescot can fucking own someone as a slave for the leak, after this is done."

✧ ✧ ✧

Caron's brain whirled with the need to do something. She choked it down. She was a scientist, dammit, and scientists were methodical. They didn't plan to kill her, she couldn't be more than a few kilometers from the college, and people would be looking for her. She also still had her backup charge card and some cash in the pocket in her waistband. If she could get outside and into traffic, she'd be free.

It was an exciting prospect. Free herself. It would also shame and humiliate her captors.

She also had to get the word out about Ewan. If he'd betrayed her, he might betray others.

Still . . . first things first. She had a small amount of stuff on her person that might prove useful. She tried to itemize mentally, but her brain was still thudding with outrage and disorientation. She might be a decent observer, but her cognitive function was still impaired.

Were her observations correct? She spent a moment reviewing the area in immediate view. Yes, probably.

She wandered about, hugging herself, scratching, shifting. She made a point of using the toilet both for relief, and to get a stall door in between her and any observation of her inventory. *I just hope there's no perv cams,* she thought.

She wound up with a lumpy pile of objects in one jacket pocket. It wasn't much, but it might matter.

This was going to take some time, she decided.

The watch imprinted on her shirt cuff said she'd been here thirty minutes. Was that all? She felt as if she'd been slow and discreet, but all her activity had to have been done in a rush.

Still, no one had come to disturb her. She had to be secure enough so far. If they wanted her for ransom or political clout, they had no reason to let her putter around unless they didn't know or didn't care. So she should continue. It would keep her mind busy.

She stepped right up to the corner of a locker bank and pulled out her handful of stuff, laid it down.

She had her stun ring, a pipe lighter, eighty-seven marks and some change in cash, her still-hidden emergency credit card, a flash stick with personal data and codes on it, a small light, a key that was not a key; it had a tiny knife folded into it—what use did she have for keys? People opened doors for her. She had a tiny pair of pliers, a couple of meters of fine cord, a pair of light gloves, a spare capacitor for her computer interface, two safety pins she kept for attaching loose buttons, her emergency condoms—as if she'd ever need *those*, and some lint. Oh, the phone hidden in her hair clasp.

She felt stupid for not remembering the phone, but a quick test showed there to be no signal. This was a metal frame building, but that alone shouldn't stop reception. Someone had a damping field set up. Likely her earlier call had gone unheeded.

However, even if she couldn't escape, if she could get where she could place the phone to be traced, that should do it. Too big a field and it would cause interference on the street. People would complain, a technician would show up, and might question the dead zone. The building ends or corners might just be outside.

That just gave her another reason to get above that ceiling, if she could.

She swept her property back into her pocket, and turned back to the room proper.

She had planned to listen at the door. There was a scuffling sound outside it right at that moment. She cursed, but it came out as a "meep."

Then the slot at the floor opened and a tray was shoved in.

"Here, miss," she heard Ewan say.

Anger welled up, and her first impulse was to kick the tray right back out. The slot closed, though.

She wasn't at all hungry, and the food didn't look that appetizing. It was okay—a sandwich, an apple, a piece of pie and a bottle of Juice-ade—just not thrilling.

She wondered if they'd return for the tray in say, an hour, or if they'd wait until the next meal, or just let them pile up. Then she added tray, thermoset plastic, one, to her list.

Thermoset didn't burn, she recalled. On the other hand, there was a lot of paper here that would, and lockers, and the cot, and the benches. She could start a sizeable fire in here. Would that trigger an outside alarm? Or had whoever had kidnapped her arranged for that possibility?

Too many variables. The only reasonably certain one was that they needed her alive. Would their claims be low enough *Tad* would just pay it? High enough the entire government would come looking? Enough to hurt the family but leave them solvent enough for a repeat performance? Would they keep trying to demand more, then dump her alive . . . or dead?

Too goddam many fucking goddam fucking goddam variables. She growled quietly but with clenched teeth.

Then she reached down and grabbed the apple. She might as well clench her teeth on something nutritious and a little tasty.

She bit, chewed and stared at the floor. It wasn't a very tasty apple.

The apple was half gone when she realized she'd been staring at a folded wad of paper, straw colored like the tray, that said "read" in tiny letters.

She unfolded it, and recognized Ewan's writing at once. She almost crushed it up in rage, but made herself read it.

It read in Welsh: "Caron, I'm sorry. Blackmail works with enough leverage. I did what I had to. They promise you'll be unharmed. It's just about your money. We're south and west of Oxford about fifteen kilometres, in Abingdon.—Ewan."

Bryan Prescot tried to focus. He knew his brother was upset also, but he was too worried about Caron to really care, or to listen.

Joe said, "I just think it's a bit too convenient that they weren't around at the time."

"We told them they could trust Ewan. Nor do they have any reason to sell out. This is what they do. It's much easier to believe one bad apple than a crate." He wanted to believe it. He also didn't want to. Ewan's family had been with them for generations. Ewan and Joe and he had played Robin Hood together in the woods, gone to school together . . . would he rather not trust his friend, or his highly paid experts?

Joe said, "Hell, he or whoever he works for may have paid them to join in. Or they may have suborned him. The only people we can trust are family. There shouldn't be any outsiders anymore."

"I wish that were true. Lots of distant cousins would like in. Our gifts are basically unspoken bribes. There are limits, though, or we're just dispensing charity and creating jealousy, and at that level, we'd be affecting entire economies." He tried to keep calm and rational. He needed to stay grounded, because his head was spinning with nausea. Caron was missing and there was nothing he could do. He didn't even know where she was, yet.

"Better that than this!"

"I'll take it under advisement." Dammit, he didn't want to fight with his brother over this.

Joe must have finally seen his expression, because he took the hint and nodded, then left, closing the door behind him.

Bryan took a deep breath, and considered what to do next.

Aramis said, "Dammit, we have to do something. She's our principal!"

They were all in a Prescot-owned hotel in Oxford. When you were Bryan Prescot, you could get air travel authorized in seconds, at high speed. An ultramodern, ultraexpensive craft delivered him to the roof about the same time they arrived by car.

Prescot was across the hall in an office. They were in a parlor for a deluxe suite. There were basic refreshments but no one was interested.

He probably wasn't here to dismiss them. Corporate would handle that. It could be a vent and bitch session. He could even scream at them. They hadn't failed or violated anything, though they might take the heat anyway. He didn't seem the type, though.

Alex replied to Aramis, "We can't do anything unless asked. If we indicate we have that kind of intel, some principals will freak. If we fail in recovery, same thing. We're not on the spot and want to stay completely out of it."

"She's kidnapped at the least, and certainly scared, probably with good reason," Aramis said.

"And a total scorcher, yes?" Alex asked with a cocked eyebrow. "Look, Aramis, I feel sick about it, too. But we did not lose her and can't get blamed. If we try to get back into it, we *will* get blamed."

"It happened the same day, too." Aramis twitched in frustration, but clearly knew the score intellectually.

"Of course," Jason said. "They were waiting to exploit that, and obviously had inside intel."

Cady stuck her head in the door and interrupted, "Alex, Mr. Prescot is across the hall. I've cleared the room and swept for bugs. The building is secure. He says he'd like to come in and talk to us."

"Roger that," he said. He breathed a deep, steadying breath. "Time for me to earn my pay. Invite him in." Still, the man was asking politely and coming to them, not demanding they fall on their swords on his carpet.

Alex would have felt better if the team hadn't waited in stony silence. On the other hand, they were reviewing the event and planning and worrying. This part was all his.

Cady opened the door, nodded and stepped past. Prescot walked in and assessed them with a glance. He looked tense, but nonthreatening. He nodded curtly, and spoke.

"I'm wondering, Agent Marlow, if you can do something to recover my daughter."

That was direct.

Alex spoke carefully. "Sir, personally I'll do whatever I can. We all will. But it has to be formally contracted for liability reasons, and I don't know if Corporate will do so. If things go south, the whole company suffers, not just us."

Prescot looked troubled.

"As a businessman I of course understand that," he said. His tight and controlled reserve cracked. "As a father . . . please, tell me what I can do? If it's money, I can guarantee you'll never need to work again."

"Yes, sir, but it's not just money," Alex said. "All our friends and associates would suffer for our mistakes."

"No amount of money will persuade you."

"Sir, I won't say no amount would . . . but I'd rather not find out what my price is. My, our services, can be bought. Our loyalty has to be earned. Our loyalty to them comes first, unless we are already contracted. I'm sorry."

Goddam, it sucked. But there were limits. How many millions would this man offer? Alex really didn't want to know.

Prescot leaned back.

"I respect that," he said with a slow, thoughtful nod. "If I call the company, will you give them an honest assessment of your interest and ability? Please?"

"Yes, sir," he agreed. "If they give the word, we'll do it."

"Very well. If you'd please wait here? And do avail yourselves of refreshments."

"Yes, sir," Alex said.

In the broad parlor, Jason said, "Do you think they'll go for it?"

"I don't know," Alex said. Morally, he wanted to help. Professionally, it wasn't really what they did. Investigation and security were related, but discrete specialties.

His phone rang, and it indicated scramble. He enabled encryption, accepted the algorithm, and connected.

He was on the phone with Ripple Creek CEO Don Meyer himself.

"Alex, man to man, can you really do something?"

"I think so, sir. We have biometrics, those others no one knows about, we have intel on some of the hostile parties, and we'll have the resources, obviously."

" 'Think so' isn't enough," Meyer said brusquely.

"Sir, if I don't think we can do it, I won't start an actual op. I'll just share intel."

"That's fair. We'll talk again in a moment. Stand by."

"Holding, sir," he agreed.

Shortly, Meyer was back, as was Prescot.

"District Agent Marlow, I have finalized negotiations with Mr. Prescot. You are to attempt location and recovery of Miss Prescot if it can be done without violations of law. You should provide any necessary information to appropriate government agencies if they ask or if you deem it prudent."

That was a pretty ass-covering set of limitations, Alex thought, but that was to be expected on record.

"Understood, sir," he said.

Prescot spoke for record, even though he was just in the other room.

"I will provide any legal services needed should there be any questions regarding your actions on this matter," he said. "Personally, not through company assets." That was good. It wouldn't be subject to a board vote or otherwise called to question. It was Prescot's word, and they knew they could trust that.

"That's all," Meyer said.

"We'll get on it at once, sir," Alex agreed.

"Good man. We'll talk later. Meyer out."

"Marlow out."

He cut the phone, and Prescot came through from the other room.

"Thank you, all of you," he said, looking at them. Aramis rose from the seat he'd sprawled in. Elke stood politely. Bart came over from near the door. The rest were already standing.

"We'll do our best, sir," Alex said, and the rest spoke agreement.

"As to legal aid," he said, "I won't ask you to do anything illegal, but if there are questions, I have excellent lawyers with both Parliament and General Assembly connections, and I'll spare no expense."

You're asking us to do anything illegal that will help, Alex thought with a mental grin. Well, they'd been on the wrong side of someone's law more than once.

"Understood, sir," he said. "We'll start now."

"Thank you. I don't require updates, but if you have any, please, make them to me personally. Only."

"Of course." He extended a hand. Prescot shook it, then, with a troubled expression, turned and left.

"Well, we have his office to work from," Jason said. "Let's avail ourselves of some massive information power."

Caron twitched when the door rattled. She hurried back to stand facing it, hands out of her pockets, feeling like a schoolgirl trying not to look guilty. Had they seen her?

One of the goons came in, closed the door and laid down his gun on the vanity.

"They'll be arranging your release soon," he said.

"Thank you," she replied. Communication was a good sign.

"Our people promised you'd be unhurt."

"I appreciate that," she said. She really did. A rush of relief swept over her.

Then he stepped closer.

"Hurting would be bad," he said.

Her stomach shriveled into a ball and dropped.

"The way I figure it," he said, "as long as there's no marks, it's a fair exchange. Just a sample of the merchandise, so to speak."

At least he was clean physically. She shuddered and couldn't control it. They planned to return her alive, good. They weren't above raping her for fun first, though.

She'd had a class in this way back, on how to negotiate, but she hadn't paid attention. Caron Prescot would never be unescorted in a place where that might happen.

She wasn't sure how she wound up against the wall, but he was pulling at her clothes with creepy hands. They were caresses, almost loverly, but he was not a lover, and the imposition was already criminal and terrifying.

She cringed, and wondered if this justified using her ring. It would definitely put him down, but how would they react? Violence on top of rape? Gang rape? Take the possessions she had, which might or might not help her escape?

He slipped a hand down her slacks, and she decided yes, she should stun him. She tried to angle her hand to make contact.

Someone shouted, "What the fuck are you doing?"

Two very large men yanked her rapist away and slammed him over the sink counter. One of them proceeded to pummel him, while the other turned to her.

"Miss, are you okay? Do you need a doctor?"

Decide fast. Doctor, certain to be an insider. She might lose the gear she had, might be secured somewhere else. No actual injuries, creeped out, *I want to be left alone. Please, just leave me the fuck alone!*

"No. I'm fine," she said, and pulled her disarrayed clothes back. She realized she wasn't making eye contact, and should. She did, but he was masked anyway.

The guard turned to his compatriot and said, "Take him out and shoot him. Do it now!" He turned back to her and said, "I apologize for the behavior. It won't happen again."

They half-dragged the aspiring rapist out the door, as he cursed and screamed and called her a "filthy elitist whore!"

The door slammed, the shouts continued, and then a loud *BANG!* echoed tinnily. There was a thudding sound, and the curses stopped.

For some reason, she didn't find it reassuring.

She cried again, and hugged herself tightly, sinking down to the floor.

Joe wanted to know how Ripple Creek was handling the situation. Bryan had met with them in person as fast as he could. His own flight was later, but as fast, and hang the expense. It was an investment, even if personal.

He knocked at the door, and that Jason Vaughn answered. Vaughn seemed like a reliable man. Behind him the room was abuzz.

Joe gave them this, they were good at reacting. The suite had comms all over, wires, antennae and chatter.

Vaughn asked, "Yes?"

"Is there anything I can do? How is it proceeding?"

"Your offer is appreciated, but this takes professionals in the field. Thank you, though." Vaughn said, and didn't that sound like a rote speech for such occasions.

"Sorry, it's just that I feel partially responsible."

"No incriminations at this point. First we'll handle recovery. Discussions are for afterward. Sir, we are rather busy, with all due respect."

"Sorry. As CFO, can you give me an update?"

"This is not a company matter."

"Of course not. It's a family matter, about my niece."

"Well, your brother has the information."

"He hasn't gotten back to me yet. Busy."

"Then, sir, I suggest you will have to wait."

The door closed, leaving Joe feeling put upon and left out. Dammit, he needed to know. Bryan would be too personally involved to get any actual information. This was where Joe could best help.

Grumbling, he figured he'd better go help his brother. That was useful, too, and he'd find something out that way, eventually.

Caron shook off the incident. That just made it more imperative she get out.

If she got above the ceiling, could she get a message out? Her phone had an override that was line of sight, and supposed to get through interference. Would it get through a deliberate screen, though?

It was worth a try. They wanted her alive. They wanted her intact, at least officially—she shuddered again. That decided her. She didn't want to face anyone else who wanted favors.

They might have a camera, so she'd have to do this fast. She walked back, stepped on a bench, opened a locker and used it as a high step, stretching to reach it, shoving a tile up and gripping the frame precariously as it bent.

There was extruded concrete behind it, and she got fingers atop that. Not the most secure hold, but enough to let her lean and stretch and get both feet onto the edge of the locker. Then she was through the panel, grit and dust and spiderwebs all around and on her.

The top of the locker bank was sloped, but she leaned and got both hands over the concrete wall, and shimmied. Her belt caught, and she wiggled to free it.

Her slacks tore at the knee and she felt a burn as something gouged her. It wasn't severe, though, and she was now into the dead space, under a sheet polymer roof and over the dropped ceilings, with old insulation crumbling all around, and barely any light, though she could see pinholes of daylight here and there.

A quick look revealed her luck or training had paid off. The main part of the room below had a solid structural sheet over it. This corner and an access above one commode stall were all the openings there were. Either they'd assumed it was all covered, or figured she wouldn't do anything.

Her phone still got no signal.

Sweating, and not just from the heat, she wondered about trying to throw it through a crack and hoping it would work outside. Of course, this could be an abandoned building in the middle of nowhere, given the way new construction was shifting everything. But that would leave her where she was—no phone service, and someone might find it and report it.

She looked around at the slits and holes of light, and saw one that might be long enough to be pried open. She squatted onto the concrete and pretended it was a balance beam in school. She used her hands above her against the roof—it was that low.

Perhaps she should have reached down to close the locker and put the tile back? They'd waste some time looking for her. But she didn't want to turn around, and she was on her way now.

It got darker as she moved away from the opening, even as her eyes adjusted.

The wall was rough and crumbled, and she shuffled along, sweating and itching and aching. Her pulse hammered and she wondered when they'd notice.

Jason and Elke shouted in unison.

"Yes!" "*Prosim!*"

Alex said, "Talk to me."

Jason said, "We have a faint but definite pheromone trace. We've got it within three blocks."

"Tell Cady."

"Yup." He keyed a mic. "Cady, you there?"

"I am."

"I have a general location for you. Get over there and look for phone signals or pheromones."

"I see. We'll be there in three."

Alex said, "That's a lot of buildings, and we can't search them. Though the odds of seeing them if they try to E and E are better."

"Tracers in the food were brilliant," Jason said. "We need to make that a regular option with the company."

"Not too regular, or word will leak."

"Ah, yes. That's why you make those strategic decisions. I'm just going to supervise while Elke does aerial analysis."

Elke said, "Already have done. There, there or there are my first choice," she said as she pointed. "This pair is second. Then these." Her accent was a little thicker under stress.

"Why?"

"Disused, access is on quiet streets and usually recessed or sunken. Major operations will not use their own buildings, nor will most people use their employer's location."

"Sound enough. That gives us six areas, but spreads our people thin."

Cady said, "We'll pop sensors all over. I have aerial coming."

Alex said, "Do it." Good people. It was still a large area of big old warehousing and industrial capacity, though.

Below her, Caron heard clattering and shouts. They were coming for her now.

There was a gap in the sheet plastic she might squeeze through. The ground was four meters down or a bit more, but that was manageable if she could hang. It would bang her up if she tried to jump. First, though, her phone. She reached down under the crack and tossed it straight out.

Shouts behind her. She didn't look, but it sounded like they were much better in the scaffolding than she.

She felt nicks and tears and gouges as she bent the plastic back, stuck her legs down and felt for a grip. She had wobbly plastic on one side, extruded concrete on the other. She tried to squeeze through and hang, slipped, banged her elbow enough for electric tingles, and landed hard enough to smack her teeth, then hit her chin on her knee. She staggered and stumbled but stayed mostly on her feet, and was on the ground.

She ran for her phone as noise up above turned to what was probably stunner fire. She scooped the phone and a handful of sharp rubble and ran.

The gap between these buildings was overgrown with two-meter stalky weeds, rubbish and construction debris from decades before. She picked her way fast and hoped the growth would stop any stuns.

Then she was out on an old, disused street that served these derelict blocks.

Right across the way were three men in suits, obviously muscle, and with bulges she recognized as body armor and weapons.

Shit, shit, shit, shit, shit.

And they definitely recognized her and started moving faster.

There was no traffic to dart into, and she was limping and couldn't run. She punched at the panic button, visibly, because it didn't matter now.

Then the men were on her.

"Miss Prescot, Agent In Charge Marlow sends his regards. I'm Agent Marlin Barnard with Cady's team. You may have heard of me. Are you all right? Do you need medical attention?"

Caron heaved a deep breath.

"Can you prove that?" she asked. Not that it mattered, but . . .

"Of course. We will wait here until you are satisfied," he said, and kept speaking into the air, "Playwright, please give Miss Prescot a call."

Her emergency phone rang.

"Hello," she said at once.

"Caron, this is Alex. I'm almost as relieved as you and your father must be. Mr. Barnard is one of our agents, you may have seen him at the house. Here's your father."

There was a pause and then, "Caron?"

"*Tad*," she said, and relief washed over her.

"The code is *Ysbaddaden*. And now we'll have to change it."

"That's fine, *Tad*," she said, tears welling out. "I'm safe. I'll be home in a few."

"I love you, *Merch*."

"And you."

She lowered the phone slowly, and breathed deeply.

"Yes, Agent Barnard, please take me home."

"Yes, miss. Right this way."

Their car pulled up a few seconds later. It was a heavily reinforced Mercedes sedan. She sank into the cushions and closed her eyes, trying to pretend the world didn't exist.

CHAPTER 9

Alex thought he'd enjoy this after-action review. He held good cards and Bryan was indebted to him.

After the thanks and grins and all around ice cracking, he got to the point fast.

"One of the positive things, if there is such, is that it's helping the claim with the government to allow us heavier weapons."

"Obviously I support safety, and the best tools for the job," Prescot said. "However, there's also a PR issue and a personal moral issue. I can't have anyone killed, no matter how richly they deserve it, by my daughter's security detail."

"That complicates things for us, sir."

"I'm aware of that and I'm sorry," he said firmly. "I hired you in part based on the expertise and dedication you showed evacuating President Bishwanath. However, there was a lot of bad PR over injuries, death and property damage."

"Yes, sir, though that was a war zone with different rules of engagement. Obviously, the streets of Greater London are not the place for that, though we have a shooting and a kidnapping to deal with. The best weapons available act as a deterrent prior to any threat, and can serve to de-escalate a situation in progress. In worst case, selective, very selective fire can end an event before it gets out of hand."

"I trust your expertise, Mr. Marlow. I do find de-escalating a situation with the presence of firearms and explosives to be an ironic statement."

"I know it sounds that way, sir. It is proven, though. Jason Vaughn is probably one of the ten best combat shooters alive, and at target shooting is Olympic quality. More importantly, he's very unlikely to shoot unless the situation is beyond salvageable by any other means. Likewise, Bart Weil has a decade more experience up close in civilian quarters than the rest of us. I trust them both completely."

"If it's that unlikely they'll use them, I'd rather just suggest that they are armed and let that serve as the threat. What do you think?"

Alex hesitated. He'd almost talked himself into a corner.

"Sir, the problem with a threat is that if you do have to carry it out, you have to carry it out. At that point, things get bad. They're worse if you've only provoked it."

"When all you have is a hammer, every problem looks like a nail."

Hah, got him, Alex thought.

"Conversely, sir, when you have a nail, you can bang at it all day with a screwdriver, a shoe or your hand and get nothing except hurt. Whereas one good blow with the hammer makes the problem go away for good." *Well, until the next time, but we won't say that.*

Prescot nodded slowly.

"I see your point," he said. "Very well, I'll authorize firearms and police stunners at my end. We'll have the lawyers and your people argue with the government. But I must reiterate that their use be absolute last resort, and I'd much prefer any attackers be left alive. I can more readily absorb the cost of legal action than the bad PR of shooting someone."

And that, Alex thought, *was the real age old justification for weapon control.*

He moved on.

"Has Ewan offered anything else?"

"He says it was all private blackmail and threats, and I believe him. They went after his daughter, and forced him into doing it. She was recovered, unhurt. I've never seen him so remorseful. The only lead he offers is that they were true to their word. Neither girl was hurt. Someone who tried to hurt Caron was shot by their own people. He was promised a cut of the ransom, which was apparently only to be a few million. I might even have paid it."

"While that's not a good idea, sir, we at least don't have to discuss that option now. I am going to have to suggest again that all the security be ours. Your brother can stick with Ex Ek outside this house and in his own matters. But we must lock this place down."

"I agree, and I already told him so. He concurred and didn't object."

"Good."

"Agent Marlow, I apologize for holding back, and I'll try to do less of it. I do have long-term PR concerns for our development, and personal issues with violence, but I will give you much greater credence. I wish I'd done so before this."

"Thank you, sir. We're quite happy to continue the contract and we'll give it our best."

He hoped the man took that very diplomatic hint that they could pack up and leave if they chose. Prescot wasn't the only man with stupid amounts of wealth who would pay them.

"The last item is we need more follow-up. The kidnapping was very professional, but several holes were left. When it failed and Caron escaped, they knew we were nearby and just ran on foot in several directions. We have no leads. Nothing in the building was traceable. Very, very professional, except that they couldn't hang onto her."

"I understand. You think it was intended to be a scare."

"Not necessarily. It could be meant as a scare or acquisition of funds, a probe of our abilities, or all three. Very tactical, which again, is professional. Not big enough or long enough to bring the entire government down, just a major nuisance that might yield them assets and did yield them intel. We'll need to watch that."

Alex would. That was twice now something had gone that way. That was a pattern.

Caron stormed into her father's office, brushing off that African doctor-turned-bodyguard. He followed her, but stopped at the door. She pushed on in. Her father's own guard sat in the corner, looked her over, and stood carefully. Truly, the bastards didn't trust anyone. She pointedly ignored him and turned to her father.

"*Tad*, what's going on with Ewan and his family?"

He looked up from his three screens.

"Are you asking what or why?"

"Why! Dammit! It's cruel!"

"Yes, it is. I discussed it with the lawyers and with our security agents, and—"

"*Fuck the security agents!*" she shouted. "Those mercenary arseholes act as if everyone on the planet has a personal vendetta against me!"

"Apparently enough do that Ewan was persuaded to violate three generations of trust, help kidnap you—and he mentioned something about attempted rape." Her father looked rather angry, which said something.

She flushed in scorching anger and violation. Dammit, no one needed to know about that.

"He was not part of that," she said.

"No, and he was very apologetic. At the same time, enough leverage made him break. I'm truly sorry to have done what I did, but there must be a lesson that hurting us carries a penalty."

"But they'll starve. *Tad*, our retainers are better paid than most barristers. They had their house, salaries, use of the facilities and lands—"

"Yes, and now they have nothing, are blacklisted, and can only get menial jobs. I realize that Leslie and the children are going to be hurt. But, *Merch*, he helped people who wanted to hurt you, badly. If we don't respond, it will happen again."

"So have him imprisoned. Don't hurt the family."

"Enough money will make prison an acceptable exchange for quite a few people on this planet. The only viable response was completely economic. They've gone from very upper middle class with upper class perks, to poverty-stricken wretches."

He put his hands carefully on the desk and breathed a slow, deep breath. "Caron, I played with Ewan and his father when growing up. He was my friend for forty-eight years, but he helped kidnap my daughter. If he'd come to me, I'd have readily thrown a billion marks at the problem to prevent it, but he didn't believe I would, or that I could be trusted, so he went along with a series of felonies and betrayed my trust. He can't be my friend. He can't be a trusted employee. The word is out that hurting us will get the instigator destroyed. I'm very sorry it came to that, but it means the rest of our employees are safer, and so are we."

She wanted it not to be true. Most people thought money was a good thing. If they had it, they'd realize what a curse it really was.

"I know that look, Caron," he said. "Don't even think of making a personal or anonymous donation. I generally don't track your finances, but I will if you even consider that. I want your word."

She closed her eyes and sighed. It was as much punishment for her as for Ewan and Leslie and Connor and Adam and Wynn and Andra.

"I promise. I'll let my friends starve in the gutter before I'll betray my family." She tried desperately not to tear up, but did anyway.

He looked very sad. "I hate that it came to this, girl. I really, really hate it. If you get any workable ideas, I want to hear them."

"You already know what I think," she said, turned, and stormed out.

He wanted a hug. Her friends wanted a roof over their head. He could suffer.

Bart and Elke were at the bottom of the stairs as she swept down.

"Take me to my flat, please," she said in her best regal tone.

They read her well enough not to offer any conversation.

CHAPTER 10

Alex sat back, stretched and tried to relax. The responsibility was crippling his mind.

"Okay, I'll consult with the younger three when they get back. What I want to do now is discuss the known and potential threats."

He looked at Shaman and Jason and waited for the discussion to start.

Jason said, "Bryan is not a threat to the daughter. The daughter seems genuine in not wanting the hassle of the money. I think it's unlikely she's a threat to him."

"I concur," Shaman said. "The staff are corruptible, as we have seen, but I don't think they are a direct threat. They've had lots of opportunity, and they are treated well. They also know the repercussions now."

Alex said, "Her uncle Joe's a tightwad. The threat he poses is that he's more concerned with a few marks than with maximum safety. He wants every penny staying in the family. He even got second-rate security for himself."

Jason nodded. "Yeah. He's also been managing the mine the last year. He's apparently great with figures. He does the books, the father does the engineering and is the official face, because he's a much nicer person."

Shaman said, "I expect Uncle Joe's going to push to get rid of us as soon as the threat level drops. In that regard, we should certainly not give him any information, and we need to express that concern, diplomatically, to the father."

"Definitely," Alex agreed. "What about the mother?"

Jason said, "I did a news search. She got a large chunk when they divorced. She's got decent investments, and salaries from several charities. She puts on a pretty face to raise awareness and money. No one here likes her, not even the staff. She's gotten a couple of presents from Bryan when the company struck big, graciously presented for her help in getting them started. It seems likely those were intended to avert lawsuits or such. She's got no legal claim on anything because of prenups and such, and even if she had ill will, she'd have a huge legal battle to get anything, after the fact. It would also be very suspicious if all three died and she then filed suit. It wouldn't be rational, but she's not entirely rational herself. A bit narcissistic. Lots of people suspect the charity is as much about keeping her name out there as giving."

"But she hasn't angled for more?"

"She cashed the transfers from Bryan but never asked for anything, and has legitimate salaries from the charities. Her books look honest from all reports and the overhead is moderate according to the groups that watch charities. So she doesn't seem to have any motives."

"So, threats are external, and might involve duplicity of staff."

"That," Jason said, "and schoolmates who might see a few potential marks. Hangers on, not real threats, but there could be a lot of them."

Shaman had a look of concentration around his coffee.

"They'll distract us from actual threats. I suspect that's how they'll be used, rather than directly. We'll have to maintain a cordon against any random contact."

"She'll hate that."

"We'll hate it as much."

Bart sat in the house office, watching everyone. Joe had his man from Ex Ek, Maur Junet, who had a good reputation as a professional. Bryan had Helas and Nick Haugen from Cady's team. Caron had Bart.

He remained a stone in the corner. He wasn't really needed here, so of course, he was alert. Threats could come from anywhere.

Still, Bryan's office, with his daughter and his brother, with all the physical security, and Elke and Jason outside, should be secure.

This was the very typical and boring aspect of bodyguarding. They were talking, he was standing. He'd note anything Alex might need to address, or anything he might find useful for protecting Miss Prescot. Otherwise, he was the goon against the wall. His opinion was not wanted, so he didn't listen too closely, even though he heard everything.

Joe Prescot had an interesting concept.

"We have plenty of room for charity. We can give a few billions where it's needed, and generate a lot of goodwill."

"We already do," Bryan said. "I'm concerned that too much will engender further demands until we start losing capital, or that when we do peak out, which inevitably will happen, we'll have to cut charity to retain financial soundness. That will create ill will. You know charity is something to be cautious with. We can't have entire nations dependent upon us. It's bad for them and for us."

Caron said, "Not any one place, of course. I think Uncle Joe is right, though. If we spread it out, small amounts in wide dispersal can accomplish a lot, create a lot of positive feeling, and if we can even knock a naught off our ridiculous total, we'll look a lot better. I hate to say we're trying to appease the socialists—"

"But that's what you are proposing," Bryan said. "Look, I'll consider it. We have billions going out anyway, and I'm gratified my family is charitable, even given the odd circumstances. Possibly I can send more, and we agree we don't mind. Remember, though, that the ore won't last forever, we won't be without competition forever, and time spent doing that is time not managing the income side."

Joe said, "I know people we can hire or contract. They are reliable too, because I know that is a concern."

"That helps. I'll look at that, too."

"*Tad*," Caron said, "I know how much we give, and I don't care about how it's perceived. I'd just like to have a normal life, or something close to one."

"I know, *Merch*." He sighed. "Whatever we can do, I'm willing to try, but I don't think you can ever be less than a billionairess."

"Even that would be an improvement," she said. She rose. "I've made my case. I'll help however I can between classes. I need to go study some more."

"I love you, Daughter," he reminded her.

"And you, Father. And you, Uncle."

She nodded coolly at Bart and headed for the door. He joined her.

That was a problem her father couldn't begin to address. He just wished her well with it.

Once back in her rooms, Caron looked at Alex.

"I'm going to a concert," she announced. She needed to get away and do something.

"Yes, miss. When?"

"Right now. You said impromptu was fine?"

"It is. Bart, Jason, please get cars. Where are we taking you?"

"Berit is performing at Hedgwick. My family owns a box there."

"Excellent. We'll just show up then? No one else will be using it as a favor?"

"No, I checked the schedule. It will be vacant."

"What are you planning to wear?"

"A basic dress and one of the bodices, why?" She was getting used to personal questions, but they still took her off guard now and then.

"So we'll wear slacks and casual shirts with blazers."

"Ah, so. I'd like to arrive early. I may be able to talk my way into backstage. I was considering calling ahead, but I presume that's out?"

"Yes. We'll work on it when we arrive. We can leave in a few minutes."

Even an "impromptu" trip involved a lot of planning, albeit done very fast. One of Cady's people would drive and stay with the limo. Alex would remain to coordinate as needed. The rest would go along. Gear, commo, armor, water, supplies, vehicles and guards all moved in a ballet. It took Caron twenty minutes to change into a dress and wrap, by which time the team was formed up to escort her.

Downstairs, into the carriage house, into three vehicles, and off in three directions.

En route, Caron busied herself with the office, shuffling messages and invitations and mail. That was part of the passive measures used to keep her safe—all the communication funneled back through the house, and gave no indication she was on the road. An expert could probably determine lags and digital coding differences, but Agent Cady had people to take care of that, too. Anyway, she hated being bored and tried to use her time wisely.

The drive was uneventful, though the team kept looking out the windows in all directions while moving, and remained in constant coded contact with Alex. They were paid to do so and always did. She appreciated it, but it just emphasized the danger as much as it reassured her.

The limo pulled up to the entrance, the driver braked smoothly but quickly, and Aramis hit the door. Bart and Jason were half a step back.

Caron was used to the idea now, and stepped out a moment behind them. Shaman and Elke filled in the sides and Aramis brought up the rear.

Other people used this aerial walkway, but most of them didn't recognize her, only that it was someone surrounded by a block of guards.

They flowed down a walkway, into the atrium, and into an elevator for the restricted area.

They had the elevator alone, and nothing happened. The door opened, Aramis led the way to a courtesy cart, and they rolled down a tiled and muralled hallway, around two turns. Caron flushed in embarrassment. It was like being royalty. She was a country girl who did some mining. It still felt wrong.

"Right here," she said, indicating the door to the box. They already knew that from maps and earlier reconnaissance trips, of course.

Jason and Elke went in first, scanners out. Their inspection took seconds, Jason nodded, and the rest came in.

From the polarized window, Caron could see scaffolding and equipment running up. It was two hours until showtime, but stage setup was still in progress.

She used her current throwaway phone rather than the courtesy phone in the box. It seemed so paranoid, but she'd play by their rules.

A generic female voice answered, "Hello?"

"Would you tell Miss Berit that Caron Prescot of the Prescot mining family would like to meet her, when and if it's convenient."

"I can relay the message. Stand by, please."

While she waited, she watched her escorts check the box over again, scan for mics and cameras, move furniture and decorations around, and generally inspect down to the paint. Most everything they displaced went exactly back where it came from, though anything that could be turned was, and some furniture was relocated. Planned randomness.

The voice came back on the phone, "Miss Prescot, Berit says she can welcome you in about fifteen minutes, but not for long."

"That's wonderful. Thank you very much."

Elke asked, "She said yes?"

"Fifteen minutes."

"Very good. Bart and Aramis will go with you. I'll secure here and come along if time permits. Jason's managing. Jason?" she asked as she turned to him.

Without looking up from his terminal he said, "Sounds good."

Another few minutes carting down tunnels brought them to a well-lit corridor of dressing rooms. Some were open and vacant, others closed. A roped and screened barrier led to the stage, and handlers moved around that way, finishing the set.

There were several rooms in use for various members of the band, dancers and crew. One in particular had an obvious bodyguard in front. He was muscle in a suit, with a practiced faint scowl. He looked reasonably competent and alert, but didn't project much presence. On the other hand, the Ripple Creek guards didn't either, generally. When they did, though...

"May I help you?" he asked.

"Caron Prescot. I hope I'm expected," she said.

He looked over the entourage.

"The invitation is for Miss Prescot, and males are not allowed in Berit's dressing room."

Aramis looked the man over. He was big, bulky, reasonably well-trained, and he had to know Prescot's detail were Ripple Creek. The way he looked at Elke said he knew she could kick his ass and wasn't comfortable with their presence. Bart and Aramis made him very twitchy. That was silly. No one was going to fight over this.

"Please inquire," Elke said. "We cannot leave her unattended."

Bart added, "Please tell her Bart Weil is with the party and would like to meet her again."

"I'll relay that," the man said, looking put upon. He opened the door and slipped inside.

A few moments later he opened it again and ushered them through it. Beyond that was a phone screen and another door.

Inside that, the room was brightly lit, had makeup smells and jabbering artists, someone with a tray of snacks, someone at a rack of outfits, all of them female and most of them young and supple.

From a makeup chair, a woman called, "Bart! My favorite German!" She bounced to her feet, bounded over and threw herself on him.

The hug looked like a giant with a doll. Berit was small and perhaps sixty kilos. Bart was near two meters and more than twice her mass. She looked comfortable in his presence as she stepped back. She sighed.

"I see we're both moving up in our jobs. I could not afford you now."

"I hope you will not need me," he said. "It's nice to see you again, though. You look well, and I'll enjoy the show."

"Thanks! But I'm being rude." She turned and said, "Miss Prescot! So interesting to meet you."

Berit was probably quite pretty with those Nordic cheeks and black hair. Her makeup, though, was designed to make her look like a pop star, and to do so under the bright houselights. Up close it was overdone and garish.

Her body, however, was the product of money and exercise. She might not have biosculp—her curves looked very natural—but she had rock hard muscles. She fit an ideal very few people even bothered with. It made her very visible.

Caron's response was interesting. She was partly meeting a celebrity, but she had her own visibility now, with all that money. She was also meeting someone who knew Bart fairly casually, who was attractive. Bart had spurned her teases. She was probably wondering how he felt about Berit. Aramis watched, curious and amused.

Of the two, he'd choose . . . well, both, of course. He wasn't going to think about that. Berit was older—thirty-two, he thought he recalled—and had just barely faint wrinkles and almost visible age from gravity. Caron was twenty-two and still flush with youth. She had nothing to be jealous of, but Bart's prior snubbing and the warm greeting he received here threw her off a little.

Meanwhile, he was on duty. He was professionally expected to examine everyone and everything here in detail and he did so. Not bad. Eight attractive women chattering in Norwegian, giving him the eye, which he could coolly ignore behind his ballistic shades while enjoying every minute of it. Nothing obviously a weapon, no threatening movements, no trouble at all. So he eyed them right back.

By the time he was done, Elke was in the process of snapping photos of Caron and Berit, with their cameras and her own. The two were comfortably close and swapping contact info, and a signed picture with attached Muzikflash from Berit.

Aramis took Berit's offered hand, accepted a gentle but firm shake with a slight bow and said, "It was good to meet you," even though he actually hadn't. Manners were part of the job, as was meeting people in passing with no time to talk. He'd met probably fifty high profile people this way, not counting principals, and been in the room for hundreds of others.

In short order they were back in the bay next to the Prescot family box.

As they moved inside, Caron grabbed a phone off the counter, then dropped into a sprawl in a reclining couch.

"Yes, Suite Seventeen. Please send up some cold cuts, cheeses and a variety of breads. Welsh rabbit would be nice, and some London broil, but medium, not rare. Assortment of beers and a sweet red please. Ta."

It was still an hour to showtime, and there wasn't much to do. They spent the time checking status, messages, news and general status. The arena filled up from scattered to packed, and the noise rose slightly, though the screens damped it a lot.

Aramis wasn't sure what to do with those. The view and sound quality would be increased with them open. So would visibility and threat level. It was one of those things they had to accept. Still, a crowded concert reduced the possibility of several types of attack. Also, the darkened box, relative to the hall, would make them harder to see.

A few minutes shy of showtime, there was a chime and flash from the door. Jason answered it, handed something back without looking. Elke snagged it, nodded, signed it and handed it back. Then Jason pulled a cart in, closed and latched the door.

"Food," he said.

Caron asked, "How was it signed for?"

Elke said, "I have an account with you, remember? So I signed."

"Ah, of course. The bookkeepers can fix it."

She stood and pulled lids off serving platters. The London

broil was rather fragrant. Fruit and cheese and crackers were in arrays worthy of a recipe page. It was almost a shame to eat it.

Caron popped a bulb of beer that foamed perfectly. It was amber and clear. She used tongs to pull a few pieces of meat and cheese onto a bed of crackers and sat back down.

"Please, help yourselves," she said.

Elke said, "Thank you," and grabbed a couple of cubes of cheese. She nibbled one, and looked surprised and happy.

That was one of the advantages of tremendous wealth, Aramis noted. Caron never had to eat bad food, nor even merely good food. It was hard not to gain weight, in fact. He'd had to up his activity level with a second session each day since the job started.

If only he hadn't stuffed himself with sandwiches right before they left.

Jason kept general watch. Elke monitored sensors through her glasses and comm. Bart and Shaman sat at the front, looking at slight cross angles. Shaman wasn't going to see much of the show, though Aramis suspected that wasn't really a problem for him.

He couldn't count how many concerts and events he'd been present at and not seen. It was just part of the job.

Roaring cheers indicated activity on stage. Aramis checked the door again and looked out and across the audience, as lights played over them.

Then the stage started flashing to bass and percussion music. Caron could see quite well at the angle the steps and balcony offered. Aramis made another ongoing assessment. Nothing was likely to come from the stage, and little could reach from other angles. So why was he nervous?

It was probably the damned lights, which were possibly just ultra bright diodes, but might be xenon or some other gas. They were enough to hurt.

Elke asked, "Shaman, have you pain killers?"

"Not OTC. I strip my kit down to major gear only. Sorry. Problem?"

"Just a headache behind the eyes," she said. "Probably all the stage lights. The color contrast is annoying."

Jason said, "I have some. You should look the other way." He handed her a package. "Might want to put your shades on, too. Your pupils are a bit pinpointed."

"Ah, that's probably residual stim. I took one earlier. Thank you," she said, and swallowed two pills. She popped open a bulb of juice and washed them down, then swapped off with Bart toward the back of the box.

While lighting was not directly a medical issue, the annoying side effects of that, and the volume, could be issues. Horace didn't appreciate it. To his mind, this was excessive. He wasn't up on modern pop music, so it was entirely possible this was some style or trend. It was not good, though. The flicker rate wasn't fast enough to cause much in the way of seizure response, but he agreed it was unpleasant. He didn't have a headache himself, but that was due to him spending most of his time watching the back of the hall. Aramis had donned his shades again, though.

Horace glanced toward the back, and rose to his feet at once, feeling a rush of concern.

Elke looked woozy, now. Her breathing was noticeably rapid and shallow.

"Elke. Toxin." That had to be symptomatic, and not of bright lights and a stim.

"Y-yes," she agreed with a slow nod, and started slumping.

Jason punched his mic and shouted, "Evac! Get Cady. Medical support. Miss Prescot, lie down, you have been poisoned."

"What? I'm fine," she insisted. Then she looked at the plate. "Oh, God."

Horace took a glance to confirm Jason had her under control, and went back to work on Elke. He was very angry, because the rules dictated he use Elke as a test subject until he knew what the problem was, then abandon her to save their principal.

Elke was rapidly losing consciousness, losing muscle control, and losing autonomic functions.

"It's a metabolic depressant or a neurotoxin," he said. "Induce vomiting."

Prescot was lying down. Jason unceremoniously rolled Caron halfway over and shoved fingers down her throat. She didn't have time to protest, but thrashed and twitched, gurgled and puked all over his hand and the carpet. He pulled them out long enough for her to gasp a breath, then did it again.

Elke, though . . . Horace tried his fingers and nothing happened. He shoved a tongue depressor far back. Nothing. Cursing, he reached for a chemical inducer.

Elke nodded her head and fluttered her eyes halfway. "Wuzza?"

"Elke, can you gag?"

"No eazly," she muttered.

He grabbed her chin, dumped a vial down her throat, and waited while it flowed down.

A few seconds later, Elke thrashed in semiconsciousness, and gushed sour-smelling, biley vomit with chunks of cheese and beef. She moaned and rolled to her hands and knees and heaved while twitching, then collapsed again.

"Use this," Horace said as he handed another vial to Jason. "Empty her as much as possible."

"Please stop," Prescot moaned. She had a sizeable puddle in front of her already, on the carpet, her hair, her dress.

As she spoke, Jason poured the syrup into her mouth and twisted her head until she swallowed and choked, then twisted her whole body back over in time for her to spew.

Bart was at the door, and pulled it open to admit Cady. She had a full paramedic kit and a gurney, one of her people had another, and the rest of her team had a perimeter set already. They had real guns. The gurneys were marked as arena property.

"Vitals," Horace said. "Apparent metabolic depressant or neurotoxin. Vomiting induced. Help Elke, keep me informed." He shifted at once to Prescot, who was twitching, moaning, sweating and losing consciousness all at once.

He reached over, unzipped her corset armor, pulled the shoulder straps of her dress, yanked it down to her waist and tore her bra off in front. Cady was ready, bent down and slapped sensors onto her skin.

"That is not a healthy rhythm," he said as soon as he glanced the waveform.

Cady said, "Move," and shoved past Jason. She snapped Elke's jacket and blouse open, and cut one strap of her body armor, then flopped it aside and sliced her elastic support shirt with a hook knife. Her assistant passed down more leads and she pressed them on. "Take care of that armor," she said.

Jason took orders at once, whipped out a knife and cut the other strap. Horace was more impressed. The man could move from leader to follower and back in a moment. First class.

Cady said, "Same rhythm, toxicity probably a little more advanced."

That rhythm was familiar, though.

"Probably a fish or shell toxin," he said.

Cady replied, "I concur. What do we have to counter?"

"Nothing on hand. Keep respiration up." He just hadn't anticipated a neural or cardiac condition in a nubile, healthy twenty-two year old, nor in an athletic thirty-two year old. There was a limit to how much gear he could carry even in a briefcase and shoulder bag, in addition to weapons and other gear.

Jason asked, "Will any stimulants work? I have three."

"No," Horace shook his head. "It takes a specific acetylcholine stimulant. Donepizil, pyridostigmine, distilled nicotine in the field."

"Cigar?" Jason asked.

Horace spun around. Jason was peeling the label off a huge Cuban.

Jason continued, "Exaltado. Genetically boosted nicotine."

"Yes, lots of smoke."

Cady said, "That's going to cause gagging if they're nonsmokers."

"It can't hurt, might help, and we don't have any time to waste. Do it."

Jason pulled out a lighter, and spun the cigar while drawing fast. He got it lit to an angry orange coal.

Cady said, "Try to breathe that fast and you'll choke out. Shaman, you monitor. I'll cover Prescot, you take Elke." She shifted sides.

Jason nodded, drew a huge puff on the cigar, handed it over and gave Elke a lungful. He just had time to reflect on how fucked up it was to be shotgunning an unconscious comrade with puke all over her lips, before he leaned back, grabbed the cigar from Cady and took another puff.

No niceties. They were trying to get a lot of nicotine in fast. The cigar was wet with spit. *Cady used to be a man,* part of him said. *Shut up and smoke.*

He had a good puff, and the lacy traces of the last one were just curling from Elke's lips as he leaned down and hit her again.

She coughed and moaned. "Wha?"

He gasped, "Nicotine as antitoxin. Shut up and breathe, Elke."

"Yah."

Dammit, he had to get a good, clean breath in between. Mouth to mouth was draining the regular way. This way . . . he was buzzing from the cigar and oxygen deprivation.

Cady coughed deeply. She obviously wasn't a smoker. Her eyes were tearing up and weepy red. That explained why she didn't know how to draw properly.

Both victims were coughing now, but that meant they were still breathing. Prescot flinched a little as Cady mashed lips on her again, but she tried gamely to inhale.

Elke moaned. "Please . . . roll over."

"Sorry, Elke." Blow. "I know it feels like shit. Hang in there."

She clutched at her guts. "Siiick," she said.

"Going to puke?"

"No."

"Good." Blow.

Elke coughed, hacked and moaned again.

Behind him, he heard Shaman say, "Transport arriving in three minutes. Keep at it."

Jason grabbed the cigar and drew again. Damn, it was going down fast. Two people drawing pretty much nonstop, and big lungfuls, kept the coal hot and bright.

"I want pyridostigmine as soon as they're here," Horace said. "Chain of custody."

"Say again?" Bart asked.

Shaman jabbed a finger for emphasis. "Make sure it's our people who bring it!"

Yes, it was paranoid, but someone had already infiltrated the food service concession on short notice. They could trust their own people . . . probably.

"We're being stupid," Cady said.

"Uh?"

She flicked ash off the cigar, shoved the mouth end between Caron's lips, said, "Seal on this," and pinched her nostrils. Then, carefully, she wrapped her own lips past the coal and blew. She didn't get as much inflation, but that had to be twice the nicotine with none wasted in her lungs.

"Brilliant," he said as he took the stub and did the same with Elke, pressing her lips around it. Smoke eddied out of her nose before he was done. He didn't burn his tongue on the coal, but he could certainly feel the heat.

Horace kept an eye on the map. There was a chronological juggle between being exposed, and not moving fast enough.

"Transport now," he said. He grabbed Caron's legs, Jason grabbed under her shoulders, and they raised her onto the gurney. When he looked up, Elke was already on the other. He quickly threw a sheet over Prescot's bare breasts. It wasn't that critical but he didn't want paparazzi selling pics to some pervert. This was a medical emergency, not a beach.

Elke went first. Again, it was a threat issue. Better someone try to shoot her than Prescot. It was aggravating, but business. The second gurney was surrounded by all four team members; four of Cady's fell in as the cordon collapsed. A crowd stared, but didn't have time to comment before they crossed the mezzanine, into two held elevators, trailing a cloud of cigar smoke, and to hell with the hall regulations and European law.

The ride down was too slow to suit him, but there was nothing he could do at this point.

At the ground floor, they pushed through the door before it fully opened. The operators went into goon mode and just shoved people out of the way, waving batons and shouting as needed, though they managed to cut a pretty good hole just from presence. Cady's eyes streamed tears and she still coughed from the smoke, staggering and gripping the gurney for balance. Jason was upright but obviously not tracking well. Still, there was most of a cigar's worth of genetically enhanced nicotine in the bloodstream of the two women, and their EKGs were faint but present.

Two ambulances were right on the curve, and they were company vehicles, with a lot of trauma gear. Perfect for someone shot, stabbed or caught in an explosion. Not perfect for a poison in the food. He'd have to make a report on that. Still, they did have pyridostigmine as far as he knew.

A man handed him two syringes. He looked familiar, but Horace wanted to be sure.

"Vouch!" he demanded.

"Yes, he's mine," Cady said. "I'm going to be sick now." She bent over at the curb and vomited.

Horace said, "Get me a vein," and tapped the first syringe. That should be enough. Better a little low than too much. Competing neurotoxins would be really bad.

Jason got a vein by the expedient method. He wrapped a hand around Prescot's arm and clenched, and shoved her fist into a ball with the other hand. Horace saw a nice vein pop up. Cady was back on her feet with an alcohol pad, and swabbed the area off.

Phenomenal teamwork, he thought, and stuck the needle in and plunged it.

"Now Elke," he said.

"Got it," Cady agreed, grabbed the other syringe. She jabbed Elke as two men loaded Caron, then jumped back down for Elke and rolled her into the second one.

The vehicles were not intended for more than one caregiver. Horace went with Miss Prescott though he really wanted to be with Elke. He had Aramis and Bart up front. Elke had Cady for care, with Jason of course, and one of Cady's drivers. Cady's team piled into two limos and drove block and tail.

"Where are we going?" Bart asked. "Family hospital is Mercy Gardens."

"Negative. Divert somewhere else right now."

"Understood, though there isn't anywhere closer."

Horace said, "All the more reason not to go there."

"Diverting to Lady of Peace."

"Do not announce that anywhere."

"Roger, obviously." He heard a radio comment cut off in the middle. Aramis had killed the radio.

Bart juggled radio, shouted instructions, driving and phone. Horace heard him say, "AIC Cady, we will need immediate security at the door. Armed. Do you have weapons with you?"

"Shotguns and a couple of carbines."

"Excellent."

"The hospital won't like that."

"Fuck them."

Horace raised an eyebrow. Had Bart ever sworn in English? That laconically? It was probable he was more worried about Elke than Prescot.

Aramis flipped his phone.

"Boss, scramble me at once and dial me back out. Thanks... Yes, we have an emergency and are en route to your location. Stand by for medical staff."

He handed the phone to Horace, who grabbed it. Aramis then lit a monitor and zoomed in on the hospital.

"Hello. Attending physician speaking. Two victims. Paralytic toxin with muscle flaccidity and no tetanus. Nicotine is palliative, so it's likely to be a cholinergic antagonist. They'll need ACE inhibitor, full cardiopulmonary support and dialysis."

"Er . . . sir, is this a nerve gas attack?"

"No. Ingested poison. There is also a security issue. Patients will be escorted by armed undercover officers."

"I can't allow that unless it's cleared through the police."

"Then please start clearing. We're arriving in two minutes. I have your floorplan on screen. Where are we going?"

"Sir, we'll take care of that after triage."

"I will have our supervisor call you at once and explain the situation. Expect the police to be advised, too."

"Very well, sir. We'll have a room standing by as soon as we can verify."

"Very good. Arrival pending," he said, and clicked off. They'd discuss it all right, though they were not likely to like his method.

Aramis took the phone back and called Alex.

"Aramis here. Please call the hospital and the police and clear our arrival and equipment with them ASAP."

Horace checked the monitors again. Still alive.

He faced Aramis and said, "Stow weapons on the gurney. We'll secure the facility from the inside," he said. "Inside, turn left, Isolation Room One. If it's occupied, we'll proceed to Two."

"And if that's occupied?"

"That would mean a serious disaster already happening, and someone with lesser needs getting unceremoniously shoved out the door by Bart."

"We have an open bay," Bart announced as he whipped into the hospital ER zone. He'd driven manual the whole way without a hitch.

"Arriving. Out fast."

Bart led the way, Aramis a moment behind. They looked big, intimidating, and their expressions suggested no one should argue. They shoved the doors wide faster than the servos could open them, then turned left immediately inside the door, pushed into the isolation room. Horace rolled Caron in, two others wheeled Elke in right behind. The lead men kicked the releases. The doors wooshed shut and sealed. Aramis shoved a manual bolt in place. Jason ripped the panel off the controls with a pair of pliers and cut wires.

"Who's outside?" Bart asked, snagging a shotgun from under Caron's gurney.

"Both original drivers and two of mine," Cady said. "Stand by." She rapidfired into her mic, then said, "They have the outside door under surveillance and cover, discreetly."

"Good," Bart said. "I have escorted a high profile patient before. I expect we will have security at the door—"

Bang! Bang! Bang! "Open this door!"

"—about now."

Horace went to work. He wanted everything set up before he allowed anyone else in, and he would supervise the procedure until the end.

"Cady, I need a high dose of stim for me, please."

Cady was good. She had the IV lines hung, and a tray of every acetylcholine stimulant or inhibitor he might need. She rolled over a dialysis machine and an external pacemaker. She reached into a drawer and grabbed out a pack of stimulants, peeled one out and slapped it onto his neck where it would absorb faster than the arm, but without shocking his system too much.

Jason knew enough to roll sensor pads up, slap them on, and step back. He'd correctly placed them on the upper curve of the right breasts and just outside and down from the left.

"I can hand implements if you need, or help with the door."

"Help with the door," Horace said.

He sprinkled a pinch of powder over each of them, more as a tradition and habit for himself than from any expectation it would help. Neurotoxins were very powerful natural magic themselves. One had to actually cleanse the blood, and fast.

"Watch for V fib," he told Cady. "Advise me if you see it and prepare to shock or pace. I'm going to cut down for dialysis."

Behind him, he could hear Bart and Alex arguing with hospital security.

Aramis said, "I don't care who you are. We have our own doctor, we just need the facilities. Everything else can proceed as normally, and we apologize for the inconvenience."

It was obvious there wasn't going to be any shooting. The doc sounded as if he was trying to guess if they were undercover UN cops or soldiers. For now, that was fine. They were not going to admit that a Prescot was in there, and they were not going to let anyone else in.

"You've shut down the whole ER! We have to cordon and evac, and—"

"And if I'm really a threat you should not be discussing your security protocols with me, should you?" It sounded as if Aramis was enjoying being reasonable with someone so distraught.

That seemed to shut the man up. Then Aramis got on his phone and talked at length. That was not Horace's concern, though. Right now, he had two young women to save. He ignored everything but their vitals and treatment.

Jason knew he was stressing out. There was nothing more he could do, except let a real physician and an advanced EMT handle things. It would be a waste of a beautiful woman to lose Prescot, and a black mark they didn't need, but he was more worried about Elke. Beautiful. Deadly. A good friend and a fine operator. He also knew if she did die, he wouldn't have anyone to take revenge on. It would just be one of those things.

One of his character flaws was not dealing well with not getting his way. He wasn't as bad as Alex, but his anger lit off when he was blocked, and there was not a damned thing he could do about this. He steamed and twitched. He was moderately nauseated from the cigar as well.

At least I have plenty of adrenaline if I need to kick someone's ass, he thought. It helped calm him just a few percent.

He was too pissed to think straight, so he left the ugly expression on his face, the one that said, "I want to kill you. Please give me an excuse," and let Aramis argue with the rentacops outside the door.

Yeah, he was pissed. He was better trained, but those guys were still colleagues, more or less, and "rentacop" was a phrase he tried not to use, even about mall security.

He looked over, and Bart seemed twitchy, too. Bart almost never betrayed emotion. That was a little reassuring, but then he remembered why they were both nervy. They had a woman down, with a neurotoxin.

If he prayed, he'd pray for Shaman to outdo himself. The man was a master with a knife, pliers and cargo tape. How was he with all the high tech gear and a high tech problem?

Horace breathed a sigh and stretched kinks from his back. It had taken an hour, but he was sure he had both women stabilized and breathing normally. They'd need some recovery time, but they were definitely going to live.

Somehow, Alex was in the room. How or when that had happened, Shaman didn't know. Somehow, he'd gotten in, and none of the crowd of staff outside had.

Horace looked over at him and asked, "How is the burden?"

Alex looked as exhausted as Horace felt.

"New Scotland Yard, UN Bureau of Safety, British Region. Local police. Board of Health. Corporate. National and UN Disease Vector Control. A bunch of pissed hospital administrators. It doesn't end. The important thing is, we're all alive."

"We should all stay that way, too. I am confident both women will survive, barring unforeseen disasters."

Alex grinned and looked younger and more awake at once. "Good. When can we transport?"

"At once, and we should. The longer we're in a hospital, the longer someone has to mix up drugs, food, atmosphere or other issues."

"Understood. I'll get us transport. Five ambulances. Jason, let's make calls."

"Yes, sir!" Jason agreed, with a grin of his own. He let his weapon down on its sling, took three bounding steps, and grabbed Horace in a tight embrace.

As Horace returned it, Jason said, "Well done, my friend. You have confirmed your reputation as a miracle worker."

"Was there ever any doubt?" he replied. Hugging was not normal for him. This wasn't the most comfortable act, but it was heartfelt.

"Not of your abilities, just that some things are not fixable."

"Luckily, sometimes a cigar is not just a cigar."

Another man was very upset with that turn of events. They'd saved her. A neurotoxin he was assured killed in minutes, before it was possible to reach a hospital, and they'd saved her, and that frightening freak of a woman with them, nor had any of the others suffered. It was impressive, and Bryan Prescot was certainly getting his money's worth, but that just drove home that he had to go down. He cheated businesses, governments and now death.

How to reach him, though? The inside intel source was iffy at this point; hell, unreliable. Bloody loyalties. The guards were, grudgingly, the best. Short of large bombs, what was there?

Some of the spy gadgets were defeated, others showing obvious false images, and the "good" ones couldn't be trusted. Most of them could be abandoned, but one set of cameras . . .

She really was a very pretty girl. *Very* pretty. It was a shame he'd had to have that camera removed, but he had a good archive.

If he played it right, he might get a closer look soon enough. Move or kill the father, get the daughter, and take the money. It was not an easy challenge, but there were more zeroes involved than most astrophysicists dealt with. That made it worth it.

So, this attack had failed. It was time to change tactics. They'd be harder to reach on that desolate rock, but harder to protect as well, and channels were slow and limited. They should just be encouraged to go there. It might take a year to work it, but that was a fair timetable. Also, most of the family hadn't spent much time there. There were arrangements in place they couldn't know about, and wouldn't be able to respond to.

The game was more exciting as it progressed.

CHAPTER 11

"You saved my life . . . again," Caron said. She didn't enjoy being in a wheelchair, but it helped with mobility. She wanted to lie back down. Horace had said that as soon as medical monitors were set, she could lie down in her own bed.

From her own wheelchair, Elke said, "It's what I get paid for, but you're welcome. I didn't plan to get poisoned."

"Still, I'm sorry . . . dammit, I'm sorry about all of this. I just wanted to be a mining engineer in the family company . . . I never wanted to be some exotic trillionaire."

"We're often trapped by circumstance."

"Why do you do it? It can't be just the money."

"It's a professional challenge, and we have pride in ourselves and our company," Elke said. "I have my own circumstances, too."

"Oh? Like what?"

"Caron . . ." Elke hesitated. "I'm the only woman on our team. Our industry is ninety percent male, and few females in front line, unless they're guarding women. It's probably worse for Cady, being trans, but I know for myself, I can't ever be a woman in public."

"Why not?"

"Culture. I'm one of the team, one of the guys. Aramis especially took a long time to get used to that idea. So I have to be more masculine than he is. He has to think of me as 'Agent Sykora, nuclear explosive disposal technician and executive protection specialist.' He tries very hard not to think of me as, 'Elke, the

Czech woman he wants to bed.' It would be cruel of me to taunt him, it would be unprofessional, and it would make working together harder."

Caron flushed. She had been taunting him a lot, from sheer frustration.

"It also would mean he'd have trouble with my professional position. So as far as anyone is concerned, Elke's a nun with no interest in sex, and a cold-hearted technical bitch with no interest in anything girly. If you think you're frustrated..." She tapered off, looking bemused and slightly embarrassed.

"You're not a nun, I gather."

"If you'd seen Bart with his shirt off..." Elke grinned. "And if I hadn't been half dead, and if Jason hadn't had that awful cigar..."

"Lucky you. Agent Cady did not have a good time with the cigar, and I can honestly say that was one of the most horrible intimate experiences of my life, but I'm very grateful for it." She'd found out about Cady's background, and wasn't sure whether she didn't like that Cady was female, had been male, had transitioned between them, or that she was a stranger with a cigar. All of it was dizzying and unpleasant.

"It's odd like that," Elke said. "Very intimate, and very professional. We have a bond we'd never have as friends, lovers or family. But really, someone should have told you this early on: if you need to get spread, it's not a problem. We are not present socially, only professionally. Use your apartment, the limo, a hotel. We are absolutely going to be there, and you could invite in a horse and nothing would be said. We've guarded a lot of people with a lot of quirks. Our job is to guard you and be silent about it, nothing more."

Caron was both relieved and embarrassed. Yes, Elke had been in the toilet with her, but she was a woman and that happened. The exhibitionism had been a challenge, a protest, but...

"So why did it get you all flushed and sweaty?"

"Honestly?"

"Please."

"You were being an utter bitch to my friend and needed a lesson. So I did a bunch of push-ups and gave you a leer. Sorry."

"He had a great ass, though, didn't he?" Caron grinned.

"Yes, he did. You were being a bit of a bitch to me, too, you know."

"I didn't know. I wasn't thinking of you as a woman."

"Well, thank you."

It took her a moment to grasp that. Then she grinned.

"You're welcome, Elke."

"Next time I'm sending Bart to the toilet with you. Or Alex."

Caron cringed. "You wouldn't."

"I would, and it shouldn't matter, but I probably won't."

"But if I'm a bloody bitch again you might?"

"That, or if it turns out to be necessary. Look, Jason and Alex are married, old enough it's not an issue, and Jason is a paramedic. Shaman's a doctor. Bart's been in the dressing room with singers and actresses. I'm female. Aramis is the only one who might be uncomfortable, and he'd never let you know it."

"I just have never had this to deal with before. Ewan . . . damn him . . . was family, and I never needed a guard standing over me to take a crap."

"Pretend we're not there. It'll be a lot easier. Have we ever commented or given any indication that it matters?"

"No . . . though that's almost disturbing, too. One expects jokes, comments. Look, genetics were good to me. I *know* men like my body, but your blokes act like robots."

"That's our job. But if you make a few jokes, we might make a few back. But you have to set the tone."

Caron nodded. "Thanks. I feel a lot better. If there's anything I can do for you, let me know."

"Don't offer me any more food."

"I was going to have you test it all."

"Absolutely. I have chemical sniffers now."

"What quirks?"

"Hmm?"

"You mentioned people you'd guarded who had some unusual quirks in the bedroom. Who?"

"None of your bloody business," Elke said with a smile.

"Just checking."

Horace came in, and Elke looked relieved.

"I'm going to hobble to next door and collapse," Elke said. She raised her arm stiffly. It still showed purple bruises from needles and handling. She grabbed the manual knob and turned for the door.

"Rest well," Caron offered.

She still couldn't fathom why someone would have a job like that. She didn't like the need and she didn't like that people got hurt on her behalf, even if they were well paid.

If only she could get rid of that bloody fortune.

She mulled it over while Horace helped her through the door and into her bed, now set with bio monitors.

By the next day, Alex had resolved all the outstanding issues, with the help of Ripple Creek HQ. The Prescot family, their lawyers, the company lawyers and some friendly assemblypersons, plus the fact that two people were saved from near certain death made a good case for the team's actions being justified. Opposed to that, those who blindly supported the rules had little to point to more than those rules... which would have likely led to two dead women and a political mess that would also cause bad PR for the hospital and the arena. There'd be grumbling for a few days, but Alex's superiors told him not to worry, so he'd make occasional checks and otherwise ignore it.

After that, he sorted routine matters such as schedule charts, incident reports open and closed—most of them birds that flew into the sensors—threats sent and made in various places—most of them from whining socialists who imagined the Prescots had done them some ill by being successful. Cady had tossed most, flagged a couple for followup. He concurred and sent the list back, where she'd send relevant information to law enforcement. He smirked briefly. If those pansies imagined they'd been done some wrong so far, wait until UNPOL and their local police got hold of them.

That was when a call came up from Facilities.

"Sir, this is Roger Edge." Edge was one of Cady's men.

"Go ahead."

"There's a woman here who claims to be Miss Prescot's mother. I can't reach Mr. Prescot to confirm. She's rather irritated."

Even through the phone, Alex heard a voice that was a cultured and harpish snap, "I am not 'rather irritated.' I'm pissed off at this treatment. Let me see my daughter."

"Assuming she's clean, escort her up and we'll do personal ID here."

"Roger. Out."

Alex smiled. That poor man's name was going to be a pain for communication.

"Miss, are you awake enough for a visit from your mother?"

"Oh, god, not that old bag," Caron writhed a bit and groaned. "There's a reason my father paid forty million to divorce her. It was worth it. I'd've paid it myself."

Ouch. Not good. However...

"I'm afraid in the interests of avoiding hassle in the press, I'm interpreting that as, 'Yes, I'm fit to see her briefly.'"

Jason came over the net. "She's here now, at the lift."

Alex nodded and said softly, "Aramis, you post in here. We'll cover the hall. Make sure she gets sniffed." The young man nodded and stepped out the door at once. Then he stepped back in.

The woman who came through the door right then had to be Ashier Prescot. She was near fifty, slim and decently kept, and had a slightly more Asian cast than her daughter. The Kazakh was obvious, and the Maltese apparent after a moment. She was simultaneously beautiful and a hawk-faced bitch.

She extended an arm with a jacket in it, and said, "Thank you, young man. Would you be so kind as to hang this for me?"

"My pleasure," Aramis said with a smile, and hung it on the hook right behind her. He didn't act at all put upon. Well done.

"Thank you. And a chair, please?"

Aramis politely moved a chair a meter for her.

Caron said, "Hello, Mum," and sounded woozier than she had before.

Ashier stepped over and sat down, every bit the concerned mother. "How are you feeling, dear?"

"Alive. The Ripple Creek doctor is amazing, and so were their EMTs. My lady guard went down first. She's next door."

"Lucky that. Is she okay?"

"So I'm told."

"And the men are good looking as well, 'ey? Worth the money." The woman twisted and winked at Alex.

"Mum! They're bodyguards and very professional. I don't get involved with the help."

Her mother clutched her hand and said, "Sorry. I'm never sure what to say. I'm glad you're all right. I can move in for a bit if it will help. The South Wing is far enough your father need never see me."

Caron paused and barely stiffened for a moment, which Alex interpreted as absolute panic.

"Mum, I hope to be on my feet in a day or so. Then I have to keep up with classes."

"All right. But do stay in touch, please? I hardly hear from you."

"I will. Every morning."

"Good girl."

"But you caught me just as I had a dose. I'm drifting off now."

Ashier looked at Alex. "Is it okay if I stay? I can sit here."

Caron's expression behind her mother's was mortified. It was a reasonable request, though.

Alex said, "Yes, of course, ma'am, but do please be quiet. Dr. Mbuto gave strict instructions for her to rest quietly."

"Oh. Not Dr. Freling?"

"He consulted, and decided that since Dr. Mbuto performed the first response and the treatment, that he should continue as lead. He's checking periodically."

Actually, he was completely shut out. No one Alex couldn't vet personally was allowed anywhere near Caron Prescot for the foreseeable future. Freling got updates as a courtesy, and so he could offer input on the progress.

Caron was faking sleep by the time he finished. He and Aramis maintained stony silence at parade rest for almost an hour. Finally, Ashier rose quietly, whispered, "I'm done with the chair," and padded out, requesting Aramis hand her her jacket again.

Once he was sure she was off the elevator and away from any mics, Alex said, "It's safe, miss."

Caron twitched and sighed.

"That's my mum," she said. "Never do for yourself what you can have someone do for you, especially if it's menial and irrelevant."

It seemed safe to comment. He said, "I gather it both maintains her self image as a wealthy person of means, and keeps employees engaged. I suppose some prefer that to doing nothing."

"Yes, she has more staff than Dad. No need for it, just a status thing."

"I suggest you do call her every morning, if you don't want her dropping in again."

Caron cringed slightly. "Yes, you're probably right."

Elsewhere two people discussed the attack from a different perspective.

The woman said, "That was awfully damned close to killing her. She's not the one we want dead."

The man decided not to argue that now. Eventually the woman would figure out her place, or she'd be on the list, too. The kidnapping didn't work, and they'd lost another inside source over that. While they got a lot of useful fear factor and the remaining staff distanced themselves, all for the better, they were scared enough that they'd probably not consider any offer or threat. Dead end. Now this.

"It had to be a serious enough scare to make them consider dropping stock options, or splitting control. That's the goal." *For now.* Actually, the goal had been to kill her, then go after the father in his remorse. Most of the staff loved the arrogant little bitch, though. They'd get in the way.

"Yes, but do be careful. The man will button up if pressed enough."

I hope so. "Obviously, since that didn't work, we'll try a different approach. We'll get them off planet, which will make communication harder, and morale worse. Then we hit them again."

"Keep him here! Once he gets there and finds out what's been done . . ."

"He won't. He's too nice to suspect, and too cloistered to notice."

"I don't trust that little bitch, either. She's too clever for her own good."

"Noted," he agreed. That was the reason he kept the woman around—inside information from the house, even if it was a little out of date. Pity she wasn't tough enough to help with killing. That would make things so much easier.

"But he definitely needs taken down a peg, the arrogant sod."

He was wryly amused at that. That was an egregious case of the pot calling the Queen's china black.

He said, "We'll keep the pressure on with lots of low key stuff until they move."

"Moving will separate them from a lot of resources. But I'm not convinced they won't figure out some of our advance strategies."

My *advance strategies, you conceited bitch,* he thought. She was useful, and savage in bed, but ultimately, he might have to decide between her and the money. He didn't see that being a tough decision.

It could have been so easy, too. There was so much money involved even the help and hangers on had millions.

Vaughn said, "I do like these cars. Classy."

"Indeed," Bart agreed. He braked firmly and pulled them into the market street of some little town called Llanfair-ym-Muallt. A sleek motorcycle wove past them and into the slower traffic ahead.

The family had Mercedes, Volvos, Skodas, classic Lincolns, but the Bentley, with a three-stage turbine, variable torque electric transmission, and the mass of a small tank was just a joy. That turbine, though, threw it around like a sports car. The long wheelbase was a pain, but that was necessary for the stretched cargo area. This was a limo meant for real travel, not publicity gags.

Bart asked, "Do we need anything locally?"

"No," Jason said, "I just like seeing the area and getting a feel for it."

"As good a reason as any to be here," Bart said. He kept his eyes on the road constantly.

The team had instructions to keep the Prescots' vehicles in use, for whatever they needed. Having three or four vehicles rolling around each day kept any potential hostiles guessing as to who might be where. Between fourteen personnel locally available, and some of the household staff, it should be pretty well impossible to predict who might be in which vehicle and when. Jason estimated that as a seventy-five percent reduction in success rate for any attacks.

It was all about probabilities. Don't be predictable. Add in distractions. Confuse the enemy. Display multiple targets, most of them decoys. And if they got through the fog of probabilities, counterattack hard and viciously and bring the pain.

"I don't like how that cycle keeps pulling closer," Vaughn said. He was visibly tense.

"I see him," Bart agreed. Yes, that was possibly a threat, and definitely an annoyance. "Is he a threat or just a twit?"

Vaughn said, "Maybe both, maybe neither. We can't risk it."

"I will relocate us. It seems easiest."

"Yes, but don't let them think we're being corralled. We'll find somewhere else to shop and make it look planned."

"I understand," Bart said. He intended that anyway, but Vaughn never talked down, he just presented facts. They both knew they were thinking the same, and that was reassuring.

Bart turned left onto a major but winding street. It might have existed since just after the Romans left, or even before. They probably hadn't been here, but some Celtic tribe...

Another cycle turned in fast from a side street, and a package rolled off the cargo rack.

"*Mine!*" Jason shouted. He ducked, Bart kept driving. It was important that Bart keep the vehicle moving, and that Jason be able to respond to the threat.

They both tensed, and the limpet exploded. Armored plastic crashed in a crescendo of sparkling shards, the blast punched Jason in the head and body and ripped at his arms.

He was half deaf, but it was probably temporary, but that meant he was still alive and combatant, so he rose up and reconned again.

There was a window missing, the back seat was shredded, and the rider was close enough to reach in, though he stayed back with a pistol.

Still groggy, Jason shouted, "Brake!" and hit the door release. Bart eased into the brakes hard and evenly, and the door slammed and creaked to full open. Jason popped up over the roof, and gapped the kid, between the eyes, through the upper lip, through the throat, then dropped back down to shoot right past Bart's head, through the hole in the window, and peg the kid low in the belly.

That done, he sprung out the door, over the roof in a roll, grabbed the collapsed body as the bike started slumping over with it, and dragged. Bart already had the large cargo section open, and crept forward enough for Jason to throw the body in, then heave the bike up with a grunt and shove it alongside. He darted back around and rolled into his seat.

Bart nailed the throttle, Jason's door slammed closed from the acceleration. The big limo barely clipped another car whose anticollision circuits couldn't move it fast enough, zipped through the intersection and was gone. He pushed the button for the rear hatch. Jason keyed his phone.

"Marlow."

"Vaughn. We got hit by a hostile. Inbound with evidence. Need diplomacy with cops."

"Understood. I'll call. You heading straight in?"

"Yes. We're done anyway. Out."

As he disconnected, Bart said, "You didn't mention that we're bringing the actual body."

"Yeah, that would be hard to explain on the phone. They'll figure it out."

"Before or after it starts to stink?"

"This whole situation stinks."

"I agree."

Alex was very attentive to the threat, and made supplemental notes as Jason debriefed.

"So there are now random attacks, despite the counter tactics. That's not good."

"Right," Jason said. "They're either desperate, or amateurs."

"We already have pros trying. This could mean multiple threats."

"Yes."

The local police chief twitched when he was called.

"You removed evidence from the scene, including a body, which you allege was killed in self defense, and explosives were involved?"

That call led to a brief standoff with police, the government, Ripple Creek corporate, lawyers from all parties, and from Prescot. It would have made great headlines, if anyone had been interested in letting the press in. All seemed to agree that would just make a world class nightmare into a drug-addled horror.

Prescot was remarkably understanding when Jason explained to him.

"In summary, sir, we had to neutralize the real world threat fast. We had to egress the area in case of followup threats. A body on the street would have been worse. We needed potential intel or evidence. We had to do it all in a matter of seconds. We reported the incident at once, returned to a safe operating location, and provided all facts to the police, our management, you and the government. It's one of those situations that just doesn't have a good outcome."

"I disagree. I think the outcome was perfect. At least one enemy knows you're playing to win, and that you can protect us. It didn't become public. You demonstrated to me and my family that you can keep us safe at all costs. The money involved would have been an issue some time ago, but not the fundamental issue, and isn't that important now. However, can you think of a more discreet way to handle it in future?"

The casual and relaxed attitude caught Jason off guard, but he'd prepared for that question.

"Honestly, sir, I can't. Someone turned the street into a combat zone. I have to treat it as such while minimizing collateral damage to innocent people and property. That means I kill the threat, relocate and call for backup, both economic and with guns. As it is, there's one minor hit and run that will take some bodywork. Most people didn't even witness it, as fast as it was. A lot of them won't believe it was real. They'll assume it was some art stunt or video trick with props."

"Very well. I accept that. And I'm very glad you and Bart are both unhurt."

"Thank you, sir."

Two days later, a stolen European Army shoulder-fired rocket came over the hedgerow. It did no damage, because the debris landed fifty meters short. It landed as debris because Elke had a directional mine on the roof that blew a shotgun spread of tungsten cubes into its flight path. No one commented on either the mine, or on the damage the backblast did to some two hundred year old slate tiles. She'd obviously done the right thing.

Alex sat attentively and rather calmly, given the circumstances at the meeting with Prescot immediately following. Prescot paced as he thought aloud.

"I want to move soon. I have things to finish, but Caron is days from her degree. We'll probably have to skip the commencement."

Alex said, "I'd recommend it. It's too big to secure without the government, and they'd want control."

"Unkind to her, but necessary." Prescot sighed.

Even though calm, Alex was at a heightened state of awareness. He said, "It just seems that all these attacks are urging us to hurry up and get off Earth. Which makes me wonder if we really shouldn't. Except we can't cover the entire globe, so moving makes sense, even if it is into the vipers' nest, because we'll have better control of the situation. I suspect it's not going to be a picnic, though."

Prescot said, "At least on Govannon we will have more relative force available, better odds and at least some filtering, yes?"

He was no fool and no coward. Alex appreciated that.

"I agree. It'll make it easier to focus, but I suspect any threats will be more dedicated."

"How fast can you move Caron if you have to?"

"That depends on how fast transport is available. There are limits in the schedules."

"How fast could you evacuate here, go to ground, relocate and get to transport?"

"I'd need ninety seconds notice for a survival egress with vehicles," Alex said firmly. He liked that line of questioning. He could prove they'd done that in a war zone under fire. Here would not be a problem, relatively speaking.

"What about a permanent departure?"

"I'd ship possessions now, or duplicate, and have everything ready. Same schedule."

"Then I'd like you to set up that procedure for Caron. Don't tell anyone, including her. Don't even tell me when you're leaving. Once her class is done, you make the call for me and get her to Govannon."

"I can do that, sir. That's a very secure method."

He wouldn't even tell his own people the exact moment, in fact.

CHAPTER 12

Elke only half heard any of the lecture. It was all partly familiar, partly irrelevant. She had most of her attention dispersed for threatening movements, and an eye on Caron's seat proper.

The crashing echoes of a Superior Armaments 10mm carbine jolted her alert.

There was no mistaking that sound, even through the structure of the building. The students mumbled and some of them thought it was construction. Elke heard muffled shouts and screams, though.

She reached over, snagged Caron's arm, and yanked her from her seat.

"Get ready to move or drop when I say so," she said. She punched her transmitter and said, "Incoming." Aramis probably already knew, but he'd make the call for backup.

She popped open the doccase she'd carried these last few weeks, and grabbed a riot baton. The school had refused to compromise on any real weapons, so an electric toy with a glorified flashlight was all she had.

Caron hunkered under the desk, as everyone around them stared in curiosity and amusement. They still hadn't caught on. The lecturer said something about paying attention, but Elke wasn't listening to non-threats at this point.

Elke said, "That was gunfire. It's an attack."

This elicited a few quizzical glances, a few titters, and two knotty rugby players who stood and looked around. That's who Elke wanted.

She gestured toward them and said, "Readers, chairs, anything heavy. Stand by to throw them, and stand by to block the door."

They nodded and moved, and other students started to act a little more seriously, but it probably wasn't enough. In her ears, she heard Aramis say, "Arriving."

She said clearly and loudly, "One of my associates is coming in."

Aramis popped through the door and closed it almost in a blink, slung a bag off his shoulder and pulled out his baton.

"I am a licensed security guard and I am armed," he announced.

No one screamed, but there were more discomfited noises. This was not something soft, decadent upper class Earth kids had ever learned to deal with. The lecturer at least had the sense to get down off the lectern and duck behind a rolling cart. He didn't do anything as far as the students, though. Elke would see if she could do something for them, but Caron came first.

There was another burst of fire. This was closer and there were more screams, audible this time.

"Barricade the door," Elke ordered. "Students, get into that corner. You and you," she indicated the two athletes, "stand there out of line of fire and get ready to throw if I tell you or if you see a problem. Caron, you move right over there," she indicated a space right between both doors, "and get ready to run either way on my order. Armor up."

The two men nodded firmly and moved. Caron blushed and looked embarrassed, but did as she was told, and opened her doccase as a torso shield and tied it around her neck and waist. That plus her corset armor should stop most carbine fire.

Aramis grabbed a rolling chair and jammed it under the door latch, then ran a rod through the release bar—the door opened out, of course—and another through the chair's wheels. The first one was purpose built and from his pack. The second was a convenient carbon fiber handle from some tool. Elke had one more rod, and she tossed it to Aramis as he sprinted up the aisle. He jammed that into the second door.

Another gun burst wasn't far away. Screams sounded, and someone yanked at the lower door, which budged but didn't open.

Someone in the room shouted, "We can't leave them to die!"

Elke swung that way and scowled. She was not in a mood to argue with sheep.

Aramis saved her from a bad incident with a point and a tap of his own stun baton. The boy in question slunk back into the huddle.

What to do? She wanted to use explosive, but that would be a clear giveaway to their location. Flight was not a good idea until they knew this wasn't an attempt to channel them somewhere. Of course, once located, there was no guarantee that whoever it was wouldn't use massive explosives. Elke would.

Aramis ran to the window, dropped the folding scaling ladder and some tools, then ran back and crouched by the lower door, ready to enfilade it. He also had a slightly oblique view of the upper doors. Elke had the reverse. That put Caron at a distance that wasn't comfortable, from a defensive point of view.

She shrugged slightly and took a deep, slow breath. Her turn.

Explosive was prohibited in civilian settings. Never mind her training, the government only trusted its own agents, even though she'd been one of those until a few years ago. However, there were places in China and America where one could buy . . . toys. She pulled out a couple of devices and prepared them.

She'd forgotten about her earbuds, and Aramis's voice surprised her.

"Elke, nothing on any immediate scans from outside. I've got two of Cady's people moving in and sweeping."

"We vacate if it's clear," she said. "Do we know how many?"

"Roger on vacating. At least one. Probably no more than three."

This time, the gunfire was through the upper door's latch mechanism.

Aramis sprinted over seats, catching his foot and stumbling but recovering amazingly fast. He gently shoved Caron down behind a desk and took up position in front of her.

Elke waved and the two rugby players, wide-eyed and breathing hard, ran up the steps three at a time and took position flanking the door.

"It's going to be loud and bright," she shouted.

Another burst shattered the lock, and someone started ripping at the door proper with a wrecking bar.

One of the players overhand-snapped a notepad. It smashed hard into the hand of whoever was prying the door, who shrieked in response and dropped the bar.

One of the intruders then fired a burst through the door. Elke dropped and heard bullets crack past. Aramis swore and she heard the crackle of his stunner and another curse. That was followed by shrieks from the students, though she couldn't tell if they were injured or not. Then she heard the door splinter.

That was her cue.

She clicked the electronic igniter with one hand, stood and pointed with the other, and clamped her guts down against possible incoming fire.

The resultant fireworks were quite literal. Both athletes heaved heavy display bases at the three armored men kicking through the shambled door. Aramis fired his stunner again, the charge riding the plasma sheath in a purplish blue flash. Elke's improvised cannon screamed in a syncopated hiss.

Eight large firework rockets lit off in a sequential burst that she knew was .48 seconds, but seemed to last half a minute. The sulfurous smoke boiled chokingly around her, deflected from directly burning her by a thick plastic plate that got hot very fast. She'd punctured the stage dividers inside the rockets, so instead of zipping in free flight after impulse, they impulsed, almost immediately exploded, and threw burning sparklies at the attackers, pelting them with white hot burning metals.

One went down, clutching at his eyes and ululating in agony. One turned to face Aramis, who zapped him again full to the torso before he could raise his weapon, then stomped him with a flying leap and a smashing kick that was so well timed, Aramis stopped in midair and dropped, his entire momentum transferred to the gunman. The gunman crashed back against the doorframe and convulsed as a piece of it impaled him. The third ducked, flinched, rose, flinched again and aimed at her, only to get smashed in a tackle by two men who knew exactly how to put an opponent down in pain. Once he was down, the two started beating him in a fashion she recalled Jason describing as, "like a left-handed, red-headed stepchild." However one called it, they smashed the man half to death. Not good.

Not good, because she needed at least one alive for questioning.

Aramis grabbed the one with the burned face, grabbed a bottle and splashed water on him, and hauled him aside. The two tacklers seemed to grasp the fight was over and stepped back, looking a little mussed and out of breath, and a bit sheepish. The students shouted, cried, hooted and otherwise were a useless mob of nothing behind her. Miss Caron was just starting to shiver in reaction, but was completely unharmed, though she'd need a requisite pat down just to make sure.

In her ears, Cady said loudly, "Babs, Musketeer is not answering. Status report."

Elke smacked her mic and said, "Hostiles down, position secure, Loretta secure, need external sweep and possible fire response." She edged toward Caron as she replied. Code named "Loretta." The coalminer's daughter.

"Roger, Babs. Entering One now, coordinating with locals."

"Understood. Standing by."

One was the school building. Cady and backup should be along shortly. Elke didn't relish the thought of trying to clear the hallway, though anyone out there should be rather surprised and hesitant. It wasn't an issue, though, because her duty was to stick close to Caron and ensure her safety.

Caron stood and raised her arms, accepted a professionally intimate feeling up and down for any wounds or injuries, which Elke did while glancing back and forth at the door. Aramis stood there ready to block any intrusion, and the two volunteers held the mostly conscious prisoner they needed. She pointed at them and down toward the crowd. One of them nodded and walked down that way to try to calm the students. As was common, their reactions to surviving a gun battle ranged from whimpers to curses to laughs and zombie stares.

Elke just hoped Cady hurried. She felt a bit rubbery herself.

Right then, Cady said, "All secure, coming through the door in five." She heard Aramis respond, "Roger."

"I'm going to sit down now," Elke said, and did so.

At least she'd gotten to do her job today.

Covering the aftermath of the attack at the college took more money. Agent Eleanora Sykora had technically committed a misdemeanor by possessing the fireworks, and felony arson by using them, though her motives absolved her of guilt, except that she'd broken the law with deliberate prior intent. The school was very unhappy and wanted to charge her. However, they didn't want a legal battle with Bryan Prescot, who could crush them like an insect and make them be *not*. The governments—Welsh constituent, British state and European national—wanted to charge her, but several high ranking officials and parliamentarians and assemblypersons made calls and that didn't happen.

Prescot was somewhat amused or bemused or something, though. Alex was glad of that.

At yet another after-action analysis, Prescot said, "The legal fees are costing me several times what your protection is costing. Of course, I can afford it, and it is keeping my family safe, but I'm wondering how to avoid scaling up to where it gets out of hand. Can we?"

Alex said, "I believe there is a social limit. A smart enemy would not want to make you the underdog, nor turn public opinion against themselves. I have to say, this last attack, the last several, have been amateurish."

"Do you think it's created some kind of meme? See if you can hurt his daughter for cultural bragging rights?"

"I don't think so, sir. I think it's one primary party, who's just hiring or enticing freelance idiots to try their hand. If they get lucky, it's a win. If not, it's annoying and stressful and puts pressure on you, which is also a win for them."

"I trust your judgment. So you think this will continue?"

"It's obviously someone with enough money to waste on it. The odds are better than in a lot of gambling. Their overhead is low if they offer an upfront fee and a larger payoff."

"Logical. Did the suspects shed any light on things?"

"Nothing. They insist they don't know who hired them and provided the weapons."

Elke finally spoke up.

"They had some training. Not a lot."

"You believe so?"

"Definitely. Their trigger control was adequate. Their marksmanship was apparently okay. They worked as an element and continued once under return fire. They don't seem professional, but they do seem practiced."

"Do you believe they rehearsed, then?"

"Yes."

"Not good." Alex sighed. "Well, I'm going to query, very discreetly, as to how many lectures are necessary to attend, and if Caron can do a remote final. Her thesis is mostly done. If her exams can be proctored here, even if we pay for the professor to show up and do so, we can get out of here that much sooner."

Prescot said, "That means more work for barristers. I assume you won't be calling to ask about that?"

"I'll find out with some research, and I'll be asking in person. Nothing is entrusted outside from now on."

"Please let me know if I can help. I've also lent support, gratefully, to those two young men who stepped in to help. I'm disgusted that bare hands against gun-toting hoodlums can be considered assault with battery in today's world."

"Yeah, we'll step up for them too, if needed, sir. Heck, they might want to talk to one of our recruiters." He said it as a half joke, but realized it was a viable possibility. They'd demonstrated courage, resourcefulness and character. Well, he could make a suggestion. After that it wasn't his problem.

After that meeting adjourned, Alex had to get on the phone with his CEO.

Don Meyer had been a Recon commando and general's bodyguard, then started contracting personal protection training to various agencies and authorized companies. Shortly, he'd had his own force. They took a lot of flak in the press, but their reputation was based on the plain fact that no one in the galaxy was better at protecting a high value person. The politicians and socialites were shocked at Elke's acts, and even whined about sympathy for the "poor man" with the burned eyes. Within the company, Elke was regarded as a heroine for working around the system, and everyone regarded it as a pity that the attackers had to survive.

He came on screen at once, since Alex had an appointment with him.

"So how is it, Alex?"

"As good as can be expected, sir. Was my request clear?"

"Very. I'm glad they have deep pockets. This is going to be expensive. I notice you didn't even trust me with all the details."

"I don't trust anyone at this point, sir."

"Good, that's what I pay you for. I have a stack of codes for you, being transferred now with your chosen encryption."

"Roger, sir. It's going to be an expensive movement. More than you imagine."

"I can imagine quite a lot."

"Add a zero."

Meyer just chuckled at that.

"It's money in my pocket. I have no objection as long as the principal is safe and happy."

"I doubt she'll ever be happy, but she'll be safe."

"I'll kill you if she's not."

"That assumes I'd be alive to kill." Alex grinned back at the joke.

"What is your mission assessment?"

"Well, sir, we're still on profile. We have to get her off Earth, keep the facilities around her secure, and provide all the intel we can to track down the threats. Sir, we really need our own investigation arm."

"Yes, we do. I'm working on developing that. We have some skilled intel people, but analysis and detective work is a specialized subset. It's going to take a few months to ramp up. Still, you busted the one ring."

"Partly through luck and partly because Caron was very dedicated. Her father's supportive, and less dictatorial than he used to be. He's grasping that we need a free hand on the security matters. Caron's average for a principal, which is a compliment for a twenty-two year old just coming into this lifestyle. Her uncle's a wimp, as much as I hate to say it. Beancounter. Worried about perceptions and expenses and other things. A perfect product of this society."

"Yeah, it sucks being a sheepdog in a flock of lambs. The wolf's real, though."

"Indeed. I wish he'd gone with our services just for convenience. Ex Ek isn't bad, but they're not us, so every time we do a group movement, or cross paths, we have to have a quick talk to confirm. I don't think anyone's tried to suborn them, but I can't rule out the possibility."

"Is it easier with him already moved forward?"

"It is, so I'm not going to worry about it. Once on Govannon we'll have control and his people can do it our way or wait. Or they can complain to Bryan Prescot, who's finally deciding that he needs to be the sole authority and not run everything through a family committee. I'm just glad his ex isn't involved. She's a real prima donna."

"Yeah, when someone pays forty million to divorce you, it's not a compliment. He obviously felt it was worth it."

"It was."

"I thought you only met her in person once?"

"I did. Once was enough. She's a shallow, obnoxious, gold digging bitch."

"Wow. That's quite a statement, coming from you."

"Well, she should be happy. She'll be given access to the house again while they're gone. That's apparently what she's wanted for some time."

"Good. The more people are happy, the less they're likely to turn coat."

"She's far too snobbish for that, I'd say. Acts like a queen."

"You'll be set up whenever you're ready, Alex. Give me the stage calls as you go."

Alex understood the meeting was over. Made sense. This might be the company's highest profile mission, but it wasn't the only one.

"Will do, sir. We're at Three now and will stay that way until I shout for Two."

That wouldn't be far in the future, either.

"Understood, Alex. Carry on."

"Out, sir."

"Out."

CHAPTER 13

Alex was glad he didn't have to deal with the university. Cady took that task, and persuaded campus security that her own, officially unarmed agents, could run better reconnaissance and security. He wasn't sure how she persuaded them to violate several privacy laws, but they got access to student profiles, and made surreptitious scans of students and staff who might have method, motive and opportunity. That was probably good for a theoretical thirty percent reduction in threat.

Unfortunately, they didn't find anything. That meant the results were indeterminate. So both teams, and a couple of spares from Bryan's team, created a more obvious cordon around Caron.

The students generally avoided her now. She wasn't approachable, and there was the perception that being near her exposed one to fire. More and more, her life was conducted on the hypernet. The whole family was becoming reclusive.

Caron remoted in to three lectures, attended two others and showed up for a lab, with Elke and Jason openly guarding her, since they understood chemistry enough to cue in on threats.

Her remaining exam was proctored at one of the company's conference rooms, with her professor helpful but worried. It was awkward to have a deluxe conference room with one student, one full professor and three highly paid goons. However, Caron did well.

Alex was there personally, and noticed she never looked at anything except her notepad and the professor.

She sat back and stretched, looked up and said, "I'm done, Dr. Roberts."

He nodded, scrolled through the results and said, "Congratulations, and I make it ninety-six percent, give or take. We'll send the final results. We haven't finished with your thesis yet, but I'm sure you've passed and met all requirements for graduation." He then smiled, relaxed his formal demeanor and said, "Well done, kid."

She grinned.

"Thanks. I will try hard to make it to graduation, even if I have to sneak in. Having it sent just won't be the same." She looked up at Alex.

Roberts looked over at him, and he said, "Yes, sir, we'll see what we can arrange." It was a total lie, but if it helped her feel good at this moment, he wasn't going to deny her that.

They shook hands and congratulated all around, and she even gave Alex a brief hug, then Elke. Elke looked a little less disturbed than she usually did with human contact.

At her father's office, after passing her exam, Caron seemed delighted when Joanne rolled in a tray of pastries and champagne. She'd even brought sparkling nonalcoholic cider for Alex and Elke. They sipped, toasted and he had a bite of baklava and a scone, both looking like something from a professional bakery. Even more impressive, she'd done it under Shaman's personal supervision, with ingredients he brought personally. That done, they headed downstairs, into the vehicles, and "home" to Wales.

As soon as they were in the car, Caron said, "As soon as I get home, I'm drinking something stronger than champagne. Then I'm going to do nothing the rest of the day. Tomorrow I'm going to kill my brain with QuestGeas, and dress like a bum. After that we'll discuss my future career."

"Very good," Alex agreed cordially. "You've earned the rest."

"It's odd. We don't take holidays, really. We go places and see things, but we work whilst doing so. I don't know how to do nothing for long, and I always feel guilty when I do. But I can justify one day, however, as rest and recuperation."

"Absolutely."

True to her word, as soon as they arrived, Caron went running and whooping through the entire mansion. Elke and Jason sprinted after her, and the echoes bounced around the vaulted ceiling of the central foyer.

Damn, poor kid, Alex thought again. He had some idea what it was like for lottery winners, who didn't even have the advantage of growing up rich, to be plunged into wealth. Though Caron's wealth was that of several billionaires each winning the Globall Max.

He gave everyone a couple of hours to settle down. The remaining staff and all the Ripple Creek personnel wished her well and tried to make up for the graduation ceremony she wasn't going to get. She probably knew that, too, but why ruin the illusion?

Caron was quite astute, and Alex enjoyed that. He suspected she wasn't going to enjoy the events he was about to initiate.

He walked into the parlor, where Caron was giggling behind VR goggles, involved in some network party or other while sipping expensive-looking liquor. He tapped for attention.

"Hold on, I have some RW stuff," she said into her mic. She transparented the goggles and said, "Yes?"

"Leave your connection open and muted. We're leaving. Right now. Elke took care of shipping your wardrobe and personal effects. Anything personal you want to take with you you need to grab in the next three minutes. We have the vehicles waiting. You'll be back on net when you get to Govannon. Your father's orders."

Her expression covered all negatives. She was angry, disbelieving, put upon, shocked, saddened and lost all at once. That just left bargaining and acceptance.

Her eyes exploded in tears.

"Oh, goddammit," she said as she tore off the headset. "It would be nice to say goodbye."

"No time, and not safe. You can come back in a while, though."

"Don't lie to me," she snapped. "Unless I find somewhere to unload a few triple zeroes of cash, I'll never be back on Earth. What do I need?"

"Anything personal, miss. Toys, pictures, anything with sentimental value. Elke got quite a bit. It'll be following along."

"Why bother?" she said. "Besides, I can always order it sent. What's money? Let's get me the hell out of here before the shock wears off and I get really pissed." She strode straight for the door.

Poor kid, he thought.

Horace was impressed with the speed of departure, and was glad Caron was reacting as she did. Clearly, she was upset, in stress-induced shock, but remarkably resilient and intelligent.

He knew his part, but not all the details. He could tell, though, that a lot of money had been spent on this departure. That made sense. It was a potential point failure.

Five vehicles left in five directions. Theirs traveled only a few kilometers before stopping seemingly at random on the roadside, as a Trirotor rumbled in and landed right in front of them. They corralled Miss Prescot into it, then lifted at once. Five minutes later, they landed outside Ebbw Vale and took a waiting commuter floater, chartered and flown by a company pilot. It had four other similar-looking young women and a dozen men. He recognized some of them from the company.

The pilot took off fast, probably in violation of local flight regs, and climbed sharply.

Caron seemed to be following every detail herself. It wasn't professional interest on her part. She was probably trying to remember every moment of her last day on Earth. She didn't utter a word.

They landed in Prešov, Slovakia on a normal small pad at the aiport, and eight nondescript Renault Carryalls came from several directions. They took one as the decoys took others. Jason took one of those, as did Elke. The team was slightly split, but the additional confusion effect should help. Horace wondered why there hadn't been decoy planes as well, but maybe there were, or maybe Alex had decided that many pilots being called to do odd things would draw attention. Drivers were easy to get.

Bart drove, of course. Twenty minutes later, he pulled into a small garage. They bailed out fast, and there was Agent Cady with a completely different Peugeot, and two more decoys. Bart piled in, Cady slid over, and off they went out the back.

Caron finally spoke up.

"Isn't a ballet this complicated a risk?"

Alex said, "It would be, if more than I knew the plan, or who was where, or which vehicle we'd take at each step. I chose some at random. The others are just going to pick a direction and drive. Nor did they know why, nor have most of them even glimpsed you. This company is handling twenty or so high profile young women at the moment, and several older male executives in suits, like me or Shaman or Jason. Any one person might be a leak, but there are enough changes to account for that. Like right now. Bart, you can choose the D One or the Three Seven One Expressway."

"Thank you." He glanced at the offered paper map and nodded.

They drove from there, and changed vehicles twice more. It was a long, overland trip with few stops. They kept up a chatter of reports on potential threats, items of interest and general banter just to keep awake.

"Disabled vehicle ahead on right. Vacant, tagged," Aramis reported from up front.

"Noted."

Horace said, "We have a van with family passing on left."

"Got it. That's quite a pretty overlook with the mist sinking." Alex indicated to the left.

"It is. Behind the van is a land train, four segment, hazmat."

Bart said, "Acknowledged, accelerating." They didn't want to draw attention of local traffic control, but next to a marked hazmat vehicle was no place for them on this trip.

With Caron curled up napping in a corner of the vehicle, Horace asked, "Why ground?"

Alex said, "We can always find an escape route on the ground. Air is a bit more restrictive. It also means they can't even guess the destination directly, though the eventual one is probably obvious. However, watching millions of cars is harder than a few hundred planes. That, and low tech is less predictable. Especially since the pheromones we used could be used against us now. I'm betting whoever might be following us doesn't bother trying a pheromone search, consider the disparity of the two tech levels. Bart, how are you doing?"

"Tired, but continuing," Bart replied. He'd been driving for close to five hours, over 1000 kilometers. They were well through the Ukraine Constituency of Europe.

Horace said, "I'm assuming Baikonur."

"Assume all you like. I won't say yet."

"Of course."

Aramis had personal duty for the stop.

"Handicapped room," he said.

"Okay," she agreed sullenly. She didn't seem bothered or even to care.

Horace and Alex flanked them, and stood outside. He went in first, made a quick scan for any threats, cursorily but professionally. Then he politely faced the door so she could piss in peace.

It wasn't just manners. As hot as she was, watching bodily functions was not something he found interesting.

"I need a bloody shower," she muttered.

"We should be at a hotel soon, miss. I think we all need to clean up."

"Mmph."

She washed her hands and he opened the door, to see Jason and Elke had apparently caught up and joined the party. Both were outside the building keeping an eye on things. That was going to make the vehicle a bit tighter.

Bart was still driving. He seemed to prefer it and never complained about the time spent in the seat. Between Bart and Jason, Aramis accepted he was going to be a permanent passenger. He wasn't a comfortable passenger, but that's how it was.

Eight hours later they did pull into Baikonur, Kazakhstan. Did Caron actually know anyone in one of her ancestral countries? Did she care?

It was a rich town in one of the world's leading resource producers and space transit hosts. In centuries past it had been looted and pillaged by countless savages and barbarians. Now it was a gleaming jewel of ultra high tech and money. Aramis kept a professional eye out for threats, while part of him appreciated the almost endless parade of lightly dressed prime female flesh. Wow. This would be a good place to vacation. They were part Asian, part European, part Persian and all scorching.

Alex said, "Head for the Mandarin Oriental."

Damn. Nice accommodations, too, if that was their actual destination. His only real regret in this job was not enough time to enjoy the sights and locations. He'd stayed in some of the finest hotels and resorts in the universe, and seen almost none of them.

Bart nodded fractionally and turned onto a thoroughfare.

Elke didn't feel nervous, but kept a very cold eye out. They were close to a choke point as far as schedule went. She watched rear and right, and saw the hotel a block south.

"I thought we had reservations at the Mandarin?" Caron commented.

Alex said, "We do. Also at the Geneva, and two others. Someone else booked us rooms at the Hilton, Hyatt and Watermark. Jason, please flip a coin and pick one."

"Hilton it is."

"Good. Caron, how fast can you look like a splash rock musician?"

She said, "Um," as Elke slapped a makeup kit down in front of her, and a small case of wadded clothes.

Elke watched, or rather, studied. She could do basic color coordinated makeup for a suit or evening dress. Beyond that, she needed a pro or her attempts looked silly. She wasn't a social creature.

Caron seemed to have some talent in that direction. In a few seconds, she pulled her hair up into a good approximation of a mane and clipped it in place. She grabbed scissors and cut several geometric chevrons into a skirt, then sliced her slacks off to avoid having to remove her boots. She pulled the skirt on. With a marker she drew a quick pseudo-Mongolian text down her left leg.

After that, she applied shocking green makeup from her eyes to her temples, painted a single tear near her nose, and stroked on magenta lipstick. A quick pull popped two snaps of her blouse to show cleavage and black lace.

"How's this?"

"Very good," Elke said appreciatively. "I barely recognize you. Do me, please." She handed over her carry bag.

In short order, her face was painted, her hair plastered down and her jeans shredded into ladders of fabric, showing green elastic panties, topped by a sport coat with no bra. It was more exposure than Elke was comfortable with, from a tactical point of view, though nudity wasn't an issue for her, except as it distracted or discomfited males, which was useful or annoying depending on circumstances. However, even without seeing the makeup, she knew she looked nothing like herself.

Aramis had done well. He looked very much like a rock star, in tight clothes with the knees and sides ripped out, with exposed calves and a cape over his shoulders.

Jason was still fit enough to pull it off, mostly, even in his forties, though that slight padding over his abs needed some work. Still, he definitely looked like a percussionist or synthesist with that big padded case that could be instruments but was all tactical gear.

The others stayed as they were, to break up the image and to look like crew. Besides, Alex and Shaman were a bit too old to pull it off as splash musicians.

Alex asked, "Everyone ready?" He waited a moment for an assent, then said, "Then here we go."

Bart flung the limo neatly and discreetly into an alley, crawled a few meters in, and shut the engine down. Caron followed Elke as everyone bailed out.

Jason had already flagged down a regular taxi, they piled in fast, and off they went. He gave directions to a local, private hotel. They arrived very quickly, lugged their cases in the front, right through to the back, and flagged another cab. This one, Jason directed to the Hilton.

Aramis went in first, and it looked as if he was playing up the role, looking half-drugged and road-dazed.

He turned back to the door, and they all piled out, lugging their cases. Elke had arranged for Caron to have the heaviest and most awkward, which caused Alex to grin. He seemed to concur it was about time she got some of what she'd been dishing out.

She had learned movement drill, though. When the elevator stopped, she let Alex and Shaman go first, fell in with Elke and Bart at the sides, with Aramis and Jason in the front.

Aramis stepped ahead, keyed the lock and walked in. As he cleared the doorway, he dropped his cases, a carbine cleared his outfit and he darted forward and left. Shaman took right, Elke brushed past straight ahead to the windows. She polarized them and closed the drapes.

At "Clear!" Alex flipped on the lights.

"Ah. This isn't too bad for a cheaper hotel," Caron said and started looking around.

A Hilton. "Cheaper." "Not too bad." She apparently wasn't even familiar with the inside of a Hilton, and this was one of the deluxe suites.

Elke reflected that Caron might get a lesson in reality on this trip, and it was something that should have happened a long time ago. Her father was far too coddling.

Jason and Bart went straight to work, snapping open cases and pulling out frames and panels. In a few minutes, solid ballistic shield covered the hallway wall of the middle room, and the windows.

Caron sat back, and watched Elke. Elke was aware of it, but said nothing. She had a task.

Caron asked, "Is that explosive?"

"Of a specialized type, yes," Elke said with a nod, as her fingers worked dexterously. "You're familiar with staging charges, a primer charge, a low explosive, then high, then hyper?"

"In theory, yes," Caron said. "For mining."

"This small charge is prebuilt as a shaped charge, with specific characteristics. The primer starts the propulsion and brissance wave, the low explosive envelopes from the outside with just enough power to contain the high, which forms its own shaped charge of plasmoidized hyper explosive, with the detonation wave already traveling through it. So the damage is minimal in the enclosed space, and maximized in a cone in front of the charge."

She set it down on a small tripod in front of the door, or where the door was beyond the ballistic curtain.

Jason indicated the thick fabric. "That stuff is soft enough to soak up the propulsion of a rocket, and probably soft enough to avoid fuzing the warhead. If there is a detonation, the fabric will slow it and damp it considerably. By the way, Elke, what's 'minimal' damage?"

"It will not be lethal outside of a meter. It won't cause more than minor injuries at three meters."

"So that whole area will be toast."

"That's the plan."

"And this you define as 'low scale.' "

"I'd rather plant projection charges in the hall and douse incoming hostiles with gelled flame agents, but this culture has a positively sick fetish against giving criminals what they need." She placed a second charge, carefully adjusted it a few millimeters, then put her gear away.

"Well, if it were legal for people to kill everyone who deserved it, we'd quickly be out of work."

"I'm sure I could find plenty," she said. Did Jason really think they'd run out of people to kill? It must be a joke.

Alex was glad to see Elke back in her element. Everyone else on the team was in fine fettle, too.

Caron asked, "What are we doing about food?"

Shaman said, "We have some field rations and some sandwiches. Nothing must come in, and we must not go out."

"Well, I can manage for one night," Caron replied with a cheery smile. It had a faint, unintentional, but definite tinge of condescension. It just drove home how alien this young woman was.

"Good," he said, and handed her a standard field ration in its box.

Her expression was surprised and curious. After she found the flap, opened it and saw the self-heating envelopes she was a little less interested. Once she got the spaghetti with meat and sauce opened, she looked rather hesitant. She pulled out a neat spoonful and ate it.

"God, that's bland and tasteless."

"There's red pepper sauce in the accessory packet," Jason said with a point of his finger. He was halfway around his stewed beef with potatoes already.

Caron finished the entire ration, though Alex gathered a lot of it was from manners. She seemed disappointed rather than repulsed.

Alex said, "Anyone watching vid must use a damper cone. We need to be able to hear everything. Jason has monitors set."

Jason read for a while, but seemed agitated. Aramis pulled up a vid on his personal system, with headphones set to amplify outside noise over the audio. Bart took duty position, upright and strolling and checking. Alex watched everyone, or course. Elke had a reader, her comm and seemed to be running calculations. Caron sat morosely for a while, then shrugged and flicked on a vid. Shaman inventoried something.

After a half hour, Jason couldn't stand it anymore. He shifted and rose, checked with Bart, then wandered into the bathroom, which was his real destination.

It was as luxurious as the suite, with real cut stone tile, manual and automatic controls, broad lavatory with several choices of soap, a Jacuzzi and a multi-head shower. Since he was sharing with six others, a quick shower would have to do. He stripped fast, flipped on the water and stepped in.

Jason was frustrated by Caron's antics, her outfit, her boots, damn her for those boots. He was pretty sure the come-ons from her peers had either been aimed at his position—young women often found bodyguards to be thrilling—or were from outside parties trying to embarrass them, gain access for paparazzi or distract him as part of some kind of threat. The end result was hours a day of watching prime young pussy that he absolutely could not touch, and no one had gotten the hint that he wouldn't. Then, he was all business when he had to pat her down after action, but those were the tightest breasts he'd ever felt, even in passing.

He sagged against the stall wall, sagged down and squirmed against his hand, eyes closed and letting the water pound him, hot rivulets that didn't divert his mind. Rather, it drew his attention to the tone and trembling tension of his entire body. His biceps, pecs, abs, thighs... that.

At least she didn't know. Elke did, but Elke wouldn't admit the sun rose. He might have to ask Bart for advice, since he had a history of dealing with this kind of stress.

Not now, though. Now he was in a hurry, and wanting to enjoy the side effects of the problem for hours, but he had minutes at most. He had that picture of Elke's in his mind, and a few comments in that beautiful accent, and a memory of her applying several layers of assorted lip gloss under the lights, to those full lips.

He felt a buzzing tingle all the way to his skull, hotter than the steaming water and enough to make his toes clench. It was moments only before he tensed and twitched in release, choking back a gasp he was sure would be audible to whoever was moving outside the door. Yes, the most sensitive organ while masturbating: the ears.

Okay, that was better. Well, not better, but it took the edge off. He was going to have to buy Marisa a pair of those boots. He could only imagine what that was going to cost him, and not in the wallet.

He let the air dryer cool then warm him all over, dressed and stepped out, feeling refreshed and less edgy. Everyone was sprawled and trying to asleep, save Elke on watch. He took the hint, grabbed an empty couch, and rolled into it.

CHAPTER 14

The next morning everyone was up early.

"It gets dangerous now," Alex advised. "We have to leave weapons here. We can't take them through the port and they'd attract notice if we did. Caron, if there's a threat, you are going to be dogpiled and dragged off. Be ready."

"I will," she said, with a nervous look.

"We'll arm up as soon as we can. It's all bare hands and sharp eyes for the next few hours, though. Let's move."

"Leave it all here?" Aramis asked to confirm.

"Yes, the room is good for another day, and I'll call someone to fill in and recover stuff as soon as we're movement complete."

"Roger that." He dug into his carryon pack and pulled out a knife and another item. Reluctantly and shyly, he reached into the front of his pants and drew out a small pistol.

Jason already had a neat pile of knives, pistol and a spring-loaded baton in front of him. Elke took several minutes. She seemed to have something stashed in every container and every article of clothing. Her haul included a baton, incapacitance gas—highly illegal though very effective—a pistol, brass knucks, some kind of whiplike thing in a belt, and several containers of explosive. She sprayed and wiped her luggage and hands to minimize the residue against sniffers. She did have official ID to cover herself if questioned, but discretion was always the better option.

Shaman had a rental car booked, and they strolled downstairs in three groups, through the lobby and into the car. The man who delivered the vehicle only saw Shaman.

Thirty minutes later they rolled into the Kazakhstan National Spaceport, less busy and more discreet than the heavy launch facility at Baikonur, and with better overall security. In this case, numbers helped. Suborning a guard wouldn't be hard. Suborning several, who knew of the huge reward and credibility for stopping threats against certain families was much more complicated.

"That's our gate there," Caron said. It wasn't only the Prescots'. Several other private operators used it.

"Which is why we're not going there."

"Of course," she said, and shook her head. She seemed to be getting used to the random changes.

They stopped at the regular terminal, and Alex climbed out and walked casually to the checkpoint. He spoke to security and showed his credentials. A few moments of talking and gesturing, and he waved the rest out.

"Let's move," Aramis said, and led the way.

Jason handed over all the IDs, and wrangled people through. The security personnel had their own plan, and Jason had his. He won by only handing them one ID at a time, and pointing to each in turn. With Alex through, then Bart, he urged Caron through, then the others with himself last. That done, the block of people moved up to the counter. Alex had seven passes already, a block of four and a block of three.

"Best I could manage," he said, "but we should be okay."

"How obvious is that?" Caron asked, still inquisitive. It might be a bit annoying, but she was learning and interested and coping with a rough situation and paying them a literal tonne of money.

"Obvious if anyone looks too closely. I used several IDs to block seats, and will bribe the gate agent if we have to. It's all we can do."

Aramis had a trick, too. He pulled out light jerseys and handed them around. They bore a logo and the label "SKI TEAM." They slipped into restrooms in groups and came out adorned, with hats pulled to their eyebrows. They looked a little odd, but didn't jump out as anything other than coaches and athletes.

"Good planning," Alex complimented him as they left the facility. Blending in by standing out was a useful trick.

"Yup," Aramis replied. Acknowledgment with no hints for anyone else.

Caron kept her eyes on Elke, and followed her lead. She seemed to know the procedure for clearing security and approaching a shuttle gate, but not to have done it before. Well, lots of people hadn't. No problem. She didn't stand out, and they were shortly aboard.

The low Earth orbit flight was loud, brisk and straightforward. They jetted off the runway, feeling the scramjets kick into the spine, turbulence buffeting and fading, then they were into the blue, violet and black of NEO.

After their arrival, they debarked amid a gaggle of travelers, which made Alex cringe, but was unavoidable.

It was hard to grasp that three hours had passed, and that the planned delays for travel had barely existed because of the need to coordinate and move. Alex was tired, his eyes gritty. Still, they were in the station, security should be easier here, and they'd soon be aboard a secure vessel.

Once they were away from the crowds, Caron asked, "Should I assume we're not taking *Dylan*?"

"I hope people are assuming that. Especially as I bought seven spaces on *Rhiannon* under your name, and seven more under an assumed name whose compromised status has not been compromised." He grinned. "The family yacht is much more secure once aboard. Especially as Jason is trained as a pilot and we're also bringing our own spare."

"I'd call you paranoid, except there've been two . . . or more attempts on my life."

"You need to ask yourself not if you're paranoid, but if you're paranoid enough."

Ripple Creek CEO Don Meyer himself waited on the boarding deck with a bemused expression and two men. District Agent In Charge Massa was in Peru at Quito Port, and another DAIC at a third location. Even the company owner hadn't known the itinerary.

Alex said, "We're here."

"So I see." Meyer grinned. Alex felt good. He had free rein over this operation, and his boss hadn't questioned him once.

"These them?" Alex said, even though he knew who they were.

"Yes, these are the cleared pilots. Good luck."

"Good. Come with us. Thank you, sir." He waved and walked off, and the two joined the entourage.

"How much is all this rigamarole costing?" Caron asked.

"A few million. Cheap at the price."

"I suppose it's yet another contribution to the economy," she agreed. "Still, the bookkeeper in me is cringing."

"All the other staff are being replaced, too. Those are somewhat easier."

"How so?"

"Our hires don't have to know what mission they're serving. Just that it's 'Shipboard.' You'll have to do without a cook and maid, though."

"That's fine, you should have time to do my laundry."

To his stare she added, "That's a joke," and smiled.

"Ah. Good," he agreed. Good that she didn't actually expect that.

"I'm surprised the pilots know where we're going, though," she said.

"Well, they do now. They didn't two minutes ago."

"You really are paranoid, aren't you?"

"Miss Prescot, if I do my job right, no one takes a shot at you. That means I don't have to throw myself between you and a bullet. I will continue to be paranoid."

She looked thoughtful.

"Very good," she said.

Jason walked ahead through the access corridor. It was good and bad that he didn't have to deal with any station security. The ship would need a very quick and very thorough scan.

Once in the family's private dock, he sought the open lock, gripped the hatch edge, and swung in. The cradle the ship rode in meant that deck was down, which made things easier.

The main cabin held the crew, awaiting their employer.

"Greetings. I'm in charge of Miss Prescot's security detail. Are all the crew present?"

"Nine of us, all here," one man agreed. "I'm Command Pilot Hales."

"Pleased to meet you. Miss Prescot needs to address you for a moment. This way, please."

"Of course."

They followed his lead back into the docking bay.

"Where is she?" Hales asked.

Alex took his shoulder and turned him slightly, and Bart came up on the other side.

Alex said, "I'm sorry to say you will not be on this flight. Strictly business, nothing personal." They ushered him, with motions to the others to follow, out the side lock.

As the pilot cleared the frame, he said, "While I'm very glad her security is being taken so seriously, you understand why I'm goddamned well pissed?"

"I do, and I apologize again. You'll be credited for pay."

"Yes, that's not entirely the point. Though I'm sure a mercenary doesn't grasp that."

That old jab no longer bothered Jason.

"I grasp it very well, but Miss Prescot's safety ranks above your feelings." *And mine,* Jason thought. Yeah, he felt like a jerk.

The crew filed off. One, probably her personal maid said, "Can we say goodbye before we leave?"

"I'm afraid not. Your baggage is being offloaded now. Miss Prescot extends her regrets. This is not of her doing. You are still employed, paid and will serve again as soon as the current situation resolves."

"Ah, when they run out of money to mine," the woman said. "I see."

There was no good answer to that, so he slapped the switch and sealed the hatch, then plugged in a module to scramble the lock codes. Not even a station emergency would open it now.

Back in that hideously nice owner's cabin, Elke and Jason ran scanners, Shaman set up bio monitors, and Aramis acted as muscle.

Over his shoulder, Shaman said, "Once we have this set up, Elke, Jason or I will be monitoring your vital signs around the clock. We generally don't tell the principal when we do so, but I feel you're entitled to know."

"Because I'm a woman?" She looked a bit miffed.

"Because I'm sure you'd figure it out, and are new enough to the concept to be angry when you did."

"You're correct."

"Too many things could go wrong, miss. Until we arrive, you will have twenty-four hour guard, and keep a respirator with you, even in the toilet and shower."

She gritted her teeth for a moment. "I understand," she said.

✧ ✧ ✧

The Ripple Creek contractors took over shipboard duties. Two pilots, one engineer and assistant, one second officer/navigator, one caretaker. Their own billets were separated by a sealed bulkhead. The filters and sensors ensured the air was safe. Elke and Shaman checked all the food. Jason checked the pilot staff every shift change. Otherwise, only one was allowed in the control room at a time.

Caron stayed in her cabin and went buggy. She ate too much, then exercised hard on the compact gym machine. She slept odd hours, watched sensies then would suddenly stop in the middle. One day she decided to be nude. The next she dressed in a fine gown, then changed to an elegant suit that would somehow manage to fit a boardroom or a porn movie. The next day she changed back to casual clothes.

"It seems odd," Jason said, "but I assume it's a reaction to the circumstances and it doesn't seem dangerous."

"She should be fine," Shaman said. "It's a coping mechanism. She's not self-damaging, drinking or doing drugs, so there's no real concern."

"The naked day was interesting," Aramis said. "If she doesn't mind showing, I don't mind seeing."

"You haven't seen her with soapy water running over her skin like mountain streams," Bart said.

Jason said, "You will stop this story now or there will be a fight." He grinned, though his body language was quite serious.

Bart grinned back.

"It is all business," he said. "I don't pay attention at the time to anything other than security."

Alex chuckled. "You remember afterward, though."

"I would not be German if I didn't," Bart said.

Elke said, "You wouldn't be male. Still, if memories of me lying passed out and rubbery with vomit over my face and bare tits with defibrillator pads help your fantasies, there is nothing I can do."

Aramis said, "God, Elke, you can crush a potential fantasy with a word."

She smiled. "You're welcome. I'd be unlikely to kiss a woman like that, either."

That made him shudder.

Otherwise, the trip was uneventful. It could be the precautions worked, or that no one had attempted anything. That latter could be due to planning on their part, or chance. The results were what mattered. Ten days out from Earth, they queued up through the Jump Point. This was where the biggest risk from outside was, since the schedule was fairly close. Everyone sweated and fretted, but shortly they flashed through and were in Govannon's system. Ten days later they warped into orbit. It was nominally a seven day flight. The pilots took ten. It might allow more time for threats to be placed in system, but it kept the expected trajectory clear. That was another coin flip. Aramis made that one.

CHAPTER 15

Elke knew all the details from her brief. Bonner Durchmusterung +63°238 was an unremarkable K0 orange dwarf, smaller and cooler than Sol. Unremarkable, that is, except for having twice the metal content of Sol system, and only one gas giant, with the preponderance of the metals concentrated in three small planets, one of which had massive deposits in the crust. It was roughly the right distance for habitability, about .66 AU, but lacked anything resembling development. It was a rocky ball laden with metals and swept by a reducing atmosphere full of sulfur and ammonia.

Govannon, as Bryan Prescot had renamed it after acquiring sole title, had a nineteen hour day, which kept the temperature fairly constant, a near circular orbit, and moderate axial tilt. It orbited in 198 Earth days. It was home to ten thousand miners, support staff, administrators and a few, very few, families. In addition, there were several thousand people working the sprouting resort that specialized in volcano trips and similar *exotika*.

Even from orbit, the operation was impressive. The huge dome covering the colony and resort looked like a crystal ball stuck on the ruddy agate marble of the surface. North and west, the large pits of the metal mines spiraled down, like hollow snail shells. They were sufficiently large as features to affect weather patterns, the cloud streams roiling past them into braided or tumbling ochre ribbons.

"Very pretty," Elke commented. She could estimate the physical changes and the energy involved. She also had a good guess as to how many megatons had been used to carve those mine flutes. What an impressive work.

Jason swam alongside her.

"Those are damned big holes," he said. "It's . . ."

Caron said, "The main pits are about twenty-five kilometers across and go ten kilometers down. The current plan is to orbit out as far as the geologic province lasts, radiate as possible along veins, and backfill the tailings into the pits for best efficiency. We may eventually have the technology to go clear to the mantle."

Elke squinted and reconsidered. Those were huge holes. She upped her estimate of the charges needed.

"*Kurva drat,*" she breathed softly. What would it take to get a job here?

Jason asked, "After that, more mines?"

"There are two more bores started to southeast, and prospecting is underway in various other areas. Capital was the bottleneck on the first one. Once it proved out, the second one came online fast. I believe my father plans to bring others up as fast as possible."

"It's not as if a planet will run out soon, after all," Jason said.

"Actually, it might. Or as technology improves, either deep space mining will become more cost effective, or other systems will be found. While he . . . we . . . have the monopoly, he wants to exploit it as fast as possible, while keeping the price moderate enough to dissuade competition."

"That makes sense," Elke said. "If the cost to profit ratio is low enough, no one else can get backing."

"I think that's part of what he's afraid of," she said with a slight shiver. "We're the richest family in the universe now."

It was likely, Elke thought, that those shut out, or more accurately, who had shut themselves out through caution, wanted back in any way possible. On the one hand, allowing that would ease the risks. On the other hand, they'd let the Prescot family take all the risk. Also, once extortion worked, it would keep working.

All they had to do was keep Caron Prescot alive and safe long enough for others to get the message.

"I see why he wants you here," Jason said, paralleling Elke's thoughts. "It's defensible and controllable. There's nowhere on Earth or any colony where you wouldn't be at risk from a sniper, a guided remote, something. You'd be a prisoner behind ballistic armor around the clock."

"Instead, I'm moving to an ugly, molten rock with ballistic armor, around the clock," she replied, turning to stare at him. The expression in those beautiful eyes was not a smile, though there was a bit of wistfulness behind the depression and irony.

She was right, of course. No matter what happened, whatever traces of a normal life she'd had had disappeared two years ago. She could never trust anyone, never believe anyone didn't have an ulterior motive, even those who were highly paid to have none. Jason earned thousands a day on assignment, and lived modestly and comfortably. This young lady, though, was heir to enough money to literally have anything she desired, except normalcy and freedom.

"I need to move forward and check the backup pilot and pilot," Jason said. It sounded paranoid, and it was.

He just hoped at least one highly paid professional was honest enough not to attempt hijacking or suicide. It would be worth billions to get a chance at the quadrillions?—quintillions?—of potential here.

Alex was nervous again during docking. This was even more dangerous than the other choke points, since by now everyone knew what ship she was on and its schedule. He pondered the idea of having had four different "Carons" get on four different ships with four different teams, but it wasn't practical, and anyone paying attention would still figure out which was which. Just because the money was unlimited didn't mean there was necessarily an increase in effect in using more. As it was, a trip that could be done on a budget for M400,000, and in deluxe style for ten times that, had cost near sixty times that to ensure safety. It was a tiny blip in the family fortune, but had been of significant benefit to several companies and people who'd been paid and asked to do nothing in return.

Once they docked, he relaxed about twenty percent. When the hatch opened to reveal Cady and her team, in shipsuits, body armor and with weapons, he relaxed another twenty percent.

She smiled and said, "About time you arrived."

"About time you were waiting," he said. It wasn't a great comeback, but he wanted to say something.

"The bay is secure all the way to your shuttle, which is vacant save two pilots, ours. They handle our route regularly."

"Good. Jason can keep an eye on them. Good to see you, Jace."

"And you."

Caron stepped forward and gave Cady a brief hug.

"Thanks again for saving my life," she said.

"My duty and pleasure," Cady replied with a smile and twitch of her eyebrows. "Alex, policy is no firearms except two I've cleared."

"Oh, not this shit again."

"Sorry."

"Well, everything was in cargo."

"Yes. Was."

"Someone just isn't getting the hint. Ah, well."

As they departed, Alex wondered. It was the type of question one never asked. Cady had been born physically male, with messed up genes. She was now a larger-framed woman, with mostly female mannerisms and movements, but the hips and shoulders weren't quite right, even with stimulated bone growth. A trained observer could tell, even if most people couldn't. That aside, though, what was her preference? Men or women? Either was possible, or both, and might have nothing to do with her physiology.

He shrugged inwardly and kept walking. She was great at facility security, and good backup for personal protection. That was what mattered.

The shuttle was as new as the yacht, which wasn't surprising. Everything other than the family mansion was new, paid for with profits from below.

Jason confirmed with a nod. Elke had already cleared the rear. Alex took a plush, comfortable seat with lots of legroom and tried to relax. He'd taken every precaution. There was nothing to do but be alert and relaxed.

He didn't relax. He was worried about the precautions he hadn't taken.

They rode the shifting Gs through the thick, corrosive atmosphere and leveled out on a long approach to a runway landing, and how the hell much did it cost to maintain a runway on this ball? To take his mind off the descent, he worked on details.

"Caron, where do you wish to go first after we land?"

"The toilet," she said. "After that, probably my flat."

"Good choice. It's secure and we can relax and move from there."

"How do you know it's secure?"

"Cady's team checked it, and there are no entrances we don't know about. The lodging in all directions is vacant and sealed as deadspace. A bomb big enough to take out the apartment would risk damaging the building, or the dome, and endanger thousands. We don't think anyone wants to cause that much damage, nor affect the infrastructure, unless there's someone who just hates you enough to kill you?"

"I think a couple of college blokes thought about it recently, but not seriously."

They touched down and rolled. It was surprisingly smooth. The company hired the best pilots, and Prescot maintained excellent facilities.

Alex was almost relaxed now, to his normal quivering state of anxiety over any mission, especially this one. It was as high profile as one could get, and she wasn't an old politician who could be stoic and philosophical. She was a nice young lady caught in circumstances she didn't create. He wanted to succeed.

The landing craft rolled into a large hangar. It was possible to evacuate the native atmosphere and replace it with Earth type air, but in this case, an enclosed docking tube extended. As the hatch opened, there was a strong wind. Positive pressure ensured no atmosphere leakage, but they walked into a near gale. Once they were all clear, the tube sealed, and things reverted to near normal, except for ear popping to adapt to the much higher ambient pressure maintained against the outside atmosphere.

There were restrooms in the terminal bay, and Caron hurried in, with Elke and Bart along against threats, and Aramis with his back to the door to keep unwanted visitors out. The terminal was near empty; their trip was a special. All the better.

Elke and Jason had scanners ready for the car that met them. It was a basic battery powered buggy dressed up to look like a compact limo, and easy enough to check. Bart politely displaced the driver and took the controls. Jason plunked down next to him with a map on display, and the rest piled into the rear.

The colony was big enough to have roads, albeit strictly controlled and boxed in. Still, they drove around an arc of the dome, the local sun shining yellowly through the hazy ochre sky and the thick crystal panels. The whole dome was ten kilometers across, and not spherical. The sides rose in a steep curve, then canted over into an oblate roof. Traffic wasn't heavy, and most of it looked to be delivery vehicles and a very few limos. Slideways ran in tunnels underneath, and in some overhead skyways. Trains on magnetic rails and trains of cars on the road carried tourists to the sights and workers to their offices.

They drove right into the building that housed Caron's apartment. By her father's orders, they were not in the same building, nor was her uncle nor their execs. They also hadn't picked the tallest buildings to live in, instead choosing to have a view outside.

The garage was surreal, with pines and palms in pots and pits, reaching for a glass ceiling. The surfaces were clean stucco with what looked like black iron fittings. The presentation was California resort, not high tech mining colony.

Caron knew the routine. She stepped out into her block of guards, who peeled off ahead in pairs to check doorways and corridors, parted to let her into the elevator, and then repeated the process down the hall. They passed overlapping sensor webs that admitted them based on biometrics. Those did not have any network connections, and could only be programmed from inside the controlled area. Cady's team had done the initial setup. Jason would lock them down from inside using his own protocols. He led the way. Once past those, he moved ahead and unlocked the door.

The apartment was insane.

Caron's quarters were about 150 square meters, with a kitchen, bedroom, a private nook/study/den, and a great room. One wall and part of the ceiling were transparent and antireflection treated, looking straight out the dome located a few meters away. The racing, Easter egg bands of ochres and reds washed by in the wind, clearing occasionally to offer a blurry view of the mine pits. On a mock balcony surrounded by one-way panes was a hot tub, plunge and jet blown lap pool.

Her furniture was not all locally made. She had a very nice wood coffee table.

Jason said, "Bluemaple burl," as he knelt and took a glance at it. "Beautiful stuff."

Her kitchen cabinets across the expanse were Circassian walnut from Turkey, probably half a millennium old. Two chairs and a couch were upholstered in ostrich skin. The glasses on the rack were real cut crystal.

The floor . . . parquet wood, area rugs, and the den had sculpted carpet with five centimeters of padding. You could wrestle, or other things, on that.

Caron looked very unhappy. It wasn't her home, could never be her home, and she could never leave. Perhaps not "never," merely "decades," but to a woman of twenty-two, that would feel the same.

She can't even pick up a quick lay here, Alex thought. Poor kid.

"I'll unpack in the morning," she said. "I'm going to bed. Thank you all."

"You're welcome, Caron," he said. "Bart is on for now, then Shaman, then Elke."

"I'm in no hurry in the morning. Thanks."

She turned and walked into her bedroom, letting go a sigh as she closed the door.

The team's own quarters were as impressive. Their first assignment together had been in a presidential palace. President Bishwanath had made sure they were comfortable, but that had nothing on this.

The "dead spaces" on all sides of her apartment were actually theirs. That made sense. There was a central spiral staircase, elevator and drop tube to ensure rapid access. Bart's apartment could be reached through the kitchen. Alex was above, Jason below, Shaman canted to the rear off the study. Elke's apartment opened through a door in the bedroom, and another through a hallway to the study. Aramis was across the hall, next to a common room they could all use. Across from that was a gym.

Someone was thinking. Oh, wait, that was me, Alex thought wryly. Aramis was a good man. Why put temptation near him? And for proprietary image and personal safety, the only person who could share bedroom access had to be Elke.

The cheapest room on this ball cost M5,000 a night. The dome overhead had cost billions. Money was something that no one here worried about in any fashion. The universe's elite had a playground kept secure by simple costs.

Except that the same elite had people with the money and mindset to try to arrange a hit. Alex would have to be alert for anyone acting out of their class, whatever class that might be here.

CHAPTER 16

Jason awoke early. The quarters were far more comfortable than he deserved, but he never slept well the first night anywhere. There was also the fact that he'd spent most of his life on a world with a twenty-eight-hour day. This place ran on Earth's clock for convenience, since the outside didn't matter that much, and its nineteen-hour day wasn't conducive to any normal human schedule.

Grumbling to himself, he rose and showered, dressed and climbed up the spiral stair to Caron's main room. There was also a ladder through a hatch and a lift pallet for moving large items. Both had additional sensor webs and security equipment. The layout was his design, and he was proud of it. They all had multiple ways in to protect her, and there were limited ways in from outside. If they could channel attackers, they could slow them.

The lights were at minimum, but it was light outside, the filthy smog pretty when seen through two layers of armored composite. The wind was steady, and some trick of aerodynamics curled a brown wisp into a corkscrew across the dome.

He got quietly to work opening crates and laying out supplies. Each of the team members had small backpacks with water, emergency rations, medical supplies, lights, batteries, maps, comms. They had body armor. They had casual and formal wardrobes. They had field and military gear. It all had to be checked and distributed. They each carried their on-person gear in pockets and pouches tailored into clothes. They had discreet backup bags or briefcases as needed, and then they had combat rucks for evacuation that could sustain them for days if need be. This mission emphasized the smaller stuff, but it all could be necessary.

A low buzz indicated someone coming in. It was Aramis. Jason took his hand off his holstered stunner and nodded a greeting.

Aramis looked a bit groggy himself, and nodded back. He came over and helped arrange things on the carpeted floor.

Elke came in seconds later wearing a casual snug sweater. Her figure was leaner than Caron's, but certainly attractive. Jason nodded again and turned away. He'd seen Elke before. Right now his concern was threats and equipment.

They certainly had the melee gear they needed. The combination baton, neural stunner with contact and range settings, and a blindingly bright strobe was welcome. They'd used those on Salin. They had folding and fixed blade knives, the latter large enough to serve as small swords. Jason had a tomahawk. That made him happy. They had incapacitance gas in aerosols, stun grenades, dazzle lights, impact stun bags, wrecking bars, and knives.

"Did they authorize those?" Aramis asked softly, pointing at the wrecking tools.

Jason said, "They didn't not authorize them, but did specifically forbid firearms and limit Elke's explosives."

"*Blbe zkurveny,*" she muttered.

"But these were not mentioned. So if they don't ask, I won't tell."

The rest walked in just then. Bart said, "I firmly believe in never telling anything. What are we not telling and who to?"

Aramis pointed.

The wrecking bars looked more like something for killing zombies. They had a hammer face, a wrenchlike gap big enough to take a timber or a wrist, a claw back sharpened almost to a knife edge, and the handle had a chisel point. It looked like it could pry, punch or smash just about anything.

Alex said, "Those are a bit blatant." He frowned.

"*Yes, they are!*" Jason and Shaman said in unison, then laughed and high-fived.

Jason said, "Alex, if someone wants to screw with us, I want an obvious dissuasion. These are emergency tools in case we get stuck. Nothing more. But I figure if I brain the first one, or even just rip his kneecap off, the rest will think twice."

"As long as we have a good cover, that's great. It looks like a cross between a war hammer and a tomahawk, built on a pry bar."

"That's pretty much what it is. Beautiful, isn't it?"

Alex said, "I like the knife. You always bring the good stuff."

"Simple is better," Jason said. The knives were chisel-pointed steel with cord-wrapped handles. An old but reliable design. They were big enough to be lethal, flat enough to conceal, and pretty much fail proof. They'd also work as pry bars.

All their clothing was constructed with non-Newtonian properties. The gloves were double thick. A punch with those and the glove shell would momentarily turn into a stiff hammer. For hand-to-hand violence, they were set.

"Police stunners?" Aramis asked, hefting one. It was more obvious, but less versatile than the stunner they'd used on Celadon. It was much more powerful, though.

Jason confirmed that. "One good shot from this and the perp will be down for hours. Anyone with a heart weaker than a cape buffalo is going to need a cardiac function test."

Bart said, "I approve. This dome restricts our variance greatly. There are definite choke points on any route to anywhere."

Alex nodded. "Randomness of schedule is critical. Caron RSVPs to nothing, may or may not show up as she wishes, I dictate, or a coin flip determines. The same for food. It gets inspected, we bring several choices up from the kitchen, and most of it gets tossed. At least we know it gets recycled instead of wasted."

"It gets recycled on Earth," Elke said. "It just takes longer. But I get your meaning."

They had one shotgun, pistol sized, with breacher rounds.

"Mine," Elke said as she picked it up and cleared the action. No one disputed her.

"We need more explosive," she added.

"Are you kidding? You have enough to kill several thousand people if applied properly. I had to lie and fight to get that much."

"There's more in the mine. I can get it."

"Elke: subtlety. Do you know the word?"

"I believe it was a medieval English word for a dessert made to look like sculpture, yes?"

Her expression was deadpan.

Caron came through right then. She was clean, neatly and

casually dressed in slacks and blouse, and wore a smile that was somewhat forced.

"Good morning," she said. "At least I'm done with school."

Alex said "Good morning, miss," while the rest echoed or mumbled quietly.

Caron said, "I'm going to cook breakfast. I will be doing good English bacon, eggs, toast and grilled tomatoes. Please sit and tell me what you'd like."

Horace thought that was an excellent coping mechanism on her part. It was sociable, fulfilling and gracious.

"Over easy please, miss," he said. "Very light on the toast."

Jason caught his eye, gave a bare shrug and nod that he understood, and said, "Over medium if you can, please, and did I see rye bread?"

"Yes," she agreed.

The others placed orders quickly, from scrambled to cheese omelet to hard cooked.

Caron was an accomplished cook, who used four pans on the RF pads without any microwave heating. She grilled the tomatoes in the electric broiler and kept the rest moving. She even brought the food to them. Horace was quite impressed. Such a nice young lady.

She even had coffee up in short order, with real cream, probably frozen for transport, and raw sugar.

Between bites, Alex asked, "So what is your schedule today, miss?"

"I'm going to run up and see Dad," she said. "After that, look around. I've seen maps and charts and overlays and video, and none of it in person. The last time I was here I was fifteen and it was just a collection of sealed boxes."

Horace asked, "How long do you need to look around?"

"It might take a week," she said. "Obviously, that's just an overview. But people need to know I'm here and part of the operation. I assume that carries a security risk?"

Alex said, "Everything carries a security risk. But we'll make it work."

"Will you be with me forever?" she asked, sounding a little tight.

"Ideally, we can devise protocols that will let you get down to one personal guard and a remote team on standby. They can also work on protecting your father, uncle and any highly placed employees in the area as well."

"My uncle has Ex Ek Security. What do you think of them?"

Alex said, "For the lesser threat he faces, they are quite adequate. No one is going to try to kill him under the present circumstances. Of course, if you or your father are removed from control, his risk goes up considerably. He's far more likely to face petty blackmail and extortion. Much less threatening, much cheaper to deal with, and much cheaper to protect against."

"That's something I'd like to aspire to," she said, finally coming from the kitchen with her own plate, which was already half consumed. "I don't mind the money, but it's a bloody choke chain."

"That's a long-term plan we're really not able to help make, but we'll support you of course."

"I appreciate it," she said.

Horace was impressed. Many people would have said, "If the money's enough, right?" or something similar. She did not.

All in all, he thought she was handling the stress very well.

"In the meantime," she said, "this is my planet, so I'm going to explore it. The operations, the raw outdoors, the tourist traps. As long as we're unannounced you think I'm safe?"

"Miss, you are not safe anywhere at any time, but we can avoid a lot of threats. However, if you're known to frequent certain locations, or even certain types of locations—casinos, say, or the outdoor tours—someone can plan accordingly and wait for you. They only have to get lucky once, and recon is cheap. They just hire a shill to report when you're seen."

She wrinkled her brow in concentration.

"While it will annoy people," she said, "would it help to have occasional delays for other traffic, to keep potential threats from reaching me as fast?"

"That's one more thing we can add, yes, with permission."

"Then I suppose I better get to my sightseeing first," she said. "I'm going to take the gondola over the volcano. How do we proceed?"

"Who's going with her?" Alex asked.

"I will," Aramis said. "I've always wanted to see one up close."

Elke said, "I assume it's basaltic flows? I'd like to see that, too."

Alex added, "Jason and Bart will escort you there. They're able to meet at the far end, yes?"

"I think that will need a puddle jumper—the little executive hoppers used around the mines. I'm sure I can get one."

Elke said, "I suggest regular clothes to visit your father. You could wear a hijab or veil while touristing."

Caron thought for a moment. "That's not a bad idea. In fact, I like it. I can not be me."

"I packed some," Elke said.

Horace wondered how that suggestion would have been received from a male. It was interesting how viewpoint and perception changed.

Aramis regretted volunteering almost as soon as the tour started. The gondola was well sealed, and everyone had an emergency pack in hand. He deemed it safer to not clear it, since there was at least a chance that a killer wouldn't want to take out twenty very rich and powerful tourists as well as Caron, and the odds of one of them being a threat were significantly below average. Add in the unannounced arrival and the basic black headdress she wore over a long dress, and it should be fine. He still watched everyone, though.

Then the car shifted and swayed. The cable above was largely for stability and backup. The gondola moved on gas jets. That combined with blasts of heat from the volcano served to make the ride very bumpy, though. Then, they were over an open fucking volcano.

Yes, it was pretty. Impressive. Awe-inspiring. Terrifying. Aramis knew the cable was sufficient, the gas jets powerful enough to hold them, the car insulated and proof against the heat long enough for recovery by the crew on duty at the terminus. His brain knew all that, and his guts wanted him the hell off and out. Five seconds was plenty.

He steeled himself to look back at the passengers, who varied from delighted to quaking, depending on their knowledge of science and trust in the materials. One older couple chattered away about geology. They might be retired professionals. Not bothered. Others squeaked and shivered. Caron seemed fairly calm.

Aramis took a closer look. He was not officially medical personnel, but he was trained in battlefield lifesaving and he knew dilated pupils when he saw them. The little bitch had tranked herself.

Was this another way of punishing them for her own issues?

Maybe not, he thought. Maybe she just wanted to see it and knew she'd be afraid of the environment.

Fair enough. Of course, he and Elke couldn't medicate on duty unless injured.

He looked over at Elke. She was very stiff, very still, white-knuckling the rail and frozen-faced. Her pupils were dilated, but it wasn't from medication. He wondered as to her awareness.

Sighing inside, he made the decision to turn around and watch the other end of the car. Elke would be all business if a threat happened, he knew. Fearless in the event. He didn't like having his back to that perfectly transparent glass, though. The shifting light from the lava boils didn't help his mindset.

A few of the passengers seemed to feel likewise. They gripped at the numerous rails and clung to dignity by taking very slow, measured looks that were mostly at the inside of the car. The usual adrenaline junkies pointed and waved.

Aramis wasn't afraid of heights. He was trained in rappelling and parachuting. Here, though, he was suspended by a wire over a volcano in a toxic atmosphere. Maybe the thrill seekers just didn't grasp the threat level, and that there was nothing a human could do if things went wrong. Certainly it was safe, or Prescot would not let his daughter here . . . but the perception killed all reason.

He was only too glad for the ride to be over. He used the excuse of status and urgency to push Elke and Caron out the door first, and climbed into the armored train car with Bart and Jason.

He wound up next to Elke, and was surprised when she gripped his hand and held it for half the trip back. Once they cleared the tunnel back into the dome, she slipped her fingers free and acted as if nothing had happened, so he did, too.

Really, he didn't blame her.

CHAPTER 17

It certainly did seem safer here, Bart thought. All visitors were vetted. The tourists were worth stupid amounts of money and less likely to be motivated for crime. The management all received excellent salaries and benefits, so had little incentive to push for more. That was also true of the high ranking mine personnel. Miss Caron didn't interact with the common miners or staff. Given all that, it was a much more relaxed environment. The team escorted her when she left her apartment and remained on call otherwise.

They had a top quality gym, unlimited entertainment and access to all shows, casinos, excursions, the best food he'd ever tasted, and limited duty for high pay with no threats so far. There was nothing to complain about.

Nothing, except that it was boring, and he didn't expect it to last.

Miss Caron seemed interested in keeping them doing light work, at least.

They had their standard morning meeting and formation in her great room. She didn't cook breakfast for them as a rule, but they could help themselves to anything she had. That also helped prevent poisoning, since everything coming in was sealed, checked by automated equipment, passed up by Cady's team, checked again by Elke, then probably served to them before her. There was still a small risk of toxicity, but given the previous failure and all the attention on the matter, it wasn't likely anyone would try that method again.

Miss Caron acted as her own social secretary. She was at the coffee table she usually used as a desk, when Bart walked in. He poured himself some excellent coffee and took one pastry, and joined the gaggle.

She kept herself busy, probably as insulation against the culture shock. Also, he realized, she was going to be one of the executives here. Her entire life was planned already.

"Okay," she said, "I'll need to check in with Dad sometime this afternoon. I do need to see most of the Operation Section management offices to get a good overview. That's going to take more than a week just by itself."

Aramis said, "You'll . . ." paused for a moment, and finished, ". . . want to do that overview soon, then." He flushed slightly, but she didn't seem to catch it.

Bart ignored it, also, though he was quite sure the man had almost said, *you'll have a lot of time to look at them in detail over the next few years, though.* No, let's not say that.

"I suppose I must. Can I get you to schedule me at the most randomly inconvenient times possible for everyone, including myself?"

"Absolutely, miss," Alex said. "Then we'll make a few of them convenient, just so we're not predictable."

"Luckily I don't have a set schedule for any of it. Do with me as you will." She sipped her tea and flipped through more screens.

Bart thought that phrase could be taken two ways in English. He assumed she meant it in the nonsuggestive way.

Alex had three screens of his own laid out on the desk near the window.

"I think we should do the entire technical tour in one go. It leaves less time for future preparations, since some of the routes are choke points."

"So you suggest one long day of potential improvised threats, versus multiple trips against a time frame that allows planning."

"Exactly."

"Very well. I'll need food and water, I assume."

Bart offered, "I'll make sandwiches. You like pumpernickel and ham, yes?"

"I do," she agreed. "Thank you."

He stepped into the kitchen alcove, dumped out an entire sliced loaf, and started throwing ingredients down. It didn't take long, and then he checked his own water, emergency respirator, pistol, armor and emergency kit.

Then they were out the door, each in a suit with a stylish shoulder bag full of things that were not lethal enough to suit Bart. He wondered how Elke felt.

They cleared their way section by section down to the garage level. Bart treated every empty cross corridor, landing, and elevator as a possible threat zone. Besides, there just might be a threat, and he'd look stupid even if he survived.

Jason drove the lead vehicle. Bart took the second one. He wound up with Miss Caron, Elke and Mbuto while the other two got in with Jason. For an over-glamorized golf cart, the vehicles were not bad. They were roomy enough, had bars and power and work tables, as well as comm and entertainment. No one would ever mistake it for a real car of any kind, though. The supplemental armor would stop small arms or very light explosives. While the security protocols should prevent military munitions from entering the dome, the mine had plenty of commercial explosive.

There was nothing to do about that at the moment, though, so Bart focused on driving.

They left the dome through a passageway with a staggered series of airtight hatches. Bart had been a surface ship sailor in the German Baltic fleet, which somehow spent much of its time in the Indian Ocean chasing pirates. He knew well-engineered equipment when he saw it. These doors would easily hold against a blowout, even explosives, and there were a lot of them. Of course, the steel and aluminum were locally produced.

They angled down and then left, which would be southwest. He had a printed map to refer to. They should be reaching the division to the mine at the next pressure door. Yes, there. This section would shortly end in a parking garage from where they'd have to walk.

Alex was glad when they parked. He found the little carts to be far too flimsy for real protection, and far too obvious, even if there were others driving around. There weren't enough to do more than draw attention. He climbed out, waited while Caron was surrounded by a wall of meat, then moved into the lead. He used the paper printout map, since his phone could be traced and theoretically read.

There weren't many people in the area, but those who were clearly identified Caron's party at once. So much for discretion. Still, they'd reached here unseen as far as he knew.

Jason said, "Called and told them to expect VIPs any moment. They acknowledged."

"Understood," he said.

The door opened to a press of the caller he carried, which made it much easier to discreetly clear the entrance as he walked in. Aramis went right as he went left, Shaman went straight ahead.

One receptionist, male. One primary occupant at a plotting station, also male. No obvious threats or weapons. The man was waiting for them, looking relaxed and not even annoyed. Good actor. No one liked VIPs dropping in unannounced during the work day.

They parted to let Caron through, and kept eyes and scanners out.

She stepped forward and offered a hand, as she said, "This is our senior mining explosives engineer, John Eggett."

Eggett smiled with crinkled eyes and extended his hand. Alex reached for it, but Elke squeezed in front.

"John!" she said, with a shake that turned into a quick hug. "Wonderful to see you again."

"And you, Elke. You're looking lovely as always." He looked down at her with a fond smile.

"That's just the smell of explosive you like," she said with a hint of blush. "I envy you. I've been admiring the work since we got into orbit."

"I've heard about some of yours, and I read your last article in the *Blaster's Journal*," he said.

"Thank you, but I'm being rude," Elke said. She introduced the team, starting with Aramis.

Alex studied Eggett. He had a definite military bearing. He had a little extra weight, but good muscle tone. Decent looking guy, groomed hair and short beard. Seemed competent, comfortable and relaxed. If he was hiding anything, he was a pro. Elke had actually hugged him in public, which spoke volumes. He'd have to ask her for a brief.

Elke concluded the introductions with, "...and our team leader, District Agent In Charge Alex Marlow."

Eggett offered his hand. "Agent Marlow. Pleased to meet you."

Alex took it. Firm grip, no games. Good man so far.

"And you, Mr. Eggett," he said. "Do please tell us anything you like."

Eggett stepped back with a slight smile. "Well, we're preparing to set off the largest nonmilitary blast in history. In about another ten days, four cubic kilometers of crust is going to jump three meters to the right, pirouette, backflip and land in a bucket."

Alex smiled. Elke snickered.

Eggett continued. "What we're actually going to do is shoot a series of charges. Six will shatter the ore-bearing layer so that it's easier to process. One will cut a glory hole in the middle from where equipment can radiate out to remove the ore. One big one just above that will blow most of the overburden to vapor and it will vent into the atmosphere."

"Any risk of projectiles hitting the dome?"

"That's where the calculations come in. Most of the overburden will sublime straight to vapor. There's obviously going to be some fragmentation, and a small buffering charge—about two hundred tonnes—will create a backblast to meet the shockwave from the main charge and counter it out to neutralize debris in that cone, or divert those fragments from trajectories toward any existing structures. Also, the detonation wave shouldn't have enough energy at the surface to throw anything heavy enough. We chose a spot deep enough to contain the charge."

"Wouldn't shallower require less blast?"

"We want depth for containing the blast. We want it to blow overburden, not make a flashy cloud. Deeper means we can also get a broader hole, exposing more ore."

Shaman asked, "Are those large metal plates ballistic protection against the blast?"

"Actually, those are chilled condensation plates. There will be some metal vapor subliming out from the residual heat. They'll condense and recover it. That's not my field, though."

"How long does all that take?"

"After the geologic survey, using seismic charges to create reflectance waves, I consult with the senior mining engineer and his staff. We design the shot. Then the devices have to be manufactured or tuned accordingly. Holes are drilled, the charges placed, everything double-checked; we even use the drill cores to check the material properties. Once everything is set, we schedule a time, clear the area, and everyone in the mine needs to be in breathing gear regardless of location, in case of shockwave triggered leaks. Then I get the go ahead, push the button, and the actual detonation takes about four microseconds. Collapse of the camouflet, venting and subsumation take a few hours to be sure, then we have to let it cool for several days. Elapsed time is about eight weeks, but saves us several months of cutting and removing material, with the attendant operating costs."

"What about radiation? How soon can you actually go in, or are the vehicles hardened?"

"The equipment is all hardened. The devices are designed to be very clean. It's not my specialty; I can build conventional charges, these I just specify for someone else, but I understand there's a tritium and beryllium component to create extra neutrons."

Elke said, "Neutron booster. Concentric spheres of plutonium, with a tritium filled gap between them and a beryllium core. Detonation basically drives the fluid wave of the outer imploding fissionable through a neutron haze, reaching supercriticality before it reaches full compression with the inner sphere. The resultant fissioning supercritical mass slaps the beryllium for even greater emission. Conversion in the center of the core is close to ninety-seven percent efficient, the outer half on a rising curve from seventy-three to eighty-six percent. A heavy outer layer of iridium acts as a nonfissionable tamper. By the time the crater cools enough to send vehicles down, the radiation should be close to background."

Caron was wide eyed. "Damn, woman!" she said.

Elke shrugged. "I can show you the math if you like."

"Do you want a job?"

"I . . . really would rather not discuss that," Elke said, looking wistful.

Hmm, Alex thought. Something to wonder about. Elke liked the job, but liked explosives more. Worth mentioning. He also needed to get her some she could work with, even if they were not likely to actually need it. Possibly she could work with Eggett on a few shots, for practice and training? A good idea. Elke loved blasting more than anything in the universe, and she wouldn't be doing any on this mission unless there was a disaster.

Eggett brought up a screen with sonar and other soundings, realtime satellite images, and some taken from drones that braved the atmosphere.

"We lose those frequently, though," he said. "The weather's just too rough. We offer a salvage prize to tourists or staff who find them. There's a moderate amount of exploration going on on the surface."

The images showed the terrain, and color overlays showed ore densities. He spun the image in 3D.

"At this point," he said, "the only delays are material. We need to fabricate the machinery and fission devices. Labor's not a huge problem, though they're not thrilled with the working conditions."

"It is very dreary," Caron said.

Jason asked, "All the equipment is produced here?"

Caron said, "Yes, turbines are not that hard to produce. We even can spin cast them in microgravity. Parts casting is all done down here. It's actually a fairly small operation, possibly two hundred people."

Alex made another mental note. He would assume any weapon or tool could be made here. That put the threat level up.

Caron seemed to want to move quickly herself, which he approved of. She thanked Eggett and made to depart.

Eggett's office was just stuck into a vacant corner, since his work was mostly outside. Around the corner was a large open bay of hydroponics and a farm, under three compartmented domes with collapsible cofferdams between them.

This time they didn't make any announcement, but walked in as a group through heavy double doors with more double doors beyond, to keep the heat and humidity in. They could seal against pressure for a short time, though were probably not completely airtight.

It was several seconds before anyone noticed their presence. That was a point to note. Once someone did, a woman in coveralls hustled over. She was sturdy looking and neat enough, though sweaty and a little grimy.

She squinted slightly, looked at the mass of obvious guards, and said, "Miss Prescot?"

Caron replied, "I am. You must be Dr. Galvin?"

"Yes, ma'am. I wasn't expecting you."

"No worries. I'm just out getting a look at things, and my visits aren't announced for security reasons. Is there anyone who can give us a quick tour?"

"Absolutely. Please follow me. Are your staff coming?"

"Of course."

Alex led the way with Jason, and the formation loosened just slightly. Galvin led them past huge vats and tanks, with steam and vapor and mist all around. Some items sweated condensation. Most had drip pans to recover the water. There were occasional splotches of mold and mildew, though the place looked to be cleaned regularly.

As they walked, Galvin said, "We're improving food production for more variety. Fruits and vegetables are fairly easy. Grow lights and climate aren't a problem, we just have to worry about possible blights and keep emergency supplies on hand. The density yield is great. Meat, though . . . we have guinea pigs and rabbits fed off the prunings and waste. Chickens are in limited supply as they need too much grain. We're working on vat grown chicken, and we have beef liver in a large tank. It's trimmed daily for food and for any potential cancerous growths."

They kept walking as Galvin kept pointing and talking.

"Right now we're pretty limited. The food is edible and healthy, but really lacks variety. There's ostrich on occasion, and beef, but those are imported. Shortly, we hope to have different cultures of tissue we can use. It's no longer a money issue, but there are a few bio issues to work through. That's all grown in these tanks. You can see the matrices a few centimeters in."

Alex didn't find the pulsating pink masses very appetizing. On the other hand, it wasn't likely most people saw this end of it. The huge pen of guinea pigs, rabbits and chickens wasn't too outré, but those were things he thought of as pets or pests, not food.

He thought he might stick to the vegetables for a while. Then he remembered he was one of the elite that got to eat deluxe frozen food from Earth, Grainne and Novaja Rossia.

"Why so much metal framing?" Aramis asked. "I see a lot of aluminum. I know the power's cheap, but wouldn't plastics be more efficient?"

"They would, but plastics require hydrocarbons, which are in very short supply. Other than methane and a few organic chains from atmospheric scooping of Ceridwen, we don't have any. Of course, the waste from tourists helps. They don't realize they're providing a few kilos each that we don't have to pay for."

In fact, they got charged for it. Some of them knew that. Some of them wouldn't grasp it. None of them would care, so Alex just ignored it.

"And that doesn't go with them?"

"We pump the ships before they jump."

"Gotcha."

"Other than that, we're working on things like llama, goat and ostrich. The first two will eat anything. The ostriches are very meaty, but a pain to work with. We'll probably vat raise those if we can work it. We'd also like more lean muscle meat, obviously."

The oxygen plant was a huge series of tanks, compartmented against possible damage and loss. They were gelatinously green with algae.

"Despite panics in previous centuries, the biggest and most efficient source of oxygen on Earth is algae, not rainforest. This is good for us, as algae tanks are pretty easy to build. We just bubble the CO two in from the bottom, and oxygen comes out the top. The algae are swept slowly from one end to the other with a mineral nutrient bath, and most of the minerals are locally available. At the dead end, as we call it, the stuff is chopped off, dried up, and then either fed back in as nutrients, used in the fish tanks, or some small amount is pressed into charcoal for the fireplaces."

"There are fireplaces??"

Caron said, "Yes, some of the deluxe suites include fireplaces and cooking grills. I didn't bother with my flat."

She asked Dr. Galvin, "I assume the steady renewal is to keep it fresh?"

"Yes, and prevent blights. If we need to, we can wipe out a tank in a few minutes with a massive hypochlorite purge, but we can only do that to so many tanks before it's a problem for air supply. We also store enough tanked oxygen for a day for emergencies, every section and suite has emergency supplies, and we can get some off the ships if we need to, or use electrolysis. Diversity is safety."

"Good," Shaman said. "I'm very impressed by the thought and development."

The tour was informative and long, and yet barely scratched the surface. This wasn't just a mine, it was a research facility, a resort, a peek into the future of space habitats, and might solve several problems with all human settlements, including pollution, starvation and resource depletion. The Prescot family had certainly earned its trillions. Far from being evil capitalists, the family were contributing massively to the future of the human race. They'd developed several entire industries, and created hundreds of refinements of others, not to mention being the vanguard of development of the mining and smelting techniques. And all that was just lead up to the billions of tonnes of raw metals they shipped out of here. The frothing socialists who hated the wealth simply couldn't, or didn't want to, understand that they benefited directly from all this development, which only came about because Bryan Prescot was willing to stake his existing fortune on a bet some decades back. If it hadn't worked out, their generations-old business would have been sold off for a pittance against the debts.

Not that it mattered what he thought. His job was to keep Caron alive and well. It was always easier when you actually liked the principal, though.

That evening, Alex held an executive meeting, with an earbud tuned in to listen to Bart and Shaman and Aramis, who were escorting Caron to a show.

He looked at Elke and Jason, his chosen overkill.

"So, this is the emergency backup plan. If it all goes to hell, what do we need to have and do to keep her alive?"

Jason said, "Oxygen. Weapons to get to transport. Transport."

Elke said, "I expect transport to be out of the question, so oxygen and a hiding hole with good communications."

"Communications will also be problematic."

Alex said, "And that's why we get paid what we do. Let's find solutions."

"Explosive," Elke said. "I can get it from the mine if I need to. No one will know. I want several caches."

Alex nodded. "I agree."

"You do?" she said, sounding incredulous. "I don't have to fight?"

"I rarely disagree with the concept," he said. "I just have to answer higher up. You can probably manage several hundred kilos over a few weeks."

"We may not have a few weeks. I shall arrange it shortly."

"Well, you haven't gotten caught yet, but do be discreet."

"Of course."

Jason said, "We need a cache of good weapons, and I don't care what Prescot thinks. We won't use them unless it hits the fan, but if it does, we need to be able to kill people. This nonlethal stuff is dogshit. If a thug knows he'll survive, he's even less intimidated, especially if angry or well paid. If he knows he'll die, we gain what, thirty percent off the mark?"

"At least," Alex said. "Her father's morally okay with us breaking heads, he's just worried about fallout."

Bart chimed in, "Bah. He is already accused of being a capitalist slavemaster. He may as well get the benefit to go with the slur. Smash heads and don't apologize. They had it coming."

Aramis said, "I'm working on maps. I'll stash some caches in various places without mentioning it. Part of the problem is there's no tactical gear of any kind for sale here. The police and security have a little. There's some basic toxic atmo gear in the excursion points, but nothing we'd need. Can Cady loan us some or order us some? We have to assume we need it fast."

"Good point. I'll follow up on that immediately. We'll have to see what we can get or improvise."

Jason said, "They may be able to fabricate some of that in the mine support shops if they don't have stuff we can use. I imagine tool belts and such can serve in the meantime. The problem is that it's not very secret."

"Keep me informed. Be very discreet. Outfit with intent to commit extreme violence. I'm going to see if Cady can arrange some other caches."

Elke nodded very seriously. Aramis didn't crack any jokes. That's how Alex knew they were fully in agreement.

The tours, office visits and social events continued endlessly. Caron's coping mechanism was to be too busy to worry. It also seemed that the threat level was way down. It was possible, Alex supposed, that the increasing threats on Earth had been because she was harder to reach here, and the pending departure had made the window small. Still, he was going to treat the threat level here with all the attention it deserved, and some extra.

The tours were as informative for him, in terms of potential threats and exploitable resources, as they were for Caron as a future manager. The technology available was bleeding edge, except when it was outdated due to resources.

Plastics, for example, were expensive and little used. Hydrocarbons to make them had to be scooped from Ceridwen, the sole Jovian-sized gas giant in the outer system. Metal ores and minerals for ceramics were readily available. In that regard, a lot of the structural members and sheathing resembled the twentieth and early twenty-first centuries more than the twenty-third.

Caron started reviewing production charts, and took a trip down into the depths of the second pit. Alex, Jason and Elke went with her.

He'd heard from Aramis that Elke was nervous around heights, though the man had admitted it pushed his own limits. The inverse wasn't true, though. Elke was fine in the hole.

Though it was big enough to be more a huge valley than a hole. Still, she didn't seem bothered by the cliffs above and the towering machines, carving, grinding, ripping away at the rock, running it along huge conveyers and up to a processor that steamed even in this atmosphere.

Bart was the better street driver, but Jason excelled at construction and field equipment. The vehicle they were in could best be described as an armored personnel carrier, adapted for mining use. It had clustered trios of wheels which Jason said enabled it to scale boulders and dips "or even climb stairs." It was pressurized and had backup oxygen hoses, assorted commo and imaging gear, plugs for headsets, everything except armor and weapons. Even without armor, the shell was a very tough composite against impacts. Most of it was built here with modern coordinate tools, though the shells were imported from SHI in the Grainne system, due to the lack of local hydrocarbons.

The vehicle was more important to Alex than the mine, but the mine was staggering. From the bottom, the sides rose higher than Everest. The atmospheric pressure was substantially higher down here. Not enough to affect breathing equipment, but there were visible gradients and thick currents. The walls weren't quite round. They were cut straight to aid mining tools. A godawful-manygon twenty-five kilometers in diameter.

"Heck of a place you have here," Alex commented.

Caron's voice was a radio-distorted squawk. "The company developed all this technology. Without it, Govannon would not be exploitable. Now that we have the infrastructure, we can replicate and expand across the planet, and gradually increase exploitation of the planetoids. We definitely need more hydrocarbons; they only come from Ceridwen. We need to make our margin fast."

"How do you enforce your patents?"

She nodded. "That's a big problem. Once out of sight in a remote system, there's no way other than an inspection to determine what's being used. We'd have to pay for the inspection, then file suits which we'd only win if we proved the intellectual property theft, which gets harder all the time. In effect, we'd lose all we gained in legal fees and overhead. So we're working fast and diligently to recover it all and make a profit, at a rate low enough to inhibit competition. And despite providing the cheapest metal in history, we're considered these evil capitalist bastards." She frowned. "I was happy as a millionaire's daughter. I never wanted all this."

Alex felt sorry for her. She'd gotten through her teen years, was all set to have a prosperous life as an engineer, with nice family holdings, and now had so much she had to fear her own wealth. Her future had been snatched away. Govannon was a technical marvel, and the most opulent, comfortable resort in the universe, and it was her prison.

Nor were they sure even this place was safe.

CHAPTER 18

A week later they were outside on the upper surface, in what was effectively a tank; a military APC converted to electric power, with solar chargers and a backup capacitor bank. The seats were benches without real padding, no amenities to speak of, and suits were worn. Jason knew that he wasn't the only one who found that to be a comfort. Armored vehicles were cold metal hugs.

Because Caron was aboard, Jason drove. Next to him was John Eggett. Eggett's staff were in another vehicle. That was a minor inconvenience, but he'd graciously agreed to the split so Caron could observe with him.

Eggett said, "We could go another kilometer and be safe, but you wanted a sure distance."

"This should be fine," Alex said via intercom. "Thanks for the help."

"You're welcome. The shot is imminent, but that still means the area has to be cleared, even though it's impossible for someone to be out here. Then all my people will confirm. Then we'll use PA and radio and data network to announce it. Then and only then will I give one more warning, and fire the shot. You should be able to see two heavier concentrations of debris to our ten and two positions."

Caron said, "Thanks. Tell us when. And you say it's safe to have the hatch open?"

"The hatch can be open during the shot. It will have to close immediately afterward. I do recommend against it officially, and I insist you check the mechanism to be sure it will close. I would never allow anyone whose name wasn't Prescot to do this, you understand."

"I do," she said. "Aramis is checking the hatch now."

Aramis was missing sleep to be here, Jason thought. They all wanted to see this. It was one of the few perks of the job, if you liked this sort of thing, which, of course, they did.

Eggett had a manual checklist on paper, and went down the sheet.

"I call clear," he announced. "All units confirm."

He ticked off boxes as each of his units contacted him.

"All units confirmed. Any other units in area, please call. Is there anyone downrange? Is there anyone downrange? Is there anyone downrange?" A klaxon squawked across all frequencies, three times. "The range is clear. Shot is imminent. All personnel check your cover. Seal all commo. Last call for alibis. No alibis. I confirm on shot. Blasting in five, four, three, two, one—"

The ground ahead rose in a dome, glowed white and boiled. Several jets erupted and spewed artificial lava. A ring of ground from the secondaries rose around the center, making it look like a massive meteorite impact.

The ground started to rumble, then a massive *Bang!* raised them a few centimeters up. Jason twitched, then remembered that was the interference charge to prevent the shockwave bouncing the dome.

Just as Eggett had predicted, the jets and fountains of debris thickened in two directions past the dome. They were parked in a relatively clear spot.

Then the ground started to rumble.

"Close the hatch."

He heard it slam behind, and Elke said something softly in Czech, her voice lilting. It sounded almost sexual, especially with her panting for breath. That was from closing the heavy hatch. Maybe. He almost could sympathize. Damn, that was a beautiful blast.

They had monitors in back, though he suspected they were all manning the vision blocks, the periscope and the opening behind the driver's compartment. He wasn't going to look away himself.

The ground started to slump, back on itself, then deeper, into a dip, a bowl, a hole, and then collapsed into a kilometer wide crater that blew clouds of dust after the pillar of blast debris.

"Very nice," Jason said.

"Thank you," Eggett replied with a smile. "I even get paid for it. We need to give it a few minutes to stabilize, and I'll check readings. There will be several sets of surveys over the next month, and then proper mining can start."

There were occasional clatters of detritus, tiny globs of congealed rock raining out of the atmosphere. They sounded like light hail.

"Well, that gets things started," Eggett said. "From this point, surveyors will determine some small secondaries—low kiloton range, that will vaporize more. After that, lots of conventional explosive to cut channels and reliefs and ramps and such, then digging machines. You've seen them?"

Jason said, "Yeah, they look like something from a nightmare."

"That's the ones. This isn't much volume as a percentage, but it gets the hole started faster, and means less hauling of initial overburden, and the initial penetration is into material already crushed for transport. Given time, we should be able to develop a multiple charge shot to clear a greater volume."

As they approached the vehicle terminal, Jason said, "Well, I hate to repay your hospitality by asking you to let us clear Miss Prescot first . . ."

"I understand. I'll wait."

"Thanks. I really wish we didn't have to be so paranoid."

"Visibility does that."

"And that was a hell of a show."

"I enjoy them myself. I wish I got to do more of them."

Inside, the rest escorted Caron out and away. Jason sat with Eggett.

Once they were alone, he said, "I need to ask a favor about dome strength."

"Oh?"

"I'm trying to prove it really is proof against small arms."

Eggett winced, clearly understanding, and said, "I hate to get involved in office politics. You're not actually employees, and anything outside of mining operations isn't my place to say. You really want the dome engineers."

"I don't know them. I don't blame you for being circumspect, of course."

"Thanks. I also feel a debt to the family, and I really want Miss Prescot to be safe. So I'll get you a file on strength of materials and such. Will that help?"

"Immensely. Thank you, sir."

"Why thank me? I have no idea what you're talking about."

"Got it."

Civilian spectators were not allowed out for the blast, but lots had gathered on observation platforms wherever they could. For that reason, and to keep the vehicles on their standard routes, Alex elected to bring Caron up from the mine rather than stop at a lock.

Jason would catch up after his business. In the meantime, the five of them should be plenty.

There was a broad tunnel with the everpresent pressure seals leading from the upper areas of the mine head, where the senior staff resided and worked, to the dome itself. The dome had in fact been built off the mine, with the mall first as an executive perk, and the rest following.

They had their electric limo, and sped into the receiving area. They could continue with it, but pedestrian traffic and tight turns would make it not only noticeable, but slow. They stepped out and proceeded in a loose square.

They took an elevator with Elke's pass key that let them bypass controls and waits.

Two floors up put them on the ground level of the dome, and three short blocks—300 meters—from Caron's Haute Tour building. There was a broad entrance with an elaborate potted garden here. Bart moved ahead to check for any lurkers.

That was as it should be, and Alex drew back to cover the rear, but then . . .

Aramis walked off.

Alex didn't want to make a scene, but muttered, "Where the hell—?" Aramis was looking at some flowers behind a man on a bench reading a paper newspaper.

Then Alex watched in concern and confusion as Aramis looped a cord around the man's neck and yanked. The man's eyes bugged out, he scrabbled at his neck, but he stepped up and back over the bench rather than be strangled. In a moment, Aramis dragged him over and managed to cuff him with cable ties on the way.

Alex assumed Aramis had reason for the action, canted his head and asked, “What keyed you?”

Aramis looked disgusted. “Who the hell reads an Urdu paper from left to right when the language reads right to left?”

“Aha. Great catch.” He turned to the culprit and asked, “So, why are you hiding?”

The man shrugged and shook his head.

“Right. We call Cady. She can grill him. I’ll be very interested in the results of this. Aramis, Elke, please hold him here. We’ll proceed.”

He was nervous now he had only three effectives including himself, but the movement finished uneventfully and they were soon in her apartment.

Caron said, “That was disturbing, and embarrassing, and . . . I don’t know what else.”

“Yes,” he said. “I hope Cady has intel soon.”

“I will work here today. I’m a bit nervous, if that’s okay.”

“Please do.”

“Thanks. I’m going to check the AARs on the blast. If only every day was this interesting, without the creepiness.”

Bart was having a very interesting time. Yesterday, the nuclear blast. Today, skiing.

Miss Caron seemed to have very unstable moods. This was one of them.

For safety, she’d worn a full robe and veil in transit, like some of the very wealthy women from Qatar, Kuwait or the Ramadan colony. With different clothing and hats, he and Elke looked just like the typical meat thug and lady’s escort such a person would have. The cable car ride up the mountain offered a creepy view. The long-paned tunnel drove home how far they were from the main dome. Even with the emergency oxygen aboard, Bart thought it unlikely anyone would survive a disaster here.

Once here, though, with a ski mask to hide her face, she changed into a chevroned skintight suit with the chevrons pointing in very suggestive ways. She was almost more naked than naked, and every male on the hill was pretending not to stare at her. A few looked rather uncomfortable.

The people who cared about classifying slopes couldn’t decide if this was natural or artificial. The hill was natural—a volcanic plug southeast of the dome, sloping long toward it. Wind had eroded the far side more steeply. It was covered by an artificial roof in substantial volume, chilled and kept at twenty-three percent O_2 in steady circulation, because the top of the slope was 15,000 meters up. The snow was effectively natural, forming crystals in the high atmosphere and falling, rather than being sprayed. However, it only fell because the atmosphere was manipulated. Of course, that was done on Earth, too, to a lesser extent. The debate was over where it became artificial. Ski aficionados cared about that. They were some of the poorer guests here.

The main slope was perfect, of course, cut and blasted to shape. That was a positive. The negatives were that it was maintained regularly by staff who might be suborned, and once off the marked course was unknown and deadly. It was also twice as long as the longest slope on Earth. From top of the slope to dogleg to base of the rift was 28,000 meters. It dropped over 14,000 meters in that run, more than thirty degrees, but some areas peaked near seventy, others much more gently.

Caron didn't wait for Bart. Once cleared to the platform, she shuffled forward, grinned and jumped to the crushed, icy ramp and then onto the slope proper.

Bart took off after her, muttering a curse. He appreciated being able to run this course. He did not appreciate having to do so while looking for threats.

She was quite a good skier, and that spandex was amazing on her arse, he thought. The fluorescent green, orange and blue made her easy to follow, and those chevrons were clearly intended to point up her physique.

It was worse that she used the long, straight run to build up speed. A good skier could easily hit 100km/h. He knew she, and he, were already faster than that, with a dead straight track ahead. It was a professionally groomed, artificial slope, so the worst that might happen was she'd break a leg or dislocate one. Or Bart might.

He was amazed when he caught motion from the corner of his eye. Two other skiers actually passed him.

He analyzed in a hurry while skiing fast. If they were faster than he, they were good. They seemed interested in Caron. Was it for her amazing body, or some ill intent?

Bart couldn't tell if they were flirting or a threat. He'd have to be discreet and *abschreckend*... dissuasive?—if he could get close enough. He'd better do it quickly, too. There was no excuse for him not being closer.

He tucked in his arms and let gravity run his speed up.

It was exhilarating, and a bit scary. He was trying for maximum speed, and getting it, too. He didn't know how fast, but he was catching up.

The two skiers presented as male, young and fit. They closed in on Caron and carefully flanked her, then moved in closer, with a slight lead and brief, friendly waves. This was almost certainly nothing, but Bart must treat it as a threat. He drew in tight, as he'd seen jumpers do, and eased toward the man on the left. The snow was amazingly smooth, with few textural changes.

With a flip of his wrist he pulled his left pole from under his armpit in a fencing moulinet, and tossed it tip first between the man's feet. He watched it start to swing and pushed right as the man went down in a tumbling arse-over-heels cloud of powder.

Caron looked that way, and missed seeing him slip behind her. The other man saw him approaching and waved in panic, then tried to egress the area. Bart jabbed at him with the tip of his other pole, the man grabbed it and pulled, and Bart let him take it, to fall sideways into the snow and spin. Bart shoved back left to avoid the tangle of limbs and skis.

"Slow down!" he shouted at her.

Even under her goggles, he could see her expression. It was a mix of puzzled, shocked, angry and serious. She nodded and started slaloming in long bends.

Bart wasn't good enough to be able to look behind while skiing, especially with one pole, but he did have a small mirror. He waved it around intermittently while keeping himself from tumbling, and managed to determine the two were far behind but upright. They kept their distance, so he was satisfied for now. He buzzed for Mbuto to meet him at the bottom in case he needed help.

Many minutes later, they leveled out and stopped on the broad plain at the mountain's base.

Caron pulled up her goggles and yanked down her mask and snapped, "What the hell was that all about?" as she poled toward the shed.

"Miss, they were too close to be safe," he said. "They are unharmed. At that speed I could not warn them away. They were ahead of me."

"Yes, well, here they come now." She turned and waited for them.

They were wary of Bart, and stopped a few meters away. Bart received a buzz and saw Mbuto trudging out from the shed. Good.

Caron pulled off her mask and spoke to them. "I'm sorry. My bodyguards don't allow anyone close unless we are introduced first. I'm Caron."

"Oh," the first said, eyebrows raising. "You're..."

"Her," the other said. "We understand completely. We just wanted to ski and such."

"Very sorry," the first said.

Both men were college age, presumably from rich families, and just now found themselves so far out of their depth they were lost for words. There was no way to impress this woman, or at least not how they'd intended. "Very rich" did not apply here.

"No, please. You must join me for dinner."

"Uh, yes," the first said. "I'm Madya Vyas."

"Eric McDaniel," the other said. "Certainly."

"Tonight then, at seven?"

"Thank you, I... we will be there."

"I'm in Haute Tour. At the top, you'll need to buzz."

It took an awkward few moments for everyone to part, and Caron scowled at Bart again. Not getting her way, or having to notice security tended to annoy her.

"Well, I guess I'm done for the morning," she said. "That was a great run. I'm going to do that again."

"It's an amazing slope," he agreed. "One pass is enough for the day."

So was one look at that skintight suit.

Caron cheered up slightly on the trip back. She had her veil and robe back on, and was near invisible. The private booth in the rear of the train let her relax behind one-way glass.

"I'm being naughty, missing a half day of work like this," she said.

"Everyone needs down time," he said. "You do plenty of work."

"Yes, but there's so much to do. We have planetoid mining to develop, core mining and gas mining. That's in addition to the current operations, and all this recreation my uncle is promoting. What am I doing this afternoon? I'm sorry, I've forgotten."

Bart made a quick assessment. No, she wasn't drugged, just giddy from the ski run.

"A tour of miners' facilities."

"Ah, that'll be interesting. We've done our best to provide facilities, but there are limits on what we can do. The contrast with this—" she indicated around her "—which is paid for by lazy rich people, is awkward."

"There are three times as many miners."

"That, yes, and they're not paying for maid service or chefs. My father thinks we need to keep tabs on it, and find ways to improve quality of life. Explaining economies of scale doesn't avoid resentment."

The train was ultramodern and deceleration wasn't that noticeable. Bart kept an eye on the monitor, and tapped a signal on his phone as they arrived.

Aramis met them at the terminal head and drove back to the apartment. Caron ducked into her bedroom, came back in a clean coverall with protective gear, and looked eager to proceed.

Cady's team took charge of interrogating the suspect. She had a report in a few hours.

"It's not helpful," she said. "For one, while your actions were justified under the circumstances, they could be construed as assault and battery."

"Yes. How did that work out?"

"He knows that, and wasn't threatening, but wasn't bothered. He's Albanian, and presents as educated. He suggested he won't press charges if we don't pursue random allegations. He says he was curious and wanted to see what the paper was like."

"But didn't know which way to read it, and kept his face studiously on one page, when there are all kinds of net sources."

"Exactly. Aramis's report doesn't show him as curious. He was intent on that paper."

"Well, we found a phone on him, set up tracing and started calling numbers. Most of them are low supervisory staff. We're monitoring them now. Company authorized us. There was one anomaly."

"Yes?"

"Phone answered and then disconnected. We managed to track the general location in those seconds but then it went dead. It was down in the bottom end of mine management. Attempts to induce signal failed. I suspect it was disposed of on the surface or in the pit after being smashed."

"Understood. So it could be a threat, or mere publicity seekers."

"Correct."

"Well, I'll keep alert, but I refuse to respond to such a vague threat. We'll continue, just more alert."

"Roger. Cady out."

Joe Prescot saw things differently.

"Bryan, it's not safe to allow her down there!"

"Her guards are with her."

"They're only six. There are ten thousand miners down there who might decide to make her a target."

"It shouldn't be an issue. She's not openly announcing herself, they weren't given notice, and they can't all attack at once, even if they had reason to."

Joe hesitated. Of course his brother didn't have the situational knowledge he did. Those miners were liable to get angry, though. Of course he hadn't mentioned that. He wanted a lid kept on things, and he didn't want any hints that he wasn't able to keep order.

"Bryan, I've been here for three years, ever since we expanded. I volunteered for that because you interact better with the government and public. Three years is a long time. I know how people act and react here, I know how things move. I really must strongly suggest you not let your daughter down there."

"Well, if you're that worried, I'll ping a message down for them to hurry up."

"Please do. They really resent the tourists. I realize that's partly my fault. We're juggling the additional income with the need to keep perceptions clean. They see billionaires playing. The guests see mining trash." That was probably the wrong term to use. "It's a perception. I'm still trying to come up with some way to clear it up. It's not easy."

"I understand," Bryan said. "I'll tell them to cut it short. We can gradually increase presence and try to offer better incentives as we go."

Joe stifled a sigh, and kept it quiet. That was one potential disaster averted.

Assuming they got her out of there before anything broke loose.

He needed to get things organized better or it was going to blow up. It wasn't just the status issue and money. The hidden investors would want a return shortly. Joe had to juggle all three groups. Preferably without violence.

✧ ✧ ✧

Horace found the tour fascinating. He'd seen diamond mines at a distance. This was far different. For one, they were about as deep as the deepest mines on Earth, and still only halfway down. The facility was effectively a space habitat, connected to the surface by crawlers instead of ships. It made sense. Why transport material when most of it was slag?

The current demonstration wasn't really directly involved with pulling ore from the hole. This was slightly more technical, a lot cleaner, and inside a pressurized area. Still, there was a lot of heavy equipment and a lot of dust. Even after vacuum washing, the crushed and sorted ore spit off particles as it jostled along the belts. Then, there was some oxidized slag in the air, palpable to the nose, eyes and tongue. The smelter wasn't that close, but it fed continuously and had an opening. Vapor and particles did escape. Outside atmosphere leaked in.

What came in from the mine was slurried and dried, though it often had chunks of ice mixed in. A dizzying mix of conveyors and trucks hauled it from the pit a mountain-depth below, in soup-thick noxious atmosphere at triple surface pressure. Dumped here, it chuted in and began its process to ingots.

Their guide, Operations Officer Monique Gisaud, said, "The choke points are here, where we can't process fast enough, but we're working on third smelter. Another is our own drawing mill that is running nonstop to produce the stock we need on site. Of course, there's a limit on transport as well."

Caron nodded acknowledgement, but gave most of her attention to the data on her screen.

Looking up for a moment, she said, "I'm going to recommend relocating another thousand meters down. I think that will optimize tailing and material transport time and costs. If we get below twelve K, we'll need to move again. Ideally I'd want three smelters for a pit this wide, but it's just not viable, given the personnel transport."

Gisaud looked partly pleased and partly put upon.

"Moving will hinder us in the meantime," she said.

"Oh, I'll have a new one built, then transfer this as components elsewhere. I think we can use modular systems. They might be a little tight, but they'll be safer and quicker."

"That sounds workable, madame."

"Are you sure? I value your input."

"I'm sure. The downtime was my concern."

"I'll make sure you have the resources you need to maintain production. I recall you get a bonus based on overage?"

"Yes, madame." Gisaud looked faintly embarrassed. She hadn't raised the money issue, but it was something Horace assumed she was concerned about.

"I'd like to see some of the workers in the area. When do you break for lunch?"

"We take three shifts from eleven hundred to thirteen hundred."

"That's soon, then."

Horace saw the signal from Alex, and nodded. Closer protection. He shifted slightly and took a step, which put him off her left quarter and in a solid blocking position.

A chime indicated the first lunch break, and a few minutes later several men came in. They shook off cold, banged off dust, and peeled off masks, hardhats and gloves. The stench of atmosphere vented from their coveralls.

They noticed their VIPs at once, and glanced over. In seconds, they recognized who Caron must be, and stiffened perceptibly.

"Oh, please relax and sit," she said. "This is informal, and I'm just trying to get a feel for things."

Horace figured they wouldn't relax much while she was flanked by Bart and Aramis.

Caron asked, "How's the weather outside?"

One of them, a slightly round-faced Hispanic, said, "It's about five degrees today. Not bad when dressed. There is a lot of mist, though, from the air and the machines. Damp."

"Do waterproof clothes help?" she asked.

He shrugged. "Not really. You get sweaty and damp inside anyway. Unless there's actual rain, it's not worth it."

"How's safety?"

"The safety equipment is good, but..."

"Yes?" she prodded.

He looked around, very hesitant, but got some kind of signal from the others.

"We need longer breaks. Minor injuries happen that shouldn't. It's a long way to carry someone out, and it interrupts vehicle traffic."

"I'll note that," she said. "That's important."

Intelligent questions, Horace decided, but he couldn't help but notice she hadn't asked his name and didn't really pay attention to body language. Perhaps he should suggest some observation training manuals. There were various reasons possible, but this man didn't want to talk to her, and the rest were actively snubbing her.

Elke was at the back. Everyone was busy paying attention to Caron. She shuffled back into a hallway that led to the toilets, and went snooping.

Yes, they did store some explosive here. There was a logbook, paper type. That indicated either power was unreliable, or some kind of problem with the network. Still, it suited her needs. She picked a handful of caps, some receivers, two blocks of Orbitol and some placer clips. They slid into her pack, it went back onto her shoulders, and she signed an illegible scrawl with barely readable item numbers from the labels. Stuff got used all the time, and with three shifts, no one should know who did it, or even question it.

From there, she stepped into the toilet for a moment, as cover, then back out.

As she oozed back into formation, she felt a ping, checked the message as it displayed on her glasses, and muttered to Jason, "We've been told to hurry her out of here."

"Understood," he agreed.

It didn't seem like a bad idea. The miners didn't seem actively hostile, but certainly generally belligerent and put upon. They certainly weren't impressed or pleased with her visit. That was a bit odd, given the circumstances. Obviously things weren't happy down here.

The spokesman was saying, "—very hard work and very long hours."

Caron nodded. "At least you get to send most of your wages home, though," she said. "That's one of the benefits of the operation."

The man looked at her very oddly. Elke wondered if she'd have to step in, but it didn't seem a precursor to anything. He just seemed to not be sure what he was hearing.

She wondered about that exchange as they left. The place didn't feel of Company Store, and the prices she'd seen were very moderate, given the lift cost from Earth, or production cost locally. They had a lot of free perks. The wages were supposed to be on par with the big mines on Earth on top of all the benefits.

Elke surmised it was a combination of not enough women, too long hours, and being cooped up inside constantly. The endless dreariness would take a toll like that of combat, only more gradual and insidious, and with no relief until departure. It was common with support troops in austere locations, and this was a similar environment.

That was something to consider, and to mention to Alex to mention to Mr. Prescot. These types of men might not admit it, but a garden and sunroom and possibly an occasional campfire would do wonders for morale.

She swapped signs with Jason, and then said, "Well, I hate to be rude, but Miss Prescot is on a tight schedule. Would you excuse us please?"

Caron said, "Oh, of course. I do apologize. Thank you all very much for talking to me."

Jason nodded to Elke's sign, and he and Bart took up the rear and created a solid wall.

As they passed through the pressure hatch to their transporter, Caron looked over.

"What was that about?" she asked.

"Your father messaged us to hurry back."

"I hope things are well," she said. Then she looked over again. "How did he message you?"

Elke turned to show the glasses.

"Ballistic proof, translucent and corner image projection, realtime from various feeds and polarized against blinding attacks. State of the art and not cheap."

"Very nice. Those are company issue?"

"These are mine," Elke told her. "They issue something similar, but I prefer not to share and not to need to ask."

"Those could have great use in our space facilities and while blasting."

"I believe they're in use for that."

Caron sighed. "I really need more hands on. I've learned all the math and theory. I need to see how things actually work. That's why I was down here."

"It's going to take a while to fit in and to learn. That's a problem executives always have with the root level employees."

"Yes, and I don't like it."

✧ ✧ ✧

Pacal smiled politely as Senorita Prescot and her guards left, then grunted and spat. Gisaud was taking her lunch in the office at the rear. Typical.

"That was strange," he said.

Binban was agitated himself. He'd controlled it well until now, Pacal thought.

"It's more than strange. She comes down here made up and in brand new coveralls, talks about the work as if she's doing any, and so very gently asks about the working conditions. What a bitch."

Ahmad said, "She is a beautiful woman, but without much clue."

Once started, Binban vented.

"Her security costs fifty thousand marks a day. A *day*. For what? Why do they think it's necessary?"

Bheka said, "She must face some threats."

"Who'd do anything? They'd be easily identified and found. With that much money, they could make someone disappear just like they were never born. If they didn't have all that money, they wouldn't have to worry, either. Pure greed."

Ahmad was a generous man, and slow to anger. "They come from more expensive areas than we," he said.

"Ahmad, her guards earn more in an hour than we do in a month. She has several. There are others for the men and assigned to the port."

Ahmad hesitated.

"Not even Japan or Germany are so expensive," he said.

"No, of course not. They get paid and they rub our faces in it."

Pacal said, "We must remain calm."

"Calm? We should be striking!"

"I have discussed that," Pacal said, keeping his voice very soothing. They all spoke good Basic English as a common tongue. He wished he could use Spanish to offer more elegance. "We can't do that yet. Soon, I hear."

"Really? Is your friend reliable, now that he no longer mines?"

"He is. Also, as a Canadian, he is from a similar culture. I trust him on how they think and work. He will tell us when."

"It must be very soon. I get tired of being told soon."

"It will be. There are offers that will affect management and help us. Be patient a little more."

✧ ✧ ✧

Caron dictated and hand corrected her notes on the trip. The miners were definitely a bit frustrated. Elke's idea seemed so girly for her, but it was a good one. She suggested some "natural" environment, though it would have to be fake. The suggestion for better emergency response definitely needed followup, but someone would have to do a study on times, cost benefit and types of response needed to make it work.

It had been a busy day, and now she had a date. With armed chaperones. She clouded up and kept her growl silent.

CHAPTER 19

Jason entered the lobby and nodded to Roger Edge.

"Going in to see Mr. Prescot for negotiation over gear."

"Yup, Alex briefed me. Do you really need that for show and tell?" He indicated the case Jason carried, that he knew contained a weapon.

"I do."

Edge raised his eyebrows.

"Well, company covers me, and Alex has the rank for this op, so okay."

"Thanks. Trust me on this one."

"You realize that was the worst thing you could say, right?"

"Of course."

The receptionist didn't pick up on the cues, but gestured for Jason to let himself in.

He did so. Bryan Prescot's office was large enough for small conferences, had a great, top floor corner view out a sweeping arc of invisible window almost against the dome. Anyone talking to Prescot had to take in that awesome, intimidating view. *Well done,* he thought. It would be more useful on Earth, but it worked well enough here.

"How can I help you, Jason?" Prescot asked with moderate geniality.

Jason got to the point, and opened the bag.

"Sir, this is the one actual firearm we have. It fires rounds for breaching doors—hinges, locks and such."

"Yes. I know about them in theory."

"Engineer to engineer, may I summarize?"

"Yes."

"Thanks. There is no such thing as a weapon powerful enough to stop an opponent that won't go through an opponent, if we're talking projectiles. That's one. Point two is that known nonlethal weapons do not carry the same deterrent effect. They're fine against normally well-behaved people who might step out of line in a heated moment. They're no good against determined professionals, or sociopaths, either of which might be hired to come after Caron. I understand your concerns about the dome, but it's designed to take impacts considerably more intense than this."

"I understand the theory. My concern is a point blank hit that could damage a panel. Even a small leak would be significantly bad, if only from a PR point of view."

"Of course," Jason said. He casually swung the weapon, raised it level and fired.

The report echoed in the glassed room, seeming to bound from every surface, like very close thunder.

Prescot threw himself back and down. His reflexes were certainly adequate, Jason thought. He was down before Edge made it through the door. Jason pointed at the window, the weapon and nodded. Edge shrugged and backed out.

Then Prescot stood, his face furious.

Jason calmly said, "Allow me to point out the office glass isn't even dimpled. The dome is about forty times as strong. It will take a lot more than small arms fire to puncture it." He hadn't looked at the material as he shot and didn't look now. That added to the effect, he hoped. He knew intellectually there wasn't a scratch on it. It would be neat to see, however.

Prescot looked *angry* now. "I can have you on a flight out of here in minutes, Mr. Vaughn."

"You hired me for my expertise, sir. I'm giving you that. You want the best safety for your daughter, yourself and your operation, and I'm telling you how to accomplish that. I will never question your mining expertise. Please don't question mine regarding weapons."

Prescot was still rubbing his ears. He sat carefully in his chair.

"Do you drink, Mr. Vaughn?"

"I do, in great moderation. If you are offering I will take one and one only today."

Prescot pointed at a well-stocked bar. "Would you like Grainnean whisky or American bourbon?"

Jason looked at the rack and said, "If that's Elijah Craig I greatly enjoy it. It's hard to get on Grainne." He kept the formal, professional wall up.

Prescot nodded, rose and turned, and was silent while he poured two glasses neat. His own was a double. Jason's was a single. Prescot placed them down on coasters, took a breath and seemed to steady out, and resumed talking.

"One of the problems I suffer from is that I always get my own way. It's easy for me to insulate myself from just about anything. Even when I'm wrong."

That was the lead Jason wanted.

"That's not specific to money or power, sir. It's very common, and I think it's human nature. We want to trust ourselves first, because even if our knowledge is incomplete, it's ours."

"That's probably it. In any case, I do need to trust the experts I am paying.

"At the same time," he continued, "I both respect and fear your zealous reputation. I want my daughter kept safe, but collateral damage is worse than the money to fix it."

Jason realized he was referring to one of their earliest and most controversial missions, around President Bishwanath of Celadon. The collateral damage had been rather large, and Elke had certainly done her best to ensure so. *Hell, so did I,* he thought. Then there was that thug he'd tossed into the rear of the limo on Earth. A confirmed threat, yes, but still rather visible. But hell, he was paid to be a trouble shooter, not a trouble analyzer.

"This isn't a war zone, sir. Nor are you going to abandon us. Celadon was a specific set of circumstances. Until that point, we'd handled everything through planning and trained reactions with almost no shooting."

"I don't trust many people, Mr. Vaughn. I can't. I don't need to explain why. However, I am convinced I can trust you. Please give me a list of what you need, and I will have it delivered promptly."

"Thank you, sir. I appreciate the trust."

"Please bring the list to me personally and discreetly. I don't plan to deny anything, but it's much easier to prevent trouble if there's no publicity, and I have no idea if I can trust anyone else at this point."

"I sympathize, sir. Caron's suffering from a lot of the same fallout. I'll bring it personally tomorrow during a briefing."

"Thank you. Ten o'clock, please. And no matter what happens, please continue to ensure my daughter is safe. Her safety comes above collateral damage, random death, or even my own."

"We'll maintain our vigilance, sir. You have all our words."

He saw that Prescot was finishing his own drink, so he set his empty glass down firmly but politely on the cork coaster. Real cork. Where the hell did *that* come from these days?

"Have a good day, sir," he said, and rose slowly.

"And you, Mr. Vaughn." Prescot smiled at last. "I'll look for your list."

"Thank you, sir."

That went okay, Jason thought. Yes, the demonstration had been graphic, but it needed to be, and no one else was willing to make the play. One of the good things about Ripple Creek was it did back its people to the hilt. He'd never have made that play with any other employer. This one expected the extreme, though.

He walked through the door to their common room with a relaxed but jaunty air that was completely fake, but added to the effect, he thought.

"Guys, I need a list of everything we need as far as weapons."

Aramis looked axed. "Don't tell me he said 'yes.'"

"He said 'maybe' with a partial 'yes.'"

"How the hell did you manage that?"

"A little man-to-man talk. We both have daughters we care very much about. I approached it that way."

Elke handed him a paper sheet with a list of explosives on it in small, clear type. She had her list ready, of course. He suspected she updated it hourly. Well, at least daily.

Aramis turned and started scrawling fast. Bart was slower and more cautious. Jason expected it would be easy to read his, and not Aramis's.

Alex said, "Standard pistol and carbine should do me."

"Likewise," agreed Shaman.

Jason said, "So we'll ask for a platoon's worth of support gear, and negotiate down to what we need and then some."

"I am surprised," Alex said, "that no one has a hide out."

"But sir," Aramis said, "that would violate the terms of our contract."

"Remember that," he said. "And don't get caught violating it."

That was a pretty broad hint, all things considered.

Aramis wondered why he kept drawing duty at times like this. The scenery was beautiful, but distracting. It wasn't intentional masochism, and he hoped he'd get used to the idea sooner or later. Later seemed to be his only hope.

For her dinner party, Caron wore a basic black gown that had silver accents. For once she wasn't wearing a bodice, and looked much relieved. Her boobs were not quite as dramatically framed, but she still had plenty of shape in the snug top with the skirt streaming in pleats.

Elke escorted the young men in, and looked scorching herself. Aramis was surprised. He knew Elke was healthy and attractive under her façade. She used it on occasion, and he'd seen her naked five and a half times. However, that gown, black at the hem, shading through violet to turquoise at the right shoulder, as it had no left, did amazing things to her. Was she dressed to match their principal? Or jealous? Or just wanted an excuse to spend tax deductible money? He had no idea about her social life.

The only downside was the blatant gun belt and stunner.

"This is Madya Vyas and Eric McDaniel," she announced.

Aramis felt almost cruel now, but rules were rules.

"I'm going to search you," he said to the men, and did so at once without any further foreplay.

They looked a bit violated when he was done. Wealthy scions on ski trips did not get patted down by thugs for hire before having dinner.

Caron looked slightly put upon, but he could read amusement, too. This was the life she led now.

She smiled and faintly shrugged, then walked over and took their hands.

"Sit, please," she said.

Aramis retreated to the far end of the room. Elke took the near corner. He blended into the background and they were able to relax a little. They'd presumably been at other parties with bodyguards, though probably not this high profile.

She was much more courteous to Aramis than she had been

before. She had a second tray of hors d'oeuvres and dished some onto a plate which she slipped on the counter near him with a friendly smile. The miniature sausage rolls he'd smelled earlier.

Aramis watched her, and watched them. Her smile was genuine and she did have a good time. They ate and chatted, and looked at the swirls and the mine as she pointed things out. They looked pleased, and interested, and impressed by the attention and the details and Caron herself.

Pity, Aramis thought, that there was probably less than one chance in a thousand they'd get more than they had so far.

Elke was closer and had the same professionally bored expression he had as she watched the event. They made eye contact once or twice, and she was open, but with that blank expression she had when thinking. He wondered again why she'd shopped up. Trying for distraction? Attention? No matter.

The three ate and chatted and ignored the video wall with its music and scenes. Caron seemed reluctant to let them go, but it was at the point where she either chased them out or sat in uncomfortable silence.

She offered them each a contact code, unhurriedly moved them to the door, and kissed them lightly before Elke took them back down the hall.

Caron gave Aramis a look of part sadness and part poison and headed into her room.

CHAPTER 20

Caron's office was in the building next to her father's, for dispersal, where she worked on production schedules and energy expenditures. While an office adjoining her apartment would be safer, it was also a smart idea to have a separate work location to avoid burning out. Alex didn't mind. Her schedule was her own and not too predictable. There were three ways out of her controlled area, and four to here. Cady's team swept them irregularly but frequently, and she had three or four of the team escort her every day. He was always here when she was, and right now, Horace and Elke were across the room.

What an office, though. Another great view out the dome, this time of the old mine and the mountain where the ski dome was. The carpet was thick and brown, the walls in tan and cream swirls and the furniture very comfortable. Too comfortable. He had to stand and walk around regularly to avoid dozing off, but the size of the office meant that was possible without disturbing her. They had a small kitchen and an emergency O_2 supply, with sensors for everything all around. To keep busy he would keep her provided with tea and other amenities. He didn't have to, but it kept him alert to her condition and what else would he do? No servants would be allowed to serve her. It was one of the ironies of her wealth that she would not have servants for such tasks.

The Prescots didn't really pay much attention to sales, only to production. They could produce more refined raw material than anyone, and ship it anywhere. As long as they maximized their efficiency, they could sell it anywhere and make an ongoing huge profit. The law firm they owned dealt with the intellectual property and licensing, and they allowed the technology use for colonial and frontier development, cheap to start with, the rates increasing as the industrial base of a system increased to where it could reasonably afford to buy directly. They'd almost literally found a way to mine money.

The next morning, Caron checked her reports, sipped tea while furrowing her brow and tracking the news, which was only hours old, the company being able to afford a shunt through the Jump Point for that purpose, and scanned a few other updates.

"Alex, I have a note from my father. One of us needs to go take a quick tour of space systems, just to show the flag as it were, and get familiar."

"I presume you're the choice?"

"If you don't have any serious objections."

"I will arrange protection anywhere. I can't and won't try to keep you locked up, even though that would be easier, so I will work a detail to your schedule."

"Thanks. I'll try to arrange for it to be quick."

"Take your time."

Actually, he thought, that was a little easier. Sabotage could happen anywhere. They had backups for that, and aboard a ship, they had one hundred percent accountability of personnel. No one could swim up through space. Though they could certainly commit sabotage.

"Would it help to leave quickly?" she asked.

"Yes."

"I can leave in an hour. Please plan whatever you need to and I'll adapt."

"Jason will pilot, Elke as backup because of her technical skills, Aramis as muscle as far as the dock. I believe one of the command shuttles holds four comfortably." He was quite used to these decisions, but always felt a tinge of doubt. He couldn't always send everyone, though.

"Great," she said. "You seem to know quite a lot about our operations already," she commented.

"That's my job, miss."

"As long as it's not an inconvenience," she said.

Elke stepped over. "Not at all," she said. "I would enjoy some travel. I'll get you some things." She left.

Shortly she returned with a basic black bag with a few wrinkleless business clothes and a personal kit that mostly held Caron's static hair brushes. She rarely wore makeup and didn't need to.

Alex saw a message flash. "I see Jason is already at the ship," he said.

Elke was ready, too, and Aramis buzzed that he was arriving.

A short walk and mini limo ride put Caron and her guards into a private cabin on a shuttle up to the station. With that done, Alex had a minor break from the ongoing schedule juggling, and only needed to worry about potential threats to her apartment, and coordination for her return.

Horace found the casinos interesting. Not that he'd ever spend money in them. Only Aramis did, and he in moderation. The rest of the team knew the odds and didn't care to lose money at such trivial endeavors. Jason had tried poker and deemed the table fair, with the warning, "If you don't match the average buy in, you're starting with a handicap." The minimum buy in was a hundred, the average around five thousand, the table limits fifty thousand. Per hand.

Caron didn't play, of course. She'd be winning or losing money to herself, and what was the point of that? Nor was even fifty thousand enough to even register on her wealth, even if her allowance, well, salary now, wasn't that impressive. Bryan Prescot was trying to raise her properly. She had a professional income, against which her living expenses were deducted for tax purposes, as if it mattered a damn. Still, it was a good habit.

Horace liked the lights, the sound, the brisk but silent ventilation system that allowed for the smoking of tobacco, hash or flavored leaves, without any clouds or residue to disturb people. The floors were laid out in sections of different types of games, coordinated down to the carpet, paint and illumination. The tables started at expensive and went skyward. The croupiers were all at least moderately attractive, professional and experienced, and well paid. As the castes went, they were fairly high. Tourists not only had to but enjoyed talking to them. Below executive, but above servant.

Horace wasn't sure why he classed people like that. It was

more an Indian thing than African. Perhaps a habit picked up in Celadon? Except it wasn't casted the same way, and he hadn't been there long.

Something about that, though, gave him pause. There were castes here. The Prescots were royalty. He was a Lifeguard. The executives were nobles. The casino and hotel and restaurant staff counted as servants to them. The mine management and facility management were similar. The housekeepers, servers and cooks were menials, but domestic. They rated with the mine managers. Below them were the technical staff, and below that, the laborers. It seemed to work, probably because of the physical barriers between the groups. He imagined there would be mayhem if they were mingled.

What he did do in the casinos was enjoy the restaurants and shows. There were ladies, far too classy to be called mere strippers, who could genuinely dance, and do so erotically, while wearing clothes. There was fine food and real liquor and wine, though he took those sparingly. He even enjoyed a cigar once. He was going to avoid the habit. All of it was a perk of the assignment, covered on an encoded card faced in real gold. He had only to flash it and be seated and treated as royalty himself. He'd done so twice, just to see what the experience was like, then reverted to waiting in line as a courtesy to others. The lines were never allowed to be long, anyway. There were top-rate musicians and plays rotating through, and when schedules permitted he would catch those, too. He made sure to tip the servers and hosts. They made note of it and always treated him well, even more so than the status of the card.

Tonight he sought a steak. That was easy enough. He could almost afford the hundred marks a steak cost here, plus salad and drink and ancillary items that became a M200 meal for one. Thanks to the card, he didn't have to.

He approached THE Grill, a presumptuous name if there ever was one, but it actually was about the best he'd ever experienced.

"Good evening, Mr. Mbuto," Keti greeted him at once with a toothy smile. She was a pocket sized Ghanian and cute and lovely, and he'd never risk a liaison with anyone here, even if she clearly did appreciate him for himself.

"It is a good evening, Keti," he said. "Or so the clocks tell me. The dome says it's early morning."

"It does?" she said. "Working in the casino means I don't get to see that often." She led him smoothly toward a table overlooking the doors. Good, she remembered his preferences.

"Ah, true," he said. The light traffic indicated a weekday evening. The glint at a low angle through the doors across the casino from here indicated early local morning. These things were obvious to him. He had to remind himself not everyone was a trained observer.

She touched the chair, and he sat.

"As usual," he said.

"Ribeye medium, potato with everything, salad with sesame ginger, wheat rolls, wheat beer and water," she said.

"Thank you," he confirmed. Then he admired the view from behind as she bustled away.

It was good to relax. He didn't need elaborate measures, just a good meal, and then perhaps a game of billiards and to listen to whatever musician was in the lower lounge.

Apart from the challenge of the job, the opportunity to experience so many interesting things was what made it so enjoyable. After that was the mere money.

Though, to be honest, there was little enough here not available elsewhere. That it was covered by a dome was a gimmick, really. Joe Prescot made this work; the investment was well into the black. It was far less relevant than the mine, but it was an efficient secondary stream. The man could pinch a penny until it screamed.

The steak was incomparable, and subtly different from the previous one. The chefs were world class, and paid to travel here. Yet Joe made it profitable. A desolate, uninhabitable, gas-swirled rock, turned into a resort. Horace supposed it fit in with the Dome on K2 in the Himalayas, and the Ice Palace in the Canadian high Arctic. Similar in scope, but even more remote, more stark and thus more desirable to those with money to burn. For those not interested in hunting dangerous predators in Grainne's remote corners, this was likely the acme of decadence.

He marked a tip on the screen and let it cycle through his account.

"Thank you once again, Keti," he said as he rose. "I'm sure I'll return."

"You're most welcome, Mr. Mbuto," she said with an iridescent grin and a nodding bow.

Horace didn't want to loiter this evening. There were striking women and men on display, in areas marked so those with moral objections could steer around them. That was largely a farce. Not even the most devout Muslim came here for any reason other than fleshpots. With the cheapest excursion at least 200,000 marks, modesty wasn't a consideration for any of the tourists.

As he exited the directional glare of THE Hotel to a walkway, he heard a familiar hum. Security Officer Sauers slid by on his skateboard.

"Mr. Mbuto," the man nodded genially, looking oddly relaxed. He had exceptional balance.

"Mr. Sauers," he returned.

The skateboard was a good idea for saving legs walking, and probably faster for a response, though it wouldn't work on broken ground. However, it would be easy to hop off at a run in that case. In the meantime, it drew attention to him, and gave him a distinct image, both useful for a mundane peacekeeper. Not a bad idea at all, he thought.

He wouldn't mention it to Jason. The man would probably create one with a motor that would turn wheelies.

He smiled at the thought as he returned to his quarters. He could relax there more than here, where he must monitor and analyze every movement.

So many enticements, if he were younger. The water park that was an indoor beach, with sand and pressure-generated waves that allowed limited surfing, swimming, real fish in the water, slides and flumes and a massive UV light bank that simulated the sun rather well. The surface excursions. Already, several billionaires were building remote domes on clifftops, with views of the rocky, ochre landscape and winds. There was a sandy desert east of here, with huge dunes. There was talk of dune surfing and rally racing there. A lifeless rock, but humans could turn it into an exotic playground.

Horace decided the casino and its less extreme diversions were plenty for him.

Jason was happy with how smoothly the trip went, though he always wondered if that meant a pending disaster.

They went down to the dock with the others. Cady's men Lionel and Marlin, tall, black, muscular and intimidating, were on patrol down there, with polite, professional nods as he came through with Caron. The shuttle had a relief pilot to return it to the surface, and the man showed company ID and code as they approached. Jason knew his name. Jeremy Steel had decades flying for Space Force and Army, and was another person who lived for the challenge rather than the money. He shook hands with Jason and Elke, nodded to Miss Caron—no one other than her personals were allowed to touch her—and invited them in.

"Get comfortable," he said. "There's no real schedule since we get to set it." He sounded amused. His voice was younger than his age, but so was his physique. Fitness was mandatory for what was effectively a contract military.

The four strapped in quickly. The shuttle was not only nice, it was new.

Steel must have noticed them sniffing and touching.

"Yeah, brand new, state of the art, and I was one of the pilots who consulted on this new control system."

"How do you like it?"

"It's good. Now. They were a bit slow on the uptake. It started out as a passenger package, but it's on par with good military stuff now, and more recent."

"I'd like to take a look once we're lifted."

"Sure. Launching now." He then spoke to Control. "Canyon Three on priority. Lifting soonest. Roger. Lifting."

He boosted the engines and they were out of the hangar at once, into atmosphere and rising fast.

Jason moved up as soon as they were in steady flight, slid into the second seat and examined the controls. Yes, very modern, mostly easy to read, though that planetside compass did have annoying controls to try to synch it. Still, he could fly it if he had to.

"That's all I need, Jeremy. I'll try to get a proper class later."

"Yup, just ignore the compass and use sat if you can. If it comes down to that you're already in a combat environment."

"I hope that won't happen in the next few minutes." He moved aft as he spoke and took his original seat. "Fastened."

Steel said, "Roger."

He took them into orbit fast, intercepting the station on its current orbit rather than waiting for the next. They were there in twenty minutes and docking took less than five.

This was a private station for family, executives and the more wealthy guests—sheiks, Fortune 50 CEOs, princes, and others. It was always lightly traveled, and was empty at present, with three ships politely waiting.

They transferred through an empty bay, into the small craft, which was guarded and had an external inspection by two more of Cady's people. They weren't getting much action, but they got lots of work to keep them busy. Most of it was strictly cover, but it was still work. Jason preferred his own tasks. He'd prefer them more once they were away from the station and harder to locate or hit.

Joe was only too glad for Caron to take that trip. That meant fewer snoopy questions, since his brother was not the type to go down into the mine. Or rather, he was, but was easily distracted with more paperwork. That couldn't go on forever, but it didn't need to.

He really hoped her guards were as good as reputed. He didn't want anything to happen to her on this trip, nothing at all suspicious. The longer she was occupied, the better. He didn't like the potential threats because they interfered with business, and his plans.

He had to hold things from coming apart just a bit longer.

The payoff was huge, and the family would benefit from it. It wasn't even unethical. Being rich did not create an obligation to anything other than providing honest jobs to people. Nor was anyone entitled to a chunk of the wealth merely because they'd graced the world with their presence. That was Prescot money and they'd worked hard for it. He had an obligation to see that through. His brother could play the nice side, he'd be the tough side.

In the meantime, he'd keep pressing for Bryan and Caron to stick to the engineering side of things and let him manage the business aspects. That would be best all around. The problem was making the man believe it. He hoped to do that soon. A family fight over that kind of money would get ugly. Not that it would come to that. A peaceful resolution would be best at this point.

So, what could he do, who could he call to keep them busy up there?

He did a quick analysis. Travel time, and say a day there, and another day. It might be enough. No need for false delays, just a good tour with lots of detail.

Bryan had to be convinced that Joe was the right person for Govannon, as he was the right person for Earth. Caron could do as she wished. He'd run things and ease her into his style of management. Or else he'd send her home.

It was very aggravating. What he was doing was all legal, perfectly moral, but his brother would take it the wrong way. Bryan knew mining. He didn't understand economics. The resort was a small moneymaker, but it was also a massive political ally, with all the connected playboys coming out. As long as they had their fleshpots, Govannon would remain open, no matter how many greenies complained. Bryan was just too straightlaced to accept booze and hookers as business tools.

Joe sighed. He'd keep applying pressure until they had a proper division of labor.

The boat could actually drive around the star's gravity well. Big engines and tanks, hot exhaust and no concerns about money. Eventually, all craft would have that capability.

Jason was concerned about external control, though, so he had all the interlocks pulled and labeled. If need be, anyone could reinsert them in seconds. Until then, he was the only person who had control over the ship. He had a Ripple Creek-provided sealed astrogation unit to doublecheck against the ship's. He wasn't going to allow the chance of any accidents.

Even given that kind of power, it was a week of nothing to get a few hours on site at each of several spots in the immediate system.

The boat was comfortable enough, though. He and Elke each had a small cabin with bunk, stowage and a standard micro G shower stall, with upgraded flow and recycling. Caron had the owner's stateroom, which was a little bigger. The galley had prepacked food that just needed to be heated, all sealed and easily inspected by Elke. Cady's team had loaded that for them.

It took two days to examine two orbital stations, even though they were in low orbits, because maneuvering took time. There was little enough to see, but the staff were delighted with Caron and seemed genuinely pleased she took notice of them. Typical PR stuff, but worthwhile. After that, it was two more days to the gem of the system.

Govannon's L1 point contained the smelters for all the space mining. Or perhaps "harvesting" was a better word. Planetoids were slung in from outsystem, or out from scorching orbits near the star, with either nuclear charges or slow ion rockets, queued up and fed in front of massive mirrors. There they were melted and stratified, and then careful localized heating blew off most of the slag. The resulting spheres of high grade ore were loaded onto a gravity whip—a ten-thousand-kilometer-long, rotating cable with a counterbalance that flung them toward the Jump Point. Rudimentary engines were attached en route by a crew in a bus-sized module, who saw them through to Sol, then returned once ferry crews took over. It wasn't as fast as a direct-driven ship, but fast enough for the mass of ore being shipped.

"That's more efficient," Elke said. "Though I estimate only five percent as much metal exists out here."

"Actually about six point three, relatively high, but yes," Caron said. "When it's gone, it's gone, but it's easy to get to, just time consuming."

"Obviously, this is not a low paying enterprise."

"No, everyone here is a trained, professional deep space operator cross trained for at least two jobs. Most have metallurgical training, and a background in materials science, smelting or mechanical engineering. Some are process control experts, and of course we need some optical scientists for the mirrors."

Jason said, "I have the personnel manifest here, with credentials."

"They're a much lower threat to me," Caron said.

"I disagree. They're highly intelligent, motivated, used to problem solving, willing to work hard in dangerous environments for a commensurate pay scale. They're the ones I trust least. They can actually conceptually grasp how much money you have."

"Oh, damn you," Caron snapped.

"One of the miners might take a swing or a shot at you. That's easy to anticipate, deal with, respond to. An interested scientist might tinker with your atmosphere, ship, food, and might do so from a distance via proxy and remote operation. Knowledge is power, and threat."

"I understand, but dammit, does everyone have to be under a cloud of suspicion? Don't answer, I know." She sighed and shook her head.

"That threat is reduced by the fact that they won't encounter you much. Opportunistic attacks are unlikely. But this trip was at least somewhat promoted."

"Sort of. My uncle is cheap and obsessive. He wants to make sure we keep eyes on all the activities against potential theft, embezzlement or fraud. But it's also a good idea for us to know how things work first hand. We've been mostly isolated. We have staff we trust, but the boss does have to visit the mine now and then."

"Yeah, I don't have a moral problem being here, and protecting you is what we were hired for, so we'll do it."

Elke said, "I appreciate being along. Seeing large power applications is fascinating."

She'd been staring out the port and on screen for most of the approach, though she kept her professional radar alert for anything that might affect Caron. Of course, anything that affected her at this point would almost certainly affect all three of them. Other than making sure they all had emergency oxygen on shoulder mounts, though, there wasn't much else to do that hadn't already been done.

Jason took another look himself. The massive arcs of the mirrors were painfully bright, and a boiling nimbus of white-hot ore floated between them, held in place by light pressure and venting gas as the ore melt sat in equilibrium. A five-hundred-meter, four-hundred-million-tonne sphere of molten, half-smelted metal was enough to be a weapon of itself.

Alex made use of the time Caron was gone. It wasn't down time, per se. It was time to do another assessment of the facility and threats.

Cady came by, still in her traditional suit, with summaries and data that were easy to read.

"There's a low level of RF activity that might be surveillance. Of course, that could also be industrial espionage, which isn't really our thing, though of course I'll report it if I confirm, but I don't want to mention it early in case I scare someone into being more cautious."

"Correct," Alex agreed. "Threats first, business second. That's understood by all parties."

"Good. Now, my other concern is predictability, and that the private areas do lend themselves to directional mines."

"Elke checks that whenever she can."

"So does Marlin, my bomb tech. It's still a concern."

"Absolutely. And we have a certain amount of unavoidable predictability."

"Yes, which is why I've suggested another garage exit. It will be exit only, which reduces the potential exploitation of it the other way."

"Fair enough. I can get behind that."

Cady stretched back, sat forward again, and pulled another screen. "So let's talk about who the threats are."

"Well, we have seven official strata of personnel here—castes, if you will—from menial workers and unskilled miners up to tourists, the family and us."

"Yes, but I don't see any particular level as significant. The miners have sheer numbers. The tourists have money. We have access. The only family member with an outside interest is the mother. We have her watched. The uncle, father and daughter are all right here. Though Joe's Ex Ek security are a bit of bother to me. They're not us."

"Hell, Jace, I don't trust even us." He grinned at the irony. "And they don't get near the rest of us. From a dispassionate point of view, no big deal if the uncle goes down. He doesn't affect Caron's stock or inheritance, and he's a meddling twit. Though losing him would mean her father would be more of a target, or her. So I hope they're good enough to keep him safe."

"I agree, but we still have to keep a sidebar on him, and interact with his personals."

"How are they? I've barely encountered them in passing."

"They'll do a professional job of stopping bullets, and they're alert and attentive for tangible threats. I can't offer more observations than that. Their reputation is of course decent, though not in our league."

"We might be the best."

"Our paychecks say so. It's just one thing to keep in mind."

"So what about threat levels here and on Earth?"

"Nothing on Earth. I wondered about someone wanting to kidnap the mother, but no one seems to care much for her, so if they do, it's not an immediate threat to anyone we have contracts on. I've suggested she be given a second level of protection. That one retainer she has isn't much of anything but a lackey."

"I noticed that."

"But there's been nothing on Earth and nothing here."

"And I still maintain that all the activity on Earth was to drive us here."

"I agree. There are no indications of anything, though."

"So, our job is to assume a threat, and assume it's going to be very well planned and high tech. Then we hope we're wrong."

"Atmosphere is the most logical. With surgeons and EMTs all around, body armor, personal guards and all the other crap, getting close and shooting her, or him, is unlikely."

"Yes, though possible. We'll up our armor standards."

"Since we can, yes. I've arranged for delivery of those items you and Jason requested. They're located in these three positions." She pointed to a map and spun it through three dimensions. One in the upper mine control, one in the tower they were in, one on the far side of the dome.

"Hopefully we won't need them, but thanks very much."

"Otherwise, I've arranged for extra masks, filters and bottled breathing mix, in bottles I've personally inspected and seen the images of, to be stored in various places with coded seals. If any of those seals gets tampered with, we scream."

"Yes, absolutely." He checked over the list. "That's everywhere I'd have spares. Well done."

"A great mind thinks alike."

"So let's do some inspections, and on with the war."

Elke was absolutely overwhelmed by the EVA.

She didn't mind deep space. Nor was she afraid of the molten glob looming within touching distance, though that was an illusion; they were twenty kilometers away. She also found it fascinating and beautiful, a lovely perk of the trip.

However, she had to keep close tabs on Caron, be ready to back Alex up, watch the workers in the vicinity against possible weapons fire or even spy out large masses that might crush her principal. Then there was suit management, her own location and movement, harness fuel, helmet atmosphere, and not getting blinded by the melt, the mirrors or the local sunlight.

The layout was interesting to her. The mirrors were wired together with monstrous molecular cables, which had large drums to maneuver them around like sails in the stellar wind. One crew maintained that.

Another crew managed the melt, advising the first team on foci and distance to stratify the various metals and keep the slag outgassing.

One group managed the feeding driver that kept ore moving into the melt, which also helped balance temperature—adding more cold metal and greater mass reduced latent heat of the entire sphere, but had to be done at a measured rate to avoid instabilities.

Outside the smelter proper, another group took care of receiving incoming ore from throughout the system. Once a melt was complete, that crew would see it was maneuvered to the Whip and flung at the Jump Point.

Before that, though, the melt had to be put into shade and cooled enough to handle, a process taking weeks, and have mounts attached with what amounted to a skyscraper-sized fusion welder. One mass floated behind a black sun screen, visibly dark rather than incandescent but possibly still several hundred degrees.

Fewer than two hundred people handled all this from a control station in the umbra of the mirrors, managing it all by remote. Behind that were their living quarters; small but private pie-shaped cabins in a converted oxygen tank a hundred meters long. That would be replaced eventually. Some of the accumulated slag was being collected into a sphere around waste water. The mirrors would melt it until the steam pressure blew it into a bubble.

The lead engineer graciously let them examine his quarters and pass through the control station. Now he and Caron discussed the operation while floating tethered to one of the cables that held the station and mirrors together.

He was almost certainly safe, she knew. They were also in perhaps the most potentially dangerous peacetime location Elke had ever experienced. A simple twitch could incinerate them like ants under a magnifying glass, into a whiff of vapor. Any number of accidents could hole suits, tumble them off, or otherwise cause them to be dead.

She settled herself by calculating the awesome energy involved in the whole process and admiring its beauty, while monitoring the engineer's distance and movements.

Control came on air and said, "EVA Party, I'm seeing some splatter. It might be a good idea to come back inside."

Right then something like gravel bounced off her faceplate, leaving dimples. Then there was a lot of it. It felt like some school child throwing a handful of dirt, except it was hard enough to hurt.

Jason grabbed Caron and started hauling in on the tethers. Elke made note of that, checked the time automatically, and yanked herself in to ensure she was between the two of them and the other personnel. There were some shouts and muttered curses, both about that and about the incoming splatter. She wasn't letting anyone near Caron, however, even if it meant greater risk for them.

Jason moved well, but the tethers didn't retract fast enough and there was some tangling. Then he cursed, and shifted to free lines.

More debris pelted them, stinging slightly through the fitted suits. A blinding flash moved over them as the mirrors were adjusted. Elke cursed in Czech, as she always did, since it was more colorful for her.

Then they all piled behind the screen that shielded the airlock, and cycled through.

Once inside, Elke reset the lock fast for the next person, and turned. Caron and Jason had helmets off. She helped Jason pat Caron down through the coarse woven armor mesh, and looked for any damage or injury. There were a few minor fabric snags that didn't compromise integrity, and Caron seemed bruised at most.

Elke felt a sting and realized she had a large sore spot on one hip.

The others cycled in behind them, quickly filling the small space. Jason popped open a hatch with more curses. Then he spoke very politely.

"I would like to inquire why that warning took so long," he said. Elke could tell he was beyond pissed.

Inside the control booth, she saw a young engineer with the common shaggy haircut, scrawny in a shapeless coverall.

"Sir!" the man snapped in response to Jason's projected anger. "Interference is common, and I was also a bit distracted. Sorry, sir."

He didn't quite shy away, but clearly looked scared.

Elke said, "I was distracted, too. There was a lot going on." She didn't add that she was effectively a tourist, and someone assigned here should do better. She wanted to make sure Jason didn't choke the boy first.

The station manager was last in after his people, which was creditable. He looked at the open hatch, the expressions, and spoke up.

"Vapor bubbles happen from time to time. Either a spot of slag or a lighter metal vaporizes, and then pops out. Given the mirror area, about half the time the splash melts and is driven back by photon pressure. Half the time it misses completely. Occasionally it tears an edge or a line. I've only been sprayed once before."

"Radar?" Jason asked.

"The radar and other sensors are for monitoring volume, bolometric temperature, dross depth. There's always slag, vapor and debris. The pulses are tagged, but still have to fight the environment."

The watch stander spoke again. "I was listening to the discussion. We don't get VIPs very often, and I let that distract me. I really am sorry."

He looked it, too.

Jason turned and asked, "Elke?"

There were a lot of questions in that one word.

Was this something to discuss in public? Though there wasn't really any privacy and they needed resolution fast. Nor would whispering make anyone less uncomfortable.

Jason was obviously wondering if the warning, coming barely ahead of the molten metal storm, was intended to cover someone against an accident that might not have been. She thought over the events, then spoke carefully.

"I can't see a viable way to plan a vapor burst to actually aim this way. Even if there was, no one here would do so. They'd be as likely to kill themselves. There is a lot of clutter, slag, vapor, cables, gear and people moving around. Even with good automated interpretation, there wouldn't be much warning. The splash was mostly very small pieces that didn't cause any actual damage. I'd call it an accident, even if the timing is ironically bad."

Caron spoke up, "Of course no one did it on purpose. I appreciate your concern, Elke, Jason, but I know I can trust my senior engineers."

Jason said, "Very well. I intended no offense, I just have to put your safety first."

The engineer boss said, "We were pretty much done out there anyway. We can see the rest better from here." He seemed faintly embarrassed, and concerned about the event.

"Show me, please," Caron said.

Several hours later they finished the inspection and headed back to the boat. Elke went first, checked all her seals were in place, called for Caron, and Jason came in last.

As soon as he unsealed his helmet she said, "I'm sorry for

acting put upon. I know the threat is real, but I have to be diplomatic with my staff."

"Of course you do," Jason said. "Don't worry about it. You can even use us as an excuse for anything you don't want to do. 'Security concerns.' We're fine being the bad guys if it keeps you safe. I just had to have an answer right then."

Elke said, "It is possible to set up a splash on purpose, with a large enough mass of light metal tossed in at the correct angle. I consider it a remote risk, however."

"Yeah, getting shotgunned with metal pellets is not something I enjoy, having tried it before. I can't imagine anyone there would risk it for the money."

"Well, what else is there to see?"

Caron said, "I'm adjusting the itinerary. I really don't need to see a gravity whip up close. It's a giant cable and another control cabin. The smelter was interesting, though. I've seen the orbital docks. We're not taking this boat all the way to the gas giants. So head home. Two days, yes?"

"If you don't care how much metal I ionize and mass I consume, yes."

"I don't. It was worth showing the flag, as it were, but I'm not really accomplishing much out here."

"Right away," he agreed. He had a course plotted and ready, and commenced at once, without notifying anyone.

Aramis kept a journal of notes, with some photos and video, his and Elke's. Someday, it might make an interesting memoir. Some of the team's assignments had been on barely industrialized worlds in constant warfare. Govannon was nothing but bleeding edge technology.

He hadn't seen the space foundry, but the ones running on the surface were bogglingly huge. Plastics labs and fabrication shops did everything from casting raw billets all the way to milling finished goods, through coordinate controls and massive energy expenditure. Glass and some ceramics were easy—silicates were all over the place. The cubic cows in the research lab were rather disturbing. There were bees, bred to live in the inside farms, and the same geneticists were working on other strains for various colonies. That would generate more income. He wondered what the top limit was, but every line of development also boosted other industries and competitors, as well as providing better, cheaper resources on the whole. This one company—family—was producing so much material wealth that the entire human race was benefitting.

His musings were interrupted by a crashing sound from within the other room, and he jerked alert, grabbing his baton and reaching for a pistol that he didn't have. His senses quivered.

The door opened, and he moved to a mental state that he didn't need, when Caron came through by herself. She was roaring drunk, staggering around. She held a bottle so clear the golden liquid within seemed almost free-floating, except for the black etched label. She had no glass.

"What have you been drinking?"

She spoke very carefully, with heartbreaking elocution. "Welsh gold. Penderyn Aur Cymru Single Malt whisky from a honey-charred barrel with a sherry finish. Two hundred marks a bottle Earthside. Close to two *thousand* once imported here. I could drink myself to death on this stuff and my bankers would never notice."

The bottle slipped, and she fumbled for it and tumbled and wound up flat on her back next to the couch, bottle between her breasts, heaving so it spilt a drop with each breath, the drops moistening her lips and tongue.

A little more about her tastes I didn't need to know, he thought.

"We'd notice," he said.

"Yes, you'd notice, and you'd stop me. I can't even fucking *die* to escape."

"Caron, you're more than entitled to get drunk and hungover. Push it too far and Shaman will IV you."

"Of course he will. Do you want to spread me?"

"Excuse me?"

"You're attractive, decent, and you're not an ore miner, and I'm tired of expensive, perfectly shaped, ultra realistic dildos with no warmth or response." She yanked at her blouse.

Shit. He wasn't going to answer that question because . . . he wasn't going to answer that question.

"Miss Prescot, I'm going to call Elke for backup and see that you get to bed."

She looked disgusted and half sobered. "Yeah. I'll get there myself. Damn your professionalism."

She stood, but not without tumbling and grabbing him for support, her body pressed against his. She undressed on her way to the bedroom, leaving a trail of clothes. It would have been erotic if she had any higher mental faculties left. As it was he just felt sorry for her.

He checked that she did actually fall into bed, naked and sprawled, and how many millions could he sell the photos for?

He closed the door and retrieved her clothes, from the lacy black silk panties to the outrageously expensive blouse and slacks, and folded them neatly onto the back of the couch.

Jason entered the apartment for morning shift change. He took a professional glance around, spied the pile, and didn't visibly raise an eyebrow, but Aramis could read it.

"Passed out drunk. Said a few things she didn't mean."

"Gotcha," he said with a nod. "Do we need to call Shaman?"

"She's breathing—well, snoring. I checked periodically. We'll see how she feels when she wakes up."

"She was drinking that?" Jason asked, pointing at the two-thirds empty bottle.

"Yes."

"Damn. If they want to give me a bonus, I know what I want." Nice stuff. He'd tried it once, but it wasn't something he kept on hand in quantity.

"I'd best say nothing at this point."

Jason understood that and showed a frown. "Sorry, brother."

"Yeah. I feel sorry for her. I also hate the taunting little bitch." He delivered the last sentence with audible viciousness.

Jason thought about naked skin, fishnets and boots, and a naked woman skinning into a spacesuit. Yeah, he understood that only too well. Aramis wasn't yet twenty-eight, had a background that didn't include a lot of socializing with women, and had to be gibbering nuts inside.

He rolled a thought over for a second, hesitantly gave himself permission and decided Elke should get a photo for the man. Not that they hadn't seen all of her already, but something you could stare at for several seconds without being rude made a difference.

CHAPTER 21

Alex said, "Joe is really starting to piss me off."

They were gathered around the table in their common room, across the hall from Caron. They needed somewhere to vent and bitch where the principal wouldn't be aware of it and couldn't complain. She and Elke were on the other side.

"He is overly cautious. It interferes with our job," Aramis agreed around his food. He was demolishing another sandwich.

"No, it's more than that. It's the money grubbing, and I'm sure he's on the take somewhere."

Bart said, "We can't say so, of course."

"Not unless we stumble on concrete proof, and no one is to go digging."

They nodded in agreement. That would raise tensions at least.

Jason put down the trigger group he was tuning and said, "But he is micromanaging, meddling, and really class conscious, as well as, in my opinion, a bit of a bigot. He doesn't like any of the non-European staff. I watch him twitch when Shaman's around, too."

Shaman nodded. "I see that as well. If it's obvious to others . . ."

Alex shrugged. "Well, we have to deal with him. Just continue to remember that he doesn't give us orders, we don't answer to him, and treat him as an obstacle."

Bart said, "It is interesting that he is more reserved about movement, and it's not just his racism."

"Yeah, he reeks of cowardice," Aramis said.

"Not cowardice," Shaman said. "Deceit. He's grubbing for more money. That's why he wants us replaced with lesser security."

Alex said, "Yeah, there's definitely some of that. He's cringing at the thought of our payroll, not of us hurting him. He's somewhat contemptuous of us."

Jason said, "So, Boss, you need to make sure Bryan and Caron continue to like us. I will take the job of keeping Caron happy, and Aramis can do his best with Bryan."

Aramis raised a finger, but grinned.

Alex smiled. They were definitely a much more cohesive team now.

"That aside, we do seem to have reduced the threat level. No poisons, no shots fired, no swarms of anything. I hate to think Caron is stuck here forever, though. HQ is working on a department to do investigations. So we'll just have to let that stand. And just in case, I've put that list together with Cady. She brought in all our usual stuff and stashed it so we can get it if we need to, rules or not."

Aramis said, "I have maps, flat and imaged, paper and module."

"You keep doing that. We should never be without a couple of spare routes and access to hardware."

Jason said, "Elke's been acquiring explosive."

"Of course she has. She's psychotic about it, but she's our psychotic. Find her places to stash it."

"Do you think it's going to come to that?"

"I hope not, but these things happen. We can always dispose of it outside. It'll degrade fast and likely not be found."

"That reminds me," Jason said. "I want to take a trip outside, just for interest. We need to consider stashes there, too, outside the locks, just in case."

"In case we wind up outside and cut off?"

"It's happened before."

Alex said, "I'd call you paranoid, but that's my job and I approve. Do it."

He wondered if they were paranoid enough, and just how their principals would react to this kind of discussion.

Bryan Prescot found an irregularity in his morning scan. It was a numerical flaw. Math was his forte, and tiny errors jumped at him, as this one had. He linked through, checked again, then went looking for the source of the discrepancy. After that, he pulled up several detailed files from far down the chart, then still farther. He spent an hour puzzling over where the inconsistency was.

Then he swore. He went over the figures several times. There was just no way it was a mistake. The columns matched closely enough. The problem was, the wrong columns matched.

One column was money disbursed for certain payrolls. The other was the transfer amounts of those payrolls. Those did not match. However, the report on those payrolls did match.

It wasn't an immediate legal problem. Deductions had been taken on the proper amount, so the government had theirs. However, after that, ninety percent of those funds had disappeared. It wasn't going to the personnel in question, and it wasn't still in the disbursing account.

Instead, it went off into some remote account on Grainne. That bank wouldn't talk, and not much would make them. Of course, Bryan Prescot could make the bank talk, by outright buying it if need be. It would be cheaper, though, to ask Jason Vaughn for any connections he might have.

However, none of that was necessary, because the process in question had been initiated, initialized, and initialed by his brother, who was on his way up now, or better be if he knew what was good for him.

Joe came in, looking flustered and a little defensive.

"What's the problem?" he asked, with a put-upon tone.

"Where's the money going, Joe?"

"Money?"

Bryan spun the image around.

"That money."

"Ah. I was able to cut costs."

"You didn't discuss it with me." Bryan couldn't believe the man was going to lie about it further. It was so childish. They'd gotten past that stage forty years ago, hadn't they?

"You weren't here and there wasn't time."

Bryan slapped the desk and pointed out the dome.

"Open Jump Point. Specifically for communication purposes, because we need that more than the money. You could have reached me in twelve hours or so."

Joe stuttered momentarily but didn't respond.

Bryan shouted, "So where's the money, Joe?"

Joe was shaking, and shifted back to a chair. He sat down hard. "In a safe account. I made sure the taxes were properly paid and then some."

"Yes, and then some. Which would not be necessary if you were openly paying lower salaries. Which means you were hiding it from me!" He hadn't wanted to lose his temper, but he realized he'd lost it before this discussion even started.

"Bryan, I wanted to make sure we had a backup. Just in case of—"

"I authorized that money so our miners could be well paid, not worked as near slaves!"

"I saved the money, even through a contractor, and our operations are above predictions."

"We don't need to save money. We do need to treat people like human fucking beings!"

"They all contracted freely, and the terms are in compliance. You've talked about overpaying people and damaging the economy. They come from very poor nations and are glad to have it. They're quite well off by their home standards."

"The plan was to get professionals and pay them accordingly."

"The professionals are. They're also all European, British or American. Much more reliable than Third World rabble, if it comes to trouble."

Bryan looked at his younger brother in confused anger and disgust.

"I can't believe our parents raised such a sociopathic, racist bastard."

"I'm sorry you feel that way," Joe said. Goddammit, he was still trying to talk his way out of it. "Look, if I was wrong, I was wrong. My intent was to save the money for development and us. It was because of that that we had the capital we have now."

"Possibly some of it. We'd have succeeded and kept our honor intact. Now we'll go into the history books alongside the Arabs, Malays, Spanish . . ."

"Pretty much everyone who was successful, yes? And that bothers you?"

Everything the man said was making Bryan fume worse. He needed . . . before he . . .

"I don't want to discuss this. I'm going to fix it. Please leave me to do so, and I'll ensure you get the agreed bonus." He kept his contempt and revulsion masked.

"It'll work out. Things will be fine."

"Yes. Let me work on it. Please."

Bryan realized he didn't know his brother at all. Even with food and lodging being furnished, and entertainment, the wages were less than a pittance. They might help a family living in Bangladesh or the Congo, if they didn't mind a chance of never seeing their father or husband again.

Now he was honor bound to fix the problem, pay back wages to everyone he could have tracked down, and offer them all a small amount of stock for their work. It wasn't a lot of money from his position behind those bags of zeroes, which was the point. It would, though, take some time to accomplish. Some of the workers from previous rotations might not even have contact info. This would mean advertising, and PR to spin it.

He'd also heard rumors of safety equipment shortages. That was another several million he'd have to explore. Unbelievable.

He was going to have to cut his brother out of the operation, too. Give him his stock and a chunk to make him happy, and let him retire to Fiji or Aruba. Or Barbados.

So this is how it works out, Joe thought. *The bloody idiot had to go and meddle in accounting and payroll, my area, instead of sticking to engineering and socializing.*

He considered making another approach, then discarded the idea. Bryan actually believed those illiterate, scrabbling inferiors were their equals. There was a reason they were hired by the thousands with minimal background checks. All they had to do was produce ore. It was a nasty, low-status job, which is why nasty, low-status people were hired. All the upper echelons, doing the intellectual work, were Westerners. That was because few Third Worlders went to college, because few of them had the capacity. That was a combination of societal, dietary early development, cultural and genetic. They really were inferior. It wasn't through any fault of their individual selves, but they certainly weren't equal, and didn't deserve more than a good wage based on their origins. It was economically bad on several levels to pay them Western wages. If Bryan wouldn't accept that reality, he'd just have to be made to.

Though it was past time for that. Joe was nerving himself up, and realized he was. So on with the alternate plan.

He dug a secure phone out of his desk. It had been bought with cash and never used. Ideally, it never should be. Still. He left it wrapped in its envelope and punched a number manually.

On the fourth ring, there was an answer.

"Hello?"

"Yes, I need to implement that item I told you about."

The man on the other end said nothing and then, "You're serious."

"Yes."

"That was hypothetical."

"Well, it's real now. Don't back out on me."

"Sir, that's . . ."

"It's a distraction, an accident."

"I really am having second thoughts."

Dammit, Joe could hear the little weasel cringing through the audio.

"I'll double the money." He would, too. That made *him* cringe, but if that was the market price . . .

"Okay . . . but I'm destroying this phone. There has to be distance."

"Of course. I'll tell you when."

Joe pulled the battery from the phone and stuffed both into a faraday bag. He'd make one more call with it, then destroy it.

Hopefully, Caron would be younger and more flexible in her thinking.

Alex thought Caron was adapting to life on Govannon reasonably well. Keeping busy helped, though she was taking a break at the moment, and just enjoying cheese and crackers in her living room, with a sense-vid playing on the wall. She had afternoon appointments and numbers to crunch, which would be at her office.

While he pondered, a tremendous blast picked everything up and smashed it down. Alex thought he saw the floor actually wave as the shock passed.

As soon as the siren shrieked, everyone grabbed for masks. Alex had his next to him. Elke rolled over the back of the couch and sprinted for her kit. Caron darted to the coat rack and grabbed hers. Seconds later, the door slid open and Aramis came in, followed by Bart. Jason and Shaman came through from the rear.

Alex read off his comm and relayed the info. "Report says the outer dome is compromised. Breech is repairable, but there is substantial contamination. Masks required worn outside of buildings, at close proximity to the event inside. That includes this building. They're boosting for a slight positive pressure. They'll update as needed. They're starting air scrubbing now."

Jason asked, "What is the repair procedure?"

Caron said, "I think they use an epoxy for cracks. If a pane is actually loose, they replace it either inside or out—there are two tracks—and a future repair would be on the other side. Frame damage is with an injected polymer, or a welded metal joint, depending on which joint. They sonic weld in situ. Entire panes can be replaced with a jig that lets pressure push it into place, then it's sealed around the edge."

"No need to evacuate, then."

"If a leak is that bad, they'd tent over the area, rip out and replace. That's never happened."

"How often has a crack like this happened?"

"Um . . . it hasn't."

"That's actually not what I wanted to hear."

Alex said, "Yes, possible sabotage, or a bona fide disaster, or even a large scale hostile act."

Caron looked very sober.

"So what should we do?" she asked. "I'll need to report in to help supervise."

Right then, Alex's phone buzzed. He snagged it on voice only.

"Marlow."

"Mister . . . Agent Marlow. Is Caron well?" It was her uncle.

That was an odd question.

"Very much, and safe."

"Are you sure?"

"I get regular reports of any changes." Alex suddenly didn't want to admit their proximity.

"Good. Can I reach her? I have to give her some bad news."

"I can't put you in contact quickly. Can I inquire?"

"Yes, it's going to be public very shortly and I need to reach her first, of course. Her father died in a mining accident a few minutes ago. Big explosion and landslide."

Alex jolted.

"Are you sure, sir? He's not just stuck?"

"It was a massive collapse. Several people were down there. We're going to mine down, of course, but it will take days, and the mass of material involved, and the toxic atmosphere..."

"I understand, sir. I'm very sorry to hear of your loss."

"Yes, thank you. But I must tell Caron, and see her, and follow up on other details from there. I suppose I'm temporarily in charge until the legal snarls are over. Should I meet at her apartment? Or in the office up here?"

The man was already in the main office.

As a massive adrenaline dump roared through him, Alex said, "We'll come over, and up. It could take a little while. We're down past the casino." Or at least, the repeater for his coded phone was. He might have to make use of several of them now.

"Please. And please don't tell anyone, not even your own staff. I don't want her being alarmed."

"Understood, sir. We'll be on our way."

"Thanks."

The call ended, and Alex flipped over his phone and pulled the card. As soon as he did so, all the others did, too. Aramis pulled six more phones out of a small pouch.

"Prepaid," he said. "Harder to trace."

Alex took one, pointed and gave orders. "Mask up. You too, Miss Prescot. Elke, take out the window. Bart, grab that cable."

Caron demanded, "What's happening?"

He spoke while locking eyes with her. "Aramis, help her with her mask. Caron, your survival depends on doing exactly as you are told for the next few minutes. An attack is imminent."

"But we're... yes, sir, I will." She nodded again, very serious and attentive.

"Good."

Yes, good. He'd maintain the no-nonsense attitude until he had her somewhere safe.

No one else asked what was happening; they just did as they were told.

Aramis grabbed two harnesses from the kit, threw one over his shoulders, and helped Caron snap one over her hips and shoulders. Even that looked exciting on her.

Elke, her voice slightly muffled, asked, "Masks? Everyone clear? Fire in the hole!"

BANG! CRASH! ROAR!

The atmosphere swirled in, tinged with filthy yellow, and stirred up debris.

Aramis clipped onto the cable as Bart heaved it out the hole. There was little material around the edges, and the cable had a heavy shroud against damage.

Bart checked its deployment, then escorted Caron over and helped her clip on. He attached behind her and reached his huge arms around.

"Remember what you were taught. Grip the rope behind you, not in front, and I will, too. Here we go."

Aramis dropped off at once, face first down into the dingy brown fog.

Caron looked scared, but frozen calm as Bart kicked off. Apparently, she wasn't dropping whatever drugs she used to relax herself before her recreational stunts. Still, she didn't hinder him as they slid down and were swallowed into the tumbling, sulfurous roils.

Alex went next, Shaman barely behind, but the boots disappeared from his view as he slid down. At least this crud offered concealment. He went down slow enough to avoid running into Bart and Caron, but fast enough his glove warmed up as it soaked momentum into friction. It didn't really feel like a rappel, as he couldn't see any terrain. It wasn't dark, just boiling yellow nothing.

Knowing there were potential hostiles out there, hidden in the haze, invisible from his current position and that he was a big, fat target until he reached ground already had him bursting with sweat around the seal of his mask, and hyperventilating. He forced himself to de-escalate the mental threat level. This was nothing he hadn't done before, it was just a reaction, and the pleasant, hell, glamorous surroundings created a lot of contrast. But, no matter how opulent it was, this was now a war zone. His mind shifted around a bit and he calmed down to near normal. Then he was on the ground.

Shaman landed right after him, Elke almost at once, and she barely cleared the line as Jason brought up the rear, fast. As he cleared, he clicked a button. A wire hidden in the rope core signaled a release, and a few seconds later the mount clattered to the ground and threw chips. That would hopefully hide their actions a few minutes longer. Elke had the coil faked halfway, Alex dismounted the hook and stuffed it in his ruck, and Aramis grabbed the other end. As he and Elke met, he took both coils, twisted them and tossed them into his ruck.

A couple of shadows resolved as staff trudging through the thick smog, and one of them stepped up.

"Sir, no one can be outside without authorization."

"We're going inside now," he said, shifting around so they weren't looking toward all the activity.

He hoped that was the end of it, but one of them squinted toward the others.

Bart and Aramis dissolved in from the fog and grabbed them both from behind. As they started to shout and protest they were zapped, then Shaman slipped up and jabbed the first with a needle, then the other.

"We have about twelve hours," he said, as the two men were dragged off to be stuffed somewhere. Alex was curious, but trusted his people.

"Let's move," he said. "What's the cheapest hotel?"

Jason said at once, "There's a Crowne Plaza. Only sixty-three hundred per night. They'll peg us by tomorrow, though."

"Do we need rest or movement?"

"Movement."

"Agreed. Staff section."

Jason said, "Elke, we need to get through some doors, and in a way most people would call discreet."

"I will try," she agreed.

Aramis held up a printed flat map. "I suggest here. One of the retreats you asked me to secure."

At once Alex said, "Lead the way. Elke and Jason, crack anything Aramis tells you."

Aramis knew where he was going. He slipped ahead and had no hesitations, though he did feel for corners in the filthy air. They turned, turned again. He held up a hand with the clenched fist for "hold," and they waited, flat against the building. He waggled a thumb and Alex repeated the gesture, unsure if Aramis could be seen by the others. They stepped quietly to the middle of the avenue. Hopefully, no automatic vehicles would come through.

Vague sounds and shifts indicated a couple of people, probably staff, were on the walkway. They apparently didn't see the party and kept going. Aramis waved a hand and pointed, and Jason moved to the walkway as a scout.

The only way to tell distance in the haze was to count paces. Alex tried to estimate the traveled distance, and knew they'd come fifty meters from when he'd started. They should be close to a service road, and just then, Aramis indicated right and turned that way.

A few moments later, Alex moved in to the group as Jason popped open a door. It was a basic metal type to keep out inquisitive tourists, so it wasn't coded or otherwise restricted, though there might be cameras inside.

Jason went in first with Aramis watching through a crack, then the rest of them got the thumbs up.

Inside was still foggy, and Jason had flipped the camera so it stared at the wall. One edge of the fisheye might barely catch the door, but it should be tough to identify people in masks. Of course, there were probably other sensors, too.

Elke was at the inside door, at work with a coding box. In a few seconds, it clicked open. They swarmed through, Aramis led the way right inside the corridor, down metal stairs that everyone navigated smoothly, though Caron's steps were a bit loud. He opened a storage room door. They were underneath another building, in a fairly secure area. Bart brought up the rear and jammed a brace under the door latch.

"Keep masks on," Alex advised. The air here was mostly clear, but it looked as if a few toxins were loose, and who wanted a lungful of sulfurous crud?

Aramis had done well. He broke out extra staff oxy bottles, loose anoraks with insulated liners that would hide their shape, tool belts with B&E tools, water bottles and rations, as well as spare socks and some other sundries. He grabbed a pack of disposable atmosphere-sealed coveralls used for light maintenance. He handed out printed maps.

"Brief rest," he said, only slightly muffled through the mask. "We're moving out in five."

Jason took the time to grab some tools. Elke went straight for the chemical locker and took two bottles. Alex said nothing. He figured they knew what they were doing. It was less than five minutes before everyone was ready, with Caron still quiet and waiting for orders, wide-eyed and trembling nervous under her mask.

They split into three groups. Aramis took Bart and went on

ahead. Elke and Jason went with Caron. Alex and Shaman brought up the rear.

The map was clear enough, though it showed a convoluted route under two more buildings and then up into the staff quarters, at the west side of the dome and crawling into the bedrock. Shortly, Alex rapped softly on the indicated door, and Elke ushered him in. She snatched the map and destroyed it at once.

As Alex unmasked, Caron asked, "How bad is it?" She sat on a couch, but very upright and stiffly.

He faced her and said, "Caron, I don't know. I have reason to believe your father's in severe trouble. I also believe there's an immediate threat to you. I intend to stay hidden until we find more information."

"Was that my uncle who called?" she asked.

"Yes, it was."

"I don't trust him," she said. "I think he may be involved."

"So do I." That had good and bad elements. Good was he wouldn't have to persuade her not to contact the man. Bad was that he wished he'd known of that distrust earlier, and for the time being, the man was in charge.

She asked, "Do you think my father's dead?" The question was delivered very dispassionately, but her eyes betrayed her. The cold mask was only that.

"Caron, I don't know. Your uncle said he thought he was trapped in a landslide. He then made immediate inquiries as to your location. That's why we evacuated."

"What would that mean for your contract? And what about your compatriots guarding him?"

"If he's trapped, so are they. Obviously, I hope they're all alive and well, and that I'm overreacting. Our contract remains in force until cancelled. It's a personal contract through your father. So until he or you cancels it, we continue."

She closed her eyes momentarily, breathed slowly, and then asked, "Can you do anything to help my father?"

"I put out a squawk through our secure channel. He has good operators with him, and they're all friends of mine. My job is to protect you, and I can best do that here. Splitting up won't help anyone. I realize that's not what you want to hear, but it's the best we can do. I'm truly sorry."

He was also prepared to argue that she couldn't give him any orders until her father was confirmed dead. She didn't argue, though. She just nodded.

"What's our plan now?" she asked.

Her haughtiness, her manner, her will were all gone. She was a young woman dealing with a very sobering and frightening life change, brittle as glass and clinging to such shreds of sanity and dignity as she could manage.

"We stay hidden until we're sure it's safe, and consider possible courses of action. But for right now, I have to assume someone wants your family dead."

"They don't seem to be trying very hard for my uncle, do they?"

He first said, "It's hard to say." Then he realized she needed more than just bland reassurance. "The available evidence is that they aren't, though."

"Are you considering him a threat?"

"I have to consider everyone a potential threat, but under circumstances like this, he must be considered so and treated accordingly."

"Can I order you to raise his threat level?"

He raised his eyebrows fractionally.

"Order, no, but I will certainly take that as a valid request and serious advisory. Is there anything that leads you to feel that way?"

"Nothing specific. My father did say something about his dealings being a bit off, though. That's not much really, but . . ."

"Combined with his apparent safety, that's significant. It doesn't confirm he's a threat himself, but it means at least someone thinks he's more useful alive than either you or your father."

Caron seemed at her emotional end. She leaned over and grabbed Elke in a hard hug, and started weeping.

Elke looked very nonplussed and stiffened up, but after a moment, she returned the grip and gently patted Caron's back. Her expression was one of confusion, discomfort and surprise. Ordinarily, it would have been funny to see.

Jason had his comm terminal up. Intel was crucial, but so was being discreet. Alex knew Jason had several evasion systems working, but it was still a potential leak.

Aramis leaned into a closet, threw out a panel that was probably a false back, and tossed rucksacks out. They were filled to capacity, bulky and rounded and had company weapons strapped on them, military grade without biometric safeties.

Caron was still stuck in her own world. In a sharp tone she said, "Who authorized those?"

Alex said, "I did."

She hesitated a moment, and then reality smacked her again. It wasn't uncommon for principals to take a while to grasp threats. Which, of course, is why people like Alex got paid to grasp them all the time.

Still, she asked, "Are all rules just tentative guidelines to you?"

"Miss, I get paid to keep you alive. We've had this conversation. Someone has just violated the rules, so now it's my turn. I plan for that. I don't intend to leave you on your own, and the only use I have for the moral high ground is a place to put my artillery. Your survival still depends on us getting you safely away. You've done well so far. Please continue to do so."

"I'll shut up, sir," she said with a weak smile.

Elke had produced another phone from somewhere, and had audio up. She motioned for silence.

She said, "Hello, Pyro. What happened?"

Eggett replied, "One of our charges prematured on a truck."

"That's impossible."

"Yes, it is. Sabotage, obviously. The damage isn't severe, but there's a lot of screaming brass. I can't talk long. Luckily it was on the near side, so the mine face acted as a tamper. Blast was generally away from the dome. We lost several miners, and will have to account for some others."

"Got it. Any word on the family? I'm down in the service area right now and cut off. I will have to work my way back."

"Well, there's lots of secrecy and no word on the boss. *She* is missing. There's a million mark reward out for recovering her."

"We won't be eligible. Even if we knew where she was."

"Bullshit, lady," Eggett said. "But I don't need to know and don't want to. I'm staying out of it, but if you need resources, strictly for yourselves, let me know. I'm sure HQ will compensate the company for it, won't they?"

"No question," Elke said.

"So you get where you need to. I have to run."

"Roger. Babs out."

She closed the link and looked up, eyebrows raised.

Bart said, "That is awfully fast for a reward."

Shaman said, "Obviously, they are worried about her safety."

Alex cocked his head. "Yeah, but I wonder why they're that worried this fast, since she was not anywhere near the blast area, and her apartment wasn't damaged. Nor have they been calling us to find out."

Elke said, "Stop pretending. It adds up to threat."

Alex said, "Yes, it does. That's how we proceed. Elke, or Jason, can you get me a secure channel to Cady?"

"I think so," Jason said. "Stand by." He fumbled with his ruck, pulled out a military radio with encryption capability, and started tapping in a code.

"Got her," he said. He handed the radio over to Alex.

"Desi, this is Playwright."

"Go ahead."

"We have extracted Flatbed and gone to ground."

Flat Bed. Press Cot. Not that it would fool anyone, but any intel equipment looking for word patterns wouldn't find anything. Besides, they were encrypting and using gear not likely available to the enemy, and no one knew they had it. It was impossible to be too secure.

Cady said, "Advise me, Playwright. We're told contract cancelled."

"No doubt. That's not morally valid, but it may be legally." That was fast, too. The uncle definitely wanted control, and was willing to kill for it. Alex presumed the outside threats had all been orchestrated to this end. Damn.

"We're in a tough situation. We can't work for free, I don't want to abandon a principal."

Alex nodded. There was not only the moral issue. Being that mercenary was professionally bad. *Sold out? Sorry, kid, you're screwed* was bad for business.

"It seems likely a resolution of post-event legalities will support our position. Pay will be backdated."

Did she catch that? Caron would certainly get enough in the will to cover it all, assuming she lived, the will wasn't destroyed or corrupted, and her uncle didn't buy a few judges. With all that, maybe the odds weren't great.

"Concur, Playwright. We'll continue with operation unless directed otherwise. I'll inform management."

"Please do. Get confirmation."

"Understood. Do you need assistance?"

"Very negative. Stay away from us. I will message with a delivery request." If Joe Prescot had any brains at all, he was watching Cady's team and any other security operations to see how and where they moved.

"I understand, Playwright. Good luck."

"Out."

He killed power at once. He wanted to know if any of Bryan's detail were alive, but that information might not be available yet, and it was secondary to their principal.

"Well, that's that. We keep Miss Prescot alive. We find deep cover. We give it a week or so to steady out." *We get more weapons.*

Bart said, "To cover all bases, let me ask if we can just call the authorities?"

Alex looked at Caron. She shifted uncomfortably.

"No," she said. "First, you'd have to convince them there was a threat against me. Then, we'd have to be where they could meet us. This assumes they're able to get in, or a message is able to get out. Pretty much everything bottlenecks through the main office."

Shaman said, "What you must also consider is the long-term threat. It would be best to deal with it now, if it can be dealt with. Long term, there are other weapons and accidents that can be arranged."

Caron sighed a deep and shuddering sigh, still in tears.

"Yes, please. Let's get this over with," she said. She swayed slightly and sat down hard on a bench. She covered her face with her hands and seemed oblivious, but wasn't crying.

Aramis said, "I think we're safe here for a few hours. Ultimately, I want to get out of this area of this dome. It's too confined."

Jason said, "What's our backup? Or should we pick another bolt hole? Or fabricate one?"

Elke said, "Down in Mine Staff should be safe for now. We have a contact."

Alex raised his eyebrows. "Can we trust Eggett?"

"Yes," Elke said.

"How do you know?"

"His reputation, his skill. I've met him before. If he was part of it, there wouldn't have been an 'accident.' It would have been a disappearance, or inside radius of a nuke. Also, he's smart enough to know it's going to leak out. That would end his career."

"Money wouldn't buy him?"

"Only if it bought him enough for more work. He loves explosive the way I do."

"Okay. I'll believe you."

One of the items Aramis had handed out was a paper map book. He'd planned well. Shaman leafed through it.

"Eggett is over a square and down three levels in the Starlight Tower. Do you all remember that buildings here run up and down from the putative surface? There are maintenance corridors most of the way if we don't mind dust."

"I prefer it," Alex said. "More concealment and less witnesses. Are we calling ahead?"

"I can't believe you asked that," Jason said, sounding snide.

"Yeah, sorry. I'm distracted."

CHAPTER 22

They moved down on foot, via back access corridors along the vehicle route. The corridors were cluttered with boxes and tools, and dim. There were tinges of yellow even here. At least that meant few of the staff were about, and no tourists. Aramis led, referring frequently to the map and to hatch and section numbers. He seemed sure of their direction generally, and didn't retrace any steps.

Elke wanted explosives and a shotgun. This was a war zone and worse, and a *zkurveny* pistol-caliber carbine and baton weren't enough for any real engagement. She gripped the baton because it was the only thing handy, but she didn't like it at all.

She wasn't suffering an adrenaline dump, but there was this steady trickle of nerves. It was more than enough for reflexes. It was genuine fear. She took slow, deep breaths through her mask, and was glad when her sensors indicated clean air. She doffed the rubber octopus and felt sweat evaporate off, leaving cool stripes where it had clung to her face.

Of course, now her face was visible, and she felt exposed and vulnerable. Silly, but another indicator.

The passageways got wider but more austere, until they were cut into stone with sprayed sealant and locks every hundred meters or so.

Eventually they came to a side passage that entered the main corridor of the block occupied by the technical staff. They gathered up against the door in a huddle.

Elke punched a number into her phone manually. She waited for a moment.

Someone apparently answered, and she said, "It's the small foreign bird."

Another pause and she said, "I need to cache a Czech."

Jason made a snorching sound. She could even use English as a weapon, and it wasn't her native tongue.

She waited silently and attentively, then said, "Understood. Out." Turning to the others she said, "Arrive in seventeen minutes."

Then they waited.

Joe was not panicking yet, but not happy. He sat in the chair in his office and gave every impression of worry. It was true. He was worried.

He'd thought things were covered enough that Caron would be brought right to him. Some negotiation, some tears, some help, an offer to deal with the crisis and let her out of the golden prison, just to reduce the threats, and he'd have control. She'd be relieved, he'd have what he wanted, Bryan would have an honest grave, and he could screw Ashier without skulking around. When he got tired of her, he could toss her aside and not worry about repercussions in the family. He'd be the family.

And if someone kidnapped that little bitch Caron he could laugh at them. What would it matter?

That was all on hold. He needed her alive or dead. Alive for negotiation, and dammit, his offer was fair and charitable. Give her a million a year and a generous travel account and nothing to worry about. If she wanted a job, she could have one. She didn't want the money and power, and he did. It was an easy accommodation.

The longer this went on, though, the more likely someone would decide Bryan's unlamented demise wasn't an accident. They couldn't prove it wasn't, but just suspicion would wreck his plans. Cowards.

His own guard was in radio communication with others, "assessing the threat level." He'd nodded and looked concerned. There was no threat, of course; he controlled almost everything at this point. Still, appearances were key when dealing with normal people. One had to make the right expressions, say the right things. No one ever meant them, but they were programmed to go through the motions.

He let that thought run his outside. Inside he pondered the current problem.

It was just possible the girl and her bullet stoppers were on some unannounced trip into the mine again. Things were a mess and they might be delayed, so he'd sit still for a short while.

If they didn't bring her up here in the next few hours, though, he was going to have to move to the next stage. He really didn't want to do that. She was a very pretty girl.

Dammit, he wanted to be alone for a few minutes, but he had to stay here and act concerned.

A message popped up and he glanced past it, then his eyes locked.

Twenty-four hours. Exactly enough time for word to go both ways.

Joe, what the hell is happening? You swore it wouldn't involve violence. You fucker. Ash.

Damn the whore, it was a perfect accident. If she didn't believe it, who else didn't?

More importantly, how to shut her the hell up?

Actually, that wasn't the problem, but juggling it was. He'd better respond.

Ash. Please believe me, this wasn't any plan. It's a tragic accident. Of course I want a better share of things, but a share, not the whole mess, and certainly not with my brother, your daughter and hundreds of innocent people hurt and missing. We're still searching, and investigating, and trying to make sense of it all. I'll contact you with answers soon. Joe.

That might buy seventy-two hours, then he'd have to offer something to back up his assertions. That shouldn't be a problem. That investigator was going to do exactly as he was told.

And it was exciting in a way. Just like judging a market peak to rake in profit from all the naïve little twits who thought they could play stocks. Only this time, instead of headlines about dreams crushed and savings wiped out, it would be dreams crushed and money couldn't stop it.

Of course, money could stop it, but why would he, when he could make more money by not spending it?

Meantime, he would have to work something out for Ashier Aiday Ghirxi Prescot. Something subtle, but permanent. That was another challenge.

The next message was terse and to the point.

Joe, you have our thoughts with you at this trying moment. Prayers for your brother's safety. As potential investors, we remain supportive. Please take time to manage your family affairs.

It was not signed. It didn't need to be. Yes, Joe was well aware of his investors, who'd set him up with the anonymous accounts and cash to get things rolling, and the cut they expected back. Their percentage would be fine, and Joe had better reason than they to keep things controlled. His money was more important.

Your thoughts are appreciated. We all hope things resolve shortly, with minimal trouble for all parties and my brother. The support of investors like you is worth more than I can express in words.

He hoped that this exchange was never made public. He didn't think it was an admission of anything, but even publicity could be bad.

Eggett's quarters were right next to a service corridor. That made it a little easier to avoid notice. Elke walked straight up and buzzed, he answered, she glanced for witnesses and waved, and the others rounded the corner in a gaggle, with Aramis and Jason poking and horseplaying. Of course, detailed camera scans might still show them, but there was nothing to be done about that.

She closed the door behind them and activated the pressure seal with a slap of the large button.

"Thank you, John," she said.

Caron slipped by, almost unnoticed, until she caught Eggett with a full body slap across the face. It staggered him. Then she started punching.

"You incompetent arsehole!"

Eggett turned and took it on his back. Elke grabbed one of Caron's arms and twisted, gently enough not to break it, firm enough to restrain her. Shaman grabbed the other and reached for his kit. He tranked her before she noticed.

"And you!" she shouted when she did.

"Half dose, miss," he said, as he guided her back to a chair. "Just enough to calm down."

It took the wind out of her, and she slumped into a dark fugue, a limp snarl still stuck on her face.

Eggett stood up and turned, his expression sad rather than angry.

"I didn't set those charges, miss," he said. "I'm truly very sorry for the event, and I'm on your side. I need my reputation to work, and whichever asshole did that has damaged mine, and put me in a position where I can either keep my mouth shut and be a shill, or starve. I want them. Not as much as you do, but I know where my loyalties are."

Caron was already glassy eyed and had a dark, violent scowl on her face.

"Sorry," she said. It was clear she was just being polite, but hell, the girl had to be in severe emotional shock.

Alex said, "Well, we're hidden for a few minutes or hours. We need to figure where to go next. We need to get somewhere hidden and off the rolls."

"I know of some people who can help."

"How close are they?"

"Several days. I'll have to leave a message for them."

"Dammit, who are they?"

"Dropouts."

"As in, people who've disappeared and are still living here?"

"Yes, you've heard of them?"

"No, but it's not a new idea, and it's happened before."

Shaman asked, "How well can they scrape by on a desolate, hostile rock?"

"One that has lots of metal resources, a large transient population and the highest technology base of any mine in history? Quite well, I'm told." That grin of his gave odd emphasis to his comments.

Alex shrugged. "Well, we do what we have to."

Eggett said, "They can keep you completely invisible, if they want to." His expression said that was a toss-up, though.

"Bad news?"

"Well, I wondered about the low wages, et cetera. I even inquired. The problem is, all official communication went through that office. I don't think most miners are that inquisitive, and they don't have a lot of access to info other than the company news and porn channels, and WCN broadcasts several hours out of date. The dropouts have even less."

"So they may approve of the 'accident' and feel no obligation to his daughter?"

"I doubt most of them would kill or rape her. At least half would give her a meal if she were starving. But actually help? Unlikely."

"If we can stay hidden, first, we'll see how things resolve and use our systems."

"You can't stay here." At the return looks he said, "I'm happy to help, but an eightfold increase in oh two consumption will be noticed."

"So we need to disappear during the day?"

"I'd suggest you get onto a work detail. They'll never look for you there, and they don't check ID for food. Why would they?"

"Sounds doable. Then we hang around?"

"The bars and theaters run around the clock. Come back here in shifts to rest. At double consumption they'll think I have a girlfriend. Above that it will start to register as a leak and trigger alarms. So will just double use, but that will take hours and resets daily."

"All right," Alex said. "First thing, Caron needs to rest. Two of you stay here with her for now. Elke and Jason. Aramis, you and Bart come with me, and Mr. Eggett, if you don't mind? We'll get them onto a work shift, and I'll get an overview. Then you come back and we'll start sliding out four at a time, plus meals. Jason, can you-"

"Make a schedule, yes," he agreed. "I'll do that while you're gone. Everyone will have eight hours of downtime, but that will include cleanup and rest both."

"We'll make it work. After you, sir. Aramis, Bart, let's go."

Bart had a very mixed threat sense at the moment. He was separate from the principal but still felt pressed by duty. He had the immediate duty of being discreet and unseen, which was hard at 193 centimeters and a hundred kilos of craggy, blond German in a mine full of swarthy little men from developing nations.

That, and he was still on edge from their recent egress, made more tense by not knowing the extent of the threat. He didn't think it was likely he'd be murdered out of hand, but the possibility did exist, as did "accidents" in a mine he knew only superficially.

Still, he trusted Marlow. Aramis was a good man to have in a fight; he'd never shied away. Elke trusted Eggett. Nor was there anything else to do.

Joe knew he was shaking from stress, and caught between a need to do something now, and a bigger need to do nothing. He was fairly quivering.

What he wanted, needed to do was to start legal proceedings

to declare that snotty little bitch dead. To complete his takeover, he needed her body, or he needed a piece of paper. He didn't have the body.

Then, he had to consider how likely he was to get the body in time to bypass the long legal process. How awkward if he had to scramble to make reality match legality.

How embarrassing if she were found, even recently dead, hours, or days, after the event, for that matter.

Then there was public perception. He couldn't start proceedings to declare her dead until he'd had sufficient mourning time. For him, that was five minutes before he made the call to set the charge. The public, though, and any investigators . . .

He had de facto control for now, but there were limits on what he could change, and also limits on what the stock holders would accept. Once he had the family shares, that would not be a problem. What was the etiquette for this, though? It wasn't taught in public school.

So what he really had to do was nothing apparent, while having his rescue teams search in the most likely places that would never find her, while certain other elements searched the unlikely places where she might be, but stop as soon as there was evidence.

Business was going to take a hit when he had to depressurize whichever tunnel she was in, along with whichever staff happened to be there. Then there'd be the hiding of the body, easy enough out on the surface, once he had the damned body. Just drop it from a jumper and let the corrosive clouds do the rest.

Those Ripple Creek arseholes were bloody annoying. He should consider hiring them for his own security, after he got rid of the ones guarding Caron.

The other problem was that he'd already put the word out for that bitch Ashier to have an impressive accidental overdose. Poor tragic woman, divorced, lost most of her fortune, lost her daughter, killed herself in a fit of despondency. It just wouldn't work the same way if that happened before Caron was properly dead. In fact, it would fuck things up royally. The problem was, he'd arranged for doctored medication to get the job started, and a menial servant to dress the scene to his direction once it took effect. There was a three to six day lead time, because there was a certain amount of randomness on when she'd swallow that first pill.

After that, Joe could seek therapy himself, lock all the assets and do nothing for a month to let things settle out, then gradually take the reins and recover from the horrible series of unlucky disasters that happen on the edge of human technology. But it all depended on getting the little bitch dead in the next seventy-two hours tops.

And what the hell was this Environmental Impact complaint? After three decades of development, now some bunch of bunny-fucking ecotwits was trying that route. It was a pathetic attempt. No environment meant no impact. This meant more lawyers, and he'd have to figure out who Bryan had cultivated in the Assembly to run interference on matters like this.

It was just possible with this kind of money that groups like that could be removed, either permanently, or in such a way they feared to even speak.

Joe wasn't sure which of those he liked better. Or, he could scare them, and then eliminate them anyway. It was only money, after all. What was the point if you couldn't have fun with it?

It was less than an hour before Eggett returned.

"They're doing scut labor, running tools and lube out to the drilling crews," he reported. "It's easy to do, not far from here, and gets them lots of familiarity with the tunnels."

"Excellent," Jason said. "It's very much appreciated, sir."

"Well, you can best thank me by never mentioning it."

"Mentioning what? I'm just watching a vid on the couch."

"Of course you are. I'm going to rack out. If you need backup, let me know. I'll trust your judgment on making calls."

"Understood. We should have switched by the time you wake up."

"Of course. 'Night." He wandered into the bathroom area.

Elke caught Jason's attention.

You owe me, she mouthed.

"At least twice," he agreed.

"Say nothing."

"Okay."

When Eggett came out thirty minutes later, Jason noted the time as a matter of course, then forgot it. Eggett stepped into his room to sleep.

Elke slipped through the bedroom door behind him.

"What are you doing?" Jason heard him ask.

"Consuming extra oxygen," she said.

She closed the door softly.

CHAPTER 23

Bart and Aramis stood out amongst the workers as tall Caucasians. However, there were a few others about, and no one seemed concerned.

The issued clothing Eggett had acquired for them was not quite a vac suit, but was an elastomer coverall that was supposed to protect the skin from the mildly corrosive atmosphere outside. The face mask wasn't comfortable, but no worse than any protective mask. The oxygen bottle was for emergencies only, since this area was supposed to be pressurized. Bart had an emergency transponder he better not need for several reasons, some tools and a water tube. He carried a long pole that was part poker and part walking staff.

He and Aramis had no trouble working out how to use the gear. It seemed the contract laborers learned quickly enough. That was reasonable. Most of them had probably worked in deep mines on Earth or elsewhere.

So, looking like laborers wasn't that hard. All they had to do was show up at the pool and wait for assignments. The trick was not to do poorly enough to be noticed, nor well enough to be pulled out for promotion.

The two men were part of what had been a long line, now much shorter, as details headed off in various directions. The passage they were in was lit enough to move through, with signage posted periodically, and had reinforcement braces spaced at even distances. The beginning was railed, but this section was mostly under survey after having been drilled.

Ahead, the tunnel broke into a large pit.

The shift leader slowed, and saw them looking at the cavern ahead.

He said, "Yeah, there was a gas bubble or something here. Popped. No one knows how deep it is, but I think they said a hundred meters? And it's round, so the floor's pretty thin, too. That's why no vehicles are allowed here. The plank is safe enough, though. Just lean on the wall for support. They're supposed to put a railing in at some point, but I haven't seen it yet. It's only been a month, though."

The man skipped over the gap in three long steps.

Bart followed, keeping his eyes only on the plank and not the hole. It was actually a pretty stout chunk of plastic, about five centimeters thick and thirty centimeters wide. It hardly budged under his weight. That was reassuring.

There were other bubbles, too, from the size of froth in milk to several meters. Certainly volcanic in origin.

The leader pointed.

He said, "Okay, poke around up there and see if the ceiling has any loose spots," then moved to give directions to someone else.

Bart thought he must be joking. That wasn't just unsafe . . . was it hazing of some kind? He couldn't argue, though. No trips to the manager's office, no arguments. He raised the pike and started jabbing at the ceiling. Over his shoulder, he realized his guide had moved far back.

After a minute of poking, the man painted a mark on the wall, like others Bart had seen. Apparently, this was the way they did it.

"Okay, move five meters and do it again."

Bart did so, and his first jab yielded a half cubic meter of rockfall. He bounded back as it tumbled around his boots.

"Good. Keep doing that."

Leaning out and up, to keep his feet on relatively solid ground, Bart thrust some more. Another chunk collapsed, along with a shower of dust. As directed, he kept poking for several minutes until nothing else fell.

"Okay, we'll call them to reinforce it," the crewboss said. "Let's keep moving."

Bart followed along, with a glance at Aramis, who grinned. He grinned back. It was that or twitch in fear.

The mine did have an excellent safety record, he reminded himself. The odds were in his favor.

At least some group had what looked like a scanning laser and sonar package they set up in several places along the bore. There were lots of personnel, and they all had radios. It probably wasn't as primitive as it seemed.

At least, that's what he told himself, as he created rockfalls with a stick.

Elke felt a lot better in the morning, despite not having much sleep. What sleep she had gotten was while curled up on the couch. Jason's rest had been on the floor on a couple of pillows.

Caron was already awake. Her bangs were cut raggedly. She sat on the floor and seemed to cheer up as Elke tracked awake.

"I cleaned up without anyone standing over me. It really felt great."

"Good," Elke said. "I'd say you're as safe here as anywhere. If not, things have really gone bad."

"Can you come with me?"

"Sure." Elke followed her back into the bath cube. Caron stood in front of the lavatory and mirror.

"If I'm going to masquerade as a miner, I imagine I need to get rid of the long hair."

"You could tie it back—"

"It's also distinctive. Chop it, please. About here." She indicated a line a couple of fingers above her collar.

She held still as Elke fished out tool shears, grabbed her hair in a hank and chopped. Her eyes in the mirror were screwed tight, and her mouth pursed. She clearly wasn't happy.

"Do you want me to neaten it?"

"I do, but don't. I need to look like a laborer. I'll rub dark makeup around my eyes before we go out. I figure dirt will keep me looking dirty."

"Good idea. Also, wear something loose or a snug athletic top. You need to conceal your figure."

"Snug is good. I've felt cold since coming down here."

"I know this is tough, but you say 'hang in there' in English, yes?"

"American English, but yes."

"Our success rate is very, very high. And this particular team has not lost a principal, even though we had to blow up buildings, hijack two ships, and shoot our way into a TV station."

"I don't think most of the details were ever made public, but I'm dying to hear that story sometime."

"After we get you to safety, I'll tell you," Elke promised.

John had found some extra bread and pastries in a commissary somewhere. That and some tea had to suffice for now. Caron, Aramis and Elke ate some, drank some, dressed down and headed out.

John had said just walking into the labor line was safe. Elke trusted him, though she felt rather exposed, and more so without explosive or weapons. She would negotiate for a bonus for future assignments like this. She much preferred to be armed, even if the threat level was higher.

There was a changing room, or rather, separate male and female changing rooms. She and Caron went to the female side. It wasn't at all crowded, but there were enough women for cover. There were bins of clean thermal underclothes, teflon suits and gas bottles for their respirators.

Caron knew enough to manage, and Elke had training for vac suits, so it wasn't problematic. They dressed up and geared up, pulled on boots and work gloves, and headed back into the labor pool.

They managed to slip past the time clock. Since they didn't care about getting paid, that wasn't really an issue, and no one said anything, likely assuming they were already on the clock. So all they had to do was get out of sight.

She spotted Aramis as he wandered through the crowd, shifting and pushing and unobtrusively heading their way.

She kept a bored look on her face, under her flattened and roughed up hair. She was as unremarkable as possible, but just being female here attracted attention. Caron was remembering to slouch. It helped. Aramis slipped in to act as block behind, and no one was likely to start trouble with him. He was big enough, and Western, in the upper ten percent masswise, and clearly fit even by miner standards. They shuffled into a line against one side of the bay.

Elke leaned casually back against the wall so she could see everything going on, with peripheral vision while she stared blankly ahead. Miners in three lines moved forward, got assignments, got safety gear, and disappeared into the tunnels.

Their line crept forward, and then they were at the front. The foreman tossed her a key.

Caron was right behind, as he said, "You, over this way."

Elke touched his shoulder and said in a thick Czech accent, "Fresh meat. Also doesn't speak English. We supposed to stay with her."

"All right then. You." He pointed at where Aramis had been a moment before, and the next man in line headed off somewhere else. The three of them were together.

The man turned back and handed them keys, then said, "Fresh meat gets to chop ice on Slime Mixer Fifteen." He shoved a wheeled cart that rolled toward them before veering off to the right. Its wheels were bent and they squeaked.

Elke nodded noncommittally, while wondering, *What the* kurva drat *is a* slime mixer?

Aramis asked, "This way?"

The man nodded, "Yup," and turned back to the line.

Caron led them down the dark hole, which was lit inside, just not as brightly as the staging areas. Elke moved into the lead, but let Caron up close behind her.

"You know where we are to go?" she asked.

"Yes," Caron said. "Through this tunnel, right and then along the catwalk."

Elke said, "Got it. I lead, you direct."

Shortly they reached an atrium with warning signs. It had lockable plastic tubs for personal gear, blast and tool-chewed rock walls, and a scarred and scratched airlock. There were O_2 bottles in several racks. Caron keyed a numbered bin and pulled out the contents. The keypad had a cat's arse painted around it, tail up. Amusing.

Elke did likewise, and Aramis silently did, too. They had cleats for their boots, safety lines, parka suits and hand tools. They had a combination harness/backpack each, and some additional power tools including a jackhammer and saw. The stuff was well worn and should get replaced soon. It seemed sturdy enough to suffice for now, just not efficient.

"So what is this task?" Elke asked. "Outside, I presume?"

"It will be in the pit, near the bottom," Caron said. "The slime mixer takes powdered ore and mixes it with various liquids, starting with water, so it can be centrifuged for separation. The slurries are then piped from different density levels in the mixer to various process plants, where they might be reduced by chemical processes or smelted, or vaporized for deposition on plates."

"How awkward is it going to be to clear ice on this?"

"That depends on how afraid of heights you are."

Elke moaned softly. That wasn't what she wanted to hear.

The lock opened, closed and opened again, to the familiar thick, filthy yellow crud eddying past. The elevator was a lattice-mesh gray plastic cage. It had UP, DOWN and STOP controls, no floor numbers. Elke elected to keep her eyes fixed on a corner girder as they descended. Aramis made a comment or two under his breath. Clearly, he wasn't thrilled either.

After an interminable three minutes, they reached a platform level that was laid atop one of the road cuts. Caron pushed the cage open, straining to lift the vertical grate. It had probably been counterbalanced at one time. Now it was just heavy metal. They walked out onto the rock, which made Elke much happier, and started trudging toward the multistory hazy outline ahead of them. It looked to be sixty meters or more in height.

It grew a bit as they got closer, but not extremely, until Elke realized it went down another level, and there were more levels even below that. The scale was disconcerting. Rather than being in a pit, it felt as if they were on the side of a mountain. The concave curvature was almost imperceptible.

Then they were upon it, its shape visible, all angles and flying plates and beams, beyond foreboding in this light. Elke could figure how to take it down, and how much power it had, but it was still terrifying to look upon.

Another plastic mesh platform set on the rock led to it. Once out into space, there were stubby railings that looked spot welded on, and a ladder. Caron grabbed the rail and proceeded up. It was sturdy enough, just slender and almost freestanding. That of course was what made it strong, but it didn't make it comfortable.

Caron started along the catwalk at a cautious walk. In seconds, she slowed to a gingerly walk, then to a shuffle, then to a crawl on her knees.

Aramis was fine with that. They were in no hurry, and he did feel safer. The scaffolding swayed slightly. Intellectually, he knew that was a good thing, and expected. His guts clamped down and quivered, though. He'd much rather get shot at; he could respond to that. This went on and on and there was nothing he could do in response.

Elke definitely had courage. She didn't slow her pace, and used one hand for balance, the other to drag her tools. His own bag rattled slightly over the sections of the floor. He assumed hers did, too, but the vibrating grumble from the mixer and the buffeting air currents hid any noise.

It sure would be nice if they had enough oxygen and pumps to pressurize the mine with air, rather than the sulfur crud. Was that a logistical matter? Or was it one more way to keep the miners under control? An uprising would be difficult if you relied on your employer for a mask to breath with, and had to return inside their perimeter every six hours or so.

They were about twenty meters up from the machinery below, on a small accordion mesh platform supported by four bars of angle iron with coarse, spatter-coated welds. The railing was knee height; just high enough to trip one, without any real support for the worker.

They edged out over the huge pit, in which slime tumbled and churned. It rumbled and shook the structure, and somewhere there was a resonance. The catwalk shook in sympathetic vibration. Aramis grunted and tried not to moan himself. How many million cycles could the thing shake before it cracked? The odds against it cracking right at this moment were remote, but . . .

It got dustier and filthier the farther out they crawled. Overhead, that huge conveyor dumped megatons of ground ore into the maw.

"Here's a frozen nozzle!" Caron fairly screamed. He could barely hear her. She edged around it and snapped her line on. Elke stayed on this side and coaxed Aramis to the wide area underneath.

The nozzle was hidden within a huge sheath of ice, centimeters thick. While they chopped at it with axes, Aramis unslung the small jackhammer, heaved it up, and jammed the blade into the ice. He clenched the trigger and felt it *wham! wham! wham!* against the ice, and his chest. Chunks flew, cracks formed, and in a few seconds he had the main part clear. As a large chunk came loose, a jet of water blasted back at him, then away as it blew more ice free. A large lump weighing probably fifty kilos fell away, then another. The women chopped the thinner ice sheath all the way back to the base.

One down, nineteen to go.

As they moved on, the mist was already frosting in the air and freezing back onto the strut.

The next one looked like the first, and the third did, too. It seemed to be an around-the-clock job. It was cold, the atmosphere toxic, the platform shook and thrummed as the wind whistled. They chipped and blasted at the ice, then skated over the metal mesh to the next one.

It became a routine bad dream, with the sweat-grimed mask stuck to his face like an octopus, the cold and wind and yellow haze, the vibrating platform, roaring noise creating a combination of mental fugue and low-grade horror.

Caron slipped, grabbed the railing, and kept going. One of the welds broke, whether from defect or erosion didn't matter.

The metal bent and sprung, sending vibrations thrumming through the catwalk. Caron snatched tightly at the piece she had, and clung to it. The next section held, at an oblique angle, with Caron about two meters down.

Aramis analyzed it in an instant. If she fell, she'd die. If they called for help, there would almost certainly be some kind of after-action review, and she'd be revealed. So they had to get her now. There was no way to climb onto the railing without causing further failure, and nothing to grip on the catwalk edge. He had a safety line, but no way to attach it to her, and she needed both hands to hold onto the swaying railing.

"Elke, I can lift you both. Give me your ankles."

He expected her to argue, but she didn't. That look on her face was sheer terror, though.

She turned around on hands and knees and crawled to the edge of the platform, under the attached section of railing next to the failed portion.

Here goes, he thought. They were both trusting him. He grabbed Elke's ankles and gave a coaxing push. She crawled over the edge and bent at the hips. He kept pushing, and her knees bound up, her butt in his face, until she found some angle that worked and squeezed over.

He heard her yelp as she dropped to full extension. Then his elbows ground painfully into the metal while her eighty?—ninety?—kilos of woman and gear pulled on him.

He'd figured Elke for about sixty-five kilos, and Caron for about sixty, but that didn't include the gear, plus what he was wearing. He wasn't sure if he could lift that much now, which might mean they all died, because there was no way as a man he could let them go and then walk away. A flush and sweat broke out all over, and he felt it itching and stinging his eyes, and his hands got cold and clammy inside the gloves.

He leaned over to let his chest take the pressure, with the raised lip under his arms. Elke stretched down, though she might have her eyes closed, the way she flailed. However, she got a hand on Caron's wrist, and then gripped it with both hands. Caron clutched back, then, apparently at Elke's direction, slapped her other hand over and scrambled slowly up the ersatz hanging ladder the rail had become. That let her get a solid grip around Elke's shoulders, and Elke around hers. Then with coaxing from Elke, she nodded and carefully hung free.

Aramis strained, feeling his biceps and pecs cramp from the tension, and veins pop in his head. He got Elke's insteps over the edge, and she bent her feet to lock them in place. He paused a moment, got two deep breaths, then shrugged to his knees. That put his wrists on the angled edged of the railing, and as soon as he heaved, Elke's shins scraped along it, scratching and tearing the fabric of her parka pants. It had to hurt like hell, too.

He leaned forward enough to avoid breaking her knees, then threw himself up and back. She bent into a perverse crouch, ass up, hips grinding into the railing, and he reached under her arms and heaved, her air bottle jamming into his chest and balls. With half her weight on the platform now, it wasn't too hard to yank, drag and pull until he could reach Caron's wrists and elbows, and drag her back onto solid mesh.

They all three gasped, sweat pouring off and fogging their face shields. They just sat and let the strain and fear ease off to manageable levels.

"Let's not do that again," he said.

"Agreed," Elke nodded through a gasp.

"How long can we sit before they notice?" Caron asked.

"We can use that hut," he indicated one of the little igloos. "That's what it's for."

The two women nodded, and he led the way in a crouching huddle. The height bothered all of them now. He urged Caron in first, Elke next, and he brought up the rear.

The hut had no airlock, was just tall enough to stand in, and had chairs and a microwave, plus a stovelike solar-powered heat element. It pressurized in under two minutes so that only traces of sulfur could be detected. The back third was a tiny toilet and shower with a sheet metal screen that offered basic privacy. He suddenly realized how badly he needed to go, but they took turns again. The pressure he felt was painful by the time it was his turn.

Yes, that had been creepy.

They hadn't thought to bring any lunch. There were some basic ration containers on a shelf, but none of them was hungry. Aramis did drink water, though. He got his brain back into a calm, professional state.

"Hut Nineteen, is everyone okay?" a voice demanded through a speaker. He jerked.

Of course, it made sense that everything was monitored.

"Yes," he said. "Minor scare on the railing, we need to rest for a moment and drink some water."

"Understood. Please remember to report in upon entering the Emergency Shelter, per Company safety regulations."

"Thanks. We'll do that next time."

So, this was not a place to discuss any tactics.

Aramis waited until the thudding rush of twitching fear retreated a bit, then indicated for them to go back out. Caron's face screwed up and she blinked back tears, but she nodded and donned her mask quickly.

Yeah, he didn't like it either. Tranks would be nice, but they'd also ruin coordination and reflex.

Back outside, they moved over the mixer again, relying less on the railings, and kept on around the perimeter, chipping ice, as four one-hundred-meter-long mixing arms rotated around the bowel of the caisson. Yeah, falling into there would be pretty final and permanent. He'd keep note of that. Someone might want to arrange an accident, or they might need to. Bad news.

At lunch time, Caron led them back to the hut. As soon as the airlock latched, Aramis said, "Hut Nineteen, lunch break."

"From where?"

"Slime Mixer Fifteen. Ice removal."

"Got it. Thirty minutes."

"Yes."

Thirty minutes of Caron not talking, Elke muttering in Czech, and Aramis trying to bring his own body under control—they were all shivering from cold and stress—was not restful. They ate some of the heatable meals, which were bland but manageable, a bit better than field rations.

The rest of the day passed in a chilled, shivering, cursing fugue, hacking and chopping and beating on ice.

By the time the shift ended, and they departed around the catwalk the same way they'd come in, there was no indication they'd accomplished anything.

Aramis assumed another shift would be along shortly to repeat the process.

Dinner presented yet another problem.

It was very unlikely anyone would recognize Caron in her current state. The smeared makeup was now smudged, with sweat and dust added to it, her hair was part spiky, part matted, and she looked dead tired. Apart from that slight pout that never left her lips, she was nothing to write home about.

Except, of course, that they were surrounded by ten thousand miners with fewer than six hundred women.

She said nothing as she got jostled in line. There were no overt gropes, but lots of rubbing and bumping. Caron ignored it. Or hell, maybe it was some kind of human touch and she liked it. Probably not. Elke, though, did not like being touched, but tried not to shy away. She exuded anger in ripples he could see. Aramis knew he was seeing a human part of her. He decided to keep it in complete confidence. Besides, he didn't want her angry.

The line was long and slow, but the smells were decent. That was chicken stew, fresh bread, and some salad. The servers didn't speak English, and just tossed lots of everything onto the trays, heedless of the plates. Aramis was fine with that. He wanted a lot of calories after today.

Elke muttered, "I'm going to find a better hiding place. We're supposed to improve safety for our principal. This did not do that."

"Yeah, well, we needed to duck in a hurry," he whispered back. "This is the last place they'd look."

"With good reason. But we can do better."

They stopped talking as they approached a table that had three seats available.

The men around it looked up at the two women. Aramis might have been invisible, and he was fine with that. The less anyone perceived them as a group, the better.

One seated man said, moderately loudly, "At least we get some nice scenery now and then. Good evening, ladies."

He smiled. It was friendly enough, but he was rather coarse looking, from India or Bangladesh or somewhere else that had aged him even before he came to this rock. He spoke accented but good English.

Elke grunted. Caron rolled her eyes. Aramis made eye contact with the man and twitched his eyebrows. He had Caron next to him.

"Jack. Doing time in labor." he introduced himself. "You?"

"Emin. Crusher operator," the man said.

Aramis didn't care. He was trying to distract him from the women and create enough rapport the man wouldn't consider fighting out of hand. While doing that, he sat down and started plowing into his food.

It really wasn't bad. The chicken was a bit greasy, overall it was a little bland, but healthy enough, and plentiful. He shrugged inwardly and devoured it. It was the only food he was going to get.

He noticed from the corner of his eye that Caron started eating very neatly, pure class. Table manners would be a red flag in this place. He nudged Elke gently, she glanced a millimeter in his direction, he wiggled his fork and went back to scooping food with it. Elke turned and nudged Caron.

"Good stuff tonight," she said, shoving a mouthful of chicken in and letting a little leak out. Caron grimaced just slightly, then forked up a large mouthful herself.

"Eh," she said noncommittally, but she got much more casual with her tableware.

Damn, it had been one hell of a day. They'd have to AAR, too, whenever possible. For now, Aramis finished his institution standard meal.

Elke stood up, walked off, ignored a few brushes and came back with two ice cream bars.

Aramis was slightly annoyed that she hadn't gotten one for him, then remembered the character she was in. They were just laborers, nothing more.

One of Emin's neighbors said, "I think I'm going to have to eat at this table more often, if you ladies are going to be here."

Elke leaned forward and said, "As long as you remember she's mine." She followed that with a hug and a very serious grope. He saw Caron flinch for just a moment, then relax, then act as if she enjoyed it. At least he hoped it was an act. Or not. Damn Elke.

"Fucking dykes," one of the men said with a disgusted shake of his head.

The other said, "No problem. Do her right here if you like," in a very reasonable tone. "No one will complain."

"Right after you and your friend," Elke replied very smoothly.

Aramis thought that was actually a moderate risk, judging from his own repressed urges and the expressions on the miners' faces.

Elke caught that at once and added, "With this guy here," and pointed at Aramis.

"Hey, fuck you, bitch!" Aramis snapped back, finding it very easy to sound offended.

"Well, I can't control your dreams," she replied.

A few nervous chuckles ran around, then conversation shifted elsewhere.

"Yes, always that way with the men," Elke said. "Come, Cory, let's go." She stood and herded Caron with her, taking their trays to the cleaning window and then out. Aramis gave them enough head start that he wasn't obviously following, though who here would blame him if he did?

There were six theaters in the broad low dome the miners used as billeting, arranged in a circle near the middle. Atop them was a meeting area the size of a small parade field. The airlock doors on them suggested they were emergency shelters as well. That made sense.

Elke and Caron browsed the screens for a few moments, and Aramis sauntered slowly past as if on his way to check something else, while eying the pussy. As he passed them, Elke mumbled, "We'll sit at the back of the theater and sneak out twenty minutes into it."

He decided his best bet was to not go in, and be waiting for them surreptitiously. After that, they'd be on schedule to stop by Eggett's.

Mine security ran past and he froze. They ran past, though. He heard someone mention "Fight." That seemed believable. He noted the bars closed early, counted drinks, and that some of the miners seemed to be using khat or hash or other recreational stuff, and probably some borrowed or stolen medical drugs, too.

He considered that Bryan really should have been here more than once or twice for overviews. His trust had killed him.

✧ ✧ ✧

Jason felt fine after a day of tuning motors and sharpening tools. He stepped into their new hideyhole and decided to say nothing of it. His friends and Caron looked like hell.

"Not a fun day, I take it?" he asked. He figured it was best to get them talking.

Caron's face was empty as she said, "Frozen. Toxic atmo. Almost fell. Extreme heights. Obnoxious miners. Bruised. Pinched." She choked it off with a sob, but got it under control.

"Mine wasn't that bad," he said. Indeed. He'd managed to lurk in the back of a workshop, fiddling with motors for far longer than needed, before bringing them to the foreman. His work had been unremarkable, by intent.

Alex said, "You can rotate with me."

"Why, what did you do?"

He held up a comm slate.

"Walked around in a hardhat and half a suit, making notes and mumbling, and occasionally talking into my phone. No one wants to mess with a suit doing inspections."

Jason said, "Dammit, I should have thought of that first." Still, he'd found the repair work time consuming without being dreary, and certainly less strenuous than the kids had found theirs.

"You can swap off with me. The other issue is we can't rely on any phone or radio at this point. We need to set up some kind of contact with our HQ, though. This was made clear to me last time."

Aramis, predictably, snorted a laugh and then restrained it. It was not a laughing matter, which made it that much funnier.

Jason said, "Through a lawyer is likely doable, with an encrypted message. You have a onetime pad, yes?"

"Of course," Alex said. "I even have a message ready. You have a lawyer?"

"I had not got around to that preparation when this happened. However, I do have one in mind. We'll need to get me back inside the dome, though. Any lawyer down here works for the company and will have to talk to the main office. We need one for the tourists."

"So we need to hit the resort again."

"It's secured. Miners can't get in. Safety. Or, I gather, my uncle's mistrust. You're going to have trouble getting in."

Aramis said, "Trouble, yes, but there is an access corridor. Take spare clothes in your backpack. You're going to get filthy."

Alex asked, "How much do you need?"

"Ten thousand should get me started."

Alex visibly cringed.

"I realize the economy of scale here, but that's a lot of clandestine cash in one chunk."

"I'll bring back what I don't need, but I can't appear cheap."

"Yeah, there is that. You have a clean suit or such?"

"Where?"

"I do," Eggett said. "You're not too much smaller."

"Other than chest and shoulders, but I can make it work. I'll just look like I'm puffing out my chest to show off."

Aramis snorted again, but at least it was just humorous in that context.

Elke said, "One day hauling is a fair risk. There are not many women here. Caron and I won't blend in well enough. Work out of sight is better."

Horace said, "I agree in general, but Caron is distinctive, and you are obviously European. These women are Bantu, South American and Polynesian."

"My Spanish is awful, but I will manage," Elke said. "I also speak passable Russian. There are Eastern Slavs here. Caron also looks a bit like one. I'll do the talking."

Aramis shrugged. "We've pulled it off so far. Once I get Jason started, Bart and I can fake Russian enough."

Eggett said, "Make sure you get the right crew. You don't want to be in with the wrong caste."

"Ah . . . how distinctive is it?"

"Think of it as social classes," Eggett said. "Ruling class and certain guests, above all laws and rules. That's the company officers and possibly some department heads. Then paying guests and retainers of the ruling class, like yourselves yesterday." He nodded at the Ripple Creek team. "Some are degreed, some just inherited money with hirelings to do the thinking. Hard to touch at all because of connections.

"Then, management for mines and habitats and resorts—contract professionals with big salaries, like . . . well, me. They can replace me, but not quickly. My assistants don't have my experience. What you're going to encounter, though, are mine supervisors down here. Up above it would include household and hotel managers, logistics, engineers, major craftsmen, hires, contracts and from family connections and clans. Suits, but just employees. Professionals glad to be here for the cred. European laborers are usually trustee type mine labor managers, construction managers, support contractors. Some non-Euros are housekeepers and such up above, and janitorial and such in the casinos, and skilled equipment operators. The lower groups are down here. Some of the Asian Slavs, the Africans and the Pacific Islanders are cargo handlers, delivery, machine operators on the basic stuff, just drivers and assembly. You want to go no lower than that. Below that is just grunt labor and menials. Few of them speak much English, they get what you've been doing at best, usually much grubbier, and you'll be very noticeable.

"Basically," he said, "you want to find people who look like you and in work clothes, who speak some English or Spanish or Russian. Caron can pass as South American. Can you drive?"

"Yes," Caron said. "I'm decent with a dump truck, though these are bigger than I'm used to."

"Only if it takes a crew of two and I come along," Elke said. "Where?"

"Let me pull up a 3D view," Eggett said.

Aramis asked, "Can I get a copy?"

CHAPTER 24

Jason found the infiltration easy enough. With a suit rolled in a typical daypack and a hat on his head, no one gave him a second look. Aramis's directions were clear, and he found the bypass corridor without trouble. Eggett had a couple of different codes for access, and assured him one of them was standardized. He kept his head down as he coded for entrance and walked through the pressure-tight door.

Aramis had been correct about getting dirty. Housekeeping didn't come into this access corridor. It was thick with rock dust and dust bunnies. Stuff was stored here, which was against safety regs, but all too common in his experience. Some areas were the full two meters wide. Others were under a meter and required twisting. He did get quite dusty. The corridor was also a good couple of hundred meters long.

At the far end, he pushed through the door, which was unlatched from this side as long as pressure was normal. That left him in an alcove. He changed quickly into the suit, and examined the door ahead cautiously. This is where he might get discovered. Civilians were not supposed to be on this side.

He cracked the door and checked for traffic, then, with his trusty clipboard in hand, stepped out, carrying the pack like a doccase. A couple of people glanced his way, but none gave him a second look. There was no immediate response that indicated a threat, but he should accomplish this fast, just in case.

In five minutes he was at the level he needed to be, in the mall that ran along the back of the dome nearest the passage to the mines. That wasn't coincidence. Some of the staff came in on weekends, when the passage was open. Joe wasn't likely to let it reopen until he'd nailed down what he needed to, though.

Taking a breath to ground himself, Jason walked up to the office of the lawyer he'd picked and through the glass door.

"Good day, how may I help you?" asked the secretary behind the desk. Male secretary. Not necessarily indicative of anything, but with an Arab lawyer could mean a conservative.

"My name is Rogan," he said. "I understand Mr. Rahman is busy. I also understand that my need is somewhat urgent." He placed his hands on the desk. He projected hurried and agitated.

The secretary noticed the card under his hand. It was a M1000 cash card.

That got his attention.

"Wait here and I will inquire," he said, and carefully took the card.

In very short order, the door was held open for Jason—an anachronism, it being a powered door. He smiled, walked in, took the offered seat, and waited for the door to seal and for the hum of a privacy field. Nice seat. A cross between French Colonial and modern, along with real wood paneling transported from Earth at considerable expense.

The man behind the desk was creepy and oily, but must have respectable credentials to be here. He couldn't afford it otherwise. Besides, Eggett recommended him.

"I am Abdullah Aziz bin Rahman. How may I be of service?"

His grip was firm enough, and he understood Westerners enough not to get as close as was customary for his culture, though as a Grainnean resident, it wouldn't bother Jason much. Still, if he passed as an American, that was better.

Jason offered, *"Assalam u allaikam, sabaaH al xeer."*

"Allaikam a salaam. Ahlan biik." Bin Rahman seemed at least slightly more genial to a paying client who made a courteous attempt at bad Arabic.

Jason sat politely, accepted a mug of tea and sipped. The formalities indicated he was being taken seriously.

He placed the cup carefully down and said, "Thank you for

seeing me on short notice. I'm told you handle business matters for travelers and guests?"

"Yes, sir. I understand you're in somewhat of a hurry?"

"I need to send a lengthy legal message. It's on this zip," he said, and handed over the stick. "Its arrival and confidentiality are of the utmost concern. It must arrive at this address, but through an intermediary."

"There are many ways to send a message. I appreciate your business, though." That was a hint to the client that while it was secure, it was suspicious. Bin Rahman didn't seem offended, but he did look cautious.

Jason remained relaxed. "Very good, sir. Here's another thousand marks. Please deliver the message and I will come back for a response. I'll check in two days. I may visit, or call with this code." He laid a paper down on the desk.

"Certainly, Mr. Rogan. You have a generous retainer for these items."

"Thank you. I'll need a billed statement at the end, but in the meantime, let me know if another deposit is required."

"Of course, sir. I'll send this personally within the hour. Do please finish your tea. "

"Thank you. It is excellent."

"Yes, a wealthy Canadian introduced me to maple syrup for sweetening tea, instead of honey. It is one of God's finer creations."

"Very much. Thank you for sharing it with me. But I know your time is valuable. *Fursa saHiida*." He placed the cup down, rose and shook hands again.

"My pleasure, sir. *Allaah yisallimak*."

He bowed slightly and shook hands again on the way out. He deliberately turned the wrong way, browsed a couple of shops and admired imported leather wallets that cost forty times as much as they should, and laser-carved indigenous rocks that were pretty but useless.

Still no notice, which was what he anticipated, but it didn't hurt to be careful.

That done, he headed back the way he'd come.

Alex was out with his trusty slate when his phone buzzed. It made him twitch and flinch for just a moment.

He took a glance down. The number displayed was the one Cady had for emergencies. Good.

"I'm here," he answered, as he strode for a wall where he could see anyone approaching.

"It seems Joe Prescot wants to cancel all our contracts ASAP. No hard feelings, did the best we could, sorry about the two operators who died with Bryan. Bonus and effects to be forthcoming. Now please with all respect get off the planet."

"That is his prerogative."

"It is," Cady agreed. "However, certainly the threat level is now higher. He should be hiring additional security. He's not. A couple here and there for the local staff, but no dedicated professionals."

"Well, we already knew he was dirty. Too late, sadly."

"He played craven well," Cady agreed. "However, we publicly have to leave, so you can't get any support from us. The stuff already in position is yours, of course. M says he's endorsing, privately, the continued support of Loretta. Either it works out, or he'll write off the costs."

And write off six dead operators, if it comes down to that. But we don't discuss that.

"Understood. That's the best we can manage under the circumstances. Thank him on our behalf, and keep the intel open. We'll do what we can. Now it's time to close this channel."

"Understand your requests, and good luck."

"Out."

Bart made his way back from the commissary, toward Eggett's quarters, for the daily briefing. It wasn't ideal to keep doing that, but they couldn't use radios or phones for anything other than periodic short notes. Today he had a message telling him to do so, which meant something was to happen.

Elke had installed a discreet wired camera a few days earlier, so he timed his approach for a quiet corridor, and the door opened as he reached it. He slipped sideways and in and it closed behind him. He was last in. The others stood in a group around a stranger.

Eggett's quarters were not home, but they were a safe base, and he relaxed slightly. Of course, they might be found out, but no random notice would affect them. The man was presumably vouched for.

He was a bit shaggy. Not that his hair was long, just self-cut, it seemed, and he needed a shave. His clothing was intact and without holes, but starting to fray at the edges.

"Call me Ontos," he said. "I was mining supervisor for one of the tunnels until a year ago."

Bart asked, "And you chose to stay?"

"I like caves. I don't need a lot of luxuries. I don't like Earth much anymore." He didn't offer more than that.

"We need some privacy and food for a few days, and some access to the upper levels now and then," Alex said.

"I can probably arrange that. What's in it for me?"

"Some money. Not a lot."

"Any helps. I'll consider it."

"We don't have a lot of time, unfortunately."

"I can see that you don't. And I will do nothing if you continue to lie to me." He nodded at Caron. Clearly, he knew who she was.

"Yes, I am," she said.

"And we're not going to mention her name. It probably doesn't matter, but we're going to be paranoid."

"Yeah. You know about the wage and living conditions here?"

"I do now," she said. "That was not our intent, and I assure you I'm going to make that sick fucker of an uncle of mine pay for it."

"So you say."

"I do."

"It's a shame you didn't notice some time ago. Or your father. The money seems to have blinded you."

"The money came about in a hurry. It also seems my uncle wasn't happy with his share and was willing to cut us off from all information to boost his, no matter how many people he hurt."

"I'll accept that for now. You realize I'm putting my ass on the line legally and literally?"

"Has the Company ever violated an agreement with you?"

"No. The agreements often sucked, but they were adhered to."

"You have my word on your safety and secrecy. Neither I nor the Company will pursue charges on any administrative crime. We won't try to have you removed. That doesn't absolve you of murder or such."

Ontos extended a hand. She took it and shook it firmly.

"Then follow me," he said. "In pairs, just within sight of each other. I'm going right."

He turned, opened the door and slipped out.

At once, Alex said, "Shaman and Bart first. Elke, go with Caron. Aramis, trail them. Jason and I are last. He pointed at bundles of gear. Aramis must have recovered another cache."

That was quick, Bart thought. He grabbed stuff in a hurry and led off.

Horace came with him, and moved slightly ahead to keep Ontos in sight. Ontos punched a code into a secure door, which led into another maintenance corridor. Horace caught it just in time, and waited for Bart, then moved on briskly. Bart held the door until Caron caught it, then turned and strode down the corridor.

It was dimly lit and empty, all plain metal panels with occasional cross passages to other entrances.

Ahead, Horace checked each threat point. Bart did the same, glancing down the stark, gleaming halls. Aramis passed the two women to provide additional front cover.

The passage turned from metal to drilled stone with bare conduit between sparse lights. This led to billets and access tunnels to the mine proper. Bart scented occasional whiffs of sulfur.

He saw Horace wave to the left, and acknowledged. He reached that point, checked in front and behind and then stepped into the side passage. It was unlit and dusty.

Shortly, they bunched up as the roof got lower and the sides narrower. It was just about a meter by two at this point.

Bart flipped on a tiny light. Five lumens was plenty, with dark-adjusted eyes. He kept it angled down to illuminate their path. No need to send a bright, piercing gleam down the tunnel to anyone who might be there.

He could just make out Ontos, who turned off to the left into a very raw looking tunnel, more like a volcanic gas vent that had a hammered floor. It twisted and the floor rose and fell. A bit farther on Ontos turned right into a passage low enough to be uncomfortable, with a floor too rough to crawl on. Bart grunted as he hobbled, and tried to ignore the now sickening sulfurous odor.

Then space opened back up into a rounded bubble pocket big enough to stand in. He skittered slightly on the relatively smooth ground, but came to a stop with the others in a cluster. He held out an arm for Caron, and she steadied herself. She looked healthy enough, as far as her expression went.

Ontos reached into a couple of crevices and pulled, and a

section of rock shifted. It was a thin sheath over a metal door. Very ingenious, and it probably took some time to build.

Aramis went first, Alex reached through and went second, then Elke shooed Caron in and followed.

"Well, this is comfortable," Elke said from in front. That didn't prepare Bart for just how comfortable it was. Elke wasn't usually one for understatement.

Bart had to duck through the hatch, and rose inside. He stepped away to let Vaughn and Mbuto through. The compartment wasn't large; was barely taller than he, and the walls were bare cut rock.

However, it opened up to the left.

There were four plastic chairs, probably stolen from the mine, and a card table. The bed was built of plastic panels, with an air mattress atop. A comm was fastened to the wall. It was a few years out of date but perfectly functional. The lights were minimal but adequate. It wasn't luxurious, but was safe and far beyond a "cave."

Elke glanced around quickly, doing an assessment. She ignored the porn. It was a guy thing and didn't bother her. Caron very graciously acted as if it didn't exist, but when she thought no one was looking, she surreptitiously glanced at the images, whether curious or critical wasn't clear. It was the straightforward male interest stuff. Oral and lesbian and not much setting, just people having sex. Why Ontos chose those as wall decorations was the part she wondered about. Trying to create an impression of not being alone? Yes, he had two full-length, fully-clothed shots of a current model, too. She nodded once she understood the motivation. Some people handled lonely well, but they were still lonely. Asocial tendencies didn't negate the need for interaction.

"I'm limited on food," Ontos said. He looked them up and down. "You probably eat a lot. You get two days."

"We brought some food, too," Caron said.

"As long as it's not beef liver or chicken."

"Pork sausage, chops, some smoked herring and some cubed steak."

His eyes widened a bit.

"Ever think of sharing that lower down?" he asked.

"As far as I know, we were working on it."

"Yes, it did take a while for things to work through the system," he said. "Well, I very much appreciate your generosity. Eat all you want within reason. I'll produce more, after a fashion."

Interesting, Elke thought. Did the dropouts have their own farm, even?

"You can sleep over there, and around that corner. I don't have nor need a lot of space."

Alex said, "That's fine. We have sleeping blankets and cold gear. We'll make it work."

Ontos pointed down a dark corridor.

"Latrine is at the end. Close the door and run the vacuum pump once you're done. It'll smell a bit, but it dissipates quickly. The vacuum boils liquid, which is condensed out and filtered. I'm never short of clean water for drinking, but don't yet have enough for bathing. Working on it."

"Got it."

"I can have hot sandwiches ready in an hour. Bread's easy to get. They leave it out to be eaten so it doesn't have to be recycled."

"Sounds as if you manage adequately. This isn't a bad bachelor pad."

"It's crude and raw, but it's all mine and I have my entire life to improve it."

Caron asked, "What about your pay and bonuses?"

"That's what I'm living off," he said. "I figure I can stretch it for life here. Clothes now and then. Occasional gear like comm upgrades. A snack once in a while."

It didn't seem like much of a life to Elke, but she knew people with ascetic and hermit tendencies. It was probably safe enough. He had his own small kingdom. For some, that was happiness.

Jason was the last to clean up. The latrine was a deep pit, and vacuum dried everything to minerals in between uses, with the water evaporated for recycling, for cleaning as Ontos had said. The drinking water seemed to be smuggled bottles from the mine supplies.

He and Elke had placed a couple of tiny transponders outside Ontos's cave, just for heads up. That, and Elke had planted a charge that would blow anyone in the bubble into greasy smears, hopefully without damaging the structural integrity. She was still fabricating charges whenever not sleeping or on duty, and had her old panoply of destruction in a pocketed vest, ready to deploy.

Between the four chairs and some crates and a rock shelf on the wall, there was a seat for everyone. The sandwiches looked a bit like burgers, and had pickled cauliflower in them, with marginally fresh, only slightly brown lettuce. There was salt and ketchup in packets, but nothing else. Still, it was food and hot and calories. He grabbed one and took a bite. Not bad. The flavor was a little odd.

"Do I dare ask what we're eating?" he asked.

Ontos said, "Worms, of course."

"Worms," he said. That was a bit unexpected.

Interesting. Elke and Aramis stared at each other and refused to blink. Bart hesitated only a moment. Caron twisted up her face, but took a deep breath and kept eating. Jason had eaten a few bugs and critters in survival training. This looked like burger, so he wasn't going to freak. He was just going to concentrate on thinking burger, though it was a little chewy, like squid in a way.

Ontos lectured while he munched. "They're easier to grow than vat meat. Enzymes for compost are easy to get, the compost is free, the worms churn it into soil for plants, and they grow fast. The day before serving, you drop them into a tub of flour. They shit out the soil and fill up with flour and incidentally coat themselves. Then you either mince them or drop them into hot oil. Very high in protein and not a bad flavor."

Everyone kept eating, though there was obvious strain.

Caron asked, "Is that typical here?"

"For dropouts? Yes. We sometimes trade for steak or chicken. I snag guinea pig when I can. We've got pretty good brain power in the network. We have water condensers, hydroponics, guinea pigs. We're working on caged chickens and pygmy pigs."

Caron's expression was horrified, fascinated and pitying in turns. She said nothing, though, and kept eating. It looked slow and labored, but she minded her manners. Only occasionally did she half wince.

She asked, "What about power? Other food?"

"Snoopy, aren't you?" he asked. "Batteries and a power inverter. Solar charging at a hidden spot on the surface by another dropout who also runs a thermodifferential power farm. We're slowly running wire, as we get it, and hooking into the grid. Other food is leftover or dated from the kitchens. It doesn't save, doesn't cost the company anything, and we cut down on costs of disposal, though they don't get to compost it themselves. The batteries are stolen, but will be returned eventually."

"You don't have a pressure-tight door. What happens in event of a major leak?"

"I grab my mask and pray."

"How long can you last?"

"Not long. Seriously, though, a hole bad enough to do that would kill thousands anyway. It's not a real concern. What is a concern is that my pump and filter have limited capacity to refresh the air. You'll need to get me more batteries and filtration fluid."

"Just steal it?"

"That's an interesting question. You're the owner. Can you steal from yourself?"

"An accountant would say yes. Also, I'm not currently the practical owner, so again, yes."

Bart said, "I know where to get those. When we next make a patrol I will do so."

Alex deemed this a safe hole for now, but there was a timetable in effect. The longer Caron was missing, the more likely her uncle could get a declaration of death. Also, he had more time to consolidate his position. So, as they'd done before, they needed to get the principal through hostile territory to make a visible presence. Going out of system was probably out of the question. The tourists were well known, and the miners' transports were less than safe, easy to check, and he wouldn't put it past Uncle Joe to blow a few up, or just halt them, if there was a risk of Caron escaping. The current "delay" on departures was part of that. Joe was even graciously paying bonuses to the detained laborers.

Alex got Elke's attention, and she came over. She hunched over next to him.

"Yes?" she asked quietly.

"How's Caron holding up?"

"Brittle."

"Keep her company. You're the closest thing to a female friend she has."

"I'll try, though I'm not much for female culture. I've been a tomboy forever."

"I know. Do what you can."

Elke nodded and rose.

Caron took that moment to speak up herself.

"Alex, you were hired to protect me, not to baby me. Your blokes need to sleep more than I do. I'll manage on the rock."

"I'd like everyone to be able to move quickly and effectively. Some padding will help."

"Okay, but not more than yourselves."

"Thanks, miss," he agreed.

In short order he had everyone save himself and Shaman bedded down, with watch rotations planned. Elke was wrapped around her shotgun as if it was a teddy bear, which would creep him out if he hadn't seen it before. Jason and Aramis had weapons comfortably next to themselves and touching them, so if the weapons were disturbed they'd notice. Bart slept on his back with a holstered pistol and the carbine tucked into the blanket.

Ontos ignored his bed for now. He was watching a movie on his comm system.

"How's your access?" Alex asked.

"Fair. Varies. I'm at the edge of the connection range, so it's never great and sometimes stops for minutes at a time."

"Do they know you have access?"

"I'm partially spoofed, but it doesn't matter. The network is unshielded. It's not as if anyone can sneak in from outside."

"Good point. How amenable are you to letting us log in from here for research?"

"Can you mask your terminal ID and location?"

"Yes on the ID, and probably on the location. I'd need to talk to my experts."

"If so, okay. But I have no desire to ship back to Earth. Be careful."

"Naturally. We need to stay hidden, too."

"Point."

Horace had slept worse places. No one was currently shooting at him, and he was dry and out of the weather. However, the rock was hard and sharp and cold for sleeping. The air was warm enough, and spare clothes and packs made for a lumpy insulation. It didn't seem to affect Bart, Elke or Aramis, but they were young and flexible. Caron acted very stiff and sore on rising. Horace knew he felt as if he'd been bent over a frame and worked over.

Neither Jason nor Alex looked very happy. He tried to grab an extra nap, sitting on his pack and leaning back, and it helped.

"You snore," Jason told him when he twitched awake. He seemed to be in charge. Alex was asleep in the corner.

"Entirely possible," Horace agreed. "How are things?"

"Elke went out on patrol and found more boom."

"Good?" That sounded useful, but Jason's presentation was a little odd.

Elke spoke up, "We're going to need them. They use thousands of tons here. They'll never notice."

Horace asked, "Aren't nitrates one of the things they do import?"

"Some. They also scoop ammonia from the gas giant. This is fine."

"How are you fixed for caps?"

"Some. I'll get more."

Jason said, "We do need them, but I'm constantly leery of anyone going off, and of stealing stuff."

Horace said, "Jason, you're fundamentally an honest man. This type of thing is a problem for you. In general, that's good. In these cases, it's ultimately Miss Caron's property and she's fine with it. Approach it like that." *And try to ignore the risk we face of getting found and killed, either by gunfire or being tossed into the corrosive atmosphere.*

"That must be it. It doesn't feel like a war zone, but I should treat it as such." He seemed more relaxed at that concept, as insane as it was.

Aramis and Bart had not stolen explosive. They'd stolen rope, locking rings, boot spikes, gloves and a variety of other climbing gear to supplement what they had. Bart had a bag of filter media for Ontos.

Aramis said, "Rope is the hard part. The metal is made locally. The rope can't be."

Caron said, "One of the things on the list is fiberglass, and various silks and plant fibers. We can't get a useful result, though. Lots of splinters and fraying."

Ontos had been sitting back, politely pretending not to hear. He stood and took two steps, putting him in the group.

"So what's your plan then, as much as I need to know?"

Jason said, "I believe we're going to try finding a strong defensive position, announce Miss Caron's survival, and rely on publicity.

It worked last time, when we had actual governments trying to harm the principal."

"How are you going to make that announcement?"

"That's the question. We can tap into various sources, but it has to be fairly widespread, including to public persons who are either off planet or going that way. Then we button up until we get more support. Any harm at that point would be obvious. Then it comes down to a stock and proxy fight, which is not our concern, though we'll morally support Miss Caron of course."

"Do you think the miners will care? Let me rephrase that: right now, the miners like him a lot better than his brother and won't care about Miss Caron, the pretty debutante."

"They like him?" Horace asked.

"You realize he has control for the time being, and has just announced wage increases of fifty percent for the bottom, ten percent for team leaders?"

Caron looked as if she would undergo fission with rage.

Then she exploded.

"Fifty percent? A thousand percent wouldn't be enough, backdated to the beginning! Additional insurance benefits and stock options as well! That's what my father intended. The nerve of that . . . murdering *thief*! First he robs our employees and blames us, then he attacks our household retainers, ostracizes us from the world, tries to have me . . . argh!" She turned and slammed a fist into the wall.

"OW!"

She jolted in pain, sank to her knees, and started bawling with deep sobs and wails.

Horace stepped carefully in to look at her abraded and bleeding knuckles. He caught a glimpse of Elke looking at Ontos, who stared wide-eyed.

"We want him alive," Elke said.

"I'll do what I can," Ontos agreed with a slow nod.

Caron hadn't broken any bones, though her hand was definitely going to bruise up, and her knuckles were skinned and torn, to shiny bone in a couple of spots. That had been a dedicated punch, the poor girl. Horace sprayed a topical, then a disinfectant, didn't see any need to debride, so just used tweezers to gently tug skin back into approximately the right place as she whimpered and shuddered and cried. It was about time she cried, he thought. Her father had been murdered and she'd been in shock from that, and stressed from all the other events. It also kept her distracted while he sprayed an artificial organic for the bruising and tearing, with a sealer over the knuckles. Her hands looked even younger than the rest of her, even with the recent labor. They were fine boned, aristocratic, and soft.

Once done, he resisted the urge to kiss her hand. She felt like a daughter at this point, and even that was not a good position. He simply stood and let her hug herself and cry. Elke nodded, moved closer, squatted down and patted her shoulder gently.

Alex had awoken during the excitement, stretched, rose and came over. He assessed things with a quick glance, gave an expression that indicated he grasped it, and looked around.

Jason said, "With Alex's approval, I think we should work on something that will attract a lot of attention and make it harder to hide things. A riot might be good."

Ontos cocked his head and scrunched his eyes.

"I'm not sure you want a riot," he said. "The last time I saw something like that in a mine was in Pakistan. The Uighur and Mongolian workers ripped things apart until the army showed up."

Alex grinned. "That's pretty much exactly what we want." Apparently, Ontos hadn't heard of their reputation.

"That's going to be an awfully big, dangerous mess."

Elke said, "I like big messes." She grinned her psychotic grin, the one that almost looked sexual.

"Well, I can do it," he admitted. "It's actually not that hard."

Caron looked quizzical. Taking a breath to control her sobs, she said, "What are you going to do? Tell a bunch of scary lies?"

"Not at all. I'm going to feed them the truth, or at least enough to piss them off. Do you want this now?"

Alex said, "Sooner generally is better. How long will this take?"

"I can call some friends and meet in a couple of days. Another couple of days will get the word out. Figure two more for things to be in place and people ready. A week. How big do you need it?"

"We don't want to destroy things en masse, just shake them up enough for the press."

"A few hundred, then."

"Sounds appropriate."

"A week it is, if that's good for you."

Horace said, "By definition it is not good, but it's the proper course of action."

"Then stay here and don't touch my stuff." Ontos checked his own security camera, then pulled the door open and slid out.

After he closed it, no one spoke for about a minute, then Aramis said, "I think we've achieved a level of trust."

Khan had only the one name. He didn't feel poorer for it. In fact, he found it amusing that people might need three or four names to distinguish themselves. It was silly. The sensie he was watching had two people with complex names, though he saw them as He and She. It was a European production with a Eurocentric view, like most. He preferred the Indian or Persian productions, but this was tonight's option.

The man who slipped into the seat next to him had three names, but chose to go by one.

Khan spoke very softly, and not just to be polite to other viewers. "Hello, Ontos," he said.

"Khan. I need a favor. It is time."

Khan took a moment to think about that.

"Now, while things are improving?"

"Exactly now. They're weak and we can get more, and I have a special ace to help. Mr. Prescot will give us a lot more, and isn't in a position to make a scene. He doesn't want his brother's death investigated too closely."

"I see," Khan said. He'd wondered about that accident.

Ontos continued, "I need a small number of reliable men. I'll tell you where. A week from now." Then he rose slowly and slipped back out.

Khan pondered the news. It was exciting and a bit scary. He had no doubts that Mr. Prescot could arrange immediate or painful deaths, and would never be questioned. On the other hand, the promised wage increases had only just now materialized, and far less than promised. On the other hand, he'd heard of that from the first rotation of miners, including his cousin. The hiring people always told you how wonderful things were, and the facilities were better than any other mine he'd been to, though the working conditions were comparable and the atmosphere was toxic.

He trusted Ontos. Especially as Ontos had been urging them not to react for a couple of years now. If he said it was time to be loud, he meant it.

He waited five minutes, then wandered out himself. The sensie wasn't conducive to thinking. He didn't need to think about the instruction. He needed to consider who to tell.

In a few minutes it came to him. Pacal was a Mexican miner who enjoyed talking about the old strikes and agitations, the fights with mine owners and their hired thugs and the Federales.

He found Pacal where he expected to, sitting in the section lounge with his favorite tequila. Khan was Muslim and didn't drink, and he couldn't fathom how anyone could drink anything that even smelled like tequila.

"Ah, Pacal. I see you're more relaxed. Is your tequila budget big enough?" He took a seat. Pacal always sat well to the rear, near the emergency exit, facing the door. Khan moved into the corner so as not to obstruct Pacal's view, and to get a bit of one himself. He was nervous about this.

Pacal leaned back and laughed from his barrel chest.

"It is now. I no longer must decide between it and my family. I can afford both, and have a little left over."

"Very little," Khan said. "It's not a lot of money as it is."

"No, but it was more than we had."

"Yes, but I wonder about it. Mr. Prescot blamed his brother, but he was the one here and in charge. His brother dies, and he gives us a small raise. It was not what he had hinted. The percentage hides the fact that it is only a few marks more. They can afford a lot more. It seems the greed is still there."

"You say he talked a good game but didn't play." Pacal squinted and leaned forward.

Khan nodded. "Exactly. It was too easy. They're taking billions a month out of here, more tens of millions out of the resort, more in royalties on the equipment we helped them develop, and we're getting less than a hundred marks a week. He did not even hesitate. If he didn't have to even consider it, we could have gotten more."

"Maybe you are right."

"You know I am. Even if they paid all of us ten times as much it would not hurt the profits. Ten thousand of us at ten thousand each is one hundred million. Their profit is in the tens of billions. We are less than one percent of their overhead."

Pacal wrinkled his brow. Complex mathematics were beyond him, but it made sense. There had been a lot of talk of large benefits if Prescot could get his brother to agree. If his brother was dead, there was nothing in the way. He obviously was mourning, but was dealing with it, managing the mine, and had given them a raise, but only a token. Twenty-five marks, even to all the miners, wasn't much when looked at compared to the huge size of the operation. It wasn't just a token, it was rude, condescending, and a slap at their manhood, really.

"We should strike."

Khan smiled slightly. "You are not the only one who feels that way, my friend. We've never struck here. But while the benefits for us are good, the pay is what supports our families. The facilities cost them near nothing. What we need is wages."

"I will talk to the Latin miners," Pacal said. "I will get back to you. In person. Write nothing down. Do not chatter on the radios. Let them think they were successful, then we can make our demands with a convincing strike for support."

Ontos wanted the strike anyway, but that should be easy enough to provoke if it didn't happen by itself.

"That sounds good, my friend. Enjoy your degreasing solvent."

Pacal laughed again at that, and downed the glass in a gulp. "Another!" he said cheerfully, and raised his glass to the bartender.

Even with approval, Jason couldn't believe they were doing what they were about to.

He checked his bypasses again, hoped the codes were right and said, "And . . . go!"

Elke opened and eased through the door, crawled down and back into the tunnel, and rummaged. For three tense minutes Jason watched for anyone passing by, or showing on his readout of other entrances. For three minutes his pulse and blood pressure hammered in rushing waves.

Elke backed out ass first, and he wasn't sure how to help. She wasn't a person you touched and she seemed okay, just weighted down.

She stood and said, "I'm happy."

"I can't believe we're acquiring charges this way."

"Just walk and get the doors," she said.

"Roger."

CHAPTER 25

Aramis found the situation a bit amusing. From the finest suite on the planet, to a senior staff office, and now to a scraped-out hole in the ground. He hoped this was as far down as they got. Much deeper and he'd have to learn to breathe sulfur.

Still, Ontos treated them decently enough, and it was probably quite secure. They could plan, and lurk, and not worry about cameras or oxygen consumption or visibility. Their host was unlikely to turn them in, as he was an outlaw himself, by choice.

The plan sounded simple in theory. Stir up the miners, head for the top, take down Joe Prescot. On the one hand, less dangerous than extracting someone from hostile territory. On the other hand, there really wasn't a surrender option at this point. Caron and they had to disappear to keep Joe's side of the story.

It also wasn't going to be as simple as the theory, of course.

Since no one else had yet asked, Aramis did. He sometimes jumped the gun and irritated people, but he was sure this was a fair question.

"So what exactly are rioting miners going to fight with, and how do you avoid having Joe Prescot simply evacuate their air, or worse, vent in the atmosphere?"

"We do have some weapons. It's not as if anyone was planning a revolution, but . . ."

"But you were planning a revolution," Jason said. "Why else?"

Ontos seemed embarrassed.

"The pay is not great. Revolts have happened elsewhere with better conditions."

Caron said, "But we don't want to stop you. Not anymore. We want to help. What do you have?"

He shrugged and stepped back to another alcove behind a rock pillar in the corner of his digs. He reached in easily, pulled out a long item and handed it forward.

He said, "Well, we can laminate plastics of different tensile strengths. A little grinding gives us this." He handed the curved staff toward Aramis.

"Interesting bow," Caron said. She reached for it, and Aramis let her take it.

In one smooth motion, she raised it and drew it back to her ear, arching her body into the gap between string and limb, two fingers and thumb lightly holding the grip section, three fingertips on the string. She winced a little because of her knuckles, but the draw was steady.

Ontos said, "I use it outside in the corridor. There's a place I can set a target." He pulled out a light tripod with a thick foam disk.

"Go ahead," Caron said. "Arrows?" she asked, easing the string down.

"I'll bring some."

Alex said, "Bart, down hall. Shaman, up the way we came. Rest of us together."

With a check of all the sensors, they filed out into the bubble, and pulled their way up to the corridor. Ontos went ahead with the target.

He set it up in the dark, rocky bore. Aramis spun his torch to level five, bright enough to illuminate it. Level one was for night vision. Level ten was enough to blind.

Caron reached for an arrow from the quiver leaning against the wall. It looked like extruded plastic with cemented vanes. She spun it between thumb and finger while casting her eyes along it, flipped it over the grip, drew again, and let the string roll off her fingertips right over her jaw.

The arrow *thwap!*ped into the target, centimeters from the X.

"Nice shot," Aramis said, eyebrows raised.

"You seem surprised," Caron said with a coy smile. "Haven't you heard of the Welsh longbow?" She held it up. "This is a composite recurve, but the same principles apply."

"Yes," he said. He had. He just hadn't made the connection. "I didn't know you trained."

"Some time back, yes. Do you need lessons?"

A couple of years before, Aramis would loudly have declaimed that any civilian, especially a woman, had nothing to teach him about fighting. Elke had impressed him, though, and a Sergeant White from the Aerospace Force, and Agent Cady, and a few others. He'd never handled a professional bow, only arcade toys.

"Yes," he said at once.

"I think we all do," Alex said. "Not a bad idea."

Aramis had good instincts. The bow wasn't that dissimilar from a rifle. You held it firm but not tightly, braced but not clenched. The forward hand rested the bow, the rear hand nocked and drew, and then rolled the string, like squeezing a trigger. His first arrow wasn't close to the bull, but he managed a reasonable string with his first five. Caron adjusted his stance and the second five were a bit low and a lot tighter.

"High is better than low," she said. "It gives you a generally longer zone that will count."

"Danger space, we call it," he said. "I'll practice more. Let me swap with someone else."

"Okay... Elke?" she asked.

He'd practice, and try to forget her arms on his, her breath on his neck, and those impossible boobs against his back.

And he'd try to forget watching her do the same with Elke. Dammit.

They took five minutes each to familiarize. They could all manage the horizontal plane and keep the arrows in a few centimeters' width. Adjusting for vertical took a lot more.

"This is probably not effective for us without a lot of practice," Bart commented as they slipped back into Ontos's cave.

"No," Ontos said, "but some of us do have practice, and mass volleys will have a good effect, as well as scaring the crap out of people. I have one because it's near silent. Gunshots would draw attention. I still may need to defend myself. But as a general issue, no. Besides, we don't have enough plastics to steal a lot of it."

Caron said, "I'd like one. Possibly even a little heavier draw."

"That's twenty kilos," Ontos said.

"I think I can handle twenty-five."

"That's strong for most women, but if you can shoot it, I'll get one. A dozen arrows is about it, though."

"They'll be bulky," she agreed.

Aramis was impressed. That wasn't bad weight for a civilian.

Alex said, "I have no problem with you being armed, Caron, but do please let us act as blocks first. Defend yourself only."

"I will," she said. She seemed a lot more confident with the bow in hand. She even smiled slightly, for the first time since the evacuation and her father's death. And those eyes...

Elke asked, "What about firearms?"

Ontos looked suspicious. "What about them?"

"I was suggesting Caron get familiar is all."

Caron raised her eyebrows.

"Oh!" she said. "I don't mind, but I have moderate practice with the bow. I'm much more comfortable with it."

Alex said, "Then carry that when it's appropriate. Use what works for you."

Ontos seemed to be hesitantly on the edge of speaking. Aramis gave him a nudge.

"So you were going to say?"

Ontos shifted, took a breath, and said, "Yes, we do have some firearms. Pistols, shotguns and some carbines."

"You can't have enough guns to help," Caron said.

"Close to five hundred so far."

"How? There haven't been that many authorized total. I know. The approval went across my f-father's desk."

"We have a chemical industry and machine shops, therefore, we have firearms. No trouble at all. Stunners pose a problem, though ultrasonic transducers aren't too hard to come by."

Caron looked offended and shocked. Clearly, she hadn't considered that option.

Jason chuckled.

"I've been trying to make that point since we landed here, and to other contractees previously. If someone wants a weapon, they're going to get one. You can stop the decent people, but never the ones you need to worry about."

"More importantly," Aramis asked, "do you have people trained in their use and in proper unit discipline?" His brain entertained horrible images of reckless laborers shooting every which way.

Ontos nodded. "We have a number of veterans, and our existing background means a lot of the old timers are very disciplined and trustworthy. If they can handle mining charges, they can handle a gun, I suspect."

"Fair enough," Aramis said to avoid debate. He wasn't convinced, but he did feel a bit better with that info.

Jason said, "Okay, guns. Talk to me."

Ontos leaned back and seemed to relax a bit.

"Well, the handguns are a bit bulky. Old design, rather blocky, but reliable. The carbines are just a tube with a barrel and a breechblock. Not elegant."

"Most carbines in history were basically that. What caliber?"

"Ten by twenty millimeter."

"That's not standard. I'm guessing you have a drawing press for the cartridges?"

"Yes. Only one. That and primer production are the holdups. We have less than two hundred rounds per gun at the moment."

"You were really planning an armed rebellion?" Caron asked.

"Not so much planned, as no one ever stopped the preparation. We all knew it was coming. No one wanted to be unprepared, regardless of when or how or why or who. There was also the likelihood—no offense, miss," he said with a nod toward Caron, "—that the leadership would try to tromp on us. The only example we had was your uncle, and he was playing good boss/bad boss with your absentee father as the bad boss."

Her jaw clenched, but she smoothly said, "I can see that. I will see about fixing it."

"I'll bring one of each later, then. I don't know where they are. Someone else gets the parts and puts them together."

Jason said, "So one of your shops gets an internal job order for a component and makes it. Presumably the maker is on your list, since rifled barrels and certain magazine components, and triggers, are fairly obvious."

"Something like that, yes," Ontos admitted. "The work is broken up and distributed. Some of the finish steps are done with hand tools rather than automated, such as trigger shaping. The barrels are smoothbore. We never figured to fight at ranges where it would matter much, and the ammo is close to spherical."

"It should still give you twenty meters reasonably," Jason said. "Very effective for what you need."

Caron did not look thrilled at finding a conspiracy cabal operating in her mine.

"Things seem to be even worse than they appear to me," she said. "I wish I had been here sooner. Or my father." She sighed rather than tearing up. "But I'll make it right now."

Ontos said, "It's time for dinner." He was probably trying to avoid any embarrassing scenes. However, Caron was obviously not thrilled at the idea of more worms or vat-grown chicken or liver.

Jason said, "I'll cook."

"Sure?"

"Yes, least I can do."

"Go ahead."

Ontos seemed fine with him doing so, and Jason thought he could manage a little more elegance. He grabbed some of the real chicken they'd brought from above, then went on a search.

Rice, dry eggs, dried vegetable chunks, and a dozen leftover sauces. He could fabricate a curry from that if there was . . . yes, cumin. All good.

Converted rice took minutes. Frying it with a little egg took less. Frying and simmering the veggies and chicken with the sauces took barely longer. In fifteen minutes he had four bowls and four plates—Ontos had sets of four—of rice with steaming golden curry atop.

Elke made appreciative noises and dug in neatly. Aramis downed it before Jason sat himself, and then went for field rations. The rest ate comfortably. He tried a full bite himself. Yup, not bad.

"Oh, I do like this," Caron said. With a quick glance at Ontos, she added, "Warm and comforting."

Yeah, she'd definitely not been happy with wormburgers. Still, she put on a brave act for a spoiled kid. Her father hadn't done badly.

"Glad you like it," Jason said. "Although cooking is not in my duty description, so there will be a fifty mark surcharge."

Caron giggled and said, "Certainly." Then she turned to Ontos. "Can you tell us a story?"

He looked surprised.

"Story?"

"Anything. Something amusing about this place. It's getting to me, and it can't be all bad."

"About like a mine anywhere else, really," he said, leaning back.

"The most important thing . . . when somebody yells 'Run,' you fucking run. You don't stop to ask what's going on, or look around to see what the problem is. If it's the same direction everyone else is running you'll probably be all right.

"Okay, here goes.

"When I first got here, babe in the woods, the production was rather crude. They had trouble with purity and keeping enough power moving. This was right as the fusion plant was finished. They were using solar, which was fine, except we expanded beyond the capacity. That shortage led to problems. It was about this cold, too," he indicated the space around them. "Which is how I got used to it, and to living in a cave. We could always sleep on warm machinery, though.

"Guy showed me this huge pipe they'd extruded, that had a flaw. It was broken, cracked along the majority of its length with a fissure that had to be twenty centimeters wide in some spots. Above and below the break, in bright orange letters was the word 'Broken.' I asked the boss if that wasn't kind of obvious, he shook his head and said that if you didn't label it, sure as hell someone would load it on a truck and ship it two hours to a place that needed a pipe.

"They had an electric smelter, and some of the gauges went out. Couldn't stop, because they had to have production running. Gauges came from Earth. In the meantime, someone started catching live rats. There's always a few around, dunno what the fuckers live on, but I guess they eat rock. They used them at the sight glasses. Ran a quartz pipe across just far enough out to stop it melting, but to gauge the mass. Guy told me, 'If the rat makes it past here, the temperature's too low, if he explodes much before that, she's set too high.' Apparently it was pretty accurate, too.

"Back then, they just dug and dumped. There was a huge tailing pile, hill sized, next to the pit. It started in a depression, but filled it and kept building. Unbelievable. Toxic shit, too. It was dust that would get all over your suit, full of fine silicon, some asbestos, sodium and potassium ores, phosphorus and sulfur. Stuff they used in small quantities and tossed the rest. Lots of silicon. Irritating rather than toxic, but it got everywhere. Like being in a desert Earthside.

"They used the pipes to run pressure down to blow dust out, and suck it up, like a massive vacuum cleaner. Periodically we'd have to drop a charge up the line to blow out concretions. After a while, the pipe would fail. So I got to wait out there one day, double shift, for a replacement. We cut the bad section out, shoveled away all the gunk that looked like baby shit and smelled kind of like scouring powder and waited for the truck to bring us a new length to slide in. It got there and they rolled it off the side before someone noticed the big orange words 'broken' painted on the outside. I was the only one who thought it was funny."

"Nice," Jason said with a grin. "I've got a million military stories like that. I miss it."

Ontos said, "Yeah, you have to laugh at the stupidity, or sooner or later you go gaga. Anyway, I'm gonna rack out. Keep it quiet, please."

"Will do. Good idea anyway. Shaman, you're on now?"

"I am," he agreed, and stood up by the door.

The rest bundled under covers and got as comfortable as rock allowed.

A shift later, Ontos had a case with two guns in it. Bart kept an eye on him. He might be an ally, but there was still a lot of money involved. He sat still and watched, with his hand relaxed, open and near his pistol.

Ontos took out the samples. The carbine was an open block with a mechanism within, a barrel and a welded on pipe for a grip.

Caron gave the weapon a quick look. She did study it like an engineer.

"It's just channel steel with a spring release, and a block with a barrel."

"That's all it takes," Jason said. "Brute force and simple."

"Wouldn't aluminium be lighter?" she asked.

"It would, and wear out faster from pivot movement."

"I'll stop trying to second guess. I can see how these were easy to make."

Aramis took it and examined it.

"The barrel's not rifled," he said. They'd been told that, but it was odd to encounter it.

Bart shrugged. "Why bother at less than twenty meters?"

"Good point."

Jason said, "This will definitely outfit a respectable insurgency under the circumstances."

The pistol was a rectangular tube for a grip, and two nesting tubes for barrel and frame. It was blocky, heavy and had no safety or slide latch. It would shoot, though.

"Five hundred total?" Alex asked.

"Four hundred and sixty three," Ontos said. "The shotgun is a single shot break open job. Those were easier to make."

Bart did not think a mob outfitted with these would constitute an army. However, it would be a dangerous mob. That would prove a great distraction.

Aramis asked, "Any good melee weapons?"

"More demolition tools."

"Good."

They had their wrecking bars, and a similar tool the miners could access, with a huge gripping jaw and a chisel back for prying.

"How many of those?" Alex asked.

Ontos said, "As many as we need. I think a couple of hundred guys with these constitutes at least an armed, angry mob."

"And then some."

"Also these." He handed over a set of metal knucks. They were brutally heavy.

"Tungsten?" Jason asked.

"Yes. Cast."

"Not something we really need, but I'd like a souvenir when we're done. Most impressive."

Ontos nodded. "I can do that. I can't get another bow for the lady," he said, "but I can let you take mine."

"I'll be fine with that, thank you," she agreed. She turned to Alex. "So, do you think that can stop a hundred thugs?"

"No. He'll have the regular police try to stop the miners, and keep the thugs for us personally. However, now we *only* face a hundred paid thugs, plus a few distractions in the way and any tourists wandering across lines of fire.

"Which brings up rules of engagement," he said.

"Uh . . ." she replied, looking scared again.

"The thugs I can kill if I have to. There's no moral ambiguity there. The cops I'd prefer not to—they're your employees. But if they hinder us, we'll have to fight them, and it's a lot harder to be nonlethal than lethal."

"I understand," she said. "I also trust you to avoid a fight if possible."

"Absolutely," he said. "Not fighting is easier than fighting. Then, there's wandering idiotic tourists who may try to help, watch, or generally get in the way. I have no intention of killing them, but accidents do happen. If that happens, it's going to cost you a lot of money certainly, and it may cost us criminal charges."

She looked depressed rather than scared now, but with an odd, quirky grin.

"When I said I didn't need that much money, I wasn't suggesting just burning assets in a swath. I prefer to be frugal."

"We'll do what we can, but Miss Prescot, will you back us up in court or in the press if we have to hurt ignorant bystanders and well-meaning but misguided cops?"

"Yes," she said. "I will."

"So we'll do what we can to minimize it." Secretly, he was glad she hadn't heard details of their first, rather spectacular mission.

"I also need a really big distraction in case things screw up the plan, which they probably will."

Elke said, "I will crack the dome if we need."

"That's a bit extreme, isn't it?"

The look on Elke's face was disgusted. Did he expect any proposal of hers not to be extreme?

He had the decency to blush slightly and shut up.

Bart asked, "Do you have enough to do that?"

"I have one to do that."

Alex said, "That's a pretty potent item."

"It's actually a small nuke, about two hundred tonnes." She reached over and pulled her ruck away from the device.

He choked on his drink.

"You are fucking kidding me."

Bart felt a ripple of heat himself. Gott in Himmel.

Aramis said, "Nice! How many do you figure to kill?"

"If I do it right, none, sadly. A horrible waste of a beautiful device. However, it should prevent much violence while offering no provocation."

"You have my condolences, Elke."

"I shall mourn and drink to its memory later. Right now I must emplace it where it will do the most bad."

Aramis said, "I like you, Elke."

"Just think of me as an artist," she said with a winking grin that was mousy-cute and disturbing at the same time.

Alex said, "That's what you were doing the other day with Jason. Jason?"

Jason blushed and looked guilty.

"We went to get charges. I didn't know she had a nuke until after we left. Still, it's only a backblast charge, not one of the big vaporizers."

Caron looked as if she'd just found a grenade in her oatmeal. Well, he supposed she had.

"What exactly are you planning with a nuke?" she asked. Her tone was halfway between amused and horrified.

"The same as your uncle planned, but better. I will stir up much dust, shake the ground, crack the dome, and force everyone into emergency gear. This will negate large numbers of hired mercenaries who will be scrambling for cover, and do not all have breathing gear. They will likely be mixed in among large numbers of civilians your uncle is depending on to keep him solvent."

"What if he decides he's losing and to have them kill civilians and blame me? Since he'll blame me for any collateral damage anyway."

Shaman said, "He does not have that personality. He will not concede failure until taken down."

"I really can't endorse this," Caron said. She spoke firmly and with wide eyes.

Alex spoke just as firmly. "Caron, once we have accepted your charge, there are some orders we cannot take, such as to stand back while you kill yourself. Jason had a lengthy go round with your father about weapons for us. Bryan was a very civilized man, but in the end, he paid an awful price for it. We have all trusted Elke with our lives multiple times. I trust her implicitly, and I agree with her assessment."

Caron still looked ready to stonewall.

"That's a nuke," she said.

Elke said, "You owe me a life. I am calling the favor now."

Caron's conflicted expression was exasperated disgust.

"You cruel bitch," she said.

"I am," Elke said. "I owe you much bitch, too. Pay up."

The young woman chewed her lip. "Very well, I agree. Under protest. Only because you're likely to strap me down if I don't."

"I knew we'd come to an accord," Jason said.

Elke said, "I can only surface emplace it. It must be close enough to crack the dome, but not close enough to actually remove more than a section. We will need two holes, one low, one high, the low one preferably upwind. The dome must evacuate its air and receive the influx. The second hole will be conventional from the inside."

"Didn't we have that when this all started? It wasn't very quick."

"I will make it quick."

"That works," Jason said. "You know if she says she can do it, she can. Then, when we get into the office, I can just threaten the glass."

"That won't do anything. You proved it."

"Yes, but I made that demo to Bryan. Joseph Prescot apparently doesn't know about it. He doesn't have an engineering degree. His is in accounting, of all things. He was the one pushing paranoia on the dome, and apparently it wasn't just to hinder us. He doesn't like the environment and is clearly afraid of it, and he'll have more reason to, then."

"That fits him," she said. "He always was more figure oriented than technical, and not much for judging people, either. So they're not armed with firearms?"

"Some shotguns, with reduced loads."

Aramis cocked his head and raised his eyebrows. "Well, that's not going to breach body armor, but it will mess up a brain if they get lucky."

"There's also a lot of them," Caron said.

To that, Aramis shrugged. "They're not that good."

"Are you sure?"

Aramis said, "Yes."

She looked wide-eyed for a moment, and Alex spoke.

"Here's how it works," he said. "There are possibly three companies who could find operators to match Ripple Creek. They wouldn't take a job like that, because it smells. We're bodyguards, not strike-breaking thugs for hire. There are about five more companies who'd look at it, and realize that they don't want to fight us, because we *are* that good. Their own operators would refuse to engage. They'd be happy to guard your uncle, but they wouldn't dare come down looking for us. Ex Ek is one of those. So anyone he's got who's willing to tangle with us is second rate at best and needs the money enough not to be thinking."

"There are still a lot of them," she said.

"There are still a lot of them," he agreed with a slow nod. "So we'll be going around most of them, and using the miners to tie the rest up."

Jason put in, "What I need now, miss, is every security code you know to every entrance and piece of equipment. Yours, your father's, your uncle's, anything. Also any codes you can get from anyone. I have all ours, but ours are obviously tagged. It still may be useful to use one here and there as a distraction."

"I'll give you what I can," she said. "I'm sure mine are compromised."

"They may be compromised, and still work. People are lazy like that."

They all paused for a moment, and into the break, Elke said "I have something else."

Alex asked, "Elke?"

She pointed at a satchel in the corner.

"I was able to fabricate fifty grenades. They are crude." She walked over and pulled one out. She raised it to show as she explained.

"It's two pipe expansions with plugs at the ends, and a spring-powered striker on a section of fuse. It will burn for three seconds, then detonate. Pull this pin, release the lever, and throw. I had to use discarded fuse sections, so I couldn't test the material as a lot. Some may be as fast as two seconds. Some may push four. The filler is commercial Orbitol."

"Er . . . how much?" Jason asked.

"The lethal radius is about four meters. I kept it as small as I reliably could. This does not include fragmentation effects."

"Yeah, those look like twentieth century crude, just with better filler, though they had better radius toward the end."

"A radius over four meters would be bad in the confines of a tunnel or hallway."

"Agreed. I'm impressed. I'm also going to tape those levers against possible slippage."

"We are short on ammo," Bart said.

"Yeah," Aramis agreed. "This calls for stealth. And explosives. And a nuke. We don't seem to have much ability to scale our actions."

Caron looked nervous and her voice shook a bit as she spoke. "Should I address our allies? A speech to rouse them?"

Jason said, "A speech to the miners would be great, if it would work. At best, you'll mix them all up fighting each other."

"And worst?"

"You'll mix them all up fighting each other, and you'll die in the process. Or they'll turn you in."

Ontos said, "I think it might help. If you're okay with it, I can bring a handful here. They're not yet convinced that they want to escalate from strike to armed violence, especially as worst case is the habitats get vented and they die in tragic accidents."

"I advise against it. They'd jump at the reward," Alex said.

Caron said, "I'm not worried about money. I think I can make a competitive offer."

Alex looked very tense.

"Well, we do need the backup. I guess worst case is we move up our schedule and kill everyone involved."

Bart restrained a grin. Caron and Ontos both flinched at that. Then they looked at each other, with the mercenaries being the outsiders.

"I'll risk it," she said.

CHAPTER 26

The next morning by clock, Ontos headed out and came back with five other men. With everyone crowded into his cave, it was tight, warm and a bit humid and rank. The men were all well-sweaty and their clothes covered in the dust of hard labor.

Caron was in the back on the rock shelf, with a hooded poncho concealing her. The men—they were all men—noticed her and Elke as female, and checked the rest of the team over, presumably as potential threats.

She was nervous as hell, but there was nothing to be gained by delay.

She threw her hood back.

"Yes, it's me," she said at once.

There were exclamations and a couple of brisk profanities.

"I'm alive. I'm trusting you not to turn me in for the reward, as Ontos has trusted me not to reveal what I've learnt."

It got noisy fast, with five conversations at once.

Ontos said, "Quiet," and they shut up at once. They did respect him.

Caron said, "According to company books, the lowest paid worker here clears a hundred G. I realize that's not actually the case. All I can say is, I'm sorry for that, and I will fix it.

"My dear, beloved uncle," she sounded quite as spiteful and angry as she felt, "arranged to kill my father and wants to kill me. If he does, he owns this planet. This is the man who's been running things the past two years. You will not get a better bargain from him."

Nods all around, though some were a bit perfunctory. Still, they were listening to reason.

"So what do we get from you? And how can we trust you?" one asked.

"I want revenge for my father. I don't care about the moral high road. I want that fucker dead. Nor do I particularly care for being so rich I have to have guards in my toilet. I would like some remote semblance of a normal existence. I also think it's disgraceful and embarrassing to treat the help like that, and I've been working down here the last three weeks. I have some appreciation of what's involved."

"So give us some money now. Prove it."

"I don't have any money now."

"Yeah, a bit awkward that, isn't it? How's it feel to be without assets?" He scratched his hair and leant against the wall.

"I have well-trained bodyguards, a weapon I know how to use, a degree in engineering, a detailed knowledge of this mine and the technology running it, a good grasp of the business involved and I own the company. I have had a couple of temporary setbacks, but I'm not without assets. I'm also agreeable to sharing those assets. The only way you get to be part of that is to help me. My uncle won't share. No other stockholders will want to."

"So, you want us to get you into the dome, and then what?"

Bart said, "Then we kill anyone who gets in our way, take her to the office, and lock everything down up there. Miss Prescot resumes control and improves your conditions."

"It's that easy?"

"I did not say easy. We will make it work, though."

One man, chewing what was hopefully tobacco and not khat said, "Allah, if it kills a few of those corporate filth, I approve." He looked Bart up and down. If anyone looked like a legbreaker, it was Bart.

The lead one asked, "So what's in it for us?"

"Much better pay. At least one thousand percent. And more benefits. Continual improvement of living conditions as the mine expands."

"We just take your word on that?" he asked, casually but with a challenging smirk.

"Yes," she said.

He raised his eyebrows.

"As I told Ontos, the company has never breached an actual contract signed here. I understand my uncle lied in his recruiting, but the contract signed here, as horrific as it was, was held to."

"Sure, but I have to believe you're going to hold to one much less favorable to you?"

"How many trillions of marks do you think I really need?" she asked, sounding disgusted.

"Well, you're claiming it will be less than your uncle, but we only have his example to go from."

"So I'll toss in a down payment."

"That's interesting," he said, and there was a buzz around the others, too. "What's that?"

"If you help me, anything you can carry off from the hotels is yours. Take the interactive, the vids, the bedding, the art, anything from the casinos. I'll replace it from our accounts afterward."

"Trinkets, basically."

"Do you think those trinkets won't make your miners happy?"

"True," he said. "What about cash for us?"

"What about bullion for you?" she returned.

"That's fascinating."

She turned and pulled a small purse from under her pile, opened it and slid out several flat bars, and tossed one to him.

He looked at the proof marks through the plastic cover.

"Rhodium?" he shouted in a whisper.

"Thirty grams each. There's more where that came from." She'd judged that correctly. The miners saw ore and process. They never saw finished metal, certainly not the precious stuff. Only the upper castes saw that.

One said, "I don't care to be bribed. I'll take the money, but I do expect everyone will be treated accordingly."

"I'll pay everyone what they're worth, really worth, for the skills and the environment. I can tell you the wages we'd set were five times what everyone has been getting. That was the startup wage. I'm sorry we weren't here sooner."

"So, more money and we get to smash things?"

"Within reason," she said. "Those things and the customers bring in the income that pays you. I have no problem replacing the bric a brac, but you have to breathe the fumes if you burn anything, and if you scare off the customers, you suffer. And I will prosecute for bodily harm or assault. My customers are not worth less to me than you. They're just a source of revenue, rather than trusted workers. Make sure you stress that to the utmost. Any rapists will be tossed into the pit without respirators. Ditto for murderers."

"That's fair," Ontos said from the side. The others nodded and mumbled.

Ontos prodded with, "So, everyone agrees? Help create a distraction for our rightful employer, get some extra money and loot, don't scare the customers too much, and wind up with much better working conditions?"

"Yes." "Sure." "Right." "Agreed."

The initial stage was easy enough, Caron thought. She'd actually grown comfortable with Ontos's tunnel and cave, though she hoped never to eat worm meat again. She could do without the wall porn, too.

Out here, though, was empty tunnel she knew was safe. Ahead it turned into mine facilities that weren't.

She understood that they needed to move as a group, and that that was dangerous. She also knew she was supposed to act casual, disinterested and just blend into the scenery. She was failing at that, sweating heavily and almost shivering with stress.

At the huge lift, they waited with a few others. It wasn't shift change or they'd be crammed and constricted. There weren't enough to require more than one trip here. Still, operations ran constantly and there were a lot of people running up and down.

When the door opened, Aramis shoved her ahead and into the back corner, out of sight. The team was far less recognizable than she, though Uncle Joe had probably circulated pictures of all of them. Still, with hats and a bit of grubbiness, and weapons stuffed into tool bags and the surplus backpacks everyone used to carry their environment gear, no one looked twice, except to notice that Elke was female.

Elke had also zipped her jacket so her boobs were framed. Caron snickered to herself and relaxed marginally. Men would see chest and not face. Her own jacket was loose over a snug bra, and she was out of direct sight.

They stopped at almost every level, with workers coming in and out, and some management. No one gave them a look.

She calmed down somewhat by the time they reached surface level, and they headed out. However, a group of eight was bound to be noticed sooner or later. Elke took care of that by moving ahead with Bart and Ontos.

They entered a side tunnel that she recalled from the plans. It was an emergency bypass for the section. Jason ran a device into the lock, which she presumed was a coder to pick it. Nothing happened.

"Well, that's disturbing," he said casually. He pulled out a couple of tools, plumbed into the lines, and did something that caused smoke, but the door opened.

"They're probably going to detect that," he said.

"Noted," Alex replied. "Weapons out."

Caron pulled the long sleeve off her bow and quiver and slung the quiver. There wasn't much room, and she bumped against the others as they drew guns. She noticed, though, that none of the muzzles came anywhere near her. These people knew what they were about.

The corridor was supposed to be clear for emergencies, and just wide enough for one of the smaller dollies. Instead, it was filthy, cluttered and awkward to navigate. She made a mental note to have that fixed. It was sloppy and dangerous.

They'd gone a hundred meters and reached a broader area that led to an emergency lock and some entrance to the inside, when clatters and shouts erupted all around them. She blinked, and realized there were suddenly a lot more people in the area, armed and armored.

Ontos was next to her. All he had was the cargo strap. Instantly, he snapped out the clip end in a flat throw that bounced off a man's face shield and dropped over his weapon. A flip of his arm in a loop and a yank, and the man stared stupidly at the carbine on the ground in front of him. The return swing arced up and tangled in his harness, a loop flipped around his neck, and Ontos heaved and smash-kicked him in the head.

As thugs closed in, Ontos threw the whole coil at the next man, and it spread into a tangling web that caught his feet and weapon. That gave Elke time to shove Caron back, and Aramis and Bart time to move forward.

Caron had seen martial arts. She had never seen a melee battle like this. Bart was a big, mean brawler who went in with fists, boots and the wrecking bar. Aramis was fluid, graceful and almost as strong. He shifted in a dance of arms and legs. Elke was small in comparison, though not small for a woman, and seemed to just stomp her way through, moving right into people's faces with a stern look and swinging knees and elbows. Shaman looked like a classical boxer with a big knife in one hand. Alex next to her kept shooting even at point blank range, the reports hammering the air and her ears. Jason on the other side was mechanically efficient. He caught an arm, twisted, shoved, stomped and yanked, and a man was broken in four places, screaming in agony until Jason's boot crushed down on his skull with an egg-cracking sound. She cringed.

That just left Ontos with his cargo strap around a thrashing man's neck, straining back as his victim gurgled and turned purple and flailed and then went limp.

The whole engagement had taken ten seconds. Caron hadn't even responded.

Jason and Shaman ran their hands over her again, Jason said, "You're fine," and then Shaman said, "Elke, you're bleeding."

"Of course I am," she said, and extended her left arm as she heaved for breath, looking flushed. The pain didn't seem to affect her much, but the exertion was obvious.

She had a deep gash inside the wrist. Shaman sprayed a sealant, Jason twisted a dressing over it, rolled two loops and tied it off. She opened her mouth and he popped in two pills while Shaman poked a subcutaneous needle in with some kind of local anesthetic. She stayed standing and barely winced through the procedure.

Bart and Aramis checked the door, Alex had the rear with Ontos, and at a nod, they moved forward.

"No regrouping?" Caron asked.

Aramis said, "We are regrouped, and they're surprised, about to be on the defensive. Once you have the advantage, you press it."

Twenty meters later, they reached a turn and another door.

"Elke, open the door please."

Elke skipped lightly forward now, was hampered in the operation a little by her fingers, which seemed to have been numbed by the anesthetic; she fumbled slightly, but in moments had something small stuffed in and around where the lock bar was on this type of door. She made one adjustment, seemed to bound back three meters instantly, and said, "FireInTheHole." She pressed a button and something that sounded like a cross between a bass drum and a loud firework made the door jump in its frame.

Caron raised her bow with a nocked arrow as Bart strode forward, raised his leg, powered up and kicked it. The panel bounced, bent and flew open. He stepped back, Aramis and Shaman swarmed through, Elke third, Alex shoved Caron, and she gasped in nervousness and excitement, blood hammering in her ears.

Two more doors yielded without explosive, and then they came to the section bulkhead.

Elke moved forward, took a quick glance, and raised a hand. Jason slung his carbine and ran up. The two talked and gestured for a moment, then Jason pointed and made a sign.

Caron found herself dragged back, and the whole team ran and ducked into an access corridor. Bart closed the door and stood before it. Aramis moved a couple of meters farther down and faced any potential threats.

Alex said, "Talk to me."

Elke said, "The door is barricaded solidly, as if sealed against a breach. It looks like the entire mine has been locked off from any contact with the rest."

"Can you blow it?"

"Alex," she said, looking very serious, "I can breach it, but I don't know what is on the other side. The monitors read atmosphere, but that could be false. Someone spent the time to manually lock this down against attack or disaster. I'd need fifty kilos to break enough bars to defeat it, and that's very detectable, very dangerous, and seems to be what they're expecting."

"Right," he acknowledged. "Jason?"

"I wouldn't trust those monitors," he said. "They only show pressure. It's about normal, but I have no way to compare, and as Elke says, it could be a trap."

"Can we get any confirmation?"

Caron said, "There are easily removable panels on the outside, to allow for rescue in case someone is trapped. They take common wrenches."

Alex looked at her and seemed a little surprised.

Remember me? she thought. *Part owner, involved in the design as a student, and with a degree in engineering?*

"I guess we have to go around, then. Suggestions?"

Ontos said, "There are tunnels we can take."

Caron said, "You mean the power conduits?"

"Yes, but not just power. They run from the reactor, but also between the two pits. It was easier to tunnel through than run cables across the hole, for the far side. Once it was deep enough, we ran power across and around in the daisy chain, but the old feed is still there as backup."

"How will you get the miners through for our distraction?"

"Either the same way, or we'll just defeat the door the hard way. I don't think you're getting out of this without making a mess at this point."

Elke said, "I don't think we are, either. Keep the masks handy."

Alex got that thoughtful look again. Caron was amazed at how fast he could solve these problems. She realized the underestimation went both ways. Their skill was as technical as her own, and required more intuition and faster resolution. What threats were where, and how did those change in response?

Alex nodded to himself and said, "Ontos, show us where we need to go, any maps appreciated. You stay here and organize the breach. We'll tell you when."

"Can do," the man agreed. "Follow me. I'll get you there and peel off."

There was little point in hiding now. Aramis acted as point, behind Ontos, Bart brought up the rear, the rest in a box around Caron, and Alex constantly shifting around looking for threats. They passed very few people, all of whom did the wallslam of fear or respect. Aramis appreciated that. He'd glance them over, ensure they weren't hostiles, and keep moving.

He wasn't real comfortable moving back down into the mine, but with no exit ahead, at least there would be somewhere to hide and reconsider if this didn't work. Tunnels. Aramis liked tunnels, always had since he was a kid. It was fun to crawl and to watch the depth. He suspected cramped quarters, a long passage and the risk of a toxic atmosphere would detract from said fun.

They caught a slideway and marched briskly along, weapons half-cloaked but still visible if anyone took a good look. Either the word was out or the miners didn't care, or perhaps thought they were some kind of security. Hell, maybe it was their presentation that caused people to assume they were legit. However it worked, they were unmolested as they traversed the surface building to the far end. They didn't pass many people, anyway. It seemed that the labor leaders were following through on their invitation to create trouble, because there were few people at work.

Ontos led through a series of turns and to what could charitably be called stairs—they did have railings and one could walk down face first, with the superstrong metal mesh see-through enough to cause acrophobia as they descended around a cable trunk. Ontos galloped ahead, taking flights in three bounds.

"Slow down!" Aramis said, and glanced back as he hit a landing with both booted feet. It shook, probably as it was designed to, but enough to make him clamp down on his sphincters. This was already very not fun. He clutched at his weapon in lieu of the railing, because intellectually he knew this structure would easily support him. That didn't affect his knowledge of gravity, cheap labor, and a de facto owner/manager who really hadn't cared.

The others were in good order behind him. Caron seemed comfortable enough with the structure. Elke stared straight ahead and navigated with sure feet and a hand on the rail. Jason seemed okay, a trifle tense. Alex was pale. That was all he had time for because they were catching up quickly.

He resumed bounding after Ontos, who had slowed his leaps to something a normal person could rush to keep pace with. There were occasional side access hatches that were all secured and didn't seem to have been messed with recently. Good.

The bottom became visible, which took some strain off Aramis.

A few minutes later he reached bottom, and stared up at an optical illusion of square-spiraled mesh, pipes and rails. The others were seconds behind, and he remembered he was supposed to be point. Ontos stood at the hatch, one hand on the access pad, one on the pressure handle, waiting for a signal.

Aramis held up a hand, Ontos acknowledged by eye, punched a fast code, and stepped aside. Aramis looked through the small port and saw the tunnel they were to take. It was dingy fading to dark, but seemed safe enough.

As boots clattered around him he said, "Elke and Jason will need to clear the entrance and route."

"On it," Jason said, squeezing in front and holding up something technical while Elke raised a camera with a weird fisheye lens.

She said, "I'm first. Crack it."

Jason stepped back from the sweep of the hatch, slapped the handle in such a way to lever it down, and pressed with his carbine to open it a fraction.

After a bare hesitation, Elke yanked it wide, counted five in Czech under her breath, swung around the door, paused and eyed all around, then stepped out.

"Safe," she advised. "Come on through."

Aramis decided to move to the rear as the rest filed in. He ducked through behind Bart's bulk, and yanked the door closed. He pondered breaking the mechanism, but they might need to get out this way. Anyway, they had weapons and stealth. They'd be fine.

The air was breathable, but had a tang mixed of sulfur, petrochemicals, bare traces of ammonia, and ozone. The only discernible noise was a loud power hum. The passage was lit by periodic LED tubes. The walkway was an aluminum grating that disappeared into a perspective point, along with the walls and the low roof. It was two meters tall, with the lights and other accessories depending from the roof, as well as the center-mounted power trunk. Bart would not be able to stand.

Alex asked, "So this will get us to the old pit? Number One?"

"Yes, and from there the long way to the reactor, then the short jaunt to the dome."

Jason asked, "How long is the first leg?"

"Five kilometers. It's a crawlway only. No tram."

"Then we use vehicles around the pit. How obvious will that be?"

"Not tremendously. There's still surface mining."

"Good. And there's a tram from Number One to the reactor?"

"Yes."

"Tell me about the reactor."

"Largely automated pressure vessel, remote control room, lots of clearly marked corridors. You'll have to work around the crew. Wait until night and it's only operators, no maintenance or overload crew for the dome."

"Is there a tram to the dome?"

"Yes, but it's a maintenance trolley and monitored. They'd wonder who was on it."

"That's about another five kilometers, right?"

"Forty-seven, twenty-one meters."

"Got it."

"I'll be peeling off in two hundred meters and taking another hidden passage."

"How many of those are there?"

"Lots. Wherever was convenient due to bubbles, caverns, erosion, gullies that could be sealed over, dead cuts, whatever."

"And all this in a decade?"

"Less. It takes claustrophiles to work a mine, and most of them weren't supervised as long as the ore moved. Nor did the supervisors care. Effectively unlimited resources made it easy. We should be moving, not talking."

"Right." Alex pointed.

Elke moved ahead in a measured pace with sensors over her eyes and in hand. She gave a signal, and Aramis waited for her to move five meters, then took second position. The rest boxed up tight around Caron, mostly behind her against possible attacks from the rear.

Elke had to cant her head slightly with the space available. Aramis was crouched over and knew it was going to hurt if it went on long. He didn't want to look at poor Bart. It must suck for him.

The noise was steady. The fumes and noxious smells got a little stronger but were not overpowering.

He wondered about those. Logically, the access corridors should be either vacuum or pressurized. Pressurized with breathable air made sense to simplify access for maintenance, and to provide an emergency supply. As long as it tested safe, a low-level of contamination wasn't a serious issue. The question was, how hard was it for someone to contaminate it to stop them, if they wanted?

Given the fairly substantial volume, he figured it would take a dedicated weaponized agent or an extremely powerful industrial vapor. They should be safe enough.

Ontos clambered between two supports and under the cable trunk, waved as he did so and disappeared. Aramis hopped over to follow him, but couldn't find any sign. He didn't have time to pursue it and it wasn't on the agenda, so he shrugged and resumed his position.

They moved at a steady walk, and Aramis resumed splitting his attention between potential threats, and map and technical analysis.

That's when the lights went out.

✧ ✧ ✧

Bart was in the rear when it went black. He turned at once against any threats, and considered dropping off the catwalk to gain some maneuver room. However, he was also needed as a bullet catcher. The tactical decision between moving offense and being a portable heavy metal collection device was a complicated one. For now, he stayed where he was, with his pulse racing.

He didn't have any night vision, but Vaughn did. He heard, "Well, I don't see anything in passive, but there's so little light from monitors, and so much thermal from everything else I can't say. Alex, should I risk a source?"

Then the lights came back on. Bart blinked to recover. No apparent threats.

Miss Prescot said, "Do you hear that click? It was a power transfer glitch. Some minor inconsistency in output and the light circuit cut out to prevent damage."

Vaughn said, "Concur. Power conditioning fluctuation."

Marlow sighed tightly. "Move on."

Their steps were soft enough. The metal mesh trembled but didn't clang. They moved at a steady pace. Almost five thousand meters was five thousand paces, possibly ten percent more given the tight confines. Forty-five minutes would be a good time. Forty-five minutes in a flushable tube with no real cover, with Bart bent over and almost shuffling sideways. It got stuffy and cramped and the background hum became almost disorienting.

The unending straight tunnel was one of the creepier movements Bart had made, but apart from the light failure, nothing untoward happened.

Approximately two kilometers in, the catwalk just ended. Elke gingerly stepped to the cut floor and moved forward.

By the time he got there, Bart already knew from cues it would be a bit slippery. Whatever machine had cut it had done a clean job, then dust and particles settled on the surface, which was angled. They had good footwear, but were still cautious. Especially as Ontos hadn't mentioned that.

He was still nervous from Ontos's disappearance followed by the lights going out. It seemed to be purely coincidental, but could they be sure? Though there was nothing to be done right now.

There was debris from a roof collapse. It looked moderate but just the idea was nerve-making. The equipment could survive a collapse, probably. They could not.

Another kilometer, slipping and stumbling, and the catwalk resumed. Apparently construction went from both ends and it hadn't been finished yet, if it ever would be. He expected Miss Caron would have some words about that, though, if this worked out.

It was more than an hour before they reached the far end. He ached and his ears rang from the power hum, and he sweated from exertion and stress. He wasn't claustrophobic, but channeled threat zones bothered him a lot.

Elke and Jason cleared the door visually and then with sensors, popped it open and stepped through. Bart was only too glad to close behind them.

Buggies. One of those would carry them all, and they needed to get around to the far side of this pit, which would be about thirty-five kilometers at this depth. This was the long way around indeed.

Jason picked one at random, checked the charge and the backup fuel cell, gave a wave and climbed in. The others were in perimeter and collapsed in with Miss Caron in the middle. Jason switched to RUN and started rolling as soon as Bart slammed his door. There was an automated airlock, since this was only a service tunnel and not a real access to the mine. Outside was dirty yellow, but clear enough not to need lights, which was good. How visible would they be and would they be contacted, though?

CHAPTER 27

Jason did not like the mining pit. The evasion options were few. It was just steep enough he might try to blast down a level. He was pretty sure they'd survive mostly intact. He couldn't swear the vehicle would. There was no up. That left a very little zigzagging and hoping for poor marksmanship as defensive measures. Otherwise, speed or mass would win if the enemy was stupid enough to use a smaller or slower vehicle.

Given the alternative of walking it, he decided this would have to do. He moved steadily with minimal trail to avoid arousing any notice.

Not only was this mine not much in use, but the atmosphere did have weather including rain, and the road was never intended as a permanent structure. It was blasted and graded enough for large trucks, or had been originally. It was well eroded, and this buggy was only intended for rescue operations or inspections.

The mine was in use, though. Far below, a Brobdingnagian excavator two hundred meters high carved away at the wall. It looked like a toy from here, when it could be seen at all through the dust and swirling crud. Jason decided he should not be able to see it, and moved closer to the wall than the precipice.

Kilometers-long bucket conveyors hauled the crushed ore to the top and into a slime mixer. Only one mixer, not six for this pit. The bottom excavation couldn't be more than a kilometer wide, and they might get one more level with that monstrous excavator. They could switch to smaller ones after that, but it likely wouldn't be cost effective.

Enough of that, he thought. He should stick to driving and threats, no matter how fascinating the engineering was.

Elke next to him had a headset on.

"We have been inquired as to our ID and work order number."

"Hell, can we fake it?" He wanted to turn and look at Caron, but settled for a rough point over his shoulder.

She said, "I don't have one handy. Is there a recent one in the comm or a note somewhere?"

Elke said, "No paper. Apparently miners don't rate the import. I find no scraps."

Jason said, "We play stupid. Don't respond."

Alex said, "I don't see any other course. Stall them with half messages if they get belligerent."

"They have been belligerent," Elke said. "We have been threatened with docking of pay."

"Oh, anything but that," Aramis said. He did sound nervous, but probably for much more practical reasons.

Jason goosed the vehicle.

"Nothing to be gained by being slow. We've got twenty-seven kilometers to go. I must compliment you on the size of this gaping hole, Caron. Very impressive. More so from the inside."

The vehicle bounced, then actually smoothed out at speed. The tristar wheels weren't sprung, but relied on low pressure tires and rotational effects over the terrain to balance the ride.

"Center of gravity is a bit high," Jason muttered. "Not bad, but it could be lower."

Caron overheard and said, "It would take a wider wheelbase. I'll certainly suggest the idea, though."

"Please do." Were they actually discussing product improvement while fleeing for their lives?

They rumbled forward. The vehicle ran off capacitor banks, so that sound was all road, or in this case, track and dirt noise. Jason leveled off at 50 kmh, which would get them there in another eighteen minutes.

Elke said, "They have responded. Two vehicles are going to attempt to intercept. Profanity is frequent. I expect this happens on occasion when someone is pissed off."

"Where are they coming from?" Jason asked. His shoulders

were aching from pushing the controls. There was no way to automate it, nor would he under the circumstances, but he was driving what amounted to a construction truck at high speed in rough terrain on a cliff ledge in poor visibility.

"One above, one below. I don't know what tactics they plan to employ."

She looked over her shoulder at Caron, who replied, "I don't know either."

Bart said, "There is also a pair of pursuit vehicles behind us."

"I guess we got their attention. So much for discretion." He edged the speed up slightly, but this was skirting what he felt was unsafe. They bounded over rocks and slipped on the looser soil. Underneath was firmly compacted, but the looser top had regular dust settlement and spills, debris from falling off trucks and blasting.

Movement caught his eye to the left and high.

He said, "Landslide. Shiiiit!" And started braking.

Elke's voice echoed tinnily. "Drive faster," she said. "I timed this. Emplaced charges."

"Faster, roger," Jason said and stomped the accelerator. His nerves and hindbrain absolutely didn't believe that was true, but this was Elke. If she said she knew how long the collapse would take, he was going to trust her. And when the hell had she gotten charges up there? Of course, she excelled at anticipating uses for explosive, so . . .

Then a huge cloud of dust led the fluid wave of broken rock and dirt right in front of them, right over them. A small rock clanged off the cab, then a larger one dented it, springing a seam and letting dust eddy in as air hissed out. The road and sky disappeared in a roiling, dirty brown cloud that spit chunks of ore and gravel. Jason stared at his hands, gauging the road by the attitude of the wheel. He puckered up tight, but there was nothing else to do.

The view ahead cleared, wisps of gritty, agitated sand flying. He corrected his steering, not wishing to sideswipe the outer cliff face.

Another oily wave of the same avalanche flowed ahead of them.

The throttle was already floored, but he slammed it again and leaned into it. This crude vehicle had no capacitors to feed to the brakes, no wastegate to close, not much of anything. He picked the smoothest probable track and held the wheel to the right curve as they swept under a cascading shower of dun rubble.

They were slowing down, and the wheels digging in, as dirt piled down on, under and around them. As it built up underneath the truck started to slip.

He clenched the wheel and urged it on, leaning back as he forced the pedal down, hoping and gritting his teeth.

Then they were through, the wave behind shooting over the ledge of the track and falling into the pit. Traction increased, the ride got bumpy, and Jason slacked off the throttle. Behind them, one chase vehicle was buried under kilotonnes of fill. Their pursuers were going to die slowly if they didn't just yank hoses and choke fast, unless someone came out with a lot of heavy equipment and did a lot of digging starting right now.

The other truck was nowhere to be seen. It had probably been swept over to bash on the level below.

"You're good, Elke," he said, breathing out a breath he'd held the last two minutes.

"So good I had nothing to do with that."

"Er?"

"I didn't set any charges. That was a lucky coincidence."

"And you said to keep driving?"

"It worked, didn't it?"

He was starting to think that deadpan of hers was an act. It had to be. He'd seen her crack and be human on occasion.

They all had their acts. It was part of their professional presentation. He shrugged and kept driving. He'd trusted her; it worked. She may have just estimated the fall rate well and figured the odds were in their favor. Or she may have figured the odds were better with the avalanche than with the thugs behind. Jason shivered and shook and clenched down to stop it. It would be ironic and embarrassing to die because jittery hands caused him to slip.

Landslides were not that uncommon, with all the earth being displaced, large and small explosions, the vibration of massive equipment, tidal effects and even wind eddies. However, the recent civil war, since that's what it was, had greatly increased the scope and number of such events.

So the radio frequencies were awash with inquiries, curses, shouts, demands for information and general ranting in English, Arabic, Russian, Spanish, Hindi, Chinese and probably Swahili. The miners were not happy, and it certainly wasn't an event to help discretion.

Jason sharply asked, "Eyes. Is there anything that can intercept us?"

Bart said, "We have clouds of dust. Hard to make visual."

Alex said, "Clear downhill at least. Also rather sobering. It's a long drop."

Elke's voice was very calm. "One vehicle above, in parallel course. No hostile movement. It could be reconning us."

Nodding, he said, "Then we keep driving."

Caron said, "This isn't the level we want."

"What?" Jason asked. Crap.

"We need to go down a level. That's an entire circuit."

"At least it's down, not up. I thought this was the right level?"

"So did I. I'm sorry."

"No apologies. Shit happens. I guess we get to try debris braking."

Aramis asked, "What do you have in mind?" His voice was tight.

"I have nothing," Jason admitted. "Elke?"

"I hate you," she said, and cursed in Czech, then German, then "Asshole," in American English. "I will need the back open and some kind of restraint. I will cut a relief. You will back down. Remember your steering will overcompensate. We are probably going to crash."

She didn't say *die* in front of the client, but he heard a faint tremor.

Aramis said, "Two hundred meters down."

"Shut up, Aramis."

Elke said, "Check masks. I'm opening the hatch."

Jason had airflow, so he was safe. "Check," he agreed. With a chorus, the others confirmed.

Elke popped the hatch, stood wide and stable, knees bent, raised her shotgun and fired twice, the drum spinning to pick recon rounds. She dropped back down, yanked the hatch strap. It slammed and she ran a hand around to confirm seal.

Jason saw the two slugs arc through the atmosphere leaving star-shaped, conical parabolas. Very pretty.

The cameras in those were tiny, but adequate for what they were doing. Elke had the images on her visor. She brushed a control and was obviously searching and panning.

"Two kilometers ahead. There's an area of partial slip, mostly small stuff. We'll do it there."

"Thanks. Can you also distract those clowns following?"

"I live to serve," she said, and climbed back up. She popped the hatch, tossed something from her harness, and dropped down once more. "Sensor mine," she said. "It might take off a wheel. Or not."

"Anything helps, thanks. We're coming up on that spot."

"Yes. See that sign marking the slip? Very convenient. Aramis, help me back, and hand me some cable."

The back of the truck had a cargo area, currently littered with trash and tools. Elke popped the hatch and tossed the contents out. Aramis handed her a strap, and she threaded it around her shoulders and latched one end to an eye. Aramis twisted and tied the other end to a frame member.

"And back, you say."

"On my order, yes."

Alex offered nothing. Jason caught his eye and his boss just shrugged. He seemed calm enough, or maybe just frozen. This was one of those things you couldn't think about. Caron whimpered again, with a soft sob. Aramis, Shaman and Bart just gripped frame and seats and looked scared.

Jason swung the wheel, turned toward the wall, then backed slowly toward the drop. His sphincter puckered and spasmed at the idea.

Elke said, "This is going to be a series, with a large blast. I will want you to back solidly over the ledge and then brake."

"Over completely, then brake, understood." Oh, fuck me.

He felt her shift and toss something. He gripped the wheel, foot on the pedal and ready to move.

The blast wasn't large, but did throw debris that rained down and puffed in in a cloud.

The second blast wasn't as loud, but he felt the ground shake. A little more rocky rain fell.

The third charge lifted the rear of the vehicle with a loud, low *Crump!* He heard ground giving way and there was even some clattering rubble from in front that bounced off the cliff ahead of him.

"Now!" Elke shouted.

He eased into the throttle quickly and smoothly, trying to stop his knees from wobbling and shaking. Then he stomped the brakes, as the truck angled, tilted, skidded and slipped. The road rose and disappeared above the screen, and they were tobogganing backward down two hundred meters of quarry. He lost sensation in his hands from white-knuckling the wheel.

"Drive forward to reduce slippage!" Elke said.

"Forward!" he acknowledged, his voice cracking and squealing like a little girl's. He ran the revs up and felt the wheels biting at the collapsing wave of gravel and stone, then slipping, rolling and churning through the entire planetary gear. To either side he could see the walls, with a cut above him. All the debris from that cut was underneath them. They were surfing on a falling column of rock, at about a sixty degree angle.

His next concern was that at bottom, they might bounce straight over the next cut and down, there to smash and bounce and smash all the way to the bottom of the pit, another nine thousand meters down.

"Halfway," Elke said. "When we near bottom you'll have to back left and hard. Not enough to roll."

"Don't want much, do you?" he shouted.

"Give me slight left now!" she said.

"Slight left!" he confirmed and pulled the wheel.

"Five seconds . . . three, two, TURN!"

He leaned into the wheel and pulled, watching the cliff above turn at an angle and move to his left as he swung. It steadied a little, to less than forty-five degrees, and he slid down the mound of rubble. Less than thirty degrees, in two directions. They were stable enough.

The road here was at least a hundred meters wide, and he had maneuvering room. He realized he was still holding a breath, and gasped and heaved.

"We're down. Forward and over now," Elke said.

"Yeah," he agreed. He engaged the gears and the wheel assemblies started them climbing up the slippery scree.

"I think that took care of that prior pursuit," he said, feeling his arteries throb and pound in his head, his hands, his feet . . . his entire body shook and trembled from the most massive adrenaline dump he could remember.

"There are others on this level, but they are looking for us to have gone over."

Alex said, "Good, that will slow them down. Elke, Jason, that was fucking masterful."

"Thanks," Jason said. He knew it was one for the books, but he was just glad it was over. "The wider road helped."

"They're all wider," Caron said numbly.

"Eh?"

"Each level is decreasingly narrow, to provide maximum stability. Lower down they're hundreds of meters."

"Oh. Makes sense."

"We can carve away more as we go. When slips happen, an area is marked off. This one still has a couple of years of expansion planned, if the ore holds out."

He realized she was talking to remind herself she was alive. He nodded, then because that would be hard to see, said, "Yes, I understand."

Jason felt a relief unlike anything he'd felt before. They'd just used explosives and an all terrain vehicle to drop two hundred meters almost straight down, while being shot at. It was too insane to grasp.

And now he had a good twenty-five kilometers to drive forward, in noxious atmosphere under high pressure, under possible fire. He welcomed that.

Aramis and Bart dragged Elke from the rear compartment. He glanced back and saw she was shivering uncontrollably. Probably delayed fear reaction. She'd been looking straight down as they fell, and directing. He didn't want to think about that.

For both of them, they did what they had to when the alternative was to give up and die. That pretty much summed up their primary job qualification. Too stupid to give up.

Still, while he had lead time, he should increase that lead. He ran the speed back up to 50, then pushed on to 70, then even to 90 kmh. What did it matter now?

Everyone was silent for a few minutes, then Elke started mumbling, volume rising, until she was cursing loudly in Czech. He was considering saying something to her, when she suddenly announced, "Okay, I'm better," and shut up. She shimmied back up front into her seat again.

"I think that's our destination there," he said. The panel lights looked dimmer than they had been.

"Yes. Dark hole."

Shaman asked, "Wouldn't something that would work as an emergency shelter be lit?"

Shrugging, Jason said, "I would think so, but it's not really a shelter, just an entrance, and they wouldn't want people running into the cables."

"There are the cables now," Elke said.

Jason saw them. Huge towers with bulky cables running across and down.

Caron said, "I'm not sure why it's not lit. Your reasoning is sound, though." She still sounded a bit distant.

"I hope that's it," Jason said. "Power's dying." He killed the lights to save a few seconds of power, and slacked off the throttle. They weren't in imminent danger, and they'd need what they could get.

"I thought they had plenty of charge?"

"We took it from a maintenance bay. And, running flat out is not efficient and causes wheelspin. Then, we spun more as we came down that slope running balls out. We probably also damaged either the packs or the feeds in the process. Nope, this is as far as we go. The capacitor bank is drained." He was now increasing throttle to keep them moving. The capacitors ran at full strength until drained, but died fast once they were. He might squeeze a few more meters, but on foot would be faster.

"We have about four hundred meters from here," Aramis said. "Run now."

At once, they kicked doors open, hopped out and formed into a fireteam. Despite all the shocks and privations, Caron was still a pretty good runner. Shaman and Elke each took an arm and moved with her at a brisk pace. Jason and Bart led. Aramis and Alex brought up the rear.

Aramis thought it felt more than four hundred meters. Rough ground, limited feed rate on the oxygen, and the nasty atmosphere that itched and burned, since they weren't in full suits, made it a lot more than a sprint. Aramis gasped and rasped for breath. Ahead, the tunnel was dark and intimidating. There was just no way to know what was inside, with the sharp shadow cutting across it.

They closed up and moved in, and the shadow became less prominent up close. Twenty meters out, Aramis could actually see for some distance. Then they were inside. The floor was cut smooth and slightly rounded, though debris made him slow to a walk. The walls were coarse with piles of collapsed rubble. This wasn't a frequently traveled route.

Ahead, things got steadily darker. Lacking night vision, Jason pulled out a torch and dialed it slowly up until it gave enough illumination to see by. Their path was blocked.

"Security door," Jason called. "Blast."

Caron said, "Emergency ingress is on the right."

Red button. So it was. Jason pressed it and a human door popped open.

That got them a cubicle with air in it. They were still not inside the powerplant proper.

"What is that door made of?" Elke asked.

Caron said, "High strength laminated composite and honeycombed ceramic to ablate any heat damage."

"Thanks," Elke said emotionlessly. She was busy pulling something from her belt.

Alex asked, "What the hell is—"

"Tungsten bore rider. Saboted penetrator."

She opened the action on her shotgun and dropped the regular ammo cassette, slid the shell home, worked the action and raised the gun as Aramis asked, "Is that a good—"

The concussion felt like getting hit in the head with a sledgehammer, even with noise cancelling earbuds. It wasn't just the tight quarters. It rocked Elke back onto her rear foot, shotgun barrel pointing crazily upward, and with a welt on her cheek where her thumb had caught it from the recoil.

Whatever she'd fired had had balls. In fact, through a blur of pain, Aramis watched as she pulled out an empty metal cartridge that looked as if it was intended for artillery.

There was a fifteen-centimeter hole right through the locking plate of the door.

Jason looked groggy as he reached in with pliers and yanked on a metal rod. The rod groaned and moved and the door popped off its supports, being well-balanced even after that assault.

"How many of those do you have?" Alex asked in what he probably thought was a quiet voice.

"Two more," she loudly replied. "And two of my special antipersonnel rounds for when it gets ugly."

Bart said, "They know we are here."

Alex replied, "Now we are inside, though," as he pulled the door and let Aramis dart through.

Yes, they'd been made, and one man was running toward them, one away, and one must be locked in the control room. Aramis went that way fast. He slung his carbine, raised his baton, and gave the charging man a two thousand lumen flash followed by a jolt of electricity.

That individual recoiled, grunted and left the fight in favor of a nap.

Bart and Jason sprinted past, heading for the fleeing operator. Jason dropped to one knee and fired. The reports were much less unpleasant here, and echoed strangely off into phase-cancelled tinny pings echoing from the far reaches of the cavern.

Aramis could hear the rest close behind him as he charged down the ramp, leapt across a gap and swarmed up the stairs. He stepped just enough aside to let Elke cut loose with a standard breacher round, kicked the smoking door as she pulled back, and took the man at the controls in a low tackle that crashed them both into the steel base of a control board.

Shaman whipped out his kit and commented, "Shift change is in three hours." He slid the needle into the struggling, groggy operator's shoulder, and the man cursed as he collapsed.

"We might not get that long."

"It's our upper limit, of course."

"Who'd you shoot?" Aramis asked Jason.

"No one. I shot the commo line."

"Wow. Nice shooting."

"Not really. I needed three shots." Jason sounded disgusted, but that was a centimeter wide target and he'd been using a carbine after a sprint and a concussion and another sprint. If he was unhappy with that level of shooting, Aramis was very glad they were on the same side.

"Now let me in," Jason said.

"Sure. What's up?"

Jason stopped in front of the controls and glanced over the screens.

"First thing is to make sure nothing affects the power. Commo out is bothersome, but wires do break. Fluctuations in power get a panic reaction. We need this to stay steady—" he reached over and tapped a function of some kind, "—while we get out of here and where we have more cover. Though I'm sure they're going to expect us now."

"As long as they can't stop us," Aramis said.

Alex jogged over, "Move it ASAP. Ontos says they can force through that section, but they need a timeframe to get stuff in place."

"That's going to be interesting," Aramis wondered.

"Ready," Jason said, and jumped out. Heights obviously didn't bother him too much.

They jogged down the ramp from the control room, across the airspace around the reactor, which was more bare stone, only some kind of agate. Where it was sheared smooth was just beautiful in waves and shimmering translucent colors bouncing the torch beams back at them. That would be something to talk about later. Then they were climbing another ramp that was rather rough, at an angle to the trolley, which was basically a powered flatbed with seats. They used all four of the seats, with Bart sprawled across the back, Elke dangling her legs off the front with her shotgun on her lap, and Caron sitting on Alex's lap.

Jason flipped switches and off they went.

The tunnel was dark. Periodically, a dim flash indicated a monitor at an airlock, opening and closing. The whole effect was very surreal, though.

It made no sense. The previous tunnel was lit constantly, this one not at all. It was one of those things there was probably no explanation for.

The tracked swerved and swooped twice, with a slight rise. That was probably partly to bring things into alignment at the surface, could be due to large masses or bubbles that weren't easy to get through, or even to break up shockwaves from going straight down the tunnel.

CHAPTER 28

Joe was increasingly pissed. Caron and her bodyguards were still alive, great. Now they were stirring up trouble and coming back. He had to keep a lid on the press, on operations, on snoopy tourists, and it was all a juggling act he couldn't share. They should have had the decency to sneak off or die in peace, and be done with it. They should not be blasting their way across the old pit, shooting their way through the powerplant and trying to cadge a ride in.

If we had time for explosives, we could just drop the roof and let the atmosphere dry the goo. Send in a drill to reopen it later, and move on with everyone "missing and presumed dead" in the original blast. But no, there hadn't been any way to get a charge down there, because his hirelings had blanched at the hint. They were "defensive." Even though they knew this was a territorial fight for control of billions, they were too much the nancies to play.

All he could do was watch the thermal image of the trolley, with all those exposed targets on it, run up the rails.

He could, however, have a reception party.

The trolley ran smoothly. Alex was sure there'd be some kind of attack, though. If it was an explosive, they were dead. There was no need to consider that, unless it might have some kind of trigger that Elke would spot. That's why she was up front with her glasses.

Of course, something sonically triggered, or just by remote, wouldn't be predictable.

And, there was no need to consider that. He should consider things they might face.

There had to be cameras along this route, and there would sooner or later be indicators of their presence from the power plant.

So, at some point, they were going to take fire.

They had no cover.

There was nothing to be done about this, except pucker up and try not to have an accident. Though, really, he wouldn't blame anyone who did.

Either they'd be attacked before the terminal end, or right there. Most likely it would be at the terminal. It wouldn't make sense for troops to come down a dark tunnel, possibly silhouetted, and give away any advantage. They could just wait for the team to come to them.

So, the only cover they did have was this cart, which was just big enough to kneel behind, and wide enough for three.

Second problem: once they bailed out, they'd be fixed in position, unable to advance. A minimal force could hold them there while air was evacuated, or heavier weapons brought.

How far apart were those cameras?

He whispered, "Jason, can we evenly ignite these seats?"

He heard Jason say, "Ah, that's brilliant. I'm sure we can. Hold on."

"Think on it. Caron, do you know where the cameras are?"

"About two hundred meters apart. They're minimal, just for supplemental tracking of problems."

"Do we incline at any point?"

"There is one twist and rise toward the end. The original survey was slightly off."

"Perfect. And the cameras there?"

"One points down from the end. I'm assuming there's one about there looking back this way."

"Jason, what do you have?"

"Some cartridge propellant and a small amount of incendiary from something Elke just handed me. Sprinkle, light with my cutting torch, but it's going to be hit or miss."

"Will it distract people long enough for us to advance and control the situation?"

"I expect so."

Aramis asked, "How violent do you want me to get?"

"Aramis, the gloves are off."

"And that's what I hoped to hear," the young man replied. He wasn't as eager as he was on their first mission, but he was certainly prepared to cut loose, accurately, with no moral qualms.

"Elke, give as much notice as you can on that bend or rise."

"You have notice," she said. "It inclines in only a few seconds, from what I can see."

"Shit, move. Torch and off the back, advance behind it cautiously."

Alex took Caron's hand and pulled toward the back of the trolley. She went along easily.

She said, "Should I time the jump?"

"Yes."

"Now."

He hopped and lit into dust and gravel, sprinted a step, jogged another and slowed to a walk. He heard other bootsteps and some half-stumbles.

"Crouch," he told her, and did so himself.

Jason reported from the darkness ahead. "Scattering. Stand by, igniting."

His tiny but hot torch hit the front bench, then the second, then he hopped down, a shadowy ghost holding a flame, and went black, leaving only a little dazzle.

The black turned momentarily orange in peaks over the seats, then subsumed to a dull glow with a whiff of ammonia and a faint residue of heat.

Alex approved. The residual heat, and the flare above the benches, could easily be mistaken for human outlines. So when the empty car arrived, that's what the hostiles would believe.

So now they had to advance.

Caron whispered, "There's actually a small alcove on either side of the dock. Is that what you want?"

"Yes!" he replied. "Lead, wait, no, get behind me. Sorry." Dammit, she was still the principal and he was expendable.

"I heard," Jason said softly, and mumbles indicated him relaying the info.

"Who's behind you?" he asked Caron.

"Shaman."

"Good, let's move."

The problem now was not to be right behind their distraction.

He advanced at a low jog, feet forward in an odd-looking step, and low to avoid tripping. A vibration came through the floor as the crashing click of the trolley docking reached his ears.

In a few moments he felt the alcove ahead. They'd have minimal cover and concealment, but it might be enough. It better be, because the doors cracked and let in a blaze of light that brightened.

There was no time for further orders, and he couldn't use radio. He'd have to rely on the team doing what they did best, which was breaking things, because there wasn't much chance of not being found shortly. He just planned to be found under his rules—by being the offense.

Weapons clicked and rustled, and someone shouted, "Dammit, it was a decoy, they're not here."

An Aussie voice said, "They must be."

"The seats are torched. It was a decoy."

"Son of a bitch, those fuckers are devious. Well, make sure they're out and go down and get them."

"One on one?"

"However many you think you can fit on that sled. You've got full armor."

"Yeah, but they're Ripple Creek. You know what happens when they get pissed off?"

"You want to get paid, right? We're just negotiating. Locate them, call back, and we'll discuss how to settle it. The boss doesn't want violence."

"Yeah, that's why he suggested explosives. I know. Paid goon and all that. Okay, let's load up. You're staying here, Captain?"

"I'll follow with more, on foot if we have to. Just make sure they stay down there."

Alex fished into his pocket and pulled out a fiberoptic periscope. Yes, twelve of them crammed onto the trolley.

Caron, Shaman and he mashed tighter into the corner. They'd be seen as soon as that thing rolled, in either ambient light or enhanced goggles. He couldn't think of a quiet way to stop them, either.

"Rolling," the team chief said, and power hum presaged the wheels turning.

Alex thought to himself really hard, *Jason, take out the captain as the doors close.*

The doors started to close, and the trolley was already in motion as they did.

He saw it edge into his view, and he saw someone raise a finger to point at them.

He thought he heard a shot. He couldn't be sure, because the trolley bounced off the guide rail, scattering the occupants. The ground erupted in firecracker goodness, which kept them plenty distracted. A definite shotgun blast sounded, and he took that as an opportunity to swing around the corner and vault up onto the platform.

As he did so, he felt a couple of those firecracker things himself. Whatever Elke loaded them with was enough to cause a hotfoot. Rolling on them had to be painful.

But the team captain was down from an impact load from Aramis, the door was jammed open, the dozen goons were shouting and thrashing. It sounded like Bart was using his trick of just repeatedly shooting people wearing reflexive armor, so that reflex stiffened and held them in place. Caron's bowstring slapped and an arrow bounced off one, giving less of the same effect. That should make them wonder, though. Then she tossed a flashbang.

The sparkling blue blast took him by surprise. Shit, she still had those? It was more of a surprise to the others, though, and another arrow and two more shots tapered the threat off to nothing.

Then they were through. Jason shot the control panel open, hit an override, and the doors slammed shut on pressure safeties. Elke sprinted to one, then the other, and two sharp *bangs* locked the mechanisms.

There was no time for congratulations.

"Run," he said. "Bart, you're hit."

"I'm functional for now."

Alex waved Bart and Aramis up front. So far, so good. Now they had to make it through the city.

Aramis wondered if it was possible to get addicted to the endorphin rush of combat. That could be dangerous. But shit, this was a kick to the system.

He knew where they were.

"Elke, when do you want to pop that package of yours?"

Alex replied, "Once we're in position to clear the civilians."

"That's now," Aramis said. "We're going up a floor, across two streets, right and into the office."

"So find us a hidey and we'll do it."

"There are cameras here, too," Caron advised.

"Thanks," Aramis said, and that rush tickled him again. "Service hall here."

Elke said, "I'll need a clear reception area for signal."

"This just never gets easy. Up, then."

He led, the rest followed, and they took emergency stairs, which he knew were less monitored.

At the first landing he said, "We have three routes from here. Patch Bart."

Well enough so far, Bart thought. He always looked naturally calm outside. Inside, though . . . they would take fire soon. He and Aramis were point, so one of them was likely to go down. They didn't have enough firepower for this. He forced his breathing to normal so he wouldn't hyperventilate, and relaxed his grip on his weapon. That just made his toes curl, trying to grip the deck. Something had to happen soon.

Mbuto bandaged his arm, and he winced. He'd lied. He was functional, yes, but the pain was disorienting and nauseating. Something Mbuto poured into the wound numbed it to a cool ache, and a few breaths let him recover enough to consider himself properly functional. It wasn't a critical structural injury, but . . .

"You've got torn muscle and a tendon," Mbuto said. "I don't have time to fix it here, but it's about a ten minute job if we get the time. I have cleaned, dressed and sterilized, with a local nerve block and general analgesic."

"I can move for now. It's a bit weak." About sixty percent, but he would manage.

Aramis said, "Move," and gestured while turning.

Up another level, and then two turns and into an access corridor that seemed to match with the large cargo elevator near the trolley station below. It was sealed and sectioned.

"Have the masks ready," Bart said. "This is where there could be a blowout."

"Concur," Alex said. "Especially as it's been evacuated of civilians."

"Stop," Elke said.

Bart stopped. The rest stopped behind him.

Elke slid over to the wall and along, probed at something very delicately, then reached for wires. She fiddled and manipulated like a watchmaker, shaking her numb and injured wrist a couple of times before proceeding.

"Single file," she ordered.

Aramis gulped and went first. Bart followed while feeling a flush. What had she disarmed?

As he reached the pressure door, Jason pushed past carefully and tapped a code into the control console. It flashed angry red. Sighing, he plugged his DataMob into it and went to work. More seconds wasted, but the door accepted his overrides and opened. As it clicked, Bart raised his carbine.

Still nothing.

That was disturbing.

They cleared and entered the next section and pushed on.

A loud *bang!* was followed by a sudden drop in pressure. Bart reached for his mask as shapes erupted from behind a panel.

Aramis was quick. He was already masked, and fired suppressing fire that made three of the first five figures flinch.

Another explosion, behind them, shook the air and walls. Bart forced himself not to react. His position was forward. He got his mask in place and commenced fire.

Jason dropped in front of him and skittered sideways, and was not wearing a mask. Bart wondered about that, but he kept shooting.

It was over quickly. The five attackers went down, leaking blood and with some twitching, and Aramis unmasked, so Bart did, too, once he confirmed the rest weren't having trouble.

Wind howled and roared. It came in through a hole in the door behind them that Elke had apparently blown, and vented up through the corridor roof. That hole had been intended as a boobytrap, and Elke had provided a field expedient air supply. Of course, air was now venting, which would require more maintenance in a hurry, but that wasn't a problem for them. Or rather, it was more of a problem for their enemy.

Over the roar, Jason said, "This door is locked out due to the leak."

Alex said, "They'll definitely know we are here. Break it."

"I have an override code," Jason said. "Until they change them or override them."

A moment later the door moved, then jammed because of air pressure, then moved a bit more. It was enough for them to squeeze through in single file, and it lessened the howl from the other leak a bit. Bart had to really squeeze. His arm dragged past the door edge and he winced and grunted. Pain.

Once through, he poked his knife into a crevice on the door and helped shove it closed. The force and strength needed took some of the edge off the screaming nerves.

Caron could see another short squad poke its muzzles out behind cover. Aramis fired a burst and went prone, needlessly shouting, "Contact front!"

Bart followed suit, and then Elke tossed something that bounced around the corner—one of her grenades. She shouted, "*Fireinth—*" *BANG!* and the blast made Jason's brain shake inside his head. His ears rang even with the earbuds in, and he knew it was devastating to whoever was around that corner.

Still, a handful of others jumped in from a side door and tried to either threaten or hose them down. Two got shot and one looked very surprised at an arrow that suddenly grew from his throat. He gurgled, though Jason could only see it, not hear well, and the man went down in convulsive twitches.

Bart and Aramis rose, rolled into the cross hallway, stood and panned, and shouted, "Clear!" together.

Shaman patted Caron down. She looked rather disturbed.

"It's always tough the first time you shoot someone," he told her softly.

"No, it's not that," she said. "I shot earlier. I had to shoot past your shoulder, about ten centimeters."

"Oh. Thanks."

Perhaps it would hit her later, he thought. Or perhaps she was too pissed off to really care. Or was she the same type of sociopath her uncle was? No, not likely.

They turned left at the corner, and Jason moved to herd Caron along. She didn't need to see bodies broken and bruised by the grenade.

"We have movement down that hall!" Aramis reported.

Then Alex's phone buzzed. He glanced at the number on display. Ontos.

"This is me," he said.

"Hello me, this is the other me. I believe we're close."

"Seems like. Are your people ready?"

"Yes, give me the word."

"I don't want to meet a crowd. No offense."

"Understood. I'm coming with two."

The connection dropped.

Alex looked up and said, "Be prepared to kill them, just in case."

Caron didn't seem surprised anymore.

Ontos appeared clearly down the hall, with two others, who were armed but not presenting. One of them was Sauers. The other was a bearded, graying man with a large rifle.

"Mr. Sauers?" Alex asked.

"I never liked that son of a bitch, and I didn't want to wind up drafted. So I defected."

"Welcome, then. And you, sir?" he asked of the other.

"John Hammill," the man offered in a gravelly voice. "Former Recon. I do a little demolition for Mr. Eggett. He sent me along. I brought this." He held up an antique rifle.

Jason squinted and said, "That's a Garand . . ."

" 'The finest implement of battle ever devised,' according to General George Patton."

"Didn't he say that quite some time ago?"

"Nineteen forty-two."

"You mean the year and not the time, right?" State of the art, two centuries past.

"It's a fine weapon," he insisted.

Alex shrugged. "Heck, it's a weapon. Bring it along."

Caron furrowed her brow and asked, "How did he manage to get that here?"

Jason shook his head and grinned. "I don't think that's important right now."

Ontos said, "They locked down the passage to Operations hard. Then they had to unlock it to let all their staff out. Then some of the staff decided it smelled better in Ops than up here. Then they had to send their thugs down to politely request presence, or not have their safety guaranteed in the pending mine uprising."

"So that's official? And a real threat?"

Ontos looked a bit put upon.

"It's a real threat. No one is going to hurt the staff, though. They mostly treated everyone decently. You'll note I'm regarded with respect, and I was in Operations Management."

Hammill took over. "It's real enough," he said. "Six hundred armed with firearms, another few hundred with wrecking tools, none of the rest working. Some probably would, but without a minimum staff, it's not safe, so they're sitting it out and hugging their oxygen masks. And I was able to put together a . . . ahem . . . mechanized unit."

Jason said, "I can only imagine, and we are grateful, but what about the staff?"

"All evacuated by coercion, except a few dozen who came down to us. We don't trust them anymore than you trust me, of course."

Alex said, "That's a good sitrep. How much control do you have over the miners?"

"Plenty," Ontos said. "Until you find some way to open the armor, they ain't going anywhere."

Elke said, "I will fix that if no one else does."

"Actually," Hammill said with a faint smile, "I think I have that covered. Say when."

Alex looked at Elke, they had a quick conversation of expressions, and he turned back and said, "May as well be ASAP. We're going this way, out onto the ground."

"What's the plan?"

"Plan? We play this part by ear. However, Elke is going to create a distraction. You can bust in and be another distraction while we do what we have to. There will be other distractions shortly thereafter."

Ontos nodded. "That works. We'll go saddle up. I've always wanted to say that."

"How much notice do you need?"

"A few minutes. All the cameras are out in the service way. Mister Joe thinks it's depressurized. He thinks we don't know about the cameras we aren't supposed to know about, which have been hacked and are showing empty space. He's going to be very surprised. Also that the service door from construction is still functional . . . after moving enough debris."

Ontos seemed a little odd, twitchy and talkative. Alex decided it was because he was so much a hermit. No harm. The man was agitated, but didn't seem to dissemble.

"So we could have come up this way?" Alex asked.

"Eventually," Ontos agreed. "Surrounded by a hundred miners and on camera the entire way, through those airlocks."

"Yeah, this probably was better. So, either I call, or fifteen minutes?" he asked with a glance at Aramis.

"Easy," Aramis said.

"Fifteen minutes after our distraction. You'll know it when you hear it. By the way," Alex added, "how did you find us?"

"You came up the tramway. Only two routes to the surface, and this is the better one."

"Right." That was obvious. The fight and the fatigue were getting to him.

"We'll be ready," Ontos said again, as he turned and left, Hammill following.

Aramis reached back into the lower compartment of his pack. "So put these on." He held a bundle of rumpled Security shirts, with patches.

Bart said, "That is not believable."

"You'll be amazed."

"Right," Jason said and grabbed one.

Aramis said, "We need a staging area."

Jason said, "I propose the lawyer's office."

"How do you think he'll feel about that?"

Alex said, "To be perfectly honest, I really don't give a shit."

Jason chuckled. "That's Stage Five. Now we just need to get out of it mostly alive."

Jason thought the choice of the lawyer's office was tactically excellent. There weren't many people that way, and those that they encountered were as much second level staff as low end tourists. They did garner a number of looks, though the uniform shirts did seem to quell suspicion for the moment. Weapons were acceptable to most civilians, if carried by people in uniform.

Jason took point, advancing past Aramis at a fast walk. The rest shifted to keep Caron penned in.

He pointed, angled over, and shoved open the door to bin Rahman's office.

"Hello," he said to the surprised secretary as the rest rushed in. Aramis was past in a blur and into the office in a moment. There was profanity and loud orders and out the man came at gunpoint.

"*Ana assif*," Jason said. "This is momentary only, and I require your cooperation."

Bin Rahman looked around the team, focused on Caron, and looked openmouthed.

He said, "I understand, and of course I will do what I can to assist."

"*Shukran,*" Jason said. "However, you can help by doing nothing. You have my apologies in advance for some small indignities."

Shaman stepped up behind him. The man shouted and looked angry before his face went slack and he collapsed. Bart caught him, carried him into his office and laid him on the couch. The secretary looked very nervous, but didn't struggle, deducing the drug had to be nonlethal. He was set down in the chair with his feet propped up.

Alex said, "That is really becoming a disturbing ritual on this trip, and how many more doses do you have?"

"Enough," Shaman said. "I restocked in the mine clinic."

"Of course you did."

Aramis pulled a map up on the wall screen and said, "Right, we're going here, then here, then over here. Ontos is coming in here with his crew. That's frontal from the mine, and will tie up most of the goons. I expect the nonaffiliated security will be busy keeping panicking civilians corralled. Elke, you have your distraction ready?"

"Sadly, yes," she agreed.

"Then with all that, we can get to the tower, I hope."

Caron asked, "Then what?"

Aramis said, "Then we fight our way in and you stay behind a body or a hard object."

She looked hesitant.

Alex said, "We have to have you alive for it to work, and this is déjà vu. You can't go down. At this point, we may have to leave injured behind to move fast. The risk of death for a casualty is low, but the risk of capture or detention or death for us and you while up and moving is significant."

"I understand," she said. She didn't look as if she liked it, which was perfectly understandable.

By then, everyone had stripped down their rucks to nothing but weapons and ammo, with necessary communication. This was a combat assault, and there shouldn't be time to be hungry, thirsty or need anything beyond reloads and bandages. Bart and Aramis came through from the back, and Elke grabbed Caron and shoved her that way.

"Toilet, now," she ordered. "Last chance."

The women were back in very short order. Everyone kept the uniform shirts. They knew who they were and the camouflage might help.

With a nod from Alex, Aramis said, "Follow me," and pulled the door.

The mall was pretty much devoid of civilians. That suggested PR was not good, and that Joe wanted a clear field of fire.

Jason said, "We also have no bodies for concealment. We're the only people here."

Shaman said, "This happened in the last five minutes."

"It's not hard to tell where we are at this point."

"The airtight barricade is closed."

"Airtight, armored and likely to have hostiles on the other side."

Caron said, "There's a maintenance hatch to the right. Even more restrictive, but we can try my password. It was abandoned in place once the newer ones were done."

"When did you start helping with the designs of this place?"

"I was thirteen when mining commenced, and I've been helping crunch numbers to learn since then. I started designing structure at sixteen."

"Can we offer you a job?" he quipped.

She looked bemused, but led from the middle as they moved around her. The door was small, at the far edge of the overlapping sections, and had a dusty, older lock.

"No good," she said, after punching in her password.

"What is it? I'll see what I can do." He stepped up and tried an override code.

"Cymru two two three six."

"That's not a very secure password," he commented. "However, I have enough access to change it. It's now my wife's birth year instead. With that changed . . ." He tapped in commands. The user language wasn't quite SysAcc, but he fumbled through it.

"Got it," he said. "Your account still has access. Only your password was restricted. Your uncle really should have hired a professional for this."

He tapped again and the door slid open.

"Fast," he added, pulled the jack and darted inside with Shaman.

Caron said, "Now we need to let the miners in."

"Not just yet," Alex said. "We'll wait until we're in position, then let them in as a massive distraction. You realize they are going to trash things and torch the place."

"But they gave their word!"

"Are you still that naïve?"

She clouded up, then admitted, "I don't want to think that will happen. I concede that putting valuables in front of them is likely to lead to some incidents."

They all looked at her.

She looked around at them in return.

"My family developed enough resources to jumpstart colonization of the universe. We developed new sciences. In exchange, my father is dead, and my perverted uncle wants... something. The socialists hate me even though I'm creating millions of future jobs. The god damned ecotwits hate me, as if I don't have better qualified and better paid scientists here than they do. The tourists are going to hate me. Most governments hate me. The miners are coming around as long as they get money, and I'm wondering how much damage they'll do.

"At this point," she said, in perfectly cultured English, "I really don't give a shit myself."

Jason said, "You have to stay alive."

"So you don't get a bad reputation?" She sounded pissed at last.

"No," he replied. "Because you deserve to rub everyone's face in it."

She smiled for the second time since her father died.

CHAPTER 29

Bart was last through, and they were finally back in the dome. Activity appeared fairly normal, though a little quiet and mostly indoors.

Alex said, "So idyllic. We must address that. Elke, now is the season of their discontent."

"Kaboom, kaboom kaboom?" she asked with a toothy grin.

"Kaboom."

She nodded, and pulled out her detonator control, scrolled through several devices she apparently had ready, and brought up the code.

Elke seemed very hesitant, filled with obvious sadness. Bart supposed for her it was a tragedy. Such a perfectly designed device, but rather than a city, a mine or even a mass of troops, she was using it as only a distraction. She coded the sequence and pressed the firing key.

The explosion was still impressive. The glare was awe-inspiring, even through a polarizing substrate on the glass. That was in part because it reflected off hills, the atmosphere, the ski slope dome and the oblique edges of the main dome struts. The color started as a blue-white with a yellow tinge, immediately cut to a brilliant rose from the polarizing, turned a hideous bright yellow-orange, then faded through red. Barely behind that, a powerful *CRACKbang!* made the ground bounce, rumble and twist. Bart was lifted a good fifteen centimeters off the ground, and his feet stung as he hit. *Scheisse.* The dome was definitely compromised. He heard a series of cracks and almost musical clangs as large chunks of the heavy plastic broke free. The response was perfect. Alarms shrieked, people ran, the staff went into disaster mode, grabbing tourists and urging them into buildings designated as shelters. Two gaggles of guards, visible at nearby facilities, sprinted straight toward the casino and a hotel tower.

Elke had managed to clear the decks of civilians, terrify everyone into hysterics, crack the dome, shake the ground, light the sky all in one go. And now crumbled dirt was raining down on the dome.

"That will be enough to cut a little light and disturb people," she said. "Most of the debris is going to land between here and the first pit."

Caron said, "You know entirely too much about this."

Elke only smiled and said, "I love my work."

Jason said, "I see a problem."

Caron looked up and said, "Yes, the air is stratifying."

Elke said, "Alex had me plan for that. I must reach a building top."

Alex shook his head. "I need you on this assault. I can spare Shaman at this moment."

He said at once, "What am I to do?"

Elke reached into her long bag and pulled out a collapsible antiarmor rocket. It was last generation and too light for modern armored vehicles.

"Do you know how to use this?"

"In theory," he agreed.

"We need a hole in the top, too, to improve ventilation."

"Understood. I believe I can hit the dome from the inside without too much trouble."

"Typical African marksmanship," she said with a toothy grin. "Better sprinkle it with some powder."

"There is more than enough magic in this little pointing stick of yours," he said. "I shall endeavor to poke a hole."

He turned and jogged toward Central Tower. The rest of them moved off the side and down the long ramp-road toward the ground level.

Bart said, "I believe we have achieved a level of panic."

Jason said, "I believe we should dial it up a bit."

Alex said, "Stand by."

Moments later, Hammill's clandestine charges cut the doors.

"They didn't fall," Bart said.

That was when a mining drill crashed through on the ground, in the main tunnel, splintering ceramic foam into jagged shards. Behind it, pulling alongside it, was a standard bucket. Hammill sat in the bucket, his beloved Garand to his cheek, and fired. He jerked in recoil, dust whipped at the bullet's passage, and one of the remaining guards flailed like a rat in a rottweiler's mouth.

That gun was loud. It fired a 7.62mm cartridge, was it 63 millimeters long? That was much more potent than the glorified pistol rounds in the improv carbines. It was probably also a lot less efficient, too. It created bow waves in the translucent atmosphere with every shot.

Then a dozen other miners charged in, dove in a relatively well-executed maneuver, and fired ugly little carbines.

Their form didn't appear to be bad, but the carbines had poor sights and worse accuracy. A couple of them got hit as Joe's security rallied.

Bart almost wept in laughter. The mining drill, on huge wheels that threw residual dust, rolled into the security team. The bucket loader was not impressive by comparison, but still sufficient to crush men. And right behind them, now pulling into line abreast, was a large pumper. It couldn't be intended for fighting fires, but was likely used to wash debris from a collapse. His estimation was proved correct when the crew started spraying with the turret. The pressurized stream was strong enough to hurl men back like rag dolls, flailing and tumbling.

That did it for the remaining security, who simply turned and ran.

That wasn't all. The next vehicle was some kind of portable power rig, and it was equipped with an air cannon and catapult.

Bart wondered just how badly they'd underestimated the potential threat from the miners. Granted, these were not only the labor, but included many of the managers. Still, it was considerably more sophisticated than they'd anticipated, and had a massive element of brute force he respected. The combination was disturbingly dangerous. Luckily most of them were allies.

"Well, that is good and bad," Jason commented. "We don't have to fight them here, but we will have to fight them in the offices." A *whoomf* from the air cannon punctuated his comment, and a delayed *bang!* emphasized it. They were launching bombs.

Caron said, "Of course my uncle will surround himself. I don't care. I will see the bastard taken down, or there is nothing for me to live for."

Bart said, "That should not be an either/or choice. And we will take him down."

Ontos came over with several others. He waved for attention as he did so. Bart still covered them with his muzzle for the duration.

Ontos noticed it, not that Bart was trying to be discreet.

"Yeah, don't trust anyone. We have a stray group that broke off, and a few other defectors. There's some shooting down in the mine now. Seems they don't like the odds."

"Not unexpected," Elke said. "However, my explosive is limited. I only had the one."

Bart had no idea if she was being serious or humorous, but he chuckled despite himself.

Alex asked, "Suggestions?"

Aramis said, "Move fast. What else is there?"

Jason nodded. "Shaman knows our destination, and we should have some commo. Brief as always."

Bart didn't wait for confirmation. He turned and took point.

Horace felt like a salmon. Crowds fled the buildings for "outside" even though they were safer inside. The legitimate security, and their own bodyguards, tried to herd them back in. Luckily, they weren't very effective. He managed to fight his way into Central Tower just as the doors started locking and the pressure seals activated.

Someone with a bullhorn announced, "Please remain calm. There is plenty of oxygen and no danger to the structure of the building. Everyone will be safe..."

It seemed to have some effect on those closest to the speaker, and none on those pounding on the doors. That wasn't his problem, though, so he shimmied through the crowd, hoping no one noticed the weapons. One or two glanced down at him, but seemed to assume he was some kind of guard.

Well, he was. Just not the kind they expected.

He made it to the elevator bank, to find the elevator cars all locked on the bottom. They'd be unlocked eventually, but that would take time and coordination and he needed to reach the top now.

He really didn't relish a climb up all those stairs. *There must be some other way,* he thought, and headed back into the staff corridor. That elevator was also blocked. Still, a building this modern and . . .

Yes, the pressure shaft. It was used to get service equipment around in a hurry. He ran over, adjusted the sling on the rocket over his shoulder, and climbed onto the plate. He grabbed the power handle and twisted.

He dialed the speed up bit by bit, then backed it down again toward the top. It almost certainly had safety interlocks, but he wasn't convinced they'd work. Twenty-five stories seemed like a lot, but as huge as the suites were, the tower didn't hold nearly the people it could. He assumed some of the crowd below were from elsewhere, visiting the casino and lounge.

He stepped out on the top floor, and looked for a control to hold the plate. That seemed to be the switch, marked with "Hold," which he pressed. He turned for the first door, presuming any suite would have windows and they were all close enough to the center to work. The door was locked, didn't respond to a kick, but did respond to bullets through the locks. On the one hand, that was bad security. On the other hand, no one came here who'd be a petty thief, the hotel had its own security, and they probably assumed they had one hundred percent control of anyone departing. That, and a combination of cost and tradition.

He forgot that in a sprint through a beautiful parlor, with imported furniture that looked Indian and handmade.

The easiest place to accomplish his task was off the balcony. He slid the door, rolled to the ground, and wrapped the sling firmly around his arm. It wouldn't do to drop it now. Then he checked the instructions on the side, muttered to himself, and slid the caps off. It extended as he thought, then he squeezed it through the railing, abrading his fingers as he did so.

He fumbled, dropped it, and had to haul it back on the sling. Sighing, he twisted it into position again.

"What the hell are you doing?" someone shouted.

Sighing louder, Horace fumbled left handed, swung up his baton and fired.

The hotel rentacop uttered, "Son of a bitch," and dove behind the couch, probably fumbling for his own stunner of some description.

Horace dropped the baton, pulled on the sling, pressed with

his fingers, got the thing as straight as possible, and yanked the trigger. The rocket bang-hissed in a wave of ammoniac heat, and he dropped the assembly. Hit or miss, it was useless now.

A beam chilled his left calf.

He groped around, found his own baton, fired back, and missed. It was now a case of two men swapping shots a second apart until one got stunned. Three exchanges later, he scored. The guard went down in a heap.

Horace shivered in relief and looked up.

The rocket had blown out a meter-wide hole that cracked in an arc, but didn't cause any further fall.

The difference was dramatic, though. He pulled his mask on quickly.

The outside atmosphere dropped through in an ugly ochre column. It started adding to the layer below, causing it to billow in waves. Not that it would fill quickly, but it was another provable threat that would keep building. It was almost pretty, like a pillar of smoke in reverse.

No time for that. He had to limp back to the team and hope the tingle wore off shortly.

Alex looked up when Jason said, "I see something."

Yes, a definite hole, and a definite leak. Good man, Shaman. That would get everyone inside faster, which would reduce the traffic and the threats, though it would make them more visible, too.

It also took care of most of the miners. They had short-term breathing gear with them as they always did, but it was only short term. Once the yellow clouds swirled in, they started retreating, and even the laggards were gone in a few minutes.

Bart said, "You do realize there will be some excessive force and possibly rapes?"

"I'd hoped to avoid it," Caron replied. "I will deal with them afterward, since we have everyone's DNA on file."

"Who has legal jurisdiction here?" Aramis asked.

"We do," she said, looking a bit vicious. "It's not as if any complaints will go anywhere."

Bart raised eyebrows at that. Absolute power had many benefits, if used wisely. However, absolute power had created this mess.

Alex swapped glances with him. Their job was to protect her, not judge her morals. Nor was she unjustified in having a vengeful streak. That was something to discuss later.

Aramis still had the lead.

"Through the Palazzo," he said, pointing at a casino. "We can connect through a service tunnel."

Alex wasn't sure the most direct route was the best, but they were in a hurry.

The main doors were obviously sealed, but Aramis led the way to a service door, about a meter and a half high. He waved, and Jason stepped forward to run the lock. These were easy. Joe had done a piss poor job of changing codes on stuff he controlled, and completely neglected everything else. Aramis pulled the door open and in they went.

The corridor inside was tall enough and industrial. It had positioning tags a robot might use, and was obviously meant for maintenance access behind the main kitchen. They followed him down, and around another corner. Alex was glad the man knew where he was going. He must have the maps memorized, as no one was risking a locator of any kind, and there hadn't been a dead reckoner handy.

Around the corner, though...

It was surreal. One moment they were in a sere, faded corridor, then through a door and they were in a deluxe function room, reinforced but pretty.

Of course the basement was a shelter. Foundation grade concrete, reinforced, with thick sealant and with shock foam underneath. It was the safest place to be on this planet.

Two of the regular security guards, who were basically EMTs with supplemental authority, acted as shepherds for a hundred or so rich socialites.

Aramis said, "Good evening," as he disarmed the first. The second made to protest, then decided he was outnumbered.

"No harm," Alex said. "Just passing through."

Someone loudly asked, "Miss Prescot? You're alive!"

Well, there went that.

"She's alive," Alex said, "and we're planning to keep her that way against the current threat."

"Current threat?" a man in a silk dinner jacket replied. "I believe the current threat affects everyone. That's the second nuke this company's had trouble with."

The noise picked up, lots of people commenting and arguing. Alex saw the team fan out slightly to widen the area around Caron.

The dinner-jacketed man asked, "Miss Prescot, what do you plan to do about all this?"

She looked at Alex first, who nodded fractionally. He couldn't appear to be manipulating her, which was one of the things he hated about public missions.

Caron said, "First, I have to get to my office and consult with my staff. I can't do anything from here."

One of the guards said, "The problem is that the doors have sealed against contamination and won't open."

That wasn't a problem for Elke, he was sure. However, if those safety protocols were in place, it did mean the atmosphere was toxic enough to be a risk.

"Caron?" he asked quietly.

"I'm not entirely sure," she said.

Naturally, the moment she said that was the moment all other conversation paused.

Jason asked the staffer, "Got backup pressure and filters?"

"They're already in effect," the man said. "They can manage a few minutes at most. That's the whole point of this shelter."

That probably wasn't the kind of thing he should say in a conversational tone in front of panicked guests, Alex thought.

About then the comment sank in and the crowd started buzzing again, with nervous and frightened comments, some demands, some shushes and fewer reasonable tones. Things got a bit pushy, and Alex wondered how long it would last.

Right then, the man in the dinner jacket said, "Well, I would guess we need to take a vote on what to do."

"We're not voting," Alex said. There was always someone who couldn't figure out reality.

The crowd pushed a bit more. They looked on the verge of a full blown panic.

And this is where I earn my pay, and risk my employer's wrath, he thought.

"I don't see where you, as a mere bodyguard, get off on telling the rest of us what to do. Do you have any idea who I am?"

That was a useful opener. Alex settled for his baton. He raised it, clicked and zapped, and the man fell down twitching.

To the place where he had stood, Alex said, "You are not Miss

Prescot, therefore you are merely in the way. You will do as you're told. Now, I need a clear path to that door." He pointed at the far side.

The wide eyes and silence from the rest indicated that he had their attention. They drew back and left a clear passage three meters wide.

Alex fixed the local guard with a gaze.

"You will stay here. We will get things fixed."

He led the way down the parted sea, and through the door.

Once they were through, Aramis said, "Sorry about that, boss. I made a map. I didn't check the secondary emergency pressure doors, only the primaries."

"We didn't anticipate needing them, and there are a lot of buildings, but we'll learn from it. Elke, can you do minimal damage to the door so they can keep partial pressure? I'd hate to kill a few hundred prize customers. Especially as they're also potential customers of ours."

"You fucked that when you shot the *blbe*," she said. "But I will try."

She slipped in front and had some kind of device already in hand. It was small, but while she usually went for overkill, that overkill rarely looked like it.

"Jason," she said, "Please work the lock."

"You may as well cut it," he said. "No time."

"Understood."

She swapped charges, placed the new one over the door's module, held up five fingers and pressed her detonator.

She faced the blast. Alex did also. The others pulled Caron back and faced away.

The bang was almost anticlimactic. However, it did destroy the module. That done, Elke pointed at the latch overrides, and hefted her demolition hammer. Aramis took the top one, she the bottom, and with some heavy swings they released the door's locking bars.

Bart stepped forward and kicked it open, and they proceeded through. Elke came last and slapped the door closed again.

"That was good, Elke. Remember that."

"I have a hard time remembering boring occurrences, but I will try."

"Two blocks diagonal," Aramis said, "and there's Shaman."

Mbuto came running up, and Ontos's element was just behind.

Ahead, though, was a milling blockage of armed men, facing the remaining supporting miners. They were in reasonable formation and forming a solid mass.

"Looks like Joe has a few hundred extra muscle... with familiar looking homemade guns."

"Did he pay them off?" Caron asked.

Jason almost smirked. "Of course he paid some off! He's got unlimited resources."

Aramis said, "As Ontos said, they figure his odds are better than yours, and this way, they make points and get promoted. The losers at least get sent home, maybe die. They figure the worst you'll do is send them home with legal costs."

Caron sighed. "Why is being good billed as such a good thing?"

Alex gripped her shoulder. "We're going to make it a good thing."

"We will still need our miners," Bart said.

"Yes, and this is going to get really messy."

Caron said, "Money won't fix this, will it?"

"Money will mop up the blood," Alex said, scanning the dome. "I'm not sure about the hurt and image."

Caron said, "I think it's tragic, but they've made a choice and will have to deal with it."

"Healthy answer," he said. As long as she meant it. It was a tough kind of call even for an experienced adult, much less a kid barely out of college.

Jason suddenly said, "I need height."

Aramis swung and buried his demolition axe in the extruded concrete of the wall. Following that lead, Bart did the same a meter higher.

Jason scrabbled and heaved and hauled himself up the building face as crumbling chunks fell, half-slipped and scraped himself as he reached the first balcony level with fingertips, but did so and then pulled while his muscles bulged and swung a leg up. Thirty seconds after his request, he was four meters up with a clear field of fire. He leaned over the railing and began taking slow, measured shots.

His shooting was always master class, though the short carbine was not as good as a rifle. Still, two shots out of three punched into flesh and caused a steady depletion of the enemy. They shot back, but their weapons were too crude to be of much effect at that range.

Elke raised her shotgun, sent a recon round in a high arc, then ducked behind cover. She used her palm comm to select a couple of photos and pinged them via area net to Jason and Aramis. Aramis waved to Bart, and the two of them slipped off to one side and through an access alley. Shaman and Alex hunkered down around Caron.

A sudden flurry of fairly heavy fire into the mob, from the right, had to be Bart and Aramis. That, and Jason's recon-improved marksmanship reduced the mob's threat considerably.

Then Elke rose, the cassette on her gun spinning to pluck the requisite loads and fired two more rounds. Both arced out while whistling, and burst just above the battle at head height in brilliant, dazzling flashes of zirconium—not lethal, but very scary and distracting.

The combined onslaught led to a rout. Most of the pack—since it couldn't properly be called a company—scattered in every direction.

"Yeah, I expected that," Alex said. "You're not even going to find out who they are, unless your uncle managed to get real names."

Jason rejoined them from above. He had a crease from a bullet along one arm, and some small cuts where a ricochet had sprayed lead and concrete over him.

"We're going to need the supplementals," he said.

Alex nodded and made the call.

Ontos, Hammill, and Sauers came running over. Hammill was covered in dust.

"I guess we're going through there," Alex pointed at the surface level of the main block, "and up as far as you gentlemen are willing to help." *Or until I decide you're too close for my comfort,* he added silently.

Sauers gave a slight shove and rolled forward on his board. He still had that thing. He had two of the carbines slung, and raised one. He didn't seem to fire at anything in particular, just light suppressing fire.

"Where's Hammill?" Jason asked.

The massive roar of the Garand answered that question, and in front of the office, someone armed in a mask went down with a hole in his leg.

"Ludovico's a good man," Hammill said as he sighted again. "I'd hate to kill him if I don't have to."

His second shot caught someone else.

Ontos had signaled his men by then, and the whole area erupted in small firefights. Bad, because that meant a lot of stray fire. Good, because Caron wasn't as likely to "accidentally" die in a rebellion. This was something the team was trained for.

Still, there were a few hardcases near the entrance, behind the concrete pots and other decorations that were really intended as fighting positions. They improved the defensive position of anyone.

"They can't really stop us, though they'll know we're coming."

Ontos said, "We can be another distraction for you."

"Can you?"

"Then we disappear, and you don't look for us. If it works out, I'll leave contact information for you in case we're needed. If it doesn't, we don't exist and no one ever saw us. I'm risking as much here as you are."

Caron said, "I accept, Ontos. I will see that you and your friends are properly rewarded afterwards."

"If it's all the same to you, ma'am, we don't need the money. Just improve the food and other support and we'll take care of ourselves. And the name's Lou Burke."

"Straight in," Alex said. "Time versus stealth. Gentlemen, would you?"

Ontos shook his head and grinned.

"You're a paranoid asshole and I don't blame you. All right, Ham, let's do it."

Hammill shouted, "Go!" and lit off on the oblique.

It was obvious that man had military training. He scampered low across the narrow road, rolled behind a planter and took a shot, then back across the other way. Ontos flitted from cornice to cornice, light and fast, firing potshots. Sauers zipped past firing short bursts.

Behind that, Aramis and Bart bounded out, tucked in and sprinted for the door, firing suppressing shots that were close enough to be serious. Shaman and Jason took Caron, Alex and Elke brought up the rear, with him scanning for threats and her firing all around. She had several smoke grenades from somewhere, tiny things with outrageous outputs. A couple of small but sharp bangs added to the fear, and made their fire sound significantly more potent than it was.

Hammill's rifle was beyond painful. Every round sent ripples through the haze and punched their ears. That served as an admirable distraction. Most of the fire was aimed, badly, at him.

Those planters, though, stopped their return fire. Elke cursed, sprinted in front, and Shaman responded by moving back to fill the hole she left.

Bart and Aramis kept fire irregularly, but consistently at them, to keep the men skulking behind in place. Elke pulled two somethings from her bag of tricks and tossed them one at a time. Two more of her finned footballs. These impacted behind the planters and exploded back toward them. Screams and curses presaged a tumbling chunk of mangled hand arcing up and out.

Aramis leapt in a very nontactical manner in a parabola directly over the rightmost tub. He started punching, smashing whoever was back there, a solid three hits that seemed to quell the threat. Those ballistic gloves added so much to a punch, his hand came back dripping blood.

Hammill came round the side of the building, and shot point blank at someone. More blood sprayed from the cacophonous brutality of the primitive cannon on mere flesh.

Hammill made sure to lower the rifle as the sprinting team came up the final meters of the ramp. Jason's muzzle remained covering him, at which he shrugged.

Sauers came round the other way with a carbine under each arm, slung down. The barrels smoked, which shouldn't be, because there wasn't that much ammo. Then Alex did a double take. Those were the SKs the Ex Ek troops carried, with spare magazines. So Ex Ek had picked a side here. Too bad.

"We're here, and we're going it alone," Alex said.

Hammill nodded. "You can thank me later."

"Believe me, we will. Want to hunker down inside?"

"And hold the door for you? Thanks, but no. I'm for moving out fast, becoming not an obstacle, and retiring. On the way I can shoot a few to keep them distracted, if that's okay."

Alex nodded. "By all means. Later." There was no time for a conversation. He brought up the rear as Shaman and Jason shoved Caron through the doors, Elke in the lead against demolitions, the two bruisers next to stop bullets.

He closed the door and had a moment as he waited to ensure it was secured. Hammill had already slipped out of sight, but popped up at a corner, fired two shots and ducked again. That was former Recon for you. He just moved too well to not be a pro.

Sauers kicked over his skateboard, hopped on and shoved off down the slope. By the bottom, he was in a low crouch for balance, shooting diagonally across both knees. It wasn't a lot of firepower, and it wasn't aimed to speak of, but the volume and presentation was sufficient to keep everyone's head down. He shifted left, then right, then pivoted across the road and into an access alley, punching the door open ahead of him.

He wished he'd stopped looking then, because Hammill popped up again, and went down in a splash from a flurry of hits. He probably wasn't going to get up from that. Goddammit.

The door latched hard, and it was moderately armored, nor did he think that Joe was going to allow anyone with explosive to come in against his own cowardly self, though it was something to plan backup for.

There'd been a brief altercation here, and the lobby was still being cleared. Caron was sheltered under the reception desk, with Shaman crouched down and moving his weapon in a slow pan. The other four sprinted around shouting tactical notes and kicking doors, frequently with an attached explosion. Elke had apparently shared the goods, because he saw Aramis slap something on a lockplate that shattered it just as he booted the door, straining the hinges. He swept the room behind it with his shotgun, made a single nod to himself, and came sprinting back over.

Alex noticed the body near him had a tomahawk buried in its face. He reached down, grasped and twisted, and it broke out of the crunched bone taking a flap of nose with it. He wiped it on the corpse's shirt and handed it back to Jason, who arrived from the other direction. Bart was already at the elevator bank, and Elke took up station near him.

"Looks like you ripped him a new axehole."

"Yeah," Jason replied. They were both too overloaded to comment on the bad joke.

Alex flanked Caron as they jogged over. One of the really bad tactical things about bodyguarding was the need to bunch up. It slightly improved the safety of Caron like this, but it made them an obvious, easy target.

"We need to discuss our plans. This is not something we can play by ear."

Caron asked, "Are Uncle's thugs any good? I thought you said not."

"Some of them are bound to be, and he has numbers. We have six. We also have to guard you, and we need you to access or bluff our way in."

"I must insist on lots of explosive," Elke said. "This is not a quirk. This is professional advice." She had Aramis's comm with the map and floorplan application up.

"I'll listen," Alex said. "What do you suggest?"

She pointed on the charts at several locations. "First this, then this. You said you wanted a distraction, yes?"

It took him a moment to realize what she meant. Then he grinned.

"Elke, that's just amazing. I love you."

"And I have charges prepared for entering doors, or walls if need be," she said, all business, not responding to the compliment.

Jason said, "Bart should carry the other shotgun with breacher loads, in addition to his other stuff. Elke has hers. I'll carry a couple of extra carbines, since we don't need to carry a lot of excess." He had a slung armful of the guns now.

"Agreed so far," Alex said with a nod. "Aramis?"

"Shotgun and carbine. I expect to need both."

"Really? Okay." Alex wasn't sure about that, but the man seemed sincere, and he wasn't boasting. "I guess that leaves me. I'll be directing and standing between Caron and any fire. I'll manage with just a pistol and lots of ammo. Caron gets as much armor as we can fit her with, and an extra bottle of oxygen. Caron, can you move fast enough with extra bottles?"

"Yes," she agreed, seeming a bit nervous but resolute. "They don't mass much."

"No, but they are bulky. We're going to skip them to save mass and bulk. If, or when, I suppose, we get a breach, you'll need to toss bottles to people as fast as they don masks, but stay down while you do it."

"I can do that," she nodded thoughtfully and seriously.

"We're stopping a floor down first. Going straight in would be stupid. On the other hand, taking the elevators is stupid. On the other hand . . ."

Jason said, "On the other hand, we don't have a choice, but we're taking *all* the elevators. I had that coded the first day here." He waggled his coding module.

Caron murmured, "Well done." The technical part of her brain was still engaged, even if her emotions were shocked into nothing. She seemed to grasp why her guards got paid as they did, and that considering everyone a threat made sense, at least this time.

They hopped into an elevator and Jason levered off the panel, stuck in his leads and punched buttons. It took a noticeable moment, but then the doors closed and they started rising, fast.

"Fuck. Camera," he said.

Aramis smashed it with the sharpened bezel on the muzzle of his shotgun. That probably wouldn't help, but didn't hurt.

Elke said, "It would have taken too long to find access and fix them all."

Alex shrugged. "Well, maybe they aren't manning it, won't notice, or assume this is a distraction, with them all coming." The shrug was for reassurance. He felt a cold chill and a flush of heat fight it out in his guts. Both lost. Nausea won. This was going to get even uglier, and there was nowhere to run at this point. Frontal assault was their only option.

Given that, there was only one thing to say.

"Let's do this."

CHAPTER 30

Joe was bothered. They should be running away or negotiating or giving up.

"I can't believe they're actually coming to me. Should I be scared?"

He didn't want to consider that. He was Joseph Prescot, now the richest and most powerful man in the universe. It wasn't possible that hired thugs could get through his hired thugs, and all the protection installed. And what about those worthless miners? An accident or two, a most regretful press release, then fire the lot with some hush money and insincere apologies.

He'd been right to keep their pay low. The dysgenic little savages couldn't even fight with 1000:6 odds and accomplish anything except a mess. The PR nightmare of the entire resort... he didn't want to think about that. It might not be recoverable.

"Sir, I don't think they can get through the barricades, nor the platoon. This should be over shortly."

"'Should be,' you say." That really wasn't a good sign. Though at least the man wasn't lying to him. "They shouldn't have made it out of the mine, or through the tunnel, or through the dome. So far, they've left a mess of damage I will have to pay to fix, scared lots of cash customers, and are rapidly advancing."

"I'm really not sure, sir. They shouldn't be doing this. They should be trying to get off planet, discreetly. That's what they did last time."

"Last time? You're basing your analysis on what they did on

some Third World shithole planet of dysgenic, tribalistic, swarthy-skinned little fucks?"

The man's expression said he'd gone too far. Dammit, was everyone afraid to come out and say it? Racism existed for a reason; because it was true.

The man was hesitant, but did reply.

"Sir, I don't have anything else to use for estimation. They completely avoided a numerically superior but technically inferior force there, with a government that wasn't hostile, but intended to outmaneuver them. Here, we are actively hostile, with modern training and equipment. They can't beat us. Even if they've managed well so far, they're coming into a frontal battle. Marlow knows as well as I do he needs five to one odds to make that worthwhile, and bringing their principal makes no sense. I could imagine your niece wanting to make a stand and hope for headlines, but I can't imagine they're choosing to die over the matter. I assume they plan to advance as far as possible, hoping for some kind of notice."

"Well, they won't get it. The press are locked out until I say so. If they think macho chest-thumping will impress me, they're wrong. They're pissing me off. *Everyone* is pissing me off, the longer this takes," he warned.

He pondered aloud, "Does she think that getting face to face will keep her alive?"

Instantly, the man turned to his team and said, "We didn't hear that." They nodded, some of them a bit hesitantly.

Joe was even more pissed off. That meant more silence money. There was just no way to get out of this without every second-rate and marginally-brained gutterscum wanting a share of his fortune. He might even have to pay off that bitch Ash, if she survived, and pay for her convalescence. Unbelievable. She was too incompetent even to take her medication on schedule.

It might take another five years to recoup what this was costing, between tangible overhead and lost market share.

He shrugged mentally. It was probably worth it.

The man said, "Well, they stopped on the floor below. I'm sending a platoon in to pin them down there. It'll take a few seconds. They had the elevators bollixed."

"Whatever it takes," he agreed. Yes, even if it took more money, he didn't want the man's hands tied. He wanted violence, and he wanted it without hesitation.

Joe was scared. He wouldn't admit it, but he definitely felt it. They were coming up here, which meant they intended a shootout. They should be fleeing, trying to get away. Junet was right, that's what they'd done last time. A frontal assault was suicide, but messy enough it might draw attention. That was disastrous to the point of billions to argue self-defense, and a PR nightmare.

But worse, they might actually manage to shoot him. It seemed Caron was brave enough for revenge, when surrounded by armed thugs.

"You've got to stop them," he said.

Junet nodded and pointed. A few more troops deployed, and the door was secured behind them. That left nine in here, and the shield, and a couple of booby traps.

Hopefully they'd already taken some casualties. He couldn't believe all six were still functional after the last day. He couldn't believe they were still going. He'd been guzzling coffee and popping stims, and they were running, fighting and straining. But they were still coming.

They might actually be worth the extra money they cost. That pissed him off more. If he'd pushed harder early on . . . but now . . .

"Are they cutting up through the floor?" he asked.

Junet said, "I doubt it. It's reinforced anyway, and it will take more than some portable charges to cut it."

"You better be right," Joe said. He was disgusted to realize he was shaking.

Bart knew he looked calm, but he was pounding from stress. They were shortly going to be in combat with professionals. He'd done that once. Random fire from amateurs was something one got used to. This—

The door opened and he stormed out with Aramis. Ironically, this was something the younger man did have the upper hand in. He'd matured enough to not be conceited about it, either.

They were clear. This section was completely unoccupied. It was an administration office, and nice cubicles with a few offices, with light doors for privacy and silence. The floor was in four airtight sections. Now it was vacant and looked as if people had left in mid shift not even shutting systems off. It added to the eeriness of the situation.

They really needed more than six people for this. He and Aramis had to secure the area. Mbuto and Marlow had to keep

Caron secure. Elke and Jason had to do their thing. He strained to sense any threats, because traps were quite possible, even if not very likely; no one should have predicted them stopping two floors down.

Jason did something with a control panel, and nodded. The ventilation kicked in, blowing noticeably. Elke slipped into an office and jumped on the desk, from where she set some kind of charge on the ceiling. She came down, drew a knife, and pulled the hinges off the door, then laid the door aside. She also cut through the sheet rock panels that constituted the walls.

She muttered as she came past him. "That'll have to do."

That done, she sprinted over to Aramis, they looked over another miniature map, and waved everyone toward another office.

Aramis led; Bart backed up the rear, alert for threats. It was still disturbing. The ventilation hissed, and he wondered about toxins. Occasional creaks and clicks from the building adapting to the atmosphere outside made him twitch. At least the gunfire below was inaudible, or had stopped.

Aramis had found a ceiling hatch for maintenance and emergencies. It led to the floor above, and opened easily. A basic ladder made access simple. Bart came up last and closed it. It took effort.

Elke sprinted past, and Aramis went with her. It looked as if they were done with their task already.

Bart's stomach flopped. No time to pause, they were off to fight.

Aramis came up short.

"They're behind this airtight," he said.

Alex asked, "You're sure?"

"I would be," he said. "It's also secured from that side. There's no reason to lock it, except to slow us down."

Jason said, "Could be security protocol for the office, but I concur with the threat."

They shuffled around into the proper formation without having to speak. Elke slapped a charge against the door-locking mechanism, ducked between Bart and the wall. Aramis rolled the other way, the charge went *bang!* in a bright white flash, Elke and Bart spun back around, her bringing up her weapon and covering rear as he kicked in the door. Aramis swarmed through the open side, Bart hinge side, Elke twirling through the middle. They sprinted directly for the next door, as Caron walked in a steady crouch, with the older three men around her as a moving wall.

As Elke blew the third door, several shots rattled against it, sending echoes booming tinnily down the corridor.

"There they are," Jason murmured, as Elke slid a grenade over the muzzle of her shotgun, aimed at the gap at the bottom of the door, and fired. The round ricocheted.

A moment later, two shouted curses were drowned out in another tremendous *bang!* that shook the floor and made the lights flicker. Bart kicked the door, they proceeded guns first, and Caron whimpered and turned green.

It was rather macabre, Jason thought. The grenade had been close to someone when it detonated, and that person was now a red, chunky smear around the corridor. Two others nearby were in large pieces, bruised into meat-filled sacks. Four others were just dead.

He grabbed Caron's arm and hurried her along, as she tried to tiptoe around the puddles, wincing as they went.

"It's going to get hot," Aramis warned. "Multiple contacts beyond this point."

"At least it makes target ID easy," Jason said.

"If it's not us, shoot it," Bart said.

Elke commented, "How is that different from other times?" That was followed by another *Bang!*

Shaman said, "Ammo is going to be a problem."

Alex said, "Yeah, numbers, dammit. Caron, you've done well with the bow, but it's going to get in the way now. Let us handle it."

"Okay," she said, and laid it down with obvious sadness.

Jason swung his shotgun butt up and cracked the release on a fire hose box next to him. Aramis caught on at once, grabbed the nozzle and ran for the door. Elke slapped a charge in place, Jason yanked the release and snuggled up to the wall. Elke went prone and punched a button, the door banged and bounced, water gushed, Bart crescent kicked the door while standing to the side, and Aramis fired a powerful high pressure fog into the space beyond.

That left Alex and Shaman to play catch up and fire a few shots for psychological effect, then fire more when one resulted in a scream.

Jason cut the water and they moved forward. Bart led the way, and smashed his boot into the first face he encountered. The pooling water turned frothy pink around a gurgling man.

They reached the next pressure zone and Elke started emplacing a charge, quite carefully. It was flat and thin. Platter charge, 10 cm. That was to punch a hole.

Without taking his eyes from center, Alex asked firmly, "Aramis, where the hell are you?"

"Right here," the young man answered, a little winded. "They use our caliber." He held up a satchel full of magazines and a couple of pistols, with only a little bit of bloodstain.

"Good man."

Elke quietly said, "Fire in the hole."

The explosion was palpable, but not as loud as some that day. It blew a very neat circular hole through the door. Elke shoved the muzzle of her shotgun in with another fire-through projectile mounted, and snapped the trigger. The bang was followed by a whump and a cursing shout and then panicky thrashing and banging sounds. A whiff of vapor trickled out of the hole.

"You don't want to breathe that," she advised.

"What is it and how long to clear?" Alex asked.

"Incapacitance agent. It's time someone else shit their pants for a change. Hold breaths," she warned.

She reached up, placed her second charge, danced nimbly back and popped it. The door bounced, Bart kicked it, and they all moved forward, breaths held.

Jason wondered what Caron was thinking. The previous bunch had been blown into goo. This bunch had just been gassed, and still twitched and convulsed, covered in parti-colored vomit composed of whatever they'd eaten in the last several hours, and with filthy, slimy stains where everything eaten before that had voided in a spasming mess. They writhed and gouged at their burning eyes, choking and dry heaving with their mental synapses fused. Just the residue was irritating to the eyes.

Bart announced, "We are directly under the office."

They had one turn, one door and an elevator to get them up to their goal. There couldn't be too many people between here and there, but they would be heavily armed and have firing lanes laid out.

Alex said, "And they know we're here. I expect the enemy is going to start closing back in soon, to try to pin us between forces, so we need to take them out fast, before they can shoot us. I don't think we can move that fast."

"Think psychology," Elke said. She pulled the second to last of her door-busters from her belt and slid it home. It was too large for the cassette and had to go in manually.

She signaled for backup, Aramis nodded, and she skipped past the corner in a low crouch.

The shot blew her back two dancing steps and spun her half around. Even with notice, the shock wave was deafening and painful. But the impact . . .

The lead man literally exploded in a mist that sprayed over his buddies and the walls and floor and ceiling. It was as bad as the explosive grenades, but this was worse because it was done with pure hydrostatic shock, and in full view of everyone.

The other six screamed and dropped their weapons, wiped at their faces and only managed to turn the goo pink and slimy.

Aramis and Bart zapped all of them in quick succession, and an odor with a tinge of fried bologna joined the horrific smell.

Caron seemed rather numb to it all, now. She'd seen people shot, stabbed, smashed, broken apart, pureed, blown to shreds . . . it might affect her later, but for now she was so overwhelmed nothing really impinged on her anymore. Shaman might want to have tranks handy afterward, though. Hell, Aramis could use one himself.

They were close now, and the remaining guards did not have the best morale. They were retreating, which was good. They were all going to gather at the office door, though, which was bad. This operation was getting properly military in its tactics.

Aramis said, "We're going to need full frontal assault. I'll lead."

Alex said, "Go." It sounded quite casual, almost conversational.

Aramis dug into a sprint while reloading with his last fresh magazine. They had little enough left. From now on, he'd have to run dry and reload instead of doing them hot. He could abandon the magazines, though.

Jason took second right behind him, point shooting cameras as they went. The rest strung out slightly behind him, but kept the space close enough for mutual support.

They reached the elevator as Aramis stuck his muzzle between the doors as soon as they opened.

Nothing.

Jason moved in right behind him, pulled out his wrecking bar, and ripped the cover off the controls.

"Overhead," he said. He slid the bar through his harness, reached into a pouch and pulled out a module and extension cables. He snaked his hand through the mess inside the box, chose two cables, and attached the fiberoptic leeches to them.

Bart had the roof hatch open by that time, looked up through it, nodded and bent double. Shaman clambered up his back and through. Aramis hopped up lightly, then Elke. Bart stood up, grabbed Caron and straight-armed her up through the hole for the others to haul her up. He bent again, Alex went up, then Jason. Bart simply heaved his head above the opening and they hauled him up.

Jason whispered, "Up we go," and fingered his remote. The elevator doors closed and it started to rise along well-greased rack gears.

Aramis had the hatch back in place, and Elke sprawled down with her shotgun.

"Gas round," she said softly.

The elevator was an obvious choke point to stop them, but there wasn't much choice. The emergency stairs would be slower, and an outside ascent too obvious. However, Caron gave them some slight shielding. They didn't want her shot publicly, and Alex was pretty sure that the contracted mercs wouldn't support outright murder. Killing off the team for "kidnapping" or arranging some accident for the bodies was possible. Cold-blooded killing of an interested party was just a bit risky. On the other hand, a lot of money was at stake.

Everyone was breathing hard, and it wasn't just exertion. This had become a real, if low intensity, war zone, and the threats included toxic atmosphere as well as guns.

Alex felt the elevator move, and the passing rails and structure slipped down, then slowed to a stop.

The doors opened and there was a quick, loud rattle of small arms. That was expected, and familiar, and Alex felt oddly better. A threat you understood was preferable to the strange.

Aramis yanked the hatch, and Elke fired her gas round. It ricocheted and popped. Then she fired again, then once more.

She thumbed a control and announced, "Five hostiles, farmost from door, with cover." Her last shot had been a recon round.

Aramis nodded, hopped, and dropped through shooting. He lit and bounded to the side.

✧ ✧ ✧

Jason fired at two struts on the elevator roof below in quick succession, and dropped through the damaged section, which would put him behind cover next to the door. It mostly worked. His sleeve ripped on a protrusion and he yelped in pain as the metal tore a chunk from his shoulder.

Aramis fired a long, suppressive burst, over a second, that let Shaman drop down behind Jason. Jason leaned out slightly and fired another burst, walking it toward one of the hostiles.

Their cover was drums full of something, probably dirt, that would soak up a large amount of fire.

Nope, he realized as he hit one. Liquid started spurting. Thick, viscous liquid, probably a soap. That would just play hell with traction.

Elke shouted, "Get off the floor. Mine."

His guts clamped down as he heard that, and he leapt forward and out, diagonally. That left him figuratively with his balls out.

Aramis went the other way, which at least split the hostile attention. Shaman came straight up the middle and wiped out on the soap. He'd been behind the door and hadn't seen it.

Shaman didn't let that stop him from firing in that direction, right at the bottom of the drums. That was smart. As they drained, they'd lose barrier effect.

Then Aramis stopped thinking for a moment as the elevator exploded.

Elke was right. The floor had been mined and now was no more. That complicated things a bit, and they were now split. He wondered why someone hadn't blown a hole in it earlier.

Still, the smoke, residual gas and swift assault had the five, now four, hostiles busy. A shotgun blast from the elevator shaft took out another. The three remaining swung toward Shaman and the elevator, and Aramis tagged another, right through the mask and face.

The other two decided it wasn't worth more fight, and threw their weapons down and their hands up.

Well, that was good.

Jason took a deep breath, and nodded to Aramis, who moved forward. Jason was the better marksman. He'd cover. He'd also take out that camera there. Jason swung and fired, and the detainees twitched. Aramis didn't flinch at all. They operated almost as a gestalt.

Quickly, Aramis cuffed the men together and left them back to back. He looped a bungee cord around their throats, which wouldn't choke them yet, but would definitely slow down any attempt to get upright or escape. He ripped off their belts and slashed their pockets to minimize hideouts, and pulled the magazines from their weapons. Same model as his. Good.

Shaman was back on his feet by then, and wiped off his soles with a rag. The rest of him could be slippery for now.

"Help," Elke said.

Jason turned to see her hanging by her ankles in the elevator, over the gaping hole the charge had blown. Bart and Alex held her feet, and she was upside down over a hundred meters of sheer drop, her face turning red from pooling blood and pale from fear of heights. He carefully stood at the ledge, being wary of the shredded opening himself, and extended one hand, then the other.

She gibbered slightly as they lowered her legs through, and he leaned back and yanked to get her onto the floor. As he did so, she clutched at him tightly.

Shaman and Aramis kept a close eye on things. As Bart lowered Alex, Jason took him by one hand and one leg until he could grab the door and swing through. Caron came down the same way, but had to be directed.

"Swing your right arm forward, grab the frame. Now the left. Lean onto me. Now step down," and she was in. The poor kid was wide-eyed, racing-hearted and numb. She wasn't hindering them, but wasn't much help anymore. Still, she'd lasted this long and they were down to the ending, hopefully.

Bart shimmied down through the hatch a bit at a time. His shoulders barely fit at an angle. Then he hung in a solid pull-up position, swung and released. His feet made it to the solid floor, and Alex and Jason grabbed his hands.

With everyone accounted for, and the two detainees drugged by Shaman, they had one door into the office.

So Alex said, "Elke, take us through the wall into that adjoining room, please, and proceed with what we discussed."

Elke seemed to have recovered from her suspension over a pit, and flashed a slightly lopsided toothy grin as she rolled out two strips of explosive, capped them, stepped back and fired the shot.

Aramis shrugged and took point. As lowest ranking and most

expendable, he knew his position and had a good attitude about it. They moved through into the space that had been part of Bryan's apartment. It seemed mostly vacant now. Sociopath that he was, Joe had tossed most of the personal effects. Hell, the bastard might even have sold them for a few marks. He was that kind of tightwad.

Elke went to work on a charge for the wall to the office, not the door. The rest checked ammo, sipped water, and Shaman bound up the nasty triangular divot in Jason's shoulder. Jason winced a bit, and accepted a topical and some pain pills. It was minor, but fucking painful. Shaman did good work, and it was less painful almost at once.

Alex said, "Okay, we go through here, face them down, and try to negotiate a peace. They get one chance to comply, or we take them out. They may be fellow professionals, but they picked the wrong side and it's gotten way out of hand. This is worse than diamond wars in Africa."

"I can confirm that," Shaman said. "Very messy."

"Are we sure the adjoining charges are ready?"

"Yes," Elke said. "Move now."

Alex nodded and pointed, and they stacked up for entry.

Caron was last, behind Alex, and he goosed Shaman. The grope went all the way forward to Aramis, who raised a hand and dropped it. Elke triggered the charge, the wall disappeared in a roar of dust and crud, and in they went.

Then they were in a protective arc with Caron toward the rear, Shaman next to her and the rest in front.

The desk was now protected by a thick, near invisible ballistic shield and mesh for a damping field. There were protrusions around the room that were definitely for stun fields, sonic guns, other weapons. Twelve men with pistols drawn or rifles already shouldered aimed at the door in a broad arc.

Joe said, "So, now that we are all face to face, man to man, let's discuss this like adults."

There really wasn't much choice for the moment, Alex thought. Six of them and Caron. Twelve of the others and him. Threats on three sides, with weapons drawn.

Alex stepped carefully forward and said, "Go ahead; let's negotiate." Joe's men visibly relaxed. Jason gingerly moved in behind him, with the others. They were carefully taking a wedge formation and preparing to move in six directions at once on a signal. Alex took a very slow, deep breath to calm himself. It almost worked.

Joe leaned back in his chair—his brother's chair—and said, "Mr. Marlow, Agent Marlow. I recall you apparently discussed with my brother that you didn't want to know what your price was. I believe I know what your price is."

No one said anything. The silence lasted about five seconds.

Joe continued, "Your price is a billion marks. Paid into any account in the universe. It's not enough for me to worry about, and I have no reason to betray you because I want people to understand my word is good. I never was opposed to raising wages for the drones, I just wanted to get the family, and myself, established first. It's my own security shield. It's safer for all involved. I could never get Bryan to grasp that. If one is untouchable, one has no concern about minor threats from below."

Alex sounded rather flat when he asked, "What do I do for this billion?"

"Ah, you can be reasonable." Joe smiled and leaned marginally forward, hands out on the desk. "Just leave. Back out armed if you like. I'll have tickets waiting at the port, for any destination you choose. You leave my lovely niece, and I promise also I won't kill her. She gets her turn at the fortune, after I die. It's just fair to keep the generations in mind."

Alex ran a hand through his hair.

"That's quite a substantial offer. But why wouldn't you want to keep that billion?"

"Agent Marlow, that's less than a week's income at this point. My personal assets and domestic product exceed that of half the nations on Earth. It's cost effective and worthwhile to me, as I said, to be known as a man of my word, who rewards those who help me. Long term, it's cheaper than lawsuits, petty fines, other annoyances.

"Alternately," the man continued, "I have the men, the emplaced weapons, total control of everything coming in or out of this office, building, dome, planet and system. I'm told that power corrupts. Absolute power, though, is rather nice. You can't shoot your way out, and if you decide to retreat, even through a hole, you will ultimately be stuck back in the mine. That's of no worry to me. If you want to squat in a hole, I won't stop you. I will ensure you never leave, have no support, and then I'll see about dismantling your employer. That same billion will buy me a lot of favors in the General Assembly. It's your call."

Jason watched Alex clench his left hand slowly and signal, "Ready."

That was all well and good, but had everyone else seen that? Adrenaline shock hit him as he internally prepared. He hoped it didn't show outside, though it was probably rather normal to be nervous while discussing your life or a billion marks. Or was the billion only an offer for Alex?

Alex finally spoke, "What if I ask for ten billion?"

Joe's eyebrows shot up. "Well, that's—"

Jason never found out what it was. Alex dove and dropped prone while drawing.

Jason could only think of one move. He raised his pistol and hoped it worked.

As he gripped it, he heard shuffling behind him indicating the others taking cover or raising weapons. The motley mob in front of him started scrabbling with their own guns. They were too late, he hoped. He saw everything in the icy clarity that meant he still had control of the situation, for as long as he could keep it.

He started from the waist, point shooting, and forced his vision not to tunnel. The pistol fell snugly into place, pointed straight forward, and he fired. One goon had his shotgun almost up. Jason shifted and fired and hit him. Then he started skating diagonally right forward.

Most shooters would expect an opponent to retreat. Most also were ready to deal with forward or backward motion of the target, just as typical training ranges did. Jason was advancing on the oblique, though, which threw most people off.

He turned back to his left and fired at the next threat, a man with his pistol coming up to eye height, who dropped it and clutched at the bloom high on his chest, just below the throat, before coughing, puking a gout of gore and collapsing.

Jason had his pistol at chest height now, and he fired as he panned across the scattering mass, hitting three.

Joe dove for his desk despite the shields, two guards tight around him. Mentally, Jason tagged them as the real threats. The rest were scattering with only some badly aimed cover fire.

In that time, Jason nailed two more, one in the guts, screaming, and one in the face, dead.

A shotgun blast behind him made him cringe, but it was behind him. Aramis? It didn't matter. It was friendly fire and it blew off an arm that protruded from behind a chair. The former owner howled in shock and horror as he bolted upright, stared at the gush of red spilling from the stump then collapsed.

Another blast. Rubble rained, ricocheted, pelted and scattered. As the bang echoed away, shrieking wind ripped back. That was Elke. Good girl! She'd just blown the hole into the damaged floor below.

The pressure dropped fast, and the remaining goons and Uncle Joe snatched for their emergency masks, without wondering why there was a pressure drop. It took a moment, then a couple realized the Ripple Creek troops were not reaching for theirs. They hesitated, attention caught between masks and weapons.

Then a cacophonic barrage of fire dropped them like the silhouette targets they'd made themselves. That had to be Aramis with the shotgun, and Bart to the left. Jason carefully picked off three who'd thought ahead enough to take cover before donning masks, but left enough head exposed for him to punch lead through.

Then Elke's second bomb pierced the lower section beyond the first, one that wasn't evacuated. Air started rushing back in, just as Jason gasped and had to strain for a breath.

Two breaths later, pressure was near normal and the roaring wind and blasts had mostly stopped, though his ears rang and stung. The contaminated air was not sweet, but should be healthy enough until the ventilation system cleared it out. It made his eyes water and lungs burn, but he'd trained for things like that. Not these goons.

The office parlor area was an abattoir with the stink of guts, blood, propellant, some atmosphere, explosive residue. It was actually reassuring for Jason. It was his environment.

Elke came forward briskly, slapped a charge down at the base of the ballistic bubble, and danced back. She didn't bother with a warning, just keyed a code and the device fuzed. There was a very sharp basso crash with a white flash. The team twitched, but Prescot and his remaining thugs ducked and cowered. The blast, however, did no more than crack the shield.

Elke looked wide-eyed and surprised. Then she flushed in embarrassment. Jason couldn't recall her ever having a misfire.

Without pause, she unslung her shotgun, pulled the last of those insane armor piercing rounds from her harness, and slid it home.

Jason wasn't the only one who plugged his nearest ear. He wished he could do both, even with the noise-cancelling earbuds, but he needed the other hand for his weapon.

By now, though, Prescot was smirking. Clearly, he didn't have any idea what Elke was about to—

Jason thought his head was being torn off. The shockwave literally punched him, the ballistic plastic shattered into several large jagged sections that tumbled free, Elke jumped and hopped to regain her balance, and Bart and Aramis were through.

Prescot reached for something on the desk, probably to stun everyone in the room. Aramis sprinted forward to get inside the likely safe area, and Shaman zapped and missed, but the charge grounded millimeters from Joe's hand. He snatched it back, realized his mistake, and reached forward again as Aramis shot a bullet close enough to make him squeal.

Prescot's two personal guards staggered from behind the reinforced desk. Bart and Aramis stood just inside where the shield had been, weapons cradled for snap shots, just far enough the remaining muscle wouldn't have time to do anything other than twitch and die.

Joe Prescot stared around at the carnage, pools of blood seeping into the carpet, and bodies and parts. He didn't get sick, but he did seem completely sobered.

"We win," Alex said, and, "Don't," when one of the guards looked like he might try something.

The man lowered his weapon and dropped it, and his partner followed suit.

Bart and Aramis stepped forward and kicked the guns away. Shaman moved into a covering position. He didn't bother with the casualties. They were pretty well done for.

Jason's adrenaline rush faded. He'd lived, dammit. He remembered to swap for a full magazine. Habit, but a habit that had saved his life before.

Joe came out from behind his desk. He crawled to his seat, looked around, and clutched the edge of his desk.

"Caron, you're alive! You don't know how—"

She interrupted with, "Shut your fucking face," delivered in perfect King's English. The profanity delivered like that from her seemed to slap him. He sat silently, lips moving but no sound escaping.

"That's better," she said. "I know about the theft from helpless workers risking their lives to line your pockets, because the billions you were earning weren't enough. I know how you destroyed the lives of my friends, who can never be my friends again despite this. You tried to have me killed. You killed my father, your brother." She choked on a sob for just a moment and then continued. "You disgraced our family name and our business reputation. I even found the filthy pictures you had of me."

At that, he flushed even more than she did. His breath was strained and rapid, and his pulse was clearly at a health-threatening rate.

"Should I just shoot him for you, miss?" Jason asked. He made it sound very eager, and yet almost disinterested. It was a perfect caricature of a cold killer, and Joe cringed again.

"I'd enjoy seeing the desk painted a delicate shade of brain," she agreed, and Alex choked. "However, it's too quick. Don't you agree, Uncle Joe?" she asked, fixing him with a hot, angry stare.

Jason asked, "Kneecaps, then?" He thought he might enjoy it, actually.

She babbled a bit. "Death, or a long life in jail? It doesn't really matter what you think. I now own more than fifty percent of the shares, or will as soon as the paperwork is done. I'm striking you from the Board, seizing all your stock under Rule Fourteen A Three, regarding fraud and criminal actions harmful to the company. They'll be resold. It was the income from them that kept you in that lifestyle you love... which is now done. You are not in my will, nor among the company's creditors, so you don't even have a means to fight me on this."

Joe Prescot was smart enough not to reply. He just glared back, with a scheming eye.

"Oh, I'm not that naïve, Uncle," she said. "I know you could borrow or acquire more assets and try to come back. That's why you're staying here. You won't be able to call for favors, because you'll be in disgrace and unable to gain footage. So you won't get revenge either. Though if there is to be vengeance, it's mine. You'll be down in a hole, and every time you hear a rumble, you'll have to wonder if it's just another mining charge, or if I've grown tired of the game and have it in for you, or perhaps some miner from the old days remembers who his sweat kept in finery. Or I may remember that Ewan and his family must starve in the gutter because of your deceit. Or I may remember those videos. It seems certain at some point some past or future wrong will cause me to kill you. Or someone will figure out who you are." It was a long speech, but she was obviously enjoying it.

"Now, I need you away from my seat. I have an operation to run." She gestured.

Bart reached around and grabbed Joe by the collar, dragged him up and shoved him across the room. He half tripped on a severed arm and skidded on the pool of thickening red slime beyond it, before catching himself on a table.

Caron sat gracefully and imperiously in the chair, leaned back to get a feel for it, sighed in just a little bit of relaxation, and then spoke.

"Elke, Aramis, while it's not part of your contracted duties, would you do me the favor of escorting my uncle down to the Pit and ensure he's furnished with a coverall, a cot and proper safety gear? He has a substantial debt to pay, and he may as well get started."

They complied immediately and silently. Each took an arm, pulled him around against his ineffective flails, and started dragging him. Elke slipped binders on him so smoothly it looked like a dance maneuver.

While Jason didn't get the satisfaction of shooting the son of a bitch, he found hearing his cursing screams presaging a life of hard labor in a hole to be almost as gratifying.

It was very sweet to hear Caron start giving orders for cleanup as if Joc was already forgotten, while he was still visible across the broad loft.

Jason's final thought on the matter was, *Nope, not a scratch on the glass.*

EPILOGUE

Alex almost felt déjà vu stepping into Meyer's office.

This was much easier than the AAR after Celadon. It helped that this time there'd only been one faction to worry about. Though that faction, he reflected, had had more money than the entire nation of Celadon and all the interests involved. He was glad this one hadn't escalated more than it had.

While uniforms were not involved, this was still basically a report to the colonel. Alex felt pretty comfortable this time, though.

"Sir," he said as he walked in. Meyer was in front of his desk and offered a hand.

He said, "I have the official report for review later. I'm considering some medical counseling for you, though."

"I don't feel that stressed, sir," he said. "Rather well, actually."

"Alex, you turned down a billion marks, that was almost certainly a real offer, with a guarantee of the principal's safety added to your own. You're insane. It's a madness I appreciate at my end, of course."

"Ah," Alex replied. "It may have been a real offer, but on top of the moral issue of a bribe, and handing Caron over to that old pervert, there was the fact that he'd certainly expect more favors, and could make the money disappear as soon as he chose. He was screwing his brother's employees all along. There's no reason to believe I'd come out any better in the end."

"And here I was thinking you were just that dedicated and loyal."

"There is that," Alex smiled. "And of course, I knew you'd reliably offer ten percent of that in reward."

Meyer laughed loudly. "You really do need psychological help."

Alex joined him. No, he hadn't expected that, but what harm in suggesting it?

"Still, well done, and I'll call everyone in for congrats and Scotch in a few. Ex Ek is screaming. Travis says he certainly didn't authorize his people to engage in combat against civilians, nor to engage against someone's principal in what amounts to a civil war. I believe him. However, since his people can be suborned and mine can't, I stand to profit. That also means future engagements should be safer. Others won't risk it, and if we have both sides of a contract, there's no risk. That's your reward."

Alex said, "Yes, I do prefer not getting shot at, though that is why they hire us." True, though, that the industry would benefit, and his personal safety should improve. That did make him happy.

Meyer asked, "What's your personal take on Miss Prescot?"

"Mixed. She's still recovering from losing her family, of course, and unhappy at needing the ongoing security. Professionally, she's quite happy and wants to continue our contract. I suggested we rotate personnel through on a varying schedule, and never to send anyone who hasn't had a previous field contract. That's what she's asking for."

"I saw. It makes sense, it's good for us, and it's lucrative. You wondered why I wanted to keep your team together."

"I didn't really wonder. It's just not that commonly done, but we work well."

"Good. It's likely I'm sending you out on another field assignment in about twelve weeks. Is that enough time for everyone to recover and rest?"

"It's rough on Jason, since he has to ship to Grainne Colony. He'll lose four of those in transit, but I think we can do it."

"Good. Miss Prescot paid everything up to date, by the way, with a bonus contingent on continued performance. Also something about fifty marks personally to Jason?"

Hah. She'd actually paid him for cooking the curry dinner.

"Yes, that's correct," Alex said. Then he sighed. "On the one hand, I feel no qualms at all about any amount of money she wants to throw at me. But I really feel sorry for the girl."

"I did from the moment we took the contract. There's nothing we can do about that, though. You've done your part. Time to move on."

"Right. After all, she'll have to."